SCARRED CROWN

Bellerive Royals Book 2

W Million

Stomill Books

For anyone who has ever loved and lost.

Bellerive Royals Series

Fake Crown – Posey and Brent (March 2022)

Scarred Crown – Nick and Jules (May 2022)

Heavy Crown – Alex and Rory (August 2022)

Fallen Crown – Brice and Maren (November 2022)

Contents

Julia

I stare at the king of Bellerive for a beat longer than I should, my mouth slightly agape. I must have misheard him. Embarrassing, actually, since my job as his personal secretary means I'm supposed to not only hear every single word, but act on his directives.

I close my mouth and school my features to hide my surprise. He's thrown unexpected requests at me before, and I've handled them with barely a raised eyebrow. My mother taught me well.

"I don't think I heard you properly." I'm praying the words that left his lips were a mistake, though they rarely are. He's a careful speaker, unlike two of his three sons. Lately, he has made a few mistakes, and I'm clinging on to the hope this might be one too.

I sit up straighter in the heavy wood and leather chair. The king sits across from me behind his massive oak desk that is older than him and me combined. His office has reminders scattered in every nook and cranny of the kings and queens who came before him. Knickknacks, signed photos, plaques, ceremonial swords, and other odds speak to his family's history.

"I need you to track down Nicholas and bring him home."

"Right." I scribble a note in the planner on my skirt-clad lap. As long as someone else is doing the task, I can handle this wayward son. "Find someone to bring Nicholas home."

"Not someone," he clarifies in his deep, booming voice. A voice that is both commanding and soothing, the kind meant for audiobooks on war and strategy. A second career, perhaps? As if he's not busy enough running the country of Bellerive. "You, Julia."

"Me?" I manage to squeak out, and my stomach drops. My to-do list isn't meant for trips to bring home his children, especially not Prince Nicholas.

"You've known each other since you were children. You grew up together. He'll listen to you."

He will *not* listen to me, but his father lost track of our relationship at some point. He still thinks Nicholas and I are the best of friends. To be fair, we spent almost every waking hour together until we were sixteen.

Every year for the last fourteen, we've grown further apart, and except for that first year, I haven't minded a bit.

"You know, I'm not sure he will." I doodle in the margins of today's date. "We're not that close anymore. Maybe send Prince Alexander?"

"I need Alexander here. I may not have much time left."

His comment snaps me into focus and away from my musings on his middle son. "What does that mean?" I must be misinterpreting his comment. "You're not stepping down from the throne, are you?"

He wouldn't step down prematurely, would he? A frown creases my forehead. A coronation is no small thing to plan. He can't be serious, but if he is, I'll have to call my mother after this meeting. As his former secretary, she was a key player in the last coronation, and I will need all the advice I can get.

Then I realize if George is stepping down, I'll be working for Alex. George's painting will go up in the great hall, and Alex will be my boss.

I swallow. Hard.

Who would I rather deal with—Alexander or Nicholas? Neither for completely different reasons. My favorite royal is Brice, the youngest son and the easiest to get along with.

King George clears his throat. "I will be stepping down, yes."

"Oh!" I flounder for a tactful way to mention his age. Not that George cares about my tact. I was raised underfoot. On more than one occasion, he's called me the daughter he never had. "I know normal retirement age is around sixty-five, but many monarchs go well beyond that. Your mother went well beyond that." His mother retired from royal life fourteen years ago and passed away two years ago at ninety. The memory of Nick's stricken face at the public memorial a second before he masked his expression surfaces. A chill runs through me, and I rub my arms.

"Hmm. Yes. Well." He lets out a deep sigh. "What I am about to tell you doesn't leave this room. Do you understand? At some point, I will have to tell the world—perhaps they'll notice for themselves—but not until Alexander is settled on the throne."

"Are you sick?" A spark of unease skitters down my spine. The thought brings a sheen of tears to my eyes, and I blink them away. Through my glasses, I peer at him more closely. His eyes are still a bright hazel, much like his middle son. His brown hair is thick and wavy, and he's in good physical shape. He can't be sick.

He stares at the papers on his desk and then plucks a sheet between his fingers, passing it to me.

I take the document, shooting him a questioning glance, but he won't meet my gaze. His diagnosis is bolded, and my heart thumps. Hot and cold wash over my body in waves. "This... can't be right," I whisper. While he has made some mistakes in the last few months, I can't believe *this* is the reason.

"I am afraid it is. Experts here in Bellerive, in America, and in Great Britain all came to the same conclusion. The same sinister fate. My last shred of hope vanished yesterday."

I read the diagnosis over and over, but I can't make the words register in my brain. "You have to tell your kids."

"I *have* to put Alexander on the throne while I still can. We can't have instability on the island, even if the elected Advisory Council makes most of the decisions. The sitting monarch is the tie-breaker in any close decision." He steeples his fingers and peers over them. "As for whether I tell my children, at some point they'll realize, won't they? But you will *not* be the one to tell *any* of them."

For a man who has always struck me as smart and fair, his instinct to keep this from Alex, Nick, and Brice is stunning. Of course, I'm not the one staring my own mortality in the face. No, I just have to look his sons in their eyes and claim I don't know or understand why George is suddenly, and likely, swiftly, retiring from royal life. I'll protect his secret, and I'll have to hope his sons don't resent me for it later.

"Helen agreed to this?" Having George keep his diagnosis to himself is one thing, roping me in is another, but having their mother betray their children as well is disturbing.

"Yes," George mutters. "She's not happy with me, but she understands we can't tarnish Alexander's moment. He's been groomed to take over from me since birth. He should bask in the experience without the sadness of my diagnosis clouding every move."

When he puts it that way, I understand a little more why he might want to shelter his kids, even when they're all either in their thirties or rapidly approaching it. "You want the corona-tion to be joyous."

"I don't want it tied to my death sentence. A celebration. There will be lots of time for mourning. The road may be narrow, but I fear it will be long."

"How long?" Tears spring to my eyes again, and I blink them back.

"In total? Years, I fear. They won't be good ones though, will they?"

"What—what do you want me to do?" The sheet with his diagnosis is a block of concrete straining against my fingertips, weighing down my hand and my heart. It flutters onto the desk.

"Bring Nicholas home to make a few more memories before it's too late. Your mother is coming out of retirement to help with the transition and to serve me while you're gone."

"Where *is* Nicholas?" Dragging Nick's globetrotting ass home isn't going to be fun, despite what legions of women around the world might think. He can be a stubborn asshole.

We used to be the greatest friends, so close he sometimes felt like my other half when we lay under the stars, drinking stolen alcohol, talking about what the future might hold. But lately, I'm not even sure he *likes* me. His feelings for me might be easier to decipher if he ever actually spoke to me.

"Africa." He seems lost in thought for a beat as though searching for more. "The Serengeti? He didn't leave a detailed itinerary, and he's not answering his phone."

"Typical Nick," I mutter. "He didn't take any staff with him?"

George raises his eyebrows because we both know, of the three brothers, Nicholas has the hardest time with his elevated social status. He likes the women and the wine, but the media storm isn't his forte. He's been burned many times by the press and his gaggle of crown bunnies. Loose lips sink ships, and he's got a graveyard of unveiled secrets big enough to circle the island.

Once a year, he goes completely off the grid for weeks, hides out someplace very few people will know or care who he is. I guess this year it's the Serengeti. At least Tanzania is a place I've always wanted to go.

"He might not want to return," George hedges. "It may take you a while to convince him."

"And you won't let me tell him *why* he must return early."

"The coronation should be enough."

"So, you only want him back in time for Alexander's coronation? That'll be his argument." I eye him. Even with everyone working flat out, the succession will take months. If he's not going to tell any of them the truth, he should at least give Nick a pressing reason to return.

George's lips twitch. "If he gives you too hard of a time, tell him I'm arranging his marriage. For every week he delays, the suitability of his life partner goes down. The threat should get his ass back here."

An answering smile tilts my lips. No doubt that *will* get Nick back to Bellerive. He's a man allergic to commitment. "I'm not sure he'll believe me."

"You have my permission to push every single one of his buttons as long as you get him home." George chuckles.

Now *that*, I can do.

Nicholas

My sundowner is halfway to my lips when her voice catches my ear, a tune I've tried to banish from my brain since I was sixteen. When we were kids, her voice was a comfort amongst the sea of people who wanted something from me. Then puberty hit, and her lilting tones started sending Morse code to my dick. Win-win, right? Except she didn't see it that way, and I couldn't see it any other.

Her blue-gray eyes were stuck on my older brother's broad shoulders. Remembering never stings any less.

The voice dips to a murmur, and I tilt my head, trying to soothe my curiosity without turning around. She's not here. How could she be? Strange for someone at this camp to sound so much like her. I used to think her voice was unique. Guess I was wrong about that too.

Then the woman behind me laughs. I tense. The pitch of this woman's voice might be a coincidence, but her laugh too?

No fucking way.

I twist in my lawn chair, away from the roaring fire in the middle of the tented camp. The grasses of the Serengeti stretch into the distance. Three weeks ago, I left Bellerive and the Crown behind for some peace and quiet. The last person I should be seeing in the middle of the Serengeti is Julia Jensen.

The woman beside me, who's been trying to figure out a way to get invited into my tent for the last hour, slides her hand along my forearm that's grown brown in the Serengeti sun. Our chairs are so close together that mine wobbles with hers. Earlier, she gave me some bullshit about coming to the Serengeti to 'find herself' as though this place has all life's answers. No one truly finds themselves by running away—I should know.

"Someone you recognize?"

"You could say that," I mutter and turn back to the fire. No point in letting Julia realize I'm aware she's here. She can come speak to me.

Delay. Delay. Delay.

Her presence is guaranteed to ruin my trip. If her message is pressing, she shouldn't be flirting with my personal tour guide. Whatever has happened is bad enough for her to come, but not so bad for her to seek me out with any additional urgency.

The woman beside me isn't bothered by my lack of response, and she natters away. Not a clue what she's on about, but she's invading my space like a bad rash. Her hands are on my arm, and now her lips suckle under my ear. I could stop her, and without Julia here, I probably would. These trips aren't about getting laid. *Pussy grows on trees, but solitude? Priceless.*

Instead of basking in my own company, I'm letting this woman, whose name I can't remember, smother me with attention I really don't want to prove a point to another woman who couldn't care less.

I suck back more of my sundowner and wonder if I can get drunk enough to tolerate this woman's slobbery interest for the rest of the night.

"Excuse me, Your Royal Highness," my tour guide, Kafil, taps on my shoulder that isn't occupied by the annoying woman.

She clings on tighter, and I turn my head to acknowledge the guy who's been showing me around for the last three weeks. He's tall, thin, and almost as black as the night that'll drop around us soon. A good sense of humor when he lets himself loosen up around me. The royal title strikes again.

"You have a visitor. She says she must speak to you."

"*Must* speak to me?" Sounds like Julia. No room for debate or argument. Two of my specialties. I raise my eyebrows and extract myself from the leech.

"Are you coming back?" Her big brown eyes peer up to me out of her sunburned face. She should have employed some sun cream today.

She was prettier before she heard Kafil refer to me as royalty at dinner. Now she's just another woman looking to bed a prince. "Who knows?" I grin. "I suppose it depends on why I'm wanted."

Leech woman must have used the little Wi-Fi we have to identify me after she took that *discreet* picture of the coffee maker just behind my head at dinner. She could have asked for a photo instead of the coyness I find tiring. I've been photographed enough over the years—not always for the best reasons.

I follow Kafil to the communications hut, and the ache under my breastbone resumes its dull throbbing at the mere idea of Julia so close by. Through the screened door of the canvas tent, her long chestnut hair is drawn back in a tight bun, and her glasses perch on her nose, framing her blue-gray eyes. I hate the prickling of my skin and the thin sheen of sweat dampening my armpits. Nerves. Attraction. Two reactions I've learned to mask where Julia is concerned. She doesn't want to see them, prefers they don't exist.

I hold back the edge of the canvas and mesh while I slip inside, and I stop in front of her, hands thrust in the pockets of my safari pants. Her appearance has already ruined my peace of mind. If she's come with bad news to wreck my trip, she can speak first.

Her gaze catalogs me from my overgrown hair to my beard, over my khaki clothing, to the sandals on my feet. Once upon a time, her blue-gray eyes owned my soul, and I gave her my secrets under a starry sky. *So long ago.*

"Prince Nicholas, I've come to escort you home."

Prince Nicholas. My royal title coming from her lips pisses me off. At one time, I was Nick to her, and I liked it much better. Two can play this game.

"Secretary Jensen, while I enjoy the implication you're my—" I meet her gaze with a smirk "—*escort*, I've still got three weeks left here."

"Change of plans, I'm afraid." She touches the edge of her glasses.

Not a hint of a reaction at my goading words. Disappointing. I'll have to up my game. "Why would I change *my* plans?"

"Is there somewhere we can speak privately?" She glances at my guide who is still in the communications tent with us.

"My tent." I shrug. "Though the walls are thin." I wink.

She gives a huff of disgust and throws open the canvas door. Success! She's so easily annoyed with me. Having her here might be fun after all.

"Your Royal Highness," Kafil says. "Can I speak with you before you go?"

"Sure thing, Kafil. And I said you're fine to call me Nick, especially in private."

"We have a small problem." Kafil's smile is fleeting. "Your colleague wishes to stay at camp, but we're full while you're here."

"Doesn't seem like a problem to me. She can stay in my tent." Julia will blow a gasket at having to breathe the same air as me.

"I have called for another bed, but due to our remote location, we won't have one delivered for a few days."

I rock back on my heels, his meaning clear. "Ah, right. I see the problem now." I rub the back of my neck and gaze at Julia who is sipping a bottle of water and speaking to one of the other guides just outside the canvas entrance. "Do you have an air mattress or anything?"

He shakes his head. "I've put a rush on any kind of bed we can turn up, but it may be a few days."

"Not to worry." I clap him on the shoulder. "I'll make sure Julia has a comfortable place to sleep." *On my floor.* I grin.

"Okay. I'm sorry. So sorry." Kafil passes me an extra flashlight.

"No need to apologize. Secretary Jensen showed up with no warning. Rude, really." I waltz out of the tent, catch Julia's eye, and signal for her to follow me. The grassy plains surround the isolated tent camp, and the hyenas call to each other in earnest. Despite the potential danger, I love the deep rumble that escalates into a high-pitched whoop. So distinctive. Soon, it won't be safe to be wandering between tents alone.

When she falls into step beside me, I pass her the extra flashlight. The sun is still sinking into the ground, so she doesn't need it yet. I unzip the tent and walk in ahead of her. A gentleman probably would have let her in first, and if she were anyone else, I might have too.

Once we're in the tent, I sprawl on the bed and leave her standing by the entrance. While my tent is one of the biggest at this tented camp, I requested any extra furniture be moved elsewhere when I booked. She can join me on the bed, sit on the floor, or stand awkwardly. She eyes the bed and fiddles with the arm of her glasses.

Awkward standing it is.

Funny she wears glasses now that she's taken over as my father's secretary. Contacts were standard for years. Quite a few funny mishaps with those. Not that she'd want a reminder. Perhaps I should bring one of those memories up?

"Your father would like you to come home." She crosses her arms and then uncrosses them to set them on her hips.

Is it wrong that I love how disconcerted she is? For the last fourteen years, she's been getting progressively more buttoned up. Christ, we used to make fun of her mother, and now she's becoming her. One of about a bazillion things I now find unbearably annoying about Julia.

"I gathered he was the reason you were here since you work for him, and I'm his son," I say.

"Second in line to the throne." Her pert reminder raises my hackles. I never seem to be quite the right fit in her eyes.

"Indeed. Your knowledge of Bellerive's succession is strong." I raise an eyebrow and then go back to staring at the thick green canvas roof. Looking at her causes this weird tightness in my chest, and sometimes in my pants, which is less weird, but both feelings piss me off. "I've got three more weeks here. Then a little time in Vegas."

"With your crown bunnies?"

"That's a rather derogatory nickname for the delightful harem of women who often accompany me." I rise onto my elbow and cradle my head in my hand, facing her. "Where are you sleeping tonight?"

"Your guide said he could get an extra bed delivered."

"Yes, of course. That's going to take a few days though." I stare at her expectantly.

She makes a frustrated noise. "I'll ask whether there's some-where else I can sleep. Another tent. Staff accommodations. Anything."

Anywhere but in here with me. The unspoken words cause another swell of annoyance. Am I really that repulsive to her?

"You aren't going to ask why you need to come home?" she prods.

"I figure you'll tell me eventually. If someone is dead or sick or injured, you're not the type to bury the lede. So, whatever is going on can wait." I pretend to consult a watch I'm not wearing. "For at least another—" I glance up to meet her gaze. "Four weeks. I'm on vacation from my life, and I'm not overly keen to return."

"Prince Nicholas, your father has decided to abdicate the throne. We'll be preparing for a coronation, and your father would like you home."

Now she's got my attention. I sit on the edge of the bed and rub my face. "Abdicating? He's sixty-five. Grandmother ruled until she was seventy-eight. Why would he *abdicate*?" I squint at her. "What aren't you telling me?"

"King George believes Prince Alexander is ready to succeed, and he wishes to retire while he is still young enough to enjoy his retirement."

I suck in a deep breath through my nose and cock an eyebrow. "You smell that, Secretary Jensen? It's the sharp stench of bull-shit. Or I suppose since we're in the Serengeti, elephant shit. Still a bull, I suppose. Just a much bigger pile of shit."

A muscle in her jaw twitches.

Rising from the bed, I saunter toward her. "Thank you for coming all this way, Secretary Jensen, to let me know about the coronation, which will be taking place *months* from now. But unless there's something you're not telling me, there's no need for me to return to Bellerive early."

I gaze down at her, trying not to linger on the plains and valleys of her face I once knew better than my own. She looks tired, and a pang of uncertainty strikes me at making her sleep on the floor. I shove it down. I didn't ask her to come here, and she's not giving me the real reason she came.

"I've got three more weeks here, and then a trip to Vegas. Join me or leave. I could care less. But I'm not returning early." I snatch my flashlight off the hook by the exit and unzip the flap. "It's getting dark. Don't leave this tent without an escort. I'd hate to explain to my father how his prize secretary was eaten by a cackle of hyenas."

I point the flashlight along the grassy path, and an answering light flashes ahead of me as one of the workers rushes forward to walk me back to the campfire.

Julia's voice rings out into the night, but I don't catch what she says, and I refuse to give her the satisfaction of turning around.

Spending however many nights with her in my tent was a better idea in theory than it is in reality. The coronation might be the big reason she came, but there's something else going on. Will she tell me? Probably not. Her loyalty hasn't lain with me in years.

When I get to the fire, I survey the small gathering. A distraction is in order.

Now, where's my leech?

NICK

Fourteen years ago

Brice and Alex are ahead of me on the steep path along the cliff's face at the far edge of the royal property. Guards patrol the area every hour, so our window for some fun is narrow, just like the rocky ledge.

On this side of the island, the black cliffs are high and jagged. Our parents, and likely the country, would have a collective heart attack if they realized we plummeted into the ocean on calm days. Below us, there's barely a ripple today.

"Are you sure she's coming?" Brice asks.

"She'll be here." My tone is tinged with annoyance. Jules isn't punctual even though she's highly organized. The weirdest combination. Sometimes I suspect the lateness is her way of shooting her mother a subtle *fuck you* with every minute that ticks by. My theory would work better if meeting her mother were her only instances of lateness. A few months ago she got her bike license, and she's been trying everyone's punctuality patience ever since.

"How do you know she's not going to tell Secretary Jensen we ditched security to go cliff diving?" Brice tosses a pebble off the edge, and the three of us watch it sail toward the ocean.

It really is quite a long way down.

"Jules can keep a secret from her mother. You don't need to fucking worry about that." She's kept every single one of mine—even when it would have been easier with her mom to rat me out. I glance behind me, my ears alert for the sound of her footsteps.

"Why'd you invite her?" Alex asks, scuffing his feet. "This is our thing."

"He invites her everywhere." Brice chimes in. "Surprised he hasn't asked her before. Jules this, Jules that."

"Shut your mouth." I shove him in the shoulder. "She'll keep our secret. I promised I'd invite her next time the ocean calmed."

At thirteen, Brice has decided he's an expert on everything, including my best friend who just happens to be female. Lately, everyone has been acting like it's shocking we're friends, as though we haven't always been tight, as if the fact she's grown tits will cause my dick or my heart to explode. I've got news for them. Neither one is happening, and frustration eats at me each time someone brings it up like our friendship is a recipe for disaster.

Except for my brothers, she's the only person who understands the complexities of my life. If someone offered me the world in exchange for giving up Jules, I'd tell them to go fuck themselves. We'll be friends until we die if I have anything to say about it.

Jules rounds the corner of the path at a jog, her long brown hair bouncing over the towel slung around her neck. A grin spreads across her face when we make eye contact.

"Sorry I'm late."

She doesn't bother giving me an excuse. It'd be bullshit anyway, so there's no point in pretending she's got a good reason. I've started calling her timekeeping *Jules o'clock*, and I tell her fifteen minutes before I actually need to do something. Not that she realizes I've adjusted our meet times. My little coping mechanism for her chronic lateness is my secret. Didn't think of it until too late today. Shouldn't matter. She's never hours late, but sometimes she pushes it to the point where I wonder if she'll show up.

"It's rude to keep people waiting when you're invited somewhere." Alex eyes her, his dark hair and eyes glistening in the bright sun.

She flushes and avoids eye contact with him, dropping her towel beside mine, and dragging her hair into a ponytail. Alex is three years old than us, and he never misses a chance to give me or Jules a hard time. He's home from college for the summer, and he's full of self-importance.

"Don't be an asshole, Alex," I mutter. "It's not like we've got a stopwatch for when we must jump off the cliff." I tap the back of my wrist, miming a fake watch.

"Just security breathing down our neck," Alex mutters, staring out at the flat turquoise waters. "Julia jumps first."

"No." I glare at him. "Oldest to youngest. That'll put Jules in the middle."

"And me at the back," Brice whines. "Youngest to oldest. Jules will still be second."

Before any of us get a chance to debate or discuss the order, Alex takes a run at the cliff and flies off, his feet kicking the air. His fall is silent. Weeks ago, we learned shrieks of joy will draw security. We had to hide in the water for almost an hour while they patrolled around us. It was a miracle no one sent out a search party.

We clamber closer to the edge to make sure he hit the turquoise water and not any sharp, black rocks. When his head bobs to the surface, I grin at Jules.

"That's." She swallows and doesn't take her gaze off the long drop. "Farther than I expected."

"You're not afraid, are you?" Brice goads her. "If you're too scared, you can head back home. Next time we won't wait for you."

"Shut up, Brice." Jules shoves his shoulder. "You're so hard, are you?"

He beats his chest. "Watch me." He backs up and charges the edge of the cliff, sailing off with a loud whoop.

I guess only two of us learned our lesson about being quiet a few weeks ago. Awesome.

She tugs on her ponytail and watches Brice surface. "This doesn't seem safe. Should all three heirs to the throne be cliff jumping unsupervised?"

"Unsupervised is the best part." I smirk. "Come on. Are you gonna wimp out if I go first?"

She straightens and adjusts her bikini, tightening the straps. "Should have worn a different suit."

My friends have declared Jules hot, and I'm constantly defending her over their lewd comments. Curves for days. Doesn't feel right to have them point them out. Up to now, I've tried my best not to notice her assets, but she's cupping them and moving them around like I don't have a piece of my anatomy likely to respond. Does she think I'm dead below the waist?

In a second, I'll be going over the cliff for a whole other reason.

"God, what if my suit comes off?" Her expression is agonized. "Alex would never let me live that down."

I need to jump off the cliff right now. I grab her hand and tug her to the edge, hoping she's too focused on the drop to notice the semi I'm sporting. I might not think of Jules that way, but my dick has other ideas today.

"Do we need to run to clear the rocks?"

"Nah." I shake my head and take a deep breath. "They were just showing off."

"Is this going to hurt?"

I laugh and squeeze her hand. "Look straight out. Feet enter the water first. Trust me?"

She gazes at me for a beat. "More than anyone else in the world."

My chest warms even though that's our question, the one we ask whenever we're uncertain about something. A call and response sort of thing.

"Look out fuckers!" I holler down, and then we step off together. My stomach dips at the loss of ground beneath my feet.

Jules screams, and I chuckle at her naked terror. She's a good swimmer, so she'll be fine once we hit the water. I contact the water first, and then a swirl of bubbles appears in my peripheral vision. I kick and pull to break the surface. Shielding my eyes from the glare of the sun, I search for Jules, but she's not at the surface.

Where is she?

A moment of panic seizes my chest, and I'm about to start diving blindly when she comes up, gasping for air.

"I went so deep," she chokes out, coughing and hacking beside me.

If we were on land, I'd hit her back or something. But since we're both treading water, there's not much I can do as she sputters beside me.

"Shit. Sorry. I forgot to tell you what to do once you hit the water. You have to angle your body like a banana to stop yourself from going too deep." I use my hand to show her the motion.

"Who's the asshole now?" Alex calls from the cliff face where he and Brice are navigating the route back to the top.

She makes eye contact with Alex before turning back to me. "Still him," Jules mutters.

I laugh and give Alex the finger. He shakes his head and starts climbing behind Brice.

"We have to go up the cliff now," she groans.

I splash water at her. "How'd you think we were getting back up?"

"Didn't think that far. I was too worried about dying." She gazes up to where we jumped from. "My mother would shit herself if she knew where I was right now."

"She knows you're with me, right?"

"Yeah, but she's still under the impression you're a good influence." Julia smirks.

"You'd think she'd know better by now." The only reason she doesn't is that Jules takes the fall for at least half the stupid things I drag her into. If Secretary Jensen knew that every time Jules did something idiotic, I was the ringmaster, she'd probably chain Julia to a chair to keep her from hanging around me.

Julia gives me a wry smile before taking a few strokes toward the cliff's edge. "Give me a piggyback?"

"Up the cliff?"

"I can ask Alex instead." She bats her eyelashes at me over her shoulder.

I glower at her and swim past. A low blow since she knows I hate being compared to him—at school, at home, in the press.

"Nick," she calls. "I was joking. It was a joke."

I climb onto the lowest rock ahead of her, and I offer her my hand to help her up. She eyes me warily but then takes it. When she's on the rock beside me, she says, "I'm s—"

But she doesn't get the chance to finish her sentence because I pick her up and toss her back into the ocean.

"Nick!" she screams just before she hits the water. When she pops up, she glares. "You're evil."

"I'm evil? *I'm evil*?" Maybe a little. I offer her my hand again, but she slaps me away this time and hoists herself up.

We stare at each other for a moment, both of us wary for different reasons. She rises on her toes and kisses my cheek. "You're my best friend, Nicky. I'd never pick your asshole brother over you. So... piggyback?" She waggles her eyebrows.

Good enough for me. I turn around, and she jumps on. "I'm not fucking doing this all the way up," I say.

"You're not strong enough?" Her tone is teasing, but the implication pisses me off.

"You're on fire today," I mutter.

She laughs, and something strange blooms in my chest. She's not the only thing on fire. My dick has decided to pay an annoying amount of attention to her today. It's distracting, and I'm sure as shit not used to noticing Jules like this.

"Please don't douse me with water to put me out again," she teases.

I stare at the rocky path ahead. Is carrying her a good idea? Probably not. But when my pride's at stake, I rarely back down. Not strong enough? *Please.*

"Hold on tight or I might lose you. I'm going to need my hands in a few spots." Sections of the climb are more like rock climbing than a clear route.

Her arms and legs tighten around me. "You'll have to pry me off. I'm never going to let you go. People at school will start calling you the hunchback and wonder about your barnacle."

Trust Jules to take a word of caution about thirty steps too far. "No one wants to see that," I say as I start up the path.

"Fine. I'll let you pry me off at the top." She lets out a long-suffering sigh.

"Might not have to." My breathing is already labored. She's not as light as she looks. "Might drop you first."

"You wouldn't dare," she cries, tightening her hold.

She's right. I might toss her into the ocean or forget to tell her something when we jump off a cliff, but I'd never intentionally hurt her. "I might dare. You're heavier than you look, Jensen."

She slaps my back and wiggles to climb down, but I tighten my hold on her. We're not at the dangerous stretch yet, but no point in taking any chances. Carrying her isn't so bad.

"Are you calling me fat?"

"Heavy. Not the same thing."

"Comments like that give girls eating disorders you know." She huffs out a breath at my back.

"You love food too much," I say, and she hits me again. "You'd have to have that one where you eat a lot and then puke."

"Are you telling eating disorder jokes? Jesus, Nick."

If she wasn't so fucking heavy, I'd laugh louder. Instead, I can barely get out a chuckle. "More of an observation."

"Rude," she crows. "Alex! Brice! Your brother is rude!"

"They like my jokes."

"So, you were joking? Seriously, Nick. You can't make those kinds of jokes. It's like... really a bad idea for someone like you."

"You mean second in line to the throne. If I tossed Alex off the cliff at an odd angle, I could be first. Should I? Is that a better joke?"

She slaps my back really hard, and I wince.

"All right, this donkey is going to take a break if you keep beating it," I say.

"You don't want me to beat you?"

Not my back. The thought springs up unbidden. What the hell is wrong with me today?

"Jules?" I wait a beat for her to speak, but when she doesn't, I continue, "We should play the silent game."

"You're an asshole." Her face appears in my peripheral vision. "You might as well just call it the 'shut up Jules' game."

"I'm open to naming suggestions." I grunt when I get to the cliff face where I need to go from rock to rock along a thin edge.

"I'm getting down." Julia wiggles on my back, and I want to groan for a different reason. Her breasts are going to do me in.

Instead of fighting with her, I ease her down. While I could carry her up under normal circumstances, my brain has decided to give my dick half my focus today. Fucking ridiculous. It's Julia. *Jules.*

I take her through all the handholds and footholds to navigate us back to the top. When we get there, Alex is waiting, but Brice has already taken the plunge a second time.

"What took you so long?" he asks.

"Nick threw me into the ocean and then piggybacked me up half the way as penance." Julia grins at me.

"Only halfway?" Alex cocks an eyebrow.

He tips his chin at Julia, and his gaze roams over her in a way I don't like.

"Jump with me, and I'll carry you all the way back up."

She laughs and shakes her head. "Nah, I'm good." She steals a glance in my direction. "I need the exercise."

A hint of a smile tugs at my lips, and I'm pleased she turned him down, even if she made a dig at me in the process.

"Your loss," Alex says, and he hurls himself off the cliff.

We stand at the edge and watch Alex surface below.

"Are you going first, or am I?" I ask.

"Me," she says, playing her belly like a drum. "I'm pleased to report this teeny tiny bikini held it together."

"Uh-huh." They're the only sounds I can get past my lips because she's drawn my attention to her pert figure again. When did she start looking like this?

"See you at the bottom!" She does a pirouette off the cliff face, and when she hits the water, an unbearable tightness seizes my chest, as though I can't breathe. Then she surfaces again, and I suck in a deep breath of relief.

What the fuck is wrong with me?

Julia

Anger bubbles up at his easy dismissal of my arrival and sleeping predicament. Where's the chivalrous gentleman he was raised to be? Throwing back the flap, I step into the grassy path.

"I'm not returning to Bellerive without you!" I call to his retreating back.

He waves above his head in a dismissive gesture. Asshole. Probably headed back to the crown bunny at the fire who was sucking on his neck while I talked to Kafil. One whisper of 'Your Royal Highness' and women cream in their panties. I've seen it enough times, especially since Nick and I went to the same college.

Nick's physical appearance is secondary to his princely status. That nugget of truth irked him in high school and likely college, but I wouldn't know about that. Would a prince have women falling at their feet even if they looked like Shrek? Probably. But Nick is no Shrek, as much as it pains me to admit it. He works out obsessively, eats healthy, but drinks too much. He inherited the best physical characteristics from both his parents and like a fine wine, he's aging extraordinarily well.

During college, he modeled 'for fun'. His arrogant strut down a runway was a sight to behold with his shaggy brown hair falling over hazel eyes. Privilege oozed out of him. I may have been forced to watch those fashion shows on repeat by a friend or two. For a surprising number of women, his *I don't give a fuck* attitude is a sweet elixir, impossible to resist.

However, there's a difference between artfully tousled and a disheveled mess. He's tipped the scales in the wrong direction. His hair's too long, his beard untrimmed, and his clothes are rumpled. Not a single member of staff is here to talk him into caring about his appearance. It's maddening for him to still be attractive, a magnet for women, when he's not even trying. I huff out an annoyed breath in the empty tent.

"Hello?" Kafil calls from outside the zipped entrance. "I have your bags, Secretary Jensen."

I unzip the flap and hold it open for him. "Thank you. You can call me Julia. There's no need for the formality."

"Right, yes." He gazes around the tent and sticks my bags in the far corner. "Did Prince Nicholas tell you about the bed situation?"

"He did. Not to worry. He's offered me his. I think he must be sleeping somewhere else tonight."

Kafil frowns but nods his head. "Perhaps."

"He's back at the fire, is he?"

"Yes. Our American guest is very interested in Bellerive."

I bet she is.

"Would you like tea or coffee in the morning? We deliver it an hour before we leave for safari."

"We're going on safari tomorrow?" A rush of pleasure flushes out my annoyance at Nick. At least if he won't come home with me right away, I can enjoy a day or two of sightseeing before brandishing my winning card. It's a sound strategy. Showing my hand too early will increase his suspicion about his father's abdication.

"Yes. We've been following a pair of mating leopards. Prince Nicholas mentioned you have a keen interest in elephants? We should have no problem tracking some tomorrow."

"Who doesn't love elephants?" Though I suspect Nick said that in reference to his elephant shit comment earlier. His response to King George's request to return is exactly as I predicted. There's no way he'll willingly come back to Bellerive with me.

"Tea or coffee?" Kafil inches toward the door.

"Tea, please. Thank you! What time are we leaving in the morning?" Exhaustion spreads across my body, and I stare longingly at the bed. Jetlag is the worst.

"Prince Nicholas requested we leave at seven." He gives me a small smile. "I'm sure you're tired from your day of travel."

"I am, yeah. But I'm excited about tomorrow. I've never been on safari." I might not be quite as excited about spending the day with Nick, but sometimes sacrifices have to be made.

"After three weeks with me, Prince Nicholas is an expert. If you have any questions in the morning, I am sure he can answer them." He must see my uncertainty because he adds, "And of course you're welcome to ask me too." He unzips the tent and ducks out. "*Usiku mwema.*"

I frown, unsure what he's just said. Goodbye? Goodnight? Tomorrow I'll get a list of the local phrases so I can respond appropriately.

Once Kafil's heavy footfall departs, I survey the room. There isn't a suitcase in sight. Nick's things must be packed away in the drawers and small standing closet. Well, if he's going to make me stay here, he can damn well share his space. While I unpack my suitcase, I rearrange as many of Nick's things as I can. The man used to be meticulous about everything having a place. Asking me where his things are will drive him nuts.

With a satisfied smirk, I grab my sleep shorts and T-shirt. Protocol demands I take the floor. I am, technically, an employee of The Crown, even if I've known them since I was a baby. If Nick and I were still friends, I wouldn't even be hesitating at the side of the queen bed. I'd slide under the sheets with a satisfied smile, certain he wouldn't mind.

But we aren't friends, and so I'll slide under the sheets in a few minutes with a satisfied smile for a different reason. He'll be livid when he returns to his room and finds I've left the floor for him. Just to make his place crystal clear, I take the extra sheets from the small closet and lay them beside the bed, dropping a pillow at the head.

Perfection.

Consider his buttons pushed, King George.

Now, he just needs to come back to his room at some point to see my masterpiece. I sprawl across the bed in a star shape in case the bed on the floor isn't a strong enough message and let sleep pull me under.

###

I wake to strong arms and hands sliding under my shoulders and knees. I'm momentarily disoriented by the dim lighting and the unfamiliar location. Then, I'm flying. I land with an *oomph* on the other side of the queen bed.

"Not gonna happen, Jensen," Nick grumbles as he throws back the covers, hitting my cheek.

I leave the blanket across my face for a beat to orient myself. I was in such a deep jetlagged sleep, I forgot I flew to Tanzania to sabotage Nick's escape from royal life. For the brief moment I was cradled in his arms, his scent invaded my senses, and I was transported back to when the smell of him brought comfort. Unexpectedly, an ache blooms across my chest. It's been years since I mourned the demise of our friendship, but there it is, the remnants of grief swirling through my body.

No way I'm dwelling on that feeling when I fought so hard not to feel it the first time. "Do you mind?" I fling the sheets off my face to glare at him.

He snaps off the bedside lamp, already snug in bed, his broad back to me. "Not at all."

Oh, God. Is he... is he *shirtless*? Didn't he get enough naked cuddling with his conquest? "You threw me across the bed."

"If you didn't want me to touch you, you shouldn't have been in my bed."

"I wasn't about to sleep on the hard floor."

"Then be thankful I didn't throw you there instead." He huffs out a frustrated breath. "Just go to sleep. If I wanted to talk to someone, I'd have stayed where I was."

"Oh, wonderful. You're comparing me to one of your crown bunnies? We might be sharing a bed, but I am *not* having sex with you." The words leave my mouth with more confidence than I feel, and my cheeks heat. Thank God it's dark in here. Pressing his buttons used to lead to my embarrassment all the time when we were younger. Nick has no shame, and I have far too much.

"I really hate that fucking nickname," he mutters.

"Yes, your cultural appropriation of *harem* was so much better earlier."

"You're relentless." He chuckles.

"Not to mention the implication that the women sleeping with you are somehow slaves."

He fakes a very loud snore.

I would hit him, but then I'd have to touch him, and I'm not convinced that's a good idea. "You're not sleeping."

"Will be soon if you keep this up. You'll bore me into a coma. Cultural appropriation. Slavery. I'm on holiday."

"Those are not subjects you can take a holiday from."

"Apparently. Funny, I was managing just fine before you showed up." The covers rustle.

Is he on his back now? It's pitch-black in here, and I can't even see my hand in front of my face. With his back to me, I had the confidence to figurately poke him. Less so when there's a chance he might literally poke back.

"Are you quite done?" His voice is closer, and I'm sure now he's on his back instead of turned away from me.

"Quite," I agree, and I struggle to get under the blankets since he threw me on top instead of placing me nicely underneath or even nudging me awake and asking me to move. Of course, I probably *wouldn't* have moved.

He helps to lift the covers with a deep sigh. "You gonna be okay?"

"Why?"

"Obviously, you didn't want to share a bed with me, but you also didn't want to sleep on the floor. I'm not leaving the bed…"

"So, why are you even asking? It's not like we haven't shared a bed before."

A heavy silence falls between us, and I curse myself for drawing attention to what we used to be to each other. The plan is to make him so desperate to get rid of me, he'll return home early. It's not to slice open my old wounds in the process.

The covers tug out of my grasp, and he must roll away from me again. "Night, Secretary Jensen."

"Goodnight, Prince Nicholas," I whisper into the darkness. Not a word of denial or confirmation about our shared past. Expecting any other reaction out of him at this point is naïve. He's shown me over and over again that whoever we used to be to each other, we're not those people anymore.

Nicholas

As I would expect, Julia woke before me and skittered out of the bed. She's been rattling around the bathroom area for a few minutes, and I'm wondering at what point she'll ask for help. Knowing her, I've probably got another ten or fifteen minutes before absolute panic and frustration overcomes her stubbornness.

This camp is a mid-range one in terms of amenities. Doesn't bother me. I'm not here for the conveniences I can get at home. I'm here for the animals, the experience, and the blessed fucking solitude. My tented camp selection does mean you have to pour water down the toilet to get it to flush, and the showers are of the bucket variety. Guests have to order a shower in advance. Did I forget to mention that to Julia last night? Shame.

I grin and shove my hands behind my head, staring at the canvas ceiling.

"Your Royal Highness?" Kafil calls from outside the zipped door. "Breakfast for you and Secretary Jensen."

"Come in." Normally, I'm up and dressed when he arrives, and I help him set up the little table. With Julia in the bathroom for a stupid amount of time, I'm still lying in bed.

When Kafil enters the tent, he takes in my appearance. "Are you feeling all right, sir?"

"Glorious. Secretary Jensen is in the bathroom. I'm just waiting my turn."

"You explained to her how the bathroom works?"

"Of course." I adjust the covers and plant my feet on the ground, rubbing my face. "You know women, always taking three hours to get ready when it could have taken five minutes." I drag on the pants I dropped on the floor last night to help Kafil set up breakfast.

When I came in and discovered Julia in my bed, I was stunned. Hadn't occurred to me she'd pull that fast one. My inner gentleman debated taking the floor space she so kindly set up for me. My not-so-inner asshole won out after I watched her sleep for a minute or two, my heart squeezing painfully at the sight of her so exhausted, no glasses, her hair loose on the pillow. A snapshot from another life.

Someday, I'll look at her and feel nothing. I've been praying for that day since I was sixteen. Ignoring and avoiding her hasn't snuffed out these lingering emotions, though I always think I've managed it until I see her again.

Maybe the next few days with her until she leaves will smother this lingering crush. How many years can someone carry an unrequited flame of longing? *Pathetic.*

We finish setting up the tea and food on the small folding table. Everyone else at camp has a communal breakfast at the meal tent. Since my preference is toward privacy, I requested only one common meal. Dinner. I can regale people with tales and play pretend for one meal and a few drinks a day. Otherwise, I want to relax and not worry about what someone's going to write about me on social media, the photos they'll post, the stories they'll tell. A trained fucking monkey. Some days, not particularly well trained.

"Do you need anything else?" Kafil asks. "Will Secretary Jensen require anything else?"

"We're fine, Kafil. We'll see you at the vehicle in an hour."

He nods and ducks out the tent, the metallic click of the zipper louder than usual.

"Nick." Julia's voice comes out of the canvas-enclosed bathroom area. "I can't get anything in here to work."

"Oh." I feign confusion. "You need a man to solve your problem?"

"A man?" She pokes her head out of the zippered area. "There's a man here?"

"A prince among men." I smirk.

She rolls her eyes. "Might be beneath you, but can you tell me how to flush the toilet and turn on the shower? After such a long day of travel yesterday, I cannot go anywhere without scrubbing off the dirt."

She has no idea what she's in for today if she thinks yesterday was a dirty day. The roads are dust pits, and our vehicle often has the windows down because I prefer that over air conditioning. No shower now, and perhaps no shower later. She's going to be filthy. Won't be sleeping in my bed tonight.

"I'll show you." I unzip the door to the bathroom and duck in. "Happy to take a look."

"Oh, um." She clutches her towel closer around her.

I swallow down the rise of desire at the sight of her so vulnerable. The towel covers more than her T-shirt and shorts did last night, but one slip of the hand would send the fluffy material sailing to the ground.

Brain, do not go there.

To distract myself, I peer into the toilet. "Just pee?"

She turns a lovely shade of red. "Well, yes."

"Leave it, then. We only worry about shit." I point to the brimming water bucket next to the toilet. "You pour that into the toilet to make it flush."

"Oh." She draws the towel tighter around her. "Okay. What about the shower?" She steps into the enclosed fabric room and peers up at the wide metal showerhead.

I tug on the cord next to the pipe, and I fake a frown of puzzlement. "Huh. That normally works. Must be broken."

"I need a shower." She groans.

"'Fraid it won't be this morning. I'll speak to Kafil." I have to turn my back so she doesn't see my smile. "Breakfast is here."

"Nick, is it really broken or is this some frat-boy trick?"

Having her refer to me as Nick instead of Prince Nicholas in that snooty tone is an improvement. I school my expression into one of confusion before I turn back to her. "Why would I trick you?"

"I stole your bed last night, and I rearranged all your stuff."

I raise my eyebrows. *She rearranged my stuff?* Hadn't discovered that yet. *Delightful.* She can stew in her own stench today, and I'm not going to care one lick.

"You didn't steal my bed, you kept it warm for me." I let my gaze roam over her towel in a suggestive way she'll hate. "My official bed warmer." I lean against the tent pole and cross my arms.

"Please. Spare me. I'll buy you a hot water bottle."

"No need. If you hadn't fallen asleep so early last night they'd have put a hot water bottle between the sheets to warm them up before I came back."

"Impressive."

Funny, she doesn't sound impressed. "Sometimes," I say, pushing off the pole. "It's good to be me. Always a joy when I find a woman in my bed instead of a water bottle."

"You're disgusting."

"By the end of the day, we'll be disgusting together."

"Except mine will wash off." She tries to cross her arms and thinks better of it when her towel slips.

"Your disgust for me will wash off? That I'd like to see." I eye her with a smirk.

"God, was your crown bunny so terrible last night that any woman will do this morning? Or do you flirt with everything that walks?"

"Secretary Jensen that's shockingly ableist."

Her cheeks glow again. "I'm glad to hear you're not discriminating."

"And yet, that doesn't sound like a compliment." I make a tsking noise. "What would your mother think about you speaking to a member of the royal family this way?" I cock an eyebrow.

"She's retired now. She'd probably tell me to give as good as I get."

"Seems like a good motto for life, doesn't it? Give as good as you get?" I coat the words in sexual innuendo, but she just rolls her eyes. Christ. She *is* immune to me. Stunning, really. When was the last time a woman didn't part their legs when I used that tone and gave them my best smoldering look? Not sure it's ever happened.

"I'm sure you give and get far more than you should." She glances over her shoulder toward her toiletries.

"There's such a thing as too much?"

"Look in the mirror. You're the very definition of it." Julia sighs. "I need to get ready since a shower seems to be out of the question." She shoos me out with one hand while the other clutches her towel to her chest.

I duck out the bathroom door and zip it closed. In the main bedroom, I search through multiple drawers until I find all my clothes. No way I'm asking her where anything is located. She didn't even organize my items in a logical manner, which had to be on purpose. Though she's messy, she's *never* disorganized.

At the little table, I stare down at my crepes. Of all the breakfast options here, these are my favorite. I should be happy—good breakfast, tracking cool animals, solitude. Except...

So strange having Julia here. I glance at the zipped door, her rustling clear through the thick fabric. We've fallen back into an easy pattern of verbal parries and thrusts. I've barely exchanged more than a few polite phrases with her for years, and in twelve hours, we've regained our footing. The thought makes the ache in my chest pulse. She was... we were...

"Ready." Julia pops out of the bathroom and zips it closed.

Her hair is back in a ponytail, and her makeup is minimal. The ever-present glasses are perched on her nose. Her curvy frame is clad in jeans and a T-shirt. By mid-morning, she'll be too hot in the jeans. First thing this morning, she'll be too cold in the T-shirt. A terrible outfit.

"Crepes. Amazing. Please tell me there's tea," she says settling in a chair.

"Right here." I pour her a cup.

"Will this be okay?" She gestures to her clothes.

"Yep." I nod and take a bite of my breakfast. Whoever cooks these is a God-damned miracle worker.

"Hmm. You're wearing a sweater. Maybe I'll grab one." She stirs milk and sugar into her tea.

I might not tell her what she should wear, but I won't steer her wrong when she makes a good deduction. Whether or not Julia and I have fallen into long ago patterns, she came here to drag me home, and I'm not ready to leave. So, my best bet is to get her to leave without me.

"Is there anything I should know about today?" When she sips her tea, her eyes close, and she groans.

My dick groans with her. *Jesus.* That expression mingled with that noise should be outlawed. "To get the true experience, let yourself be surprised as much as possible."

Her eyes pop open and narrow. "That's Nick-speak for 'I'm going to find a way to enjoy your discomfort all day.'" She peers at me more closely, taking in my outfit. "I need to change. God, that stupid shower probably actually works, and you just aren't telling me." She tosses her napkin on her seat and storms toward her suitcase. "Wouldn't it have been amazing if you'd actually grown up in the last fourteen years?"

"I'm a prince. I don't need to grow up until I'm the king, and since that's never happening…"

"Playboy for life. I suppose all those crown bunnies come in handy in that case."

"Oh, they're handsy." I wink.

She shudders. "I don't need to know where their hands have been."

"Would you prefer I talk about their mouths or their—"

"Nick!" She snorts out a frustrated breath. "It's quite possible I liked it better when you weren't talking to me." She snatches a pair of shorts out of a drawer and wrenches the zipper up to the bathroom.

"You can always go home!" I call to her through the fabric, polishing off my last bite of crepe and cutting off a section of hers, plopping it on my plate.

"Not going to happen, Prince Nicholas." She throws open the flap and tosses her jeans in the general direction of her bag.

They flop on top and then slowly slip to the floor. I stare at them pointedly.

"I'll pick them up later." She waves off my annoyance.

"You're staying in my room."

"Our room now." She gives me a sweet smile.

It's fake. She doesn't smile like that. Julia's real smile causes her blue-gray eyes to spark with mischief, and a lightness overtakes her posture. No point in thinking about that.

"Do you need me to book you a flight home?" I ask.

"Depends. Is the ticket built for two?" She flutters her eyelashes and leans across the table in a flirtatious manner.

An annoying jolt of pleasure rushes through me at her coy demeanor. Jules doesn't talk like that or act like that, and the idea of being turned on by her behavior seems oddly wrong.

"Doubtful. Not much in life that's truly fun is only built for two." I give her a wicked grin.

"That's disgusting." She picks up her fork, and her mouth drops open. "You *ate* some of my crepe?"

"Tick tock, Secretary Jensen. We leave in five minutes." I stack my plates and head to the bathroom.

When I come out, I grab my water bottle, camera, and binoculars.

She shovels the crepe into her mouth. "This is delicious. I wish I had time to savor it."

"Now you understand my dilemma when I realized you weren't going to eat it."

"Yes, I'm sure *that's* why you ate some of it." She downs her tea and sets it on the table. "I did it."

"Don't be late." I unzip the main door and slip out before she can ask me any questions. A jerk move? Sure. But I don't want her here, and the longer I spend with her, the more I start remembering how much I used to want her everywhere.

JULES

Fourteen years ago

Nick peruses the cellar wine racks humming and hawing over which bottle to steal tonight. There are hundreds, possibly thousands, of bottles down here. A difficult choice for someone who knows wine and wants a particular flavor? Probably. Alcohol percentage is all I care about.

"Can you just pick one? Someone is going to catch us." I've already landed in waist-deep manure with my mother once this week thanks to Nick taking one of the motorcycles for a joyride with me on the back. We weren't even gone that long. But we didn't notify security, at Nick's insistence. I told my mother the ride was my idea, and we forgot about guards. A lame excuse. Sometimes I enjoy saying stupid things to see how quickly my mother's head pops off and spins around.

"I'm just debating how expensive I should go." Nick rubs his chin and strolls the rows of outrageously expensive wines.

"None of those." I stride to the opposite end of the cellar and pull out the newest bottle, which is likely to be the cheapest.

"They'll realize that one is missing, Jules." He gives an exasperated sigh.

"And they'll be pissed if they realize we stole a thousand-dollar bottle of white wine to drink while watching a meteor shower."

"Ah, white? That's what you're after? Helps narrow it down." He plucks a bottle from one of the slots.

"I don't want to know how much that bottle costs. Easier to plead ignorance." I hold up my hands and half turn away.

He takes a closer look at the label. "Only a couple hundred, likely." He grins. "They'll think it was pulled during one of their state dinners."

A door opens somewhere upstairs, and Nick and I freeze.

"Oh, God. We're going to get caught," I mutter. "They'll throw me in the dungeon."

"We don't do that anymore." Nick teases. "Your mother, though..."

I slap his arm, and he rubs his bicep.

"No mother jokes tonight?" He tucks the bottle of wine under his arm. "I've got a corkscrew. We drinking out of the bottle, or do you need your sparkling water and a glass?"

"I'll get the water and glass from the kitchen. Meet at the barn balcony?"

"Best seat on the island," Nick agrees heading for the walkout exit to avoid going back into the main house. "Try not to get caught."

"Shut up," I hiss in a fierce whisper. Of the two of us, I always end up spotted by someone whenever we're scheming. I creep up the stairs, avoiding all the spots on the wooden stairs that creak. At the top, I crack the door and listen for anyone in the kitchen. Most of the staff should be gone by now.

I breathe a sigh of relief at the silence and prop the door open just enough to squeeze through. Stupid thing gives a loud squeak if you open it too far. Light from the clear starry sky streams through the kitchen windows bathing the excessive space in moonlight.

"Stealing from us again?" Alex comments from behind me.

I jump, and my heart kicks and then races before I whirl on him. "No! No. I would never."

"Just decided to go for a walk in the wine cellar. Does your mother know?" He raises his eyebrows and pops a piece of orange into his mouth.

"Why are you eating oranges in the dark like a creep?" I circle the island and take out the wine glasses from the cupboard and the bottles of sparkling water from the fridge. Alex is the least of my worries. If I don't get to the barn in good time, Nick will be annoyed at my lateness. *Did it really take twenty minutes to get two glasses and some water?* His tone will be tinged with annoyance. I walk a fine line with my tardiness.

"I happen to like oranges. Why are you drinking water out of wine glasses?" He points to my full hands.

"*Sparkling* water. It's fancy water. Needs a fancy glass."

Alex's lips twitch. "You've got all the ingredients for a wine spritzer, just need the wine." He stares pointedly at the door I came from. "Want someone legal to get you a bottle?" He meanders toward me.

My bravado vanishes when he gets closer, and I can't seem to get any words past my lips. Nick's always been my person in the royal family. The one I turn to, the one I look for in a crowd, the one who'd form a one-man team to drag me back from the peak of Everest if I got lost. That's an actual conversation we had once while drunk after we read *Into Thin Air* for extra credit. There's nothing I wouldn't do for Nick, including keeping my confusing feelings for his older brother in check. Alex has dark and mysterious nailed down to the highest level of cliché. Almost everything about Alex mystifies me.

"Where'd you stash the bottle, Jules? Or did my rebel brother run off with it and leave you to do the dangerous glass and water gathering?"

"This is hardly the dangerous bit," I scoff.

"What's going on between you two anyway?"

"What do you mean?"

"Drinking under the stars together. Attached at the hip." He gives me an assessing gaze. "Hardly a leap to think there's more to this friendship."

I laugh self-consciously. "Nick's been my best friend since forever. I don't know why everyone all of a sudden thinks our behavior is weird." I tuck a stray strand of hair behind my ear. "Nick has a girlfriend."

"Does he? And he's lying under the stars with you?" He invades my personal space, the tang of oranges circling me.

My back is pressed against the island, and the citrus scent mingles with his cologne. My stomach flutters. "You didn't know he had a girlfriend?"

"Never met her. You, though, you're here all the time."

"If you were home more, you'd meet her." My words sound convincing, but Alex has a point. Nick doesn't spend a lot of time with Vicky now that school is out for the summer. Might be because I mocked him for picking a girlfriend with a name that rhymes with his. Nicky and Vicky. *How cute.* He ignored me for almost an hour after my heavy-handed teasing. Tough exterior with the softest, gooiest center, that's my Nick.

"Uni keeps me occupied." Alex leans against the island beside me. "There's really nothing going on between you and my brother?"

"We're friends, Alex." I push off from the island, the glasses clinking together while I storm to the side door. Talking to Alex is a waste of time, and Nick will be pissed I've taken so long.

I wave to the guard at the edge of the road while I hurry up the narrow path to the old barn. By the time I get to the bottom of the ladder, I'm out of breath. Nick peeks out from the roof hatch that leads to a balcony big enough for us to stretch out beside each other on a blanket.

"Jesus, Jensen. Did it really take twenty minutes to get two glasses and some water?" Nick takes the items from me so I can climb the rest of the way up.

"Alex caught me," I admit. "Offered to get me wine to go in my glasses."

Nick opens the wine and mixes the spritzers before passing me one. "Give you the whole *I'm legal* bullshit?"

"That's exactly what he did. How'd you guess?" I plop onto the blanket beside him, and he tosses another blanket over my legs. The roof is breezy at night, and we've been here so many times, we have our roles down. We've been stealing alcohol since we were thirteen—stray bottles of beer and cider split between us—but we've upped the ante to full bottles of wine since my sixteenth birthday.

A sigh escapes me when I take the first sip of spritzer and catch sight of a shooting star. "There!" I point to the streak in the sky.

"Been going on for twenty minutes now, Jules." He leans back, his hands behind his head.

We watch the meteors, pointing them out to each other, and exclaiming at their brilliance. But Alex's comments in the kitchen niggle at me every time Nick's shoulder rubs mine. We've always done these things together, and I don't know why I'm second-guessing us now.

"Does Vicky ever get annoyed at how much time we spend together?"

"Why?" Nick's tone is wary.

"Just wondering."

"She's mentioned it a few times."

"We don't have to spend all this time together if you'd rather spend more time with her." The offer tastes sour on my tongue though. Nick is mine in a way I never want him to be anyone else's.

Nick catches my gaze. "If you were a guy, we wouldn't even be having this conversation. So, let's not. You're my best friend. Some girl, *any* girl, isn't going to change that. So just shut up, okay? No one tells me who I can and can't hang out with." Despite his harsh words, his voice is gentle.

"Do you really think your future wife will be cool with us hanging out all the time?"

"If she's not okay with it, I can guarantee she's not my future wife. Besides I'm not sure I'll ever get married."

"Really?"

"I barely tolerate people, and I don't know about subjecting anyone to my life. I might not be the future king, but the royal title's not that simple, is it?" He shrugs. "Even if I did get married, I can't see it happening until I'm forty or fifty. I'll be the silver fox." He waggles his eyebrows at me.

"I swear to God, if you're fifty and try to marry some twenty-five-year-old model, we won't be able to be friends anymore whether or not she likes me."

"Twenty-six is cool, though?" He ruffles my hair.

"Ugh. Don't be that guy."

"Which guy would you like me to be?"

"*This* guy." I ruffle his hair in return. "Don't ever change, okay?"

"Got it. Remain stagnant for the rest of my life. Sounds easy, actually. Could probably manage that."

I laugh and sip my wine.

We fall into a companionable silence with small bursts of pointing out a streak in the sky while we drink.

"Won't your parents make you get married at some point?" I ask. A vague memory from my Bellerive history class surfaces.

"In theory, Bellerive Royalty can be married off via arranged marriage any day after their thirtieth birthday if they haven't managed to make a love match." Nick gulps his wine. "I'll be counting on you to save me in that situation, Jensen."

"Save you?"

"You'll have to marry me. Keep me out of trouble."

My heart kicks. Nick. Mine. Forever. I search his face, but it's brimming with sincerity. "Why would you marry me?"

"Why not? I know I can tolerate large doses of you. To be fair, there's at least one thing you haven't mastered from my wish list. I always expected any wife of mine would be able to read a clock. Sort of a vital life skill."

"Tonight was not my fault." I slap his chest, and he grunts.

"How about the fifty thousand other times?"

"Hyperbole."

"Barely."

"Oh, look!" I point to the sky.

"Distracting me from the point with pretty things."

"Isn't that my line?" I tease.

"Will be if we get married. I'll shower you with jewels."

"You'll need to. Marrying you would be a tremendous sacrifice."

"Becoming a princess is such a hardship." He scoffs.

"We both know according to Bellerive custom, I would not be a princess."

"True. You'd have to marry Alex to get that title." He chuckles. "Whoever does that deserves more than jewels. She might need to be heavily medicated."

"Oh, please," I say, taking another gulp of my drink. "Alex isn't that bad."

Nick goes still beside me. "Since when?" He searches my face.

"I don't know," I say carefully, thinking of Alex in the kitchen who was almost civil to me for once. "Don't you think he's mellowed a bit in college?"

Nick draws his knees toward his chest, and his drink dangles from his fingers before he chugs the spritzer. "No, I don't think he's mellowed."

Since we were little, Alex has acted like he's the smartest person in the room, even when he isn't. He constantly niggles Nick about being the 'spare.' His favorite phrases start with *When I'm king* and often get worse from there. I'm not convinced Alex does any of it with malice—it's just him. Arrogant and cocky and oblivious to everyone else's feelings.

He pours himself another generous drink but doesn't say anything more, just stares out over the property, not even watching for meteors anymore.

My opinion of Alex softening even slightly has ruffled his feathers. Luckily, smoothing them is my specialty.

"Do you think she'd need anti-depressants or a hard-core drug addiction to marry him?" I muse.

Nick glances at me, and the tension eases from his shoulders. He grins.

Just like that, we slip into our easy banter while another meteor streaks across the sky above us. I could stay on this roof with Nick for the rest of my life and never regret a moment.

"I promise," I say, my voice tinged with humor, "if your father tries to arrange your marriage, I'll sacrifice my freedom for you. Fall on the sword. Take one for the team. Drink from the poisoned cup."

Nick clinks his glass with mine. "Cheers to that. That's one promise you won't be getting out of."

Luckily, I can't imagine I'd want to, anyway.

JULIA

Once Nick is gone from the tent, I sink into my breakfast chair and check my phone signal. Nothing. No bars. Kafil told me last night I can purchase data from the camp's Wi-Fi, and they have a satellite phone I can use to get my messages and make phone calls. Outside the camp, I may get a signal, but here it's unlikely.

The king asked me to check in after I gauged Nick's reaction to coming home. Although we didn't compare notes, I'm sure neither of us expected him to jump at the chance to return to Bellerive.

A phone call to the king is best. He doesn't answer his emails. His secretary does. My mother doesn't need to be aware of my tit-for-tat with Nick. Her sense of humor isn't quite the same as King George's.

Will he even answer his phone? The lack of goodbye yesterday was strange. He and Alex were holed up in meetings with my mother all day, but since I was leaving, I wasn't privy to their discussions. After becoming his right hand the last few years being cut off so abruptly was disconcerting like they were hiding something from me. An overreaction, I'm sure. I'm just not used to being excluded.

I watch the clock turn over on my phone. How long will I need to sit here to guarantee Nick will be frustrated with me when I turn up?

Last night when I chatted to Kafil I learned he's at this camp until Nick's adventure is done. Whether we leave on time or not today is no concern to him because he's got nothing else to do but serve Nick's needs. I'm not inconveniencing him by showing up late. However, I remember well how much Nick likes to be punctual. Early, even. Odd for a boy and a man who has often prided himself on being a rebel.

My tardiness will drive him bonkers.

When almost twenty minutes have ticked by, I gather my camera and water bottle. I unzip the flap and keep a watchful eye on the long grasses along the path. Kafil said the dangers were mostly at night, but no one can afford to be complacent in the middle of the Serengeti. Animals can wander wherever they like. Thrilling and terrifying to think of coming close to such big, dangerous wildlife.

I frown when I get close to the meal tent, and I adjust my prescription sunglasses. Hadn't this been where Kafil said the vehicle would be parked? Not a single person anywhere.

"*Habari za asubuhi*. Are you looking for the prince?" a male voice calls to me from inside the meal tent. "He left you a note."

"He left?" I squawk. Seems I've underestimated my opponent.

"Yes. They departed at seven, sharp." He ducks out the canvas door and passes me a slip of paper. "He said you had changed your mind about going out this morning. Too jetlagged? He asked me to give you this when you arrived for some more food. Are you hungry? He mentioned you only ate half your crepe."

Because he ate the other half. Am I angry or impressed Nick took off without me? Dropping me on my ass, figurately or literally, never used to be his thing. Who knows what his thing is now? I guess I'm learning. He obviously takes his punctuality just as seriously as he did when we were kids. Being raised on dinners with leaders from other countries, diplomatic trips, fundraisers, and public outreach has honed Nick's sense of responsibility in some ways. Made him rebellious in others though.

I finger the folded note and contemplate not even opening it. Maybe he left me instructions on how to meet up with him? Younger Nick would have. I flip it open and suppress my eye roll.

Told you not to be late.

That's it. No indication he'll be back for me later or how to fill my time since he's abandoned me. I huff out a breath and rip up his note. So frustrating.

I follow the worker into the spacious tent and gaze at the big family-style table in the middle.

"Do you serve breakfast in here?" I address the staff member who let me in. Other people are buzzing around us, clearing dirty dishes, scrubbing surfaces, and readying the table for the next meal.

"For everyone but His Royal Highness. He enjoys his breakfast and lunch in the tent. More privacy, I believe."

Ah, right. Makes sense. Nick only ever enjoyed an audience on his terms.

Well, if I'm stuck here, I might as well check in with King George and pretend like this rescue mission is going great. *So great.*

"Can I use the satellite phone? I need to call the king." I give the worker a fleeting smile.

"Yes, no problem. In here, in the corner." He waves me past the table to a corner desk housing their communications systems. Radio. Phone. Wi-fi connection. "Food? I can have something prepared for you."

"Are there any more crepes? His Royal Highness was hungry and ate mine." Nick might not want to look like an asshole in front of other people, but I have no qualms with ratting him out.

"Oh." A brief smile lights up the worker's face before he smothers it. "His Royal Highness isn't normally that hungry in the morning."

"I doubt he was this morning either," I grumble, following him to the phone. We seem to be having a pissing contest, and so far, Nick's winning. Not that I'd ever admit that aloud.

The staff member leaves me in the corner with the phone, presumably to fetch more food. With my jet lag, I'm not that hungry, but I can't turn down a chance to put in a dig at Nick, even if he's not here to witness it.

I dial the king's personal extension from memory, half expecting my mother to answer. While she's been enjoying her retirement, she has far too much time to meddle in my life and my little sister's. Although Posey has a good sense of humor about it, she and my father will be happy Mother has someone else's life to organize again.

"King George." His deep voice rumbles in my ear, and a familiar comfort embraces me. In my heart, King George and Queen Helen have been my bonus parents. Though they employ me now, they were always quick to congratulate me on accomplishments, cheer me on in my pursuits, and help me in any way they could.

"My king, it's Secretary Jensen." Then I realize my mother is also called that, and we sound somewhat similar on the phone. "The younger one."

"Julia! I was hoping you'd call. How is Nicholas?"

Very Nicholas-like. "He needs a haircut, a shave, and someone to organize his closet."

"Sounds like I sent the right person." George chuckles.

"He also doesn't want to come home. I'm going to wait a few days, and then I'll slip in some comments about his impending engagement."

There's a long silence across the line, and I'm about to say hello again when George speaks, "Actually, Alexander and I haven't had a chance to discuss his succession."

My stomach drops into my feet. That's not good. "I already told Prince Nicholas," I whisper.

"No matter. He's not communicating with anyone while he's there. Off the grid, as he likes to call it. But I would prefer Nicholas doesn't return until I've had a chance to speak to Alexander."

Okay, that's fine. I can handle my gaffe. I press a hand against my racing heart. We can't just hop on a plane tomorrow anyway. "By the time I get flights arranged and—"

"Please wait for me to let you know I've spoken to Alexander. It may be a week or two as we're collaborating on one final government project together."

A week or two? Why did he bother to send me at all? Nick is here for three weeks, and then a week in Vegas, and then he'll be home anyway. Now that I think about it, I'm really not sure why I had to come. Had the request been to go after anyone but Nick, I might have discovered the missing piece earlier.

Who am I kidding? The king's illness has also toppled me off my logic game. *He's sick.* People like King George aren't meant to be fallible to these types of illnesses. While everyone dies someday, his won't be the dignified affair any of us might have wanted or expected. It'll be messy and awful and so hard on everyone. My heart sinks.

Might as well put my thoughts out there. "Your Highness, I'm not sure why you sent me if you don't need Prince Nicholas home right away?"

"The opportunity for one final government initiative landed in my lap the day you departed. I couldn't pass it up. Once we've finished the government maneuver, I'll talk to Alexander about the coronation, and you can prod Nicholas to return."

That explained them being holed up in meetings and not giving me a proper sendoff. Still, it's strange for him to be so vague. Why not just tell me what government project he's working on? I didn't even know there was something he was trying to get done. Security sensitive, maybe? Though I'm usually privy to those. My mind is a riot of speculation.

"Prince Nicholas plans to be home in four weeks. If this is going to take a bit, do you want me to come back to Bellerive?" If there are things that need to be taken care of there, I don't know why I'd stay here.

"Haven't you always said you wanted to go on an African Safari? I was sure that was something you told me once."

My breath catches at his memory. If we ever had that conversation, it would have only been once. Since I've taken over my mother's position at her request, my hopes and dreams haven't really been a topic the king and I have delved into. My job as secretary was meant to be a stopover on the way to another life. Instead of a layover, I've been stuck, not sure where to go next, what to do, and I'm rapidly approaching thirty.

How do I abandon family, leave the island? Except for my four years in college, I never quite figured out how to loosen the strings.

Now with the king sick, there's no way I'm leaving the island anytime soon.

Perhaps I should seize this chance, even if it means I'm stuck experiencing my adventure with the asshole version of Nick who appeared out of nowhere at sixteen.

"Yes," I admit. "This is a trip I've wanted to take."

"Take it. Enjoy yourself. Your mother is cracking the whip here. Keep Nicholas in line and off the grid for a few weeks while we sort some business. Better for all my children to be happy before the news must drop, don't you think?"

Actually, he should be telling them now in case a tabloid breaks the story before George can inform them. While Bellerive might be a dot located between Bermuda and Ponta Delgada in the North Atlantic Ocean, his three sons have attracted ample attention since they hit puberty. Beauty, arrogance, and wealth attract gossip rags like bees to honey.

Consulting doctors in three different countries leaves loose ends and mouths to flap. To me, not telling his children is incredibly risky.

But I've already given my opinion, and one thing I've learned as his secretary is that I'm welcome to voice my ideas once. Beyond that lies danger and his sharp tongue. So, I decide to hold mine.

"I think you know your family best," I hedge.

"Since we've got Nicholas's location, and I now have a contact number for you, there's no need to check in unless you're leaving the camp in Tanzania. Once I've spoken to Alexander about the coronation and plans are underway, I'll leave a message for you."

A sliver of unease wedges itself under my skin. Something about this situation isn't right. Is it the change of plans after I've left? The vagueness about the government initiative he's working on, or is it simply being stuck in Tanzania with Nick for an undetermined amount of time?

My plan to needle him into agreeing to come home can't continue if I'm not supposed to goad him into leaving. The new goal requires him to stay.

"As you wish, my king," I agree. Someone knocks on his office door, and he hangs up before I have a chance to dig any deeper. I could email my mother, but she's not likely to tell me anything the king doesn't want me to know.

I replace the phone and stare at the communications center for a moment. "What time does Prince Nicholas return?" I speak to the bustling room, hoping someone will throw out an answer.

"They come back for lunch." The same person who showed me to the phone enters through a back door, a covered plate in his hand, and he passes it to me. "Prince Nicholas told the kitchen staff your favorite breakfast food was eggs benedict, so they made it especially for you."

I grit my teeth and force a smile. Eggs benedict is my *least* favorite breakfast meal ever. The sauce is disgusting. Perhaps I can scrape it off and salvage some of the eggs or English muffins. "So thoughtful," I mutter. I'll need to find a polite way to tell the kitchen staff Prince Nicholas made a mistake or I'll end up with this atrocious meal each morning, I'm sure.

"Prince Nicholas will likely take a night drive. He has nocturnal animals he wants to check off his list." The man grins.

The idea of a night drive should be thrilling, but my conversation with King George is still playing on a loop in my head. With a deep breath, I try to figure out a new strategy. Needling Nick is still my preference because the alternative is being *nice* to him. Which, given our history, doesn't sit well with me.

However, he's proven in the last twelve hours to be much better at ambushing and surprising me than I am at doing the same to him. *So annoying.*

"What time will Prince Nicholas return to camp?" I ask.

"Around one."

"Am I okay to take this to my tent?" I gesture to the plate.

"Of course. Of course. If you need anything else, please let us know."

Then I remember the one thing I want more than food. "A shower," I say. "Can you show me how to work the shower?"

"Ah, yes. You'd like a bucket delivered?"

"A bucket delivered?" Nick didn't say anything about buckets this morning.

"Yes. The showers are heated buckets of water that we pour into a holding tank and then you pull on the string to release water."

I draw in a deep breath. That *asshole*. "Right. Yes. That would be lovely, thank you!"

On the way back to the tent, I hatch a plan. While it might be better not to piss off Nick, denying me a shower is one step too far.

NICHOLAS

Julia ruined my morning. What's that stupid saying? Can't live with 'em, can't live without 'em. Too fucking right in her case.

There was no way I was waiting around like some servant to her whims. If she couldn't turn up on time, especially when all that was required of her was to walk down a grassy path behind me, she could sit and stew alone.

Except I underestimated how guilty I'd feel leaving her behind. *I* ended up stewing in the back of the vehicle while Kafil tried to entice me out of my foul mood with mating leopards, a massive herd of elephants streaming past our vehicle, a pride of lions frolicking in the long grass, and a civet, which I hadn't encountered yet. Another one ticked off my list. As a guide, he outdid himself today. I'm winning safari bingo, and I can't even be happy about it.

When we pull into camp, I'm steaming, and not from the heat. I grab my stuff from the back of the vehicle and storm toward my tent, ignoring leech-woman and everyone else from the other morning drives. Normally, we all compare notes over a drink before lunch. The drivers talk amongst themselves on radios while we're out, but I enjoy the buzz of excitement that coats the camp when we've all returned from a good morning. Who was lucky enough to see what and where?

There's no enjoyment in boasting about our sights today. Instead, I'm preoccupied with curvy brunettes who've taken over my small slice of solitude. Of all the people my father could have sent, it had to be her. Anyone else I could ignore or be a complete asshole to or tolerate or something other than *this* feeling.

Where am I supposed to spend my afternoons between drives if she's in the tent too? With everyone else in the common areas? I don't think so. Small talk for days. The idea makes me want to fall into a coma.

Last night, I figured I could chase her away and back to Bellerive easily enough, and perhaps I still can, but in the meantime, I have to put up with her presence seeping into my life. I cannot risk getting attached to her and clawing my way out of those big feelings a second time. No one would willingly do that to themselves. I'd have to be mentally unstable to wade into depression and heartbreak a second time. *No thank you.*

Standing in front of my tent, I take a deep breath before unzipping the flap. As soon as I'm inside, my sixth sense kicks in.

The one that senses food or naked women. On the two-person table in front of me is a charcuterie board, and I haven't seen one of those since I left Bellerive. That in itself might not be suspicious, but it's piled with some of my favorite tidbits, almost as though someone who knows me specially ordered it. With a frown, I glance at the bed. Not a naked woman in sight. The food must be the cause of the strange fluttering in the pit of my stomach.

"Secretary Jensen?" I call.

The door to the bathroom unzips, and she steps out. "You're back!"

I stare at her for a moment, expecting anger or annoyance or anything other than my favorite foods laid out along with a cheery attitude. Did she have a personality transplant in the hours I've been gone?

Ah, now I see. She's probably going to sit down and eat the charcuterie board in front of me and not offer me a single piece. I'll give her the opening to rub the food in my face. Least I can do after leaving her behind.

"What's this?" I gesture to the table piled with food with a raised eyebrow.

"Lunch. Do you want some? I gave the kitchen all your favorite foods while I was there talking to them about my intense distaste for eggs benedict." A hint of a smile tugs at the corners of her lips. "They were misinformed."

"Oh?" I'm still at the entrance, an intruder in my own tent. Leaving her at camp to get far too comfortable with the staff and my tent was a miscalculation on my part. "You don't like eggs benedict?" I furrow my brow in mock regret. "My memory must be faulty."

She takes a seat at the table and gestures to the one across from her. "Not to worry. I sorted it out. Eat with me."

I hang up my water bottle, binoculars, and camera by the door, my mind ticking through all the ways she could be ambushing me with food. Hot sauce coating everything? Spoiled food? Have someone come in partway through and remove the food before I've had a chance to get my fill? Dump the board on me? So many possibilities.

There's a napkin beside my chair, and I pluck it up, placing it over my lap after I sink into the chair across from her. All my senses are on red alert. "You're not upset I left without you?"

She releases a laugh that's as fake as leech woman's claim she used sun cream yesterday. "Not at all. I can't always think of myself. I need to understand that other people's time is just as valuable as mine, right?" She sips her water and meets my gaze.

I swallow and lift my water glass. That's almost word-for-word something I said to her during a fight we had when we were sixteen. Our friendship was unraveling around me, and I couldn't figure out how to spool the strands back into something resembling order. She needs to stop reminding me of things I've worked really fucking hard to forget.

I rub my face at the memory and check to see what she's put on her plate. Whatever she's eating must be safe—no hot sauce or disgusting sabotage. Would she do that to herself? I'd admire the commitment, but I doubt it.

"What'd you see?" Julia takes a bite of crunchy bread piled with cheese and shaved meat.

I make myself exactly the same combination she's eating and take a bite. What kind of meat is this? No matter. It's delicious. I close my eyes and stifle a moan.

"I did well? It's an apology board, of a sort."

"For being late?"

She shrugs and makes herself another little sandwich. "So, what did you see?"

"Leopards, elephants, lions, a civet." A frisson of satisfaction zips through me at the list. While I might not have enjoyed my morning, she doesn't need to realize that.

"Ah, the mating leopards you and Kafil have been following?" She selects another piece from the board, and I follow her lead.

"We found them a couple days ago. Kafil figures we might see them again tomorrow. They're only together for about five days."

"Five days of bliss." She winks at me. "Do they mate a couple times a day?

"Every fifteen minutes." I'm definitely missing something. She's being far too nice and relaxed given I abandoned her this morning and ensured she received her least favorite food.

"Impressive. Probably just a two-pump dump, though, right?" She takes an olive from the board and pushes it between her lips.

Watching her is distracting, and realizing we're discussing the sexual habits of leopards as though it's perfectly normal is also a bit strange. The woman sitting across from me reminds me too much of a girl I once knew.

She plucks a miniature samosa off the board and sets it on my plate. "These are my favorite."

I eye her warily. "Funny, you haven't eaten one yet." When she frowns, I say, "Since they're your favorites."

"Oh, I didn't want to hog them. The cook gave me a few while he was preparing the board." She grins and picks one, popping it into her mouth.

After she's chewed and swallowed, I decide it's safe. I pop the one she gave me into my mouth. At first, the flavors mingle and rotate around my mouth in an incredible combination. Once I've swallowed, the heat kicks in, shooting up my throat, and my mouth is on fire. I cough and take a big gulping drink of water.

She frowns and takes another one out of the samosa bowl throwing it into her mouth. This time I notice she takes from her side of the bowl, and she definitely gave me one from the *opposite* side.

"You're not getting the full experience," I wheeze out, plucking one from my side of the bowl and putting it on her plate. "They're so delicious. You should have one more."

Her lips twitch, and she pats her flat stomach. "I'm getting pretty full. No need to waste food." She lets out a deep sigh. "I still haven't had that shower yet. Did you talk to Kafil? Or can you come take another look to see whether they fixed it while I was in the kitchen?"

My mouth is on fire, and I glance around the board for anything creamy to put out the blaze. There's a small cup of what looks like rice pudding, and I seize it, spooning it into my mouth. I suppress my sigh of relief when the inferno fades to a dull throbbing. As payback for either leaving her behind or for her delicious breakfast, a five-alarm fire in my mouth isn't so bad.

"You didn't ask anyone else about the shower?" I take another mouthful of the rice pudding, holding it there to ease the burning.

"Should I have?" Julia asks, already over by the bathroom entrance. "You said you'd ask Kafil? I didn't want to get anyone in trouble."

Reluctantly, I put down the rest of the pudding and follow her into the shower. Since she hasn't figured out she needs to order a bucket, it's not going to work. But whatever. I can keep up the ruse a little longer. After all, she just blindsided me with wildfire samosas.

She crowds me into the shower area, her chest brushing against mine as she reaches for the cord. I glance up and realize I'm standing under the head of the shower. When I look back down, Julia's blue-gray eyes are wide and warmth spreads across my chest. She's not wearing her glasses.

"I pull this cord and water comes out, right? There's like plumbing or something?"

"Or something." My lips twist in amusement.

"Hmm," she says, biting her lip.

My body should not spring to attention at her proximity, at the way mischief enters her gaze the second before she yanks on the cord. A warning bell almost penetrates my haze of desire before freezing cold water douses me in a blast from above.

"Oh." Julia feigns surprise and jumps back. "I guess it works. Was it warm?"

The barely suppressed smile tells me she knows exactly how fucking cold the water was. Not that I didn't need a cold shower for the hot thoughts creeping into my mind. I'm not impressed she was the one to deliver it. I stalk toward her, ice-cold water dripping off me.

"Now, Prince Nicholas, be reasonable," Julia cries, her back pressed against the tent, hands up, gaze averted.

I'm not sure what she expects me to do, but I press a hand on either side of her and shake my shaggy head, dousing her in residual water and probably more than a little damp dust. She glances up at me, a smirk on her face.

"That's all you've got? You're going to shake over me like a dog?"

"Make no mistake, Secretary Jensen, I'm no dog." I wrap my arms around her, drawing her flush against my soaking wet body, letting the water seep into her clothes. "Better?" I ask, gazing down at her.

The look she gives me is so coy, I almost don't believe it's Jules. "I don't know. Have you cooled off yet?"

"I'm just warming up," I mutter, my gaze straying to her lips.

Her breath catches, and I scan her face, trying to figure out if the zip of attraction that just sparked between us is one-sided. Did she fake that catch in her breathing? Or is she not quite as immune to me as we both might prefer?

"Don't leave me behind again," she murmurs, her gaze stuck on my lips.

Does she *want* me to kiss her? I've got to be reading this wrong. "Don't be late again."

"No promises. Old habits and all."

Oh, I am more than familiar with how hard it is to quit an old habit. Before I can do something stupid, I let her go and step around her. "We leave right after dinner for our night drive. If you're not at the vehicle, I *will* leave without you."

On my way out of the tent, I fill a small plate with everything from the charcuterie board that's been proven safe, and then I head for one of the dreaded common areas.

Staying in here with Jules is emotional suicide.

Nick

Fourteen years ago

People are paid to dress me. At my age, the slew of women in this powder room checking my hair, steaming my tux, and treating even the hint of a blemish as though it's a national crisis should probably bother me. But if having them here means I don't have to wrestle this piece of cloth in my hand into a bowtie, I'll take their prodding.

The prodding I won't take? Alex's. My brother could try the patience of a saint.

Unfortunately, as per tradition, the three of us have been forced into the same room so the attendants don't have to flounce from room to room to ensure we present ourselves on time for this diplomat dinner downstairs.

My phone goes off, and I maneuver around Bea, who is styling my hair, to grab it off the table.

"Who's that?" Alex asks, trying to peer over my shoulder.

"Why does it matter to you?" It's a text from Vicky asking if she can see me later. Since school got out a couple weeks ago, I've only hung out with her a handful of times. Most of those involved a bedroom and a lack of clothing. When I rub my face, Bea sucks in a sharp breath.

"The treatment." She gestures to my face where she claims I'm in danger of getting a breakout.

"Sorry," I mutter, replying to Vicky's text that I have a royal thing till around ten.

"Was that Jules? Are you seeing her later?"

I toss my phone onto the settee next to me. Alex has been asking me a lot of questions about Jules the last week or so. Fucking annoying.

"She told me you have a girlfriend?"

Not sure I like the sound of this. When were he and Jules trading secrets? "Jules told you I had a girlfriend? Why would she tell you that?"

"I asked her if there was anything more happening between you and her. She said you have a girlfriend."

I narrow my eyes. "Jules is my best friend. She's been my best friend since we could walk. I don't know why everyone's obsessed with making it more." Though lately, my feelings for her haven't felt quite so platonic. Obsessive. Possessive. All consuming. Whether or not she's with me, she's all I think about, and I try very hard to make sure she's around all the time.

"So, you don't fancy her?"

"You know you're not British, right?"

"Bellerive has British influences. I go to a British school."

"You mean *uni*?" I mock.

"You didn't really answer my question," Alex says as one of the women helps him into his tux.

"Because it's insulting. There's no reason Jules and I can't be friends."

"Of course. But is that all?"

"Why do you care?"

"Curious. I find your relationship with her fascinating, and if I'd gone to an American college, my minor would have been in psychology."

Instead, he opted to go to a British university and major in being a dickhead. Brice wanders over almost fully dressed.

"What are you two talking about?" Brice asks.

"Jules," Alex says, examining himself in the mirror.

"He give you the speech about how men and women can be friends without wanting to bang each other?" Brice asks.

"Brice," Bea admonishes while she fixes a strand of his light brown hair that's fallen over his forehead.

I've been giving a less crude version of that speech for almost two years now to everyone who asks about Julia. Lately, everywhere I turn, people assume Jules and I are more than we are. Whereas before I used to burn with the fire of indignation. *How dare they suggest we can't be just friends?* Now the same claim doesn't ring as honest coming from my lips. At some point, against my will and unbeknownst to me, I became what everyone expected. Jules and I *are* just friends, but there are so many days, so many moments where I long for a relationship I may never have. The thought of kissing her no longer baffles me or frustrates me—it excites me.

But I also realize kissing her might ruin our friendship. Can best friends recover from unrequited love?

"I'm surprised your girlfriend doesn't have a problem with you and Jules. The two of you are huddled together all over the estate. If Jules was my girlfriend, I wouldn't be too pleased."

"Jules will never be your girlfriend, so I suppose you'll never have to concern yourself with our friendship."

"That wasn't actually my point," Alex says with a smirk. "I feel sorry for your girlfriend. Must be hard for her to realize she'll never measure up."

All Vicky's comments the last few months come back to me in a rush. Some of her digs about Jules were veiled, others more blatant, but once I made it clear my friendship with Jules wasn't up for discussion, she mostly dropped it. Have I been unfair to Vicky? Hadn't even crossed my mind. I've been too busy protecting my friendship with Jules.

"Impossible to maintain, if you ask me." Alex tugs on his tux while Bea finishes his bowtie.

"No one asked you," I mutter, the bowtie in my hands damp with sweat. What exactly does he mean? My friendship with Jules is impossible or my relationship with Vicky? For me, there's no choice. Vicky's had my body, but Jules has my heart.

"Someone will get jealous along the way, and the two of you won't be as close anymore." He uses the snooty, older brother, know-it-all tone that grates.

Despite my annoyance with Alex, his words turn around and around in my head all night while I'm making small talk, while I'm eating dinner, and again while I'm dancing with strangers. By the time the last guest has left, my mind is made up.

###

When I arrive at Jules's house, it's late. So late, in fact, her light is the only one still on in the house. From underneath her window, I text her. Within moments, her window opens, and she's leaning out.

"Nick, what are you doing here? It's late." She glances over her shoulder as though expecting someone in her house to burst into her room.

Posey, her younger sister, pops her head out beside Julia. She gives me a wave and a sigh. Julia pushes her away and shoos her out of the room.

When she comes back to the windowsill there's a hint of a smile on her face. "What are you doing here?"

"Come for a ride with me." It's not a question. I need her on the back of my bike, pressed against me, arms around my waist, her cheek against my back. While I waded through all the things I had to do tonight, getting this moment with her has been all I could focus on.

"Did you ditch security again? My mother will kill me if I go with you when you're unprotected."

"I broke up with Vicky. Come for a ride. *Please*."

Her expression turns from frustrated to a soft understanding, which makes my stomach clench. "Aww. Nicky. Are you okay?"

"Just get your ass down here and come for a ride with me." How many different ways can I cajole her into getting on my bike?

"Give me a sec," she says, disappearing inside her bedroom again. She shuts the window, and I can see the outline of her moving around her room. We've done enough middle-of-the-night rides she'll know exactly what to grab.

From the side door, she emerges, a leather jacket zipped tight. She eyes my outfit. "Did you come right from the dinner?"

"Vicky, then here." My tux is out of sorts, and I've thrown a leather jacket over it to break the wind. Later, I'll hang my tux neatly on the dry-cleaning hanger and hope no one notices the mud on the pant legs. If they realize it's from riding around the country escort-free, I'll catch hell.

She stares up at me, searching my face, and I smooth a strand of her hair that's come free of her low ponytail. This moment, right here, is worth any lecture from anyone at the palace.

"What's bothering you? Did you break up with Vicky or did she break up with you?"

A smile tugs at the edges of my lips. Her gaze is locked on mine, and all is right with the world. There's nowhere else I want to be, no one else I want to be with. Should scare the shit out of me. But this is Jules, the one person I trust more than anyone else in the world. We're always one hundred percent honest with each other.

"I broke up with her," I reiterate. "I was a shitty boyfriend anyway."

"Did she say that?" Her eyes light up with amusement and then she laughs.

"No, but we all know it's true."

"I never really understood why you were with her," Jules says when my hand slides along hers.

I raise my eyebrows. She knows exactly why I was with Vicky.

She tugs me toward the bike, walking backward. "Okay, maybe I remember you saying something about why you were with her."

Vicky and I might not have a lot in common, but she's fucking hot. A few months ago, that attribute was enough for me. Seems hollow now. To be fair, Jules mocked me for my shallowness, accused me of letting my dick make decisions for me. She wasn't wrong then, and I'm not sure what's in charge right now. Doesn't feel like the right head this time either.

I pass Jules a helmet, and I put on my own before climbing onto the bike. She gets on behind me and scoots forward so her arms wrap around my middle, the side of her head pressed to my back.

I place my hand over hers on my stomach before I start the bike. We idle at the end of the long driveway for a moment, and I consider the wisdom of what I'm about to say. But I can't keep holding the sentiment in or I'll do something stupid, ruin everything.

"I love you, Jules," I shout over the noise of the motor. We've given the words to each other freely over the years—sometimes mocking, sometimes serious—but I've never meant them like this before.

"I love you, too, Nicky," she says against my back. "I'm sorry things didn't work out with Vicky." She snuggles against me.

A hollowness settles in my chest. I roar out of her driveway to weave us along the nearly deserted roads of Bellerive, and I try not to examine the blithe way she said the words back to me, the sympathy in them for my shallow, fleeting relationship. If the situation were reversed, I'd be rejoicing at her singledom. Relieved she was mine and no one else's.

The love she gives me so freely isn't the kind of love I want from her anymore, and I can't decide if I'm willing to risk this love to have a chance at the other one.

What's my father's saying? A bird in the hand is worth two in the bush.

Julia

The zipper latching from the main tent, indicating Nick's exit, is loud, even from the shower where I'm standing, shaken. What the hell just happened? A joke to drench Nick for being an asshole ended in a moment I didn't want. Whatever came alive between us felt a heck of a lot like sexual attraction. But that's impossible. He's never seen me that way. One drunken kiss, and Nick's scathing indifference is burned into my brain.

I wanted to see what it would be like. Now that I know, I don't ever have to do it again.

That *kiss*. Nick scrawled his name across my heart and then cast me aside as though I meant nothing, as though we weren't best friends above all else.

I thought I dealt with all these overblown emotions when I was sixteen. Or maybe when we were in college, and he was screwing everything that walked on two legs.

Ridiculous and stupid to let even a drop of sexual tension drip between us. Nick's withering rejection years ago should have cured me forever. Who goes back for a second dose?

He's toying with me. Payback for the spicy food and the cold shower. There's no denying his attractiveness, and he's well aware of his effect on women. This flicker of sexual attraction is manufactured, a way for him to let me know he can get to me even when I've barricaded myself in royal protocol.

Except I've thrown out policy and procedure since I got here. Idiotic.

We aren't friends anymore. We don't even know each other—little better than strangers given the distance we've wedged and widened between us, as though we couldn't get far enough away.

We're Prince Nicholas and Secretary Jensen. Nick and Jules have been gone a long time.

###

Prince Nicholas doesn't come back to the tent all afternoon, and I'm too paranoid about running into him and having him pretend that moment *didn't* happen to seek him out. I'm equally concerned about him admitting it *did* happen and him trying to recreate that pulse between us again for funsies. There's no end to his charisma, and he doesn't have a humble bone in his body. I'm not feeding his ego because my body happens to think his body is attractive. Me and half the world.

He has no idea how he ripped my heart out when we were sixteen, and I intend to keep it that way. Pretending we're acquaintances is the only way I've coped for the last fourteen years.

College was the hardest. All the women who caught a glimpse of Prince Nicholas and wanted a taste. *How well do you know him? Can you get me an introduction? Is he the boyfriend type? Will I become a princess if he falls in love with me?*

An ache blooms in my chest at the memories, at the indifference I propelled out into the world, hoping it would stick. *Not well. No. No. God, no.* Any friend who showed too much interest was locked out of my circle. Didn't matter though. Prince Nicholas still found a way to insert himself, to put me in the most awkward situations.

I clamp down on the flood of memories. My job in Tanzania is clear. Keep the prince occupied and away from home until I get the all-clear from King George. Easiest job in the world since he doesn't want to cut his vacation short. Instead of stressing over him or our history, I need to relax and enjoy this once-in-a-lifetime opportunity to go on safaris for however long I get before King George summons us home.

At the meal tent, I pause at the door. Almost all the seats are taken. There's one left near the head of the table at the opposite end to the prince. I breathe a sigh of relief. No interaction required. Perfect.

Everyone already has a drink, and I ask for water. I can't even remember the last time I was drunk. In typical Nick fashion, he has two empty beer bottles and a glass of something else in front of him. Perhaps he plans on going for round two with the American woman who is so close she could be in his lap without too much effort.

There's a buzz around the table as everyone discusses their morning drives and details what they hope to see this evening.

"What did you see this morning?" the British man beside me asks.

When I turn to look at him, I'm surprised at his youth. I was so focused on Nick, I didn't look around the table properly. He's likely around 30, not much older than me, with light brown hair and dark brown eyes alight with interest.

"Oh, um. I didn't go. I just arrived last night, and I was jetlagged." A lie, but I can't throw the prince to the wolves. The camp is probably a hive of gossip.

"You're going out tonight?" he prods.

"She is," Prince Nicholas calls from down the table. "What'd you see this morning Robbie?"

Great. The prince has taken the one person who showed any sort of interest in me. After their brief exchange, Prince Nicholas regales the table with his stories from this morning, that he didn't bother to tell me, even when I asked. The gulf between us widens. We're not friends. Maybe we aren't even acquaintances anymore. Enemies, maybe, given the tit-for-tat we've been engaged in. As far as he knows, I still want to drag him home.

Dinner is samosas, rice, and some sort of fish. Each bite is cardboard while I listen to the prince work the crowd. They're hanging on his every word. When everyone but me bursts into laughter at another one of his stories, my chest constricts. Without too much effort, he's managed to eat up all the oxygen in the room.

"Is he like this when you're alone with him too?" Robbie asks, leaning close.

"You mean entertaining?" I pop a piece of fish into my mouth and chew while I wait for him to clarify.

"Larger than life." He scoops his rice onto his fork with his knife. "Every night is another outlandish story. Entertaining for sure. Never quite feels real though, does it?"

"Doesn't it?" I avoid eye contact and eat another piece of fish. "So far he hasn't told a story I know to be false." Of course, I don't know that any of them are *true* either. Whatever persona the prince wants to present to these people, I'm not going to interfere. They're strangers, and he has every right to protect himself. The number of cringeworthy stories his pretty face has inspired must eat at him. Of course, the modeling didn't help anything but his personal bank account. At heart, he's a private person coping with a public life.

"What's it like being the secretary to the king of Bellerive?" he prods, taking a sip of his beer.

"I imagine it's like any other job. Good days and bad."

"Bad days? What do those encompass when you work for a king?"

"Something goes wrong that was supposed to go right." When was the last time someone asked me questions about my job? At a press junket, probably. It's not like I'm an avid traveler for anything other than business. The people I associate with know what my job is like because they deal with dozens of staff members just like me.

"Manage to get any writing done today, Robbie?" Prince Nicholas calls down the table, disrupting our conversation. Except this time, I don't mind the interruption.

"A bit," Robbie says, leaning back in his chair, his drink dangling between his fingers. An air of arrogance surrounds him.

"I forget who you said you were working for while you're here?" Prince Nicholas mirrors Robbie's posture, and I suspect any moment one of them will whip out their dick and ask me to get a measuring tape.

"Doing a bit of freelance work," Robbie says, sliding his glass back onto the table. "As I mentioned, I've had pieces published in various papers and magazines."

Ice snakes through my veins. Papers and magazines? Are they the ones we wipe our asses with in Bellerive or the ones we read over breakfast? Sometimes the line between them is thin.

The prince's animosity makes more sense. He's come here for a vacation, and he must have discovered Robbie has worked for or is currently working for a tabloid. For all I know, he may have done stories on the Bellerive Royals. Alexander has remained largely scandal free, but Nicholas and Brice have not.

"Making the world a better place one article at a time, I'm sure," Nicholas says. "Lauren." He turns to the American woman who is stroking his arm with light fingers.

So cringy. Does she have no self-respect? He's let her touch him during the meal, but not once has he seemed to enjoy her affection. In fact, he's spoken to everyone but her.

"Didn't you say you've had a travel guide published? Perhaps you and Robbie should chat tonight, see what else you have in common." He extracts his arm from her to grab his drink from the table.

Her cheeks blaze red, and she raises her own glass of wine, chugging the contents. He's fluffed her off on Robbie in front of everyone. I'd feel bad except desperate isn't a good look for anyone—male or female.

"I'd love a chat," Robbie says, his grin almost lecherous.

Desperate one, meet desperate two. Perhaps this is why Nick—Nicholas—prefers to eat in his tent. Someone needs to save me from this mess.

Kafil appears at Nicholas's shoulder.

"Secretary Jensen," Prince Nicholas rises from his seat. "Your chariot awaits. We're heading out for our night drive."

I haven't finished eating but given that I spent most of the afternoon polishing off the rest of the charcuterie board alone, I won't be starving anytime soon. Rising from my seat, I drop my napkin beside my plate. "I hope everyone has a good evening."

I trail Nicholas out of the meal tent and back to ours to collect our things.

"Wow," I mutter as soon as we're out of hearing distance. "Lauren would have hand fed you from your lap if you'd asked."

"Ah, yes. So many Laurens in the world." He winks at me. "Robbie seemed fond of you. Asking about Bellerive or trying to crawl up your skirt?"

I glance down at the khaki skirt I'm wearing, and the thought of Robbie crawling anywhere near it sends a shot of revulsion through me. "Pumping me for information about Bellerive."

"Suppose that's the better kind of pumping in this case."

We've arrived back at the tent, so I'm spared from coming up with a response to his overt sexual comment. "What do I need to bring?"

"Camera, water bottle, sweater." He glances at my bare legs. "Pants. But if it's going to take you ages to change, just wear that."

I bristle. "It won't take me ages." My lateness was on purpose this morning, though the outcome wasn't quite what I expected.

"Whatever you say." He slips into the tent before me and grabs his things off the hooks by the door, and then he leans against a tent pole, arms crossed.

"I need to change." My pants from earlier today are still on the floor beside my bag. My silent rebellion. Instead of picking them up, I leave them there and grab another pair from a drawer.

Rather than taking my time, I change quickly, grab the suggested items and follow Nicholas toward Kafil and the waiting vehicle. We climb in, and Nicholas sits just behind Kafil. Uncertainty stirs in my stomach. There are at least twelve seats, so I could sit anywhere. Does Kafil narrate the drive? Is there a speaker, or am I better sitting across from Nicholas?

Nicholas releases a deep sigh and shifts toward me. "What's the problem, Secretary Jensen?"

"I'm not sure where I should sit."

He scans the vehicle that's more like a bus. "Yeah, that's a tricky one. So many of the seats are taken." He puts a hand to his forehead as though scanning a crowd. "Might be one seat left at the back. Have a look, will you?"

I slap the hand he has perched on his forehead like a visor, and he chuckles.

"You don't think that one's free either?" He peers up at me from his bench, a smirk balanced on his lips.

"Where is the *best* place to sit?" I let out an exasperated sigh.

"There," Kafil says, pointing at the seat across the aisle from Nicholas. "When I spot things, I'll tell you. You can't hear as well at the back, and I'll have to shout."

I glare at Nicholas and slide into the empty place. "Was that so hard? Really?"

"Not hard at all," he says, sliding me a sideways glance. "You used to have more common sense."

The temptation to hit him surges through me. "You used to be able to answer a simple question without being an asshole."

"Did I?" He stares out the window. "Doesn't seem right."

The vehicle rumbles to life, and Kafil calls over his shoulder. "I'll aim for the two male lions first. One of the other guides saw them not too long ago."

Male lions? Despite Nicholas's shitty attitude, excitement stirs in my chest. If I can focus on Kafil and the animals, this night drive might not be so bad.

Ignoring Nicholas can't be that hard, can it? Lord knows I've had lots of practice.

NICHOLAS

The sun is setting when Kafil finds a spot near a tree to park the vehicle for our sundowner and snacks. A week ago, we saw two cheetahs here.

"What are we doing?" Julia asks, tearing her gaze from the window when Kafil and I open our doors.

She's been avoiding me, which is quite a feat when there are only three of us. Not once has she directed a question or spark of excitement over an animal in my direction. While she watched the male lions, I watched her. Solitude is my thing, but her obvious and enthusiastic delight about everything on this drive is causing my too-small heart to grow a few sizes. Perhaps sharing this particular adventure with someone, *with her*, isn't so bad.

"Sundowners and snacks," I answer, though she directed her question at Kafil, not me.

"We're getting out of the vehicle?"

I suppress a smile at her panicked tone. "Yeah, we do that sometimes. Live life on the edge."

She almost had a coronary when Kafil mentioned a lack of public toilets. Coping a squat behind the vehicle hadn't occurred to Julia, and quite genuinely, I forgot to mention that tidbit before we left. She probably thinks I didn't tell her on purpose. I suspect her bladder will explode before she notifies Kafil or me she needs to pee.

"Wine spritzer?" Kafil asks, ducking his head into the vehicle to address Julia, who hasn't moved from her seat.

"Is it really safe out there?" She peers out the window at me, where I've already cracked a beer.

"Safe enough," I say. "When did you become a chicken shit?"

"Are you kidding, Nick? There are animals out there that could tear me limb from limb. They could *eat* me."

"I doubt they'd find you tasty enough." I sip my beer and avoid eye contact. The animals might not want her, but I'm not so lucky. Even sitting in the vehicle with a stick up her ass, I'm drawn to her. Is it this version of her, or the one from my memory? Jules and Julia inhabit the same body, but they *aren't* the same person.

"The chance of any sort of attack is very, very slim," Kafil assures her. "Come have a drink. His Royal Highness said you like wine spritzers?"

"I don't really drink anymore." She ducks out of the vehicle and stands beside me before moving to put Kafil's cooler of drinks and snacks between us.

"A wine spritzer is hardly a drink," I say. "Do you do anything fun anymore?"

She bristles and turns toward Kafil. "Just water is fine, thanks."

Jesus, even when I try to do the nice thing like ask him to pack her favorite drink, she shoots me down. Jules used to love wine spritzers, and at the last palace event, I'm sure she drank at least one. Didn't she? As if I don't know, keep tabs, unconsciously monitor her movements in a crowd. She had one. I'm sure of it.

I shift toward her, prepared to make another biting comment about her selective drinking, but the fading sunlight skims along her cheekbones, and the comment dies on my lips. She's luminous, staring at the Serengeti spread out before her. Jules's enthusiasm was always contagious, infected me more than once. The sheer delight in her expression coupled with the fading light steals my breath.

"Oh, my God. Are those giraffes in the distance?" Excitement lights up her face, and she points at the tall figures striding across the horizon.

The hard knot in my chest releases, and I drink my beer in silence while Julia and Kafil chat about what we may or may not see on the drive back once the sun has set.

Kafil breaks out the snacks, and we eat in companionable silence while the sun dips into the horizon, coating the long grasses in a golden glow. Thanks to her time in the palace, Julia can crank up the charm, pepper a room with small talk, and coax a reluctant guide into loosening up his perceived royal protocol. Not that I've asked for much in the way of special treatment. The location of my meals, but otherwise, I try not to flex my royal might on trips like this. I relish the chance to disappear, sink into a different life.

Not far from us, a lone hyena wanders down the gravel road, his head low while he whoops for the rest of his group.

Instinctually, I move closer to Jules, and when she glances up at me, the current of our earlier animosity has vanished. Her blue-gray gaze softens, and the joy and contentment in her expression sucks me down like an undertow.

"You worried he's going to attack us?" Her lips twist into a wry smile. "Want me to protect you?"

"Would you?" Hadn't been my own safety that drew me to her, but no point in admitting that outright. "Die for The Crown?"

"For The Crown?" Her voice is husky.

Somehow we've ended up so close our free hands are brushing together. The urge to run my fingers along hers, lace them with mine strikes me. When was the last time I held her hand? I used to drag her around everywhere until something as simple as her palm pressed to mine became a grenade. The urge to seize her hand, pull the pin, battles with my sense of self-preservation.

Fucking pheromones are still ruining my life.

"I have a gun," Kafil reminds us, breaking the moment. "No one will die, just the animal."

Julia steps back from me and gives a little shake of her head, confusion marring her features. She clears her throat, and the moment between us dissipates as though it never happened.

The world is full of attractive women, and I need to learn to leave this one alone.

"Surely you'd have to justify the killing," Julia says.

"Oh yes," he agrees. "A lot of paperwork. Attacks are rare. Animals in this country have a long history of being hunted. It's in their DNA to avoid us."

"Do you think so?" I ask though Kafil and I had a similar conversation one of the first nights after I arrived. My mind is stalled at thirty seconds ago, on the cusp of taking a chance with Jules.

"Yes." Kafil nods. "Once an animal has a bad experience with a human, the trauma lives on, stops them from trying a second time."

Now *that*, I can understand. "Shoot your shot, stick your neck out once, learn from your mistakes." My mind clears.

"Exactly." Kafil passes me another beer.

A good reminder for me. The longer Julia stays at the camp, the more likely I am to bury my first attempt and go for round two.

Kafil makes a throat slitting gesture. "Very few animals stick their neck out twice."

"Those that do go for round two," Julia says, "who don't seem to be afraid, must be dealt with somehow?"

"Monitored. Sometimes the lessons they learn from their encounter with humans aren't the right ones. A screw loosens." Kafil taps his temple.

"They seek something they can never have," I say, draining my second beer.

"Not without dire consequences." Kafil begins to repack the cooler as the last rays of sunlight slip beneath the horizon. "In the vehicle." Kafil gestures to us. "We'll make our way back to camp."

###

On the way to camp, we come across a pack of hyena cubs scattered across our path with a few adult protectors.

Julia stares at them in the headlights. "How can something so ugly also be so cute? I had no idea they could be so many different colors."

From there, she floods Kafil with questions about hyenas, packs, mothers, fathers, babies, and whatever else comes to her mind. Listening to her intellectual spiral is a delight. She's always known how to drill into a subject to find some sort of clarity. Her intelligence is wasted as my father's secretary.

Not that being my father's secretary is an easy job, but when I think back to all our conversations, she never once mentioned she wanted to become her mother. Quite the opposite, actually.

The question hovers on my lips while I watch her talk to Kafil with so much enthusiasm. *What happened to the girl I once knew?*

When we arrive back at camp, the circle around the campfire is already mostly formed by all the groups who either didn't go for a night drive or returned before us. There are three chairs left, one of which is beside Lauren the leech.

"Your highness," she calls to me as soon as she catches sight of me and Julia. "I saved you a seat."

Inside I cringe, but on the outside, I give her a broad grin. "Kind of you. But we've got some official palace business to discuss." I gesture to Julia beside me.

Julia purses her lips but doesn't dispute my claim. At least that's something.

We take the other two chairs, and while a staff member brings her some sparkling water and me a beer, she turns to me. "Did you really use me as a shield from your conquest?"

"There was no quest needed to conquer her." I give her a wry grin before taking a drink. "You want her? Pretty sure you could conquer her too."

On the other side of the fire, Lauren is drunk and sprawled in her chair, a pouty expression on her face. Before her glassy gaze can connect with mine, I slide my focus back to Julia. Not sure which is worse—a sober, disapproving Julia or a drunk, desperate Lauren.

"Why any woman would want to sleep with you when you speak of them so disparagingly afterward is a mystery to me."

I raise my eyebrows to cover the sting of her words. "You think I slept with her?"

"Why wouldn't you?" Julia sighs.

"I can afford to have standards," I mutter. "She doesn't meet them."

"Prince Nicholas has standards? This is news to me." Julia taps her finger against her chin.

"Perhaps we should call Robbie over and give him the scoop."

"He wouldn't believe it. I'm sure he thinks you slept with her too. Probably planning to write a woman scorned article."

"Wouldn't be the first."

"Not likely to be the last either."

"You really think so little of me?" I turn in my chair to meet her gaze. Her words shouldn't cut so deep. Women I've slept with, and ones I haven't even met, have sold me out to gossip rags or posted shit on social media for likes and retweets. Anything for a buck or five minutes of fame. The story doesn't need to be real—just needs to *sound* real.

Means I've had to become more selective of the company I keep. The Laurens of the world don't get a peek in my pants unless I decide I'm fine with the exact dimensions of my dick being splashed across social media again. I wish I was kidding. Youth and alcohol lead to poor decisions.

She searches my face. "I suppose if you wanted me to think more of you, you'd have to show me something different, wouldn't you?" She pats my bearded cheek and drains her water. "Bed for me. Jet lag and all that." Without waiting for a response, she strides over to a staff member with her empty glass and, flashlight in hand, is escorted back to our tent.

I stare into the fire, considering her words. What do I care what Julia thinks of me? Her opinion of me doesn't mean anything. So what if she thinks I'm a philandering man-whore? She's squandering her life working for my father. Of course, if my father is retiring, her new boss will be my older brother Alex. The thought sours my stomach. I tip up the last of my beer just as Lauren gathers her courage to approach me again.

I suppress a sigh while she wobbles over, coming perilously close to the fire.

"Are you leaving?" Lauren cries, and her high-pitched voice draws stares from the remaining safari goers around the fire.

"Did you get a chance to talk to Robbie?" Not that I want her talking to Robbie and feeding him whatever narrative she decides to construct about me, but it's a small sacrifice to keep Robbie away from Julia. She doesn't need him hounding her for palace gossip.

"Robbie isn't as much fun as you," she says with a pout. "Are you and your secretary together? You're sharing a tent."

I'm tempted to lie and tell Julia I fabricated a relationship to get Lauren out of my lap. Would Julia go along with it? When we were kids she would have. Now? I don't know.

"Lauren," I say, smoothing down her hair and framing her face, forcing her to make eye contact with me. "You should cut yourself off and go to bed."

"Do you need somewhere to sleep?" She peers at me hopefully.

"I do not." I let her go and wave to everyone around the fire and head for my tent. Julia should have been there to see me handle Lauren. Honest and not even an asshole. Pfft. Show her something different? Maybe she just needs to pay better attention.

A worker walks me to my tent, and I unzip it, prepared for Julia to be sprawled across the bed again. Instead, I'm struck dumb a second time.

On the floor in a pile of blankets is Julia, sound asleep.

How can that be comfortable? Why did she take the floor tonight?

I replay the evening, but I can't pinpoint a moment where I was a big enough dick to make her want to sleep on the hard ground. She'll be exhausted in the morning.

While I get ready for bed, Jules stirs, asleep, but clearly uncomfortable. When I'm all set, I slide into bed and consider turning out the light, leaving her on the floor. If she wants to judge me and be so fucking stubborn about it, maybe she deserves the ground.

But the longer it takes me to snap off the light, the more the knot in my chest dissipates. No point in having her grumpy tomorrow, right?

With a sigh, I throw back the covers on the other side of the bed. Then I crouch down and lift her gently into my arms, trying not to disturb her. I'm not in the mood for another fight when I'm taking the high road.

At her side of the bed, I slide her under and tuck the covers around her. A strand of chestnut hair falls across her face and with the lightest touch, I smooth it back. The urge to linger, to feather a kiss across her forehead, to curl myself around her is ridiculously strong.

God, I've missed her.

Instead of touching her, I rub my hands along my beard and suck in a deep breath.

Christ, I need to get her out of Tanzania. This slope is far too slippery. I can't let myself slide down it again.

JULES

Fourteen years ago

I'm on the palace grounds, following a trail of text clues from Nick—a little game he likes to play whenever I've tried his patience with my lateness. Guess where Nick is? Juvenile and frustrating, but at least he's still answering my texts.

"Julia!" My mother calls out one of the palace windows.

I grimace and consider pretending I don't hear her. Of course, that'll just set off an argument later about how disrespectful I can be. She never believes I'm deaf. "Yes, mother," I call back without bothering to see which window she's opened.

"I need to see you. Meet me in the library."

I text Nick that I've been caught by the Momster, and I'll have to track him down when my lecture is over.

He sends back a sad face but doesn't offer to help. Figures.

I enter one of the side doors with the keycode and make my way to the library on the first floor. During school, Nick and I spend a lot of time in here doing our homework. When we hit twelve, we were no longer allowed to hang out in his room. It's a stupid rule because half the time Nick locks the door to the library, and we could be doing anything we wanted in here. There is a couch.

Besides, the royal estate is huge, and it's not like a bed or a couch is needed for a make-out session. Not that either of us has so much as joked about being anything other than friends. Anytime someone else suggests it, Nick goes off on how platonic friendships are not just possible, but he and I are living proof that they're achievable.

Even if I were tempted to think about him like that—hello, I'm not blind—I don't allow those thoughts to creep in. I'm far better off being his best friend. I've seen how he treats his girlfriends. He'll never discard me.

"Ah, there you are," my mother says, entering the room with her notebook and pen in hand. Her hair, the same chestnut shade as mine, frames her face, and her reading glasses are perched on her nose.

"You asked me to be here. I don't know why you're surprised I showed up."

She raises her eyebrows at me, but she doesn't bite back. "Security at our house logged something interesting the other night."

Shit. "Oh?" I cross my arms. Lecture number five hundred about leaving the property without telling an adult is headed my way.

"Nick came and picked you up again—without any security." She sets down her notebook and pen and eases onto the couch.

A long lecture. She's even sitting down. With a sigh, I sink into one of the armchairs. "Yes." I can't deny it. She's got the proof from the cameras and likely Nick entering the code to get inside the gate.

"I realize you two are very close friends, and you rely on one another for emotional support. For Nick's sake, I've never tried to discourage you from spending so much time with him. But I am concerned with the number of rules Prince Nicholas feels comfortable breaking, particularly when it comes to his personal safety. If you're on the back of his bike and no one knows where you are, what happens if you're in an accident?"

"Someone would find us and call an ambulance."

"What if you're ambushed by someone wishing to kidnap Prince Nicholas, hold him for ransom?"

"On Bellerive?" I scoff. "Mom, you can't be serious."

"All it takes is for the wrong person to realize Nick is careless. Bellerive is an island, but we are not devoid of bad actors, people who will take advantage of a situation." She gives me a hard stare. "The three boys are very photogenic, and as a result, the island is starting to get more attention in the media. Neither of you can nor should assume these rides won't become a prob-lem."

"I'm not policing Nick. That's not my job."

"Then police yourself. Perhaps if you didn't hop on the back of his bike every time he showed up, he wouldn't come, or he'd go home instead of gallivanting around the country."

"He'd still go," I say, an edge to my voice. "He'd just be alone. Is that what you want?"

"I'd prefer he didn't go at all. I've spoken to his parents, but they feel this small rebellion is better than something larger." She gives me a hard look. "I doubt these rides are his only rebellion, but that's instinct, not proof." She sighs and laces her hands. "My true concern isn't Prince Nicholas, though I love him dearly, it's you. You're my daughter. I don't want you lying in a ditch or kidnapped by criminals because Nick felt like a joyride at God knows what time in the morning."

God knows what time, and so does my mother. The security cameras and keyless entry are timestamped. "Are you telling me I can't go?" I will anyway, but I'd like to know exactly how much trouble I'll be in.

"If I have to, yes. I'm hoping you'll behave like the young adult I know you can be and you'll either stop going with Nick or you'll get him to stop venturing out."

I stare at her, not committing to anything. I'm on Helen and George's side with this one. Nick's life is so buttoned up with all the things he can and can't do. Our night rides and our drinking sessions, which thankfully my mother doesn't seem to know about, are his outlets for a life he didn't choose. He doesn't even have his sexcapades with Vicky anymore. It's just me. I'm not letting him down.

"Knock, knock," Alex calls from the entryway of the library. "Secretary Jensen, my father was looking for you."

My mother checks her watch and frowns. "Julia, I need you to seriously consider what I said."

"Sure," I say with a fake smile. "It'll be all I think about."

She releases an annoyed breath and flies out the room to put out some other fire somewhere else. She lives for organizing someone's life. Most days I'm thankful she's too busy to meddle too heavily in mine, and my father is super chill. He'd have to be to live with her.

"You all right?" Alex asks from the doorway.

I release a deep breath. "Fine, yes. Just another lecture from the Momster."

"Momster?"

I flush. The nickname is one Nick and I use on text exchanges, and I forgot for a second Alex isn't in on the joke, might even tell someone else. "Never mind." I hoist myself out of the armchair, but Alex has shut the library door.

"Where are you off to?" Alex asks as I approach the door.

"Find Nick."

"He's in his Mandarin class still." He frowns. "Were you supposed to meet him?"

"Yeah, but..." I trail off as I reach the door, and Alex still hasn't moved from the small space. "I'll have to wait until he's done, I guess. I'll find something to keep me occupied."

"Mom just got some more silkie chicks down at the chicken coop, if you're interested. I could walk you down there."

I eye him with suspicion. Alex has never willingly offered to go anywhere with me. Normally, he's the one moaning to Nick about me hovering like a pest. "You're offering to hang out with me while Nick's busy?"

He peers around him with exaggerated curiosity. "You've got some better offers, have you?"

Nick mocks Alex for picking up a hint of a British accent this last year while he's been at school. In truth, the whole family has a slightly different accent than the rest of the island. If I were to defend Alex, Nick would get his knickers in a knot, so it's best to keep those opinions to myself.

Time alone with Alex. My stomach flips. No problem. I can handle this. Alex must be exceedingly bored to want to hang out with me and stare at baby chickens. One visit to the chicken coop is nothing.

"Yeah," I agree with a shrug. "I guess I could do that." Meanwhile, my stupid heart is beating triple time. Dark, mysterious, everyone is in love with him Alex wants to spend time with *me*. On the way there, I text Nick to let him know where to find me. He won't be happy I'm with Alex, but that'll be easy enough to shrug off as long as I leave with Nick right away.

"So, I know Nick has a girlfriend, but what about you? Any boyfriend lurking around pretending he doesn't mind how much time you spend with my brother?"

I laugh and shake my head, my cheeks burning. "No boyfriend." I should probably tell him Nick isn't with Vicky anymore, either, but Nick prefers me to keep his secrets. He wasn't happy I mentioned Vicky to Alex in the first place.

"Really? I find that surprising." Alex walks backward down the gravel path so he can make eye contact.

"It's sort of like what you said, most guys aren't that understanding of my friendship with Nick." The few boyfriends I've had have been short-lived and intimidated by Nick. He's royalty, and I put him first before everyone else, always.

"Does it bother you that you always have to put Nick first?" Alex asks. "Does he put you first?"

I narrow my gaze. Typical asshole question from Alex, and I can suddenly see why Nick isn't so keen on his brother. "We're best friends. We always put each other first."

"Hmm." Alex turns around without saying anything else. The rest of the walk to the chicken coop is quiet.

The chickens are Helen's pride and joy. She gets the best breeding stock and treats them all like children. Whenever she's not busy, she's down at the coop feeding the chickens in overalls. One of her most beloved used to be allowed to wander the palace rooms. For a while, as a child, Nick even had one that followed him like a puppy. Now that we're older, we don't spend as much time down here, so none of us but Helen get quite so attached.

The coop is behind one of the barns, so it's sheltered from the wind, and impossible to see from any room in the main house.

Alex lets us into the yard and leads the way to the smaller coop where the chicks are kept until they don't need a constant heater. We peer in the largest window, huddled together. His arm brushes mine, and I glance at him.

"You're not the Jules I remember from last summer." His voice is hushed, husky.

"I'm not?" I match his tone, my stomach a flurry of nervous wings. He's looking at me like he wants to kiss me. Am I reading this right?

"Definitely not." Then his hand digs into my hair and he's kissing me.

For a stunned moment, I don't kiss him back, and his lips are too hard, too firm on mine. Then I return the kiss, but it's still weird. There's no rhythm, and his lips aren't soft and pliable, but instead like he's trying to direct me somehow, someway.

When we break apart, I'm half-expecting him to laugh at me, to say he can't believe he wanted to kiss me in the first place.

Instead, he stares into my eyes and says, "Again?"

Girls all over the island, possibly all over the world, would kill to be in my shoes. Five minutes ago, I would have counted myself in the same category. Again? How can I say no? The next kiss can't get worse. We're warming up.

"Yes," I say, breathless.

The second kiss is better, but it's still mechanical, as though we're figuring each other out rather than lost in the moment. Most of my first kisses have been after I've had a few drinks.

Maybe that's the problem. It's not him, it's me. I'm too sober to properly relax.

"Jesus, Jules," he says when we break apart as though it was the best kiss of his life. "I'm only home for a few more weeks, but I want to do this all the time."

"Kiss in the chicken coop?" My brain can't process that this is happening. Alex, who thinks I'm annoying, just kissed me. Kissed me in a way that should have made me feel alive, on fire. Right? Isn't that what a good kiss does? Now I'm questioning whether I've ever had a good kiss. My expectations are likely too high.

He chuckles. "Just kiss." He plants another firm one on my lips. "You." Another kiss. "All the time."

My heart stutters to a stop. "W—what?"

His chuckle becomes a laugh. "Never thought you'd be the type to be at a loss for words."

"I can't—we can't—" Can we?

"You're worried about Nick?"

Is that my problem? Either his kiss has stunned me into stupidity, or I'm not sure I want to do it again. Do I? Only a fool would turn down a chance to be with Prince Alexander. He's hot. He's mysterious. He *might* be a shitty kisser. Or maybe *I'm* the terrible kisser.

He's hot. Hot, older, college guy. No brainer, right?

Then his comment about Nick really registers. *Nick.* If he thought I was choosing Alex over him, he'd... I don't know what he'd do, but nothing good. Nothing good.

"Nick can never know."

"If you're just friends, what we're doing shouldn't matter," Alex says, his tone annoyed.

Can't very well tell him his younger brother hates him. Though hate might be a tad strong, Nick would never forgive me for letting Alex have any piece of me. I'm not so swept up by passion that I can't think straight. Sort of the opposite, actually.

"You want these lips again," I say, pointing to them. "Nick can never know."

Alex sighs and runs his hand down my side, tugging me against him. "Fine. We don't tell Nick."

"No one," I say, turning my head to the side when he tries to kiss me again. "No one can know."

"You don't want *anyone* to know." He narrows his eyes at me.

"That's the deal, Alex."

A hint of a smile touches his lips. "Well, this will be different. A secret summer fling. Why not?" Then he tugs me into another kiss.

I close my eyes and wrap my arms around his neck, but I'm too hyperaware of the chickens, the breeze from the ocean blowing past us. The sound of footsteps on the gravel path.

"Jules?" Nick calls, far too close.

I push Alex off me and straighten my clothes, pretending to peer into the chicken coop. Alex laughs beside me, and Nick rounds the corner of the barn.

"Tennis?" Nick says when he catches sight of me, ignoring Alex.

"Yes!" My response is too enthusiastic, and I'm worried my lips look as though they've just been smashed against a brick wall. My heart is kicking in my chest. Nick can never find out, and I'm not sure I can trust Alex to keep his word.

"Pairs?" Alex suggests from beside me. "I could grab Brice too."

"He's in his Mandarin lesson," Nick says, his voice tight. "I didn't realize you liked Mom's silkie chickens so much, Alex."

"Who doesn't like soft, silky things?" He grins.

Nick frowns, and I grab his hand, practically dragging him away. "See you later, Alex."

"That was weird," Nick mutters.

"Alex is weird." My stupid heart is going to beat out of my chest. If Alex is going to make thinly veiled comments for the next few weeks, I might have to start taking anti-anxiety meds or die of a heart attack.

"Did Alex stress you out?" Nick searches my face. "You're acting strange."

I look away and shake my head. "Lecture from my mother earlier about you taking the bike out without security."

"Ah, that old staple." He sighs.

"She doesn't want me to go with you anymore."

"Or what?" He stops walking and tugs on my hand.

"Doesn't matter," I say. "If you want me there, I'll be there."

He wraps his arm around my shoulders and draws me against his side, and we start walking again. He kisses the top of my head, and I bury my face in his chest and squeeze him tight. I'll never let anything or anyone take him from me.

JULIA

When I wake up, the tent is pitch black, and there's a shuffling noise along the far wall. My heart beats in my ears while something, large or numerous, moves past the tent. *Oh God.* I hope whatever is out there isn't large *or* numerous.

"Nick," I whisper. "Nick, there's something outside the tent."

He stirs beside me, but I can't make out whether he's awake or still sleeping.

"Nick, did you hear me?"

"Bush pigs, Jensen. Nothing to worry about," he mumbles.

"How do you know? Do you have some sort of infrared camera or sixth-bush-pig-sense?" I hiss.

He gives a sleepy chuckle over his shoulder. "Kafil told me they wander the camp at night. Not a problem until the lions decide to hunt them, which has happened, apparently. Though

I doubt that's happening tonight. No high-pitched squealing? No death cries? We're good."

"High-pitched squealing and death cries? This is supposed to comfort me?" I keep my voice low even though I want to smack him. Who jokes about lions organizing a slaughter when there's only a piece of fabric between us and death?

The bed sinks, and Nick must be shifting closer. "You've watched too many horror films." His voice is quiet in the dark.

My chest aches at the tone of his voice, at how the heat coming off him crawls toward me, tempting in its comfort, its familiarity. At one time, I could have bridged the distance between us, and he would have wrapped me up, kissed the top of my head, and then made fun of me. When was the last time I let myself long for him, for what we lost? *Years*. Any hope I had that *my* Nick was still somewhere inside *this* Nick died in college. Maybe *my* Nick never really existed.

"My horror film viewing period was short-lived." Once Nick and I blew apart, none of my other friends were into watching people being cut up by chainsaws or eaten by sharks.

"You used to love those films."

I consider keeping the truth to myself, but the darkness gives me confidence. Why not tell him? "No, I didn't."

"We certainly watched a lot of them."

"Because *you* loved them." The rest of it, *And I loved you*, goes unspoken. Sometimes you realize what someone means to you just before they're gone, and no amount of wishing brings them back. He's so close and so far away.

"You never liked them?" His voice is tinged with surprise.

"I didn't *dislike* them," I admit. My enthusiasm for those movies was more for his benefit than mine.

"Well, that's not much of a standard. Why didn't you say? I never liked them much myself." His amusement is clear.

"What?" I gasp. "Why did we watch all those god-awful movies?"

"I thought *you* liked them."

"All those hours I'll never get back," I mutter.

He laughs a little harder. "Serves you right for faking it. That's what you get. Dissatisfied. Time could've been spent on something enjoyable."

The darkness hides the heat creeping up my neck and into my cheeks. He does not need to see how easily he can still embarrass me. Something more enjoyable? We tried that, didn't we?

When he kissed me at sixteen, a door opened, one I never realized was there. For him, the kiss confirmed he didn't want the door opened. If only he left it closed. I've never been able to figure out how to seal it shut again. My stomach rolls at the memories.

"Trust you to bring horror films back to some sort of sexual innuendo," I say to mask my discomfort.

"I thought that was quite clever, actually."

"You would."

Silence settles between us, and my heart pounds in my ears for a completely different reason. Now I wish I could see him, figure out what might be crossing his mind. *What happened to us?* But I know, don't I? No matter what we told ourselves, told each other, our friendship wasn't built to last.

"No more pigs," Nick whispers. The bed shifts under his weight. "You should get some sleep." His voice is farther away.

Sleep? Between being this close to Nick and the wild animals outside, I might never sleep again. Then I realize I should be on the floor. "Did you move me? I thought I went to sleep on the floor."

"I did. Had no choice. You were moaning and groaning so loudly as you tossed and turned on the floor, I couldn't sleep. My poor ears couldn't take it anymore."

"There is no way that's what happened," I scoff.

"Since you were sound asleep, you'll have to take my word for it. Would you like me to recreate your various noises?"

My first instinct is to say no, but then I change my mind. Might be a decent distraction from my morbid thoughts. He's terrible at impersonations. "I would, yes."

"Oh, I'm so uncomfortable," Nick says in a high-pitched voice. He thrashes around, tugging the covers off me and making various absurd noises.

"I think you must be mistaking me for one of the other women you've shared a bed with." I hope he can't hear the smile in my voice. His ridiculousness knows no limits.

"I can make those noises, too, if you want. They generally sound quite different." His voice is pitched low.

I swallow, and warmth surges from my belly to someplace it should not go. His ability to pivot a conversation from lighthearted to panty-dropping is something I've witnessed, but I've never been a participant before this trip. He's shameless.

"My poor ears couldn't take another demonstration," I say.

"True. Probably a bit wilder than you're used to." He rotates away from me, taking the blankets with him.

Probably more than a bit, but I'm not admitting anything in a dark room while we're sharing a bed, and my heart is threatening to gallop away.

"Any word on the extra bed?" I ask.

"Nope. Any word on your return flight?"

"You mean *our* return flight? I can book it whenever you like."

"My father sending you here makes no sense if there isn't an emergency. Is there an emergency, Secretary Jensen?"

"The coronation. Your father wants you home to help plan." His formal tone grates on me even though I made my bed on the floor to avoid any chance of us growing closer. Formal is a lot more stable than the coziness we were tiptoeing into earlier. I guess the gentleman in Nick isn't quite dead since he couldn't leave me on the floor. That door between us, the one I wish I could slam shut, cracks open a little wider. There's a chance Nick will slam the door for me when he realizes his father is ill.

"You should go back. I'm sure, unlike me, he needs your help."

The tone of his voice is like nails on a chalkboard—arrogant, dismissive. He doesn't want me here, doesn't need my help. Fair enough, I suppose. He didn't ask for me to track him down, invade his tent, his bed. But I made a promise to King George, and I'm not letting him down. I swore to drag Nick home, and when the time comes, that's exactly what I'll do.

"I'm not going anywhere without you," I say, turning my back on him.

Nick doesn't say anything, and when his breathing evens out, I curse his ability to fall asleep before me. I release a sigh and stare into the darkness. The king needs to call soon, or I must discover a way to fortify my heart. Prince Nicholas isn't getting a chance to hurt me again.

###

Across the breakfast table, Nick's gaze narrows. "You look like shit."

"Wow. You're a charmer this morning," I mutter.

There's a glint in his hazel eyes. "Please tell me you didn't lay awake anticipating a bush pig invasion."

The bush pigs ended up being the least of my worries. The man sitting across from me is twisting me into knots. "What's on the agenda for today?"

"We're driving to Ngorongoro Crater. We'll spend the day there."

"All day? Or will the afternoon be spent here?" Being in a vehicle all day with Nick might play havoc with my sanity. He blows so hot and cold, I'm never sure which version of him I'll be subjected to.

"Bit of a drive, so we won't be back here until the evening." He drains the last of his coffee and searches his drawers for his clothes before disappearing into the bathroom.

I cut into my eggs and chew slowly. Technically, I'm ready except for finishing my food, but our itinerary is giving me pause.

When he comes out, he tucks all of his things into their proper places, grabs a backpack near the door, and unzips the entrance. "Don't be late."

"And if I am?" I ask, taking another bite and meeting his gaze.

"We'll leave without you." He shrugs and steps through the flap.

Once his footsteps have retreated, I drop my fork onto my plate and run my hands along my face. My glasses have gone missing, so I'm relying on my contacts. Has Nick hidden them? Are we still engaged in a tit-for-tat or are we beyond that?

At a glacial pace, I collect my things and check the bedside clock. Two minutes to meet him at the vehicle, or they'll leave without me. Do I go for the day and risk getting closer to Nick? Or perhaps we'll bicker the whole time, and the trip won't be fun anyway?

I gather everything into my backpack and then sit at the breakfast table, the minutes ticking past on the bedside clock. Too much alone time with Nick is madness. Part of me is desperate to sink back into the easiness just on the edge of all our antagonist interactions. Our friendship dance is so familiar.

But the craters his absence left in my heart are covered with the thinnest skin. He dropped me like a barnacle from his back after kissing me. Every piece of our friendship became a lie.

I massage my temples with my fingers and search for clarity.

Seeing wild animals isn't worth the potential heartache.

Once he's gone, I'll grab a book from the common area and try to forget I've let him down.

NICHOLAS

Kafil climbs into the driver's seat, and I stare down the path, willing Julia to show up. Every time I check my watch, the heat of my frustration rises another notch. She's unbelievable.

"Should we go?" Kafil asks, starting the vehicle.

I toss my backpack through the window onto a seat and let out a grunt of frustration. How hard is it to be on time? She ruined my morning yesterday and considering I asked Kafil to make the trip to the crater *for* Jules, I'm not leaving without her.

"I'll be back in a tick." I stride toward the path to our tent.

At the door, I take a deep breath because I'm about to unleash my temper if I don't get a lid on it. I unzip the flap and storm in. Jules is sitting at the breakfast table, her backpack at her feet. In one swift movement, I swing her backpack over one shoulder and Jules over the other.

"Hey!" She slaps my side.

Her ponytail hits my legs while I haul her out of the tent firefighter style.

"Told you not to be late." I force the zipper closed on the door.

"I know. I wasn't going to come," she cries. "Put me down."

"Forget that," I mutter, carting her along the grassy path. Why wouldn't she want to come unless she's got a problem with spending time with me? At what point did I become repulsive? She's sleeping on the floor and avoiding a safari she'll love. Whatever screw that's popped loose in her head needs to be retightened. Am I really that hard to be around?

Usually, there are loads of people willing to stroke my ego, but here I've stripped all my armor away. Her attitude stings more than I like.

When we get to the vehicle, I practically toss her into the seat across from mine and throw her backpack at her.

"We're ready," I say to Kafil and avoid looking at Julia.

He raises his eyebrows in the rearview mirror but doesn't say anything. He puts the vehicle in drive, and we rumble down the gravel road.

"Why wouldn't you want to come today?" I turn the full force of my frustration on her.

"I—I don't know. I just... I thought maybe we could use a break from each other."

We had half of yesterday, and oh, I don't know, fourteen fucking years. Can't say that though. Then we'd have to talk about how she picked Alex over me, and how, even at thirty, the sting won't subside. Despite my anger, she's been back in my life for a day, and already I can't stand the thought of not having her around. That realization just amplifies my anger. Can I be any more pathetic?

"Using your words like an adult is the best way to communicate you want a break from me. Being late is passive-aggressive bullshit." I glare at her. "You want Kafil to turn the vehicle around? I can have him take you back."

"What exactly is your problem with me?" Julia asks, meeting my glare with one of her own.

"Besides your chronic lateness?" The list goes well beyond that, but I'm not prepared to talk about Alex. Whatever she has to say about what happened back then, I don't want to hear it. That much I know for sure. We weren't a good fit, would never have been a good fit romantically, or at least that's what I've told myself for fourteen years. When she had a choice, she picked Alex. A memory threatens to surface, and I shove it back down. Recalling that'll lead to nightmares, and I don't need those when she's sleeping in my bed.

"Whatever is going on with you doesn't have anything to do with me being late," she says.

A deep growling noise sounds over the rumble of the vehicle, and Kafil glances at me. "Mating leopards. Shall we stop or carry on?"

He likely came this way on purpose. The guides talk constantly on the radios to find the most interesting sights for their clients. While I've seen the leopards the last few days, if there's one thing I know for sure, it's that you can never count on encountering something a second time. Some experiences are truly once in a lifetime.

"If we can locate them easily," I agree.

"Why did the leopard sound so angry?" Julia asks, leaning toward Kafil.

"Not angry," I say with a smirk. "Triumphant."

When she frowns at me, I continue, "He makes that noise when he comes." I wink at her.

She scrunches up her face, repulsed. Was it my wink or the thought of the leopard achieving an orgasm? In truth, it's fascinating to see how much instinct drives animals. Much of humanity has become consumed with things beyond our basic needs, and there's a simplicity out here in the Serengeti that speaks to me. Food. Fight. Fuck.

Kafil locates them in a crop of low trees, and once we're parked a short distance away, Julia stands on her seat to observe the leopards through the pop-up roof. There's enough room for me, too, but the iciness between us stops me. I created the tension, and I'm not sure how to thaw it. Telling her she hurt my feelings fourteen years ago, and I'm still not over it, is the height of juvenile behavior. More proof in her eyes that I haven't grown up.

Instead, I listen to her conversation with Kafil for a moment, silently basking in her enthusiasm and curiosity before getting out of my seat and rising to my spot beside her. Tension radiates off her, but she doesn't push me away, sit back down, or call me an asshole.

I cross my arms and lean on them, keeping my focus on the leopards.

"I'm sorry I tried to bail on you this morning."

When I glance in her direction, she's still staring at the leopards. "You should be. Not everything in life gets a redo, and this is too cool to miss."

She mirrors my pose and then turns to look at me. "Thanks for letting me tag along on your too cool trip."

"I had a choice?" I chuckle.

"You could have been an asshole to me. Left me behind. Oh—wait." She holds up a finger. "That *is* what happened."

"You weren't enjoying our game? Who caves and leaves first?" I cock an eyebrow at her.

"Past tense? Who won?" A hint of a smile tugs at the edges of her lips.

"Yet to be determined. You're still here."

"As are you." She grins. "If I were you, I'd bet on me winning."

"Would you? I would not." I peer at her. "You'd need a literal secret weapon."

"Not so much a secret weapon as an ace in the hole."

"An ace in the hole," I ponder out loud. What could Julia have up her sleeve that would cause me to cave and return to Bellerive early? Can't be anything serious or she'd have played it already. "You're bluffing."

"Am I?" She suppresses a smile and stares out at the leopards. "You haven't happened to find my glasses lying around, have you?"

"You? Leave something lying around?" The pants she threw in the direction of her bag yesterday are still on the floor. It's killing me not to pick them up each time I walk past them, but like everything else that's been going on since she arrived, we're at a standoff.

"Weird, right?" She eyes me.

"No idea where your glasses are." Buried at the back of one of my drawers. Perhaps if she rearranged everything again for fun, she'd find them. "You never used to wear your glasses."

"Not never," she corrects.

"Rarely, then." I amend. Her eyesight was on the border of needing glasses. When she needed to see with perfect clarity, she preferred contacts. "You wear them all the time now."

Her lips twist, and she sighs. "Hazards of the job. When I took over as your father's secretary, I got too many comments on how young I was from diplomats, other government people. My glasses help me look the part. Fewer comments about my age, and my implied lack of experience."

Anyone implying Julia doesn't have the appropriate experience doesn't understand she grew up as close to the king as possible without being a blood relation. Her mother never left her work at home, and Julia was subjected to frequent lectures on royal protocol. She was my best friend for the first sixteen years of her life and passed those maternal lectures on to me in a mocking voice. Then she and Alex did I-don't-know-what for however long they lasted. Never been too clear on the timeline.

In many ways, she probably understands palace life better than me. Over the years, unless a new initiative, a new rule, a new piece of protocol has directly impacted me, I've ignored it. My parents are mostly focused on how Alex presents himself, which means Brice and I can get away with anything as long as we don't make the tabloids or embarrass Bellerive. Not a bad deal, as far as I'm concerned. Admittedly, I haven't always got the balance right between what's good press and what's... not.

My latest project in Tanzania will never be directly associated with Bellerive since I'm using my own money to fund it. Of course, I started it before Julia arrived, and now I'm not sure how to finish establishing the protocols with her around.

Kafil clears his throat, and I duck down to meet his gaze. "If we leave it too long, we'll be very late getting to the crater."

I look up at Julia. "Good to move on?"

She searches my face for a beat and then says, "Yeah, I could move on." With that, she hops off the seat, and Kafil lowers the pop-up roof.

I slide into my seat and gaze out the window, puzzling over what to do about Julia. The best thing for both of us would be for me to drive her away, out of Tanzania and back to Bellerive. We can't be friends. What I had with Jules I've never had with another woman, and I'm not naïve enough to believe whatever switch flipped at sixteen will miraculously flip back.

Hasn't happened yet, and I've tried everything. Anti-depressants, drugs, alcohol, other women.

"Excuse me, Your Highness," Kafil says, catching my gaze in the mirror. "Are we stopping at the villages today?"

"No," I say, my tone sharper than I intend.

"Villages?" Julia perks up and sits forward. "You've been visiting local villages?"

Kafil's gaze is still on mine, and I shake my head.

"Sometimes, yes," Kafil admits. "But you have to pay to visit them."

Ah, perfect. Good man, Kafil. He's leading her astray. We've been visiting non-tourist villages as part of my private initiative, but she can think we're talking about the Maasai mud hut settlements. The guide provides the tourists, and the tourists provide the cash. A taste of Maasai life for a price.

"Who does the money go to?" she asks.

"In theory," I say, "to everyone in the community. The Air Jordans on the men taking your cash might make you wonder about that."

"I get money for taking you too." Kafil sighs.

"Like a finder's fee?" Julia perks up again.

"More like a delivery fee." He grins. "I take you where I get the best percentage."

She stares out the window for a moment and then turns to me. "Have you been?"

"Yes." Once, and I hated every tourist trap moment of it. An entrance fee. A walk through the women's jewelry market with an unspoken expectation to purchase. A traditional dance from the Maasai with a tip expected. A tour of their 'schoolhouse' which had a jar to donate to the children's education. Raining money. That's what I told Kafil when we left. I should have taken all the money out of my wallet and thrown it into the air. I enjoy donating to worthy causes or communities in need of funds, but I hate the slimy sensation of being scammed.

"Did you like it?" Julia asks.

"No," I admit.

"Hmm." She sighs. "I'd like to see for myself. Kafil, I'll double whatever payment you get from the village if you'll take me." The sweet smile she directs at me sets me on edge. "Not everything in life gets a redo." Her smile turns into a grin. "Luckily, you're getting one today."

"Oh, joy," I mutter, but her glee at tormenting me causes my heart to kick. "Whatever will I do with all this luck?"

"On the way back we'll stop," Kafil says. "But first, the crater."

Real joy surges in me at the reminder. Julia's expression as we descend into the crater might be worth the scammy torture later. Nothing is more beautiful than Julia fully immersed in an experience. An ache spreads across my chest, and I tear my gaze from her to take in the passing scenery out the window. Thoughts like that will get me in trouble.

Nick

Fourteen years ago

The basketball bounces down the court, and Jules chases it, her sports bra and short shorts making me wish for fall to arrive. Of course I've discovered Jules is attractive during the height of summer, the endless season of barely-there clothing. I swallow when she bends over.

She grabs the ball and turns back to me, her hair swinging around her shoulders. "Are you feeling okay? You're not even trash-talking me today."

"Just... distracted." I rub the back of my head and then hold my hands out for the ball. "I thought your ineptitude at basketball was a given—no need to rub it in."

"Doesn't normally stop you," Jules says with a wry smile. "So, what's distracting you from making fun of me?"

You in that outfit. You, anywhere. "We've got a family meeting in a couple weeks to determine our next charity outreach program. Alex, Brice, and I are each supposed to bring an idea to the table."

This is the first time our parents have asked our opinion on any of their programs. Usually, we're forced into acting as the face of something we never agreed to or have no real interest in. A chance at fronting a charity I'm interested in would be a change. Except, grandmother will only select one of the three ideas. I'd never say it out loud to my parents, but they might as well give the slot to Alex. No matter what Brice and I come up with, it'll be his idea getting the green light.

"What's your idea?" Jules asks, chasing the ball after my shot. She comes close to the net and lines up her own attempt and completely misses the basket.

I chuckle while I retrieve the ball from the fence and come back to the foul line on the court. "Not a clue. Not sure it matters. They'll pick Alex's idea."

"They might not." Jules catches the ball under the hoop and bounces it out to the three-point line.

She's not going to make that shot. She just airballed inside the key.

"What would you suggest to my parents if you were sitting at the table?" I ask.

"Oh, that's easy." Jules grins before she launches another ball into the air that's sure to miss by a mile. "I'd organize something to help girls in Africa go to school."

"You do realize Africa is a continent and not a country, right?"

Jules huffs out an annoyed breath.

"And not all countries in Africa are poor." I chase down the ball.

"You do realize not everyone gets classes in international relations or stores extra details in their giant brain." Jules crosses her arms.

"Africa as a continent is basic geography though. Isn't it?" I pretend to think about it. "Yes, basic geography. My massive brain has confirmed it. I'm not asking you to give me every country's GDP."

"All right. Whatever. Mock me if you want. But you don't have any ideas, so my idea is better than no idea."

"Well, the first question my parents will ask is why Africa and why girls?" I shoot the ball, and it swishes through the net again.

"We should have played tennis. I suck at basketball. I spend all my time chasing the balls."

"My shots go in, so if you stand under the net, there's no chasing needed."

She sticks out her tongue at me while she lines up another shot.

"I'd need to figure out which African country. But assuming I can narrow the field, why girls? Why school?" I prod.

"Education is the great equalizer. Women are less likely to attend school than men. They're also more likely to be illiterate in poorer countries. Without an education, women have limited choices. Get married, have babies." She raises her eyebrows at me as though she's schooled me.

"What's wrong with getting married and having babies?" Despite my goading, I see her point.

"Nothing as long as that's what you're choosing to do and not what you're forced to do."

"Where'd you learn all this?"

"Model UN Club. You should have joined." Her smile is smug.

I might have joined if the Model UN Club hadn't been Alex's big achievement during his school years. Whatever he's done and excelled at, I avoid. "Shame they didn't teach you that Africa is a continent."

She hurls the basketball at me, and I laugh.

"That's it," she says. "You can't have my idea. Find your own."

I palm the basketball and stare at the net. "Let's say I put in the research, and my grandmother picks this idea. Are you going to help me run it?"

"You want me to help you?" She's beside me now, and she takes the basketball out of my hand.

"It's your idea. You're always saying you want a job where you'll make a difference in people's lives. Someday, when we're old enough, we can run it together."

She taps her chin and pretends to think about it. "Only if I get to be the boss, and you're in charge of fetching tea."

"I will work on my tea fetching skills," I say, stealing the ball from her and dribbling down the court for a layup. "I suppose that means we need to do some research."

###

Two weeks later when I enter the conference room where we're meeting to discuss our proposals, I'm confident Jules and I have the best plan. There's no way Alex or Brice put as much effort into their pitches as Jules and I put into this one.

I have a slide presentation, handouts, and a map of areas to target. Aside from actually visiting Tanzania, we've got our plan all laid out. Simple but effective. Provide school uniforms and supplies for girls to attend public schools. We went back and forth on whether I should pitch an actual school, but we decided it might be too much as a starter project for us as high school students. A school, training local women as teachers, developing scholarships, funding daycares are all extensions Jules and I have clearly labeled in the pamphlet. Start small and go big.

A bunch of advisors file into the room behind my parents and my grandmother, and a sweat breaks out under my armpits.

My parents suggest youngest to oldest for our presentations, probably assuming Alex's will be the best, and Brice will be first to minimize any embarrassment if his sucks.

My younger brother's presentation is on Haiti. He's surprisingly organized and informed on the earthquake and how much of the relief funds weren't properly channeled to the right people. But his idea to build a casino and offer a percentage of the profits to local communities probably isn't quite the vibe our parents are going for. Definitely not one Grandmother will approve. I swear he's going to have a gambling problem when he's older.

It's my turn next, and I pass out my information, adjust my tie, and dive in. The advisors ask a few questions that I really wish Jules could be here to answer. We worked so much as a team in the research and planning, I didn't consider the gaps in my knowledge. Between the two of us, we have everything covered. Have I gotten our thoroughness across?

Next Alex presents, and I'm tempted to tune out. Everyone in the room is sitting up straight, paying attention, clearly interested in what he has to say. Is this the difference between being the future king and being the second-in-line? Automatic respect.

There's no way he came up with his topic on his own. He's chosen disabled veterans from Bellerive who've gone to Iraq and Afghanistan to help fight the War on Terror as his charity. He wants to pump money into an accessible housing project. There can't be that many people who fit his criteria on the island, can there? Does he know that?

Doesn't matter. Right away, I realize Jules and I are sunk. Who can argue with army vets? *Disabled* army vets? No one can. No one will. His presentation is adequate, if nothing special, and our grandmother, who will ultimately give the nod of approval to the panel's selection, won't be able to resist.

Instead of doing research, he probably had a chat with Grandmother about issues that are important to her. *Fucking cheater.* I suppress a sigh, and when they leave the room to deliberate, I gather up every piece of work Jules and I labored over for hours. Burn it in a bonfire on the cliff later.

"Gran give you the suggestion?" I ask Alex, eyebrows raised.

"Don't know," Alex says with a smirk. "Jules give you yours? Seems like something she'd be into. Women's issues."

"I came up with my own," Brice says, cracking his knuckles.

"It showed," Alex says, not even bothering to look at Brice. "Well? Did she?"

"We did it together, yeah. There's a difference between getting my best friend's help and pinpointing the top judge's weak spot."

"Just means I'm smart—smarter than you," Alex says, and he rises from his seat at the table to peer out one of the windows. "Jules is very helpful, isn't she? Full of good ideas."

"She's clever, yes." I'm not telling him she called Africa a country. One, rather large, slip doesn't change her level of intelligence.

"Maybe someday she'll take on some sort of position of authority on the island," Alex muses.

If he's hinting I might marry her, for once, he's not barking up the wrong tree. When we're thirty, if we're both single, I'll shoot my shot. That's like fourteen years from now.

Fourteen years.

Can I hold out that long before I do something dumb?

###

It's late when I get to Jules's house, but I've been driving around the island solo on my bike for a while. We put so much work into the pitch that I don't want to tell her we didn't get it.

I park my bike just inside the gates after punching in the code and then I text her to meet me out back. Their patio furniture is actually more comfortable than ours, and I slouch into the couch and wait for her to appear.

The door creaks open behind me, and Jules plops onto the couch beside me. "You're not happy, so I'm guessing Brice squeaked out a win?"

"Brice wanted to build a casino in Haiti."

"Seems fitting, actually." Julia laughs.

"I lost," I say. "Or rather, *we* lost."

"To Alex?"

I purse my lips and glance at her. "Who else? It's always Alex. There was never any point in putting in all that work because I could have passed them the most brilliant plan ever, and they still would have listened harder, tried more to see Alex's idea as having merit."

"What *was* Alex's idea?"

"Accessible housing for disabled vets on the island."

Jules sucks in a breath. "There are only twenty vets in Bellerive who qualify."

"Exactly!" I throw up my hands. "Local though. And military. There was no way my parents or my grandmother would reject it in favor of ours."

We sit shoulder to shoulder in silence for a few moments, and I wonder if she's as disappointed as I am.

"Brotherhood doesn't have to be a competition, you know," she says quietly, surprising me.

"Everything with Alex is a competition. Always has been."

"Do you honestly think *he* feels that way?"

I rub my face and turn to her. "Yeah, I do. You know I do."

She doesn't say anything for a while and then she bumps my shoulder. "Someday, you and I'll do our Tanzania school project, and it'll be the best fucking thing the Bellerive Royals have ever done."

I stretch my arm around her shoulder and draw her against my chest. She sinks into me, and the loss to Alex doesn't feel quite so terrible. What's he doing right now? Not this. He doesn't have a Jules to lick his wounds, to make everything else in the world seem not so bad.

After I release a deep sigh, I say, "At least I've got you. No matter what, I know you're always on my side."

Julia

The crater is the stuff dreams are made of. Lush green grasses spread out between steep edges. On the way down, we stopped at a lookout, and the view took my breath away. Nick kept examining me as though he could crawl into my mind and reexperience the wonder of this place a second time. When I gave him a wry grin, he pretended he wasn't staring. Can't fool me. Though why he's sometimes so focused on me and other times so... I don't even know what, is a mystery.

But not even his scrutiny can ruin the day. So many wild animals in their natural habitat with perfect weather, gorgeous scenery, and tolerable company.

A few times, Nick was even helpful. Like when he spotted a hyena lurking before I got out to pee. Would the hyena have come after me? Kafil might say it's unlikely, but no one wants to die with their pants around their ankles. Needless to say, we found another place for me to squat.

Even though I didn't want to be trapped in a vehicle with Nick for hours, a switch flipped when he rose beside me into the pop-up roof and reminded me not every missed opportunity gets a do-over. He's right. How many times have I wished I seized the moment instead of letting it pass me by?

I might never return to the Serengeti, and I can guarantee I'll never have such a private, tailored experience the second time. A broody, moody, ex-best-friend, who is far too physically attractive can't ruin my enjoyment. I won't let him. Besides, when the king does call, we'll have to leave immediately, headed into a situation that'll be complicated and fraught with emotion. While I'm here, I might as well enjoy myself.

When we arrive at the Maasai community, Nick sits in his seat for an extra beat before releasing a long-suffering sigh.

"Carpe Diem," I say, practically bouncing out of the vehicle.

"Seize the day?" Nick ducks out of the Landcruiser. "Seize my wallet is more likely for this tourist trap."

His pessimism doesn't faze me. A bunch of boys rush over to Kafil with enthusiasm, all of them a chorus of *jambo, hujambo,* and *hamjambo* while their gazes travel over me and Nick. Everyone seems to greet each other with some version of *jambo,* and I haven't quite parsed out what each version is used for. In any event, I wave to them awkwardly and offer my own *jambo* in return. Nick gives me the side-eye.

I notice Nick wasn't lying about the Air Jordan sneakers, and I examine the boys without masking my scrutiny. Some of them are probably only a few years younger than us. They're talking to Kafil in excited Swahili, and I can't catch anything of substance. I've learned a few words here or there but not enough to understand when I'm about to be scammed. Kafil, even if he gets a cut, wouldn't want to ruin his relationship with us, right? As far as he knows, he's stuck with us for almost three more weeks.

Nick's hands are shoved in his pockets beside me, and he's staring out at the field of mud huts with unmasked boredom.

"Do you know what they're talking about?" I ask, peering up at him.

He sighs. "Some sort of local gossip. Kafil asked for any news, and one of the boys told him it was bad. That's all I got."

"Oh." I frown. "Should we offer to help?"

Nick shakes his head. "Not right now. We can ask Kafil later if he seems troubled. They know I'm a prince, Julia. Make of that what you will."

I stare at the group, absorbing Nick's words. I've spent the last few years ensconced in royal protocol, guards, vetted guests, and controlled circumstances. Being out in the wild with Nick, literally and figurately, takes some getting used to. At the camp, I watch what I say around Robbie, and here, I'm forced to wonder whether they're trying to prey on Nick's wealth. When we were younger, Nick worried about friendships and girlfriends.

Who could he trust and how much? Now that he's older, he's wary of everyone.

"Isn't it better to lead with kindness?" I ask, thinking out loud.

"What do you mean?" He turns to face me.

"Just—" I struggle to formulate my thought into words. "You can *afford* to help."

"Of course I can," he says, dismissively. "Perhaps I will. But I've never enjoyed being manipulated, no matter how good the cause. Give me honesty, and I'll give you the world. Lie to me and suffer my wrath."

"Life is rarely that simple," I mutter. I'm tempted to remind Nick of all the times we lied for each other to our parents or manipulated them into agreeing to something we both wanted very badly. Perhaps the choice to manipulate seems black and white, but the reasons never are. Most decisions have layers upon layers built into them. Which reminds me that I still don't fully understand why the king sent me here when there's no urgency to have Nick return home.

"We are ready," Kafil says, coming back to us.

I keep my lips pressed together to stop myself from drilling Kafil with a million questions. As long as Nick's willing to help later, I'll ask Kafil what they were talking about when we leave.

Nick gets out his wallet and passes Kafil a stack of bills. I swing my backpack around and try to take out my money.

"No, no." Kafil shakes his head. "His Highness insists on paying your entry fee."

I hesitate with my hand on my wallet. When did that discussion happen? Reluctantly, I swing my bag onto my back and smile at Nick. "Thank you."

"Consider it a perk of the job," Nick says. Without meeting my gaze, he follows Kafil into the settlement of mud huts.

One of the boys steps forward and offers his hand to shake. "I'm Koinet. I will be your guide through the Maasai village."

His English is accented but smooth. When we enter the village, a few people emerge from the huts and greet us with a smile and a nod or a call of *jambo*.

"First," Koinet says with some authority, "a traditional Maasai jumping dance." He ushers Nick and me off to the side, and a bunch of the boys come back, having changed, wearing traditional tribal gear in bright reds and vibrant blues. On their feet are sandals instead of Air Jordans. There are no instruments, but the boys use their voices to make different sounds and calls that join together in a pattern while they walk toward us and eventually form a straight line. Then two of their group break from the line and start jumping straight up and down, higher and higher, trying to outdo each other. I grin and nudge Nick.

He peers down at me with raised eyebrows.

He's such a stick in the mud. "Come on." I cajole. "That's impressive. They're bouncing on their toes and not even using their arms for leverage."

"The last time I was here," Nick says. "They tried to get me to do it."

Brilliant idea. "Excuse me," I call to Koinet. "Nick would like to try."

"Jensen," he growls.

I stifle a laugh.

"Yes, yes." Koinet gestures to one of the women, who disappears into a hut and emerges with traditional clothing.

"Oh, wonderful," Nick says, falling into royal mode. "Do you happen to have a women's set for Secretary Jensen? She's quite taken with the look. I wouldn't want her to miss out."

"Of course, of course." Koinet shoos the woman away again while he approaches Nick with an armful of heavy blue and red material.

"Carpe Diem," Nick says in a low enough voice only I'm likely to hear. "Wouldn't want you to miss out."

"So sweet. Such kindness," I say, amused. Watching Nick squirm is worth being draped in heavy material.

They truss Nick up before two women come out and do the same to me. While they tie various pieces of material around me, I can't take my eyes off Nick. While he might be cringing on the inside, he's chatting and laughing with the men like they're all good mates. He might not relish his role as the face of our country, but he understands the importance, slips into it with ease. Missteps he's made in the past have been drunken foolishness. Sober, his charisma is on full display.

"He's very handsome," one of the women whispers, glancing at Nick.

While he still needs a haircut and a shave, there's no denying the truth. "He is, isn't he?" I muse. "He used to be so much more than that."

A furrow appears in the woman's brow, but she doesn't say anything else. When they bring out a headdress, I try to protest. There's only so far I'm comfortable taking this. They wave me off, and Nick shoots another mocking, *Carpe Diem* my way over the din of the chatter. I grit my teeth and let them settle the beaded masterpiece on my head, and it comes to rest across my forehead.

When the boys start up their vocal rhythm, they drag Nick out of the line and into the open, encouraging him to jump. He laughs good-naturedly and shoots me an embarrassed grin before following the men's instructions. After a few false starts, Nick jumps along with a couple of the other boys as they tease him into jumping progressively higher and higher.

After a few other boys challenge Nick to jump higher than them, they lead us to the schoolhouse at the back and far right of the community. There, composed mostly of sticks, is a large, rectangular structure with thick grasses and what looks like mud for a roof.

"How do you keep the mud from washing away when it rains?" I ask.

"It's not mud. It's cow dung." Koinet grins.

Ah. Right. That explains the manure smell that coats the air almost everywhere we walk. Subtle, but still present. There are benches in the large, one-room schoolhouse and an oversized chalkboard at the front with letters and words printed on it. We're here in the middle of the day, and there are no children running around—none anywhere. Young men and women, but no one older or younger in sight. Perhaps this settlement is a scam, but it doesn't make the experience any less interesting.

While he explains the inner workings of the one-room schoolhouse for the Maasai nomadic lifestyle, my mind drifts to a conversation Nick and I had as kids. Koinet finishes and lets us wander around the schoolhouse where a tip jar sits near the chalkboard. I get out my money and stuff a bill into the empty jar. It looks so lonely in there, I stuff in a second note. Before I can take out a third, Nick jams another dollar into the jar.

I glance up at him, and there's a hint of a smile at the edges of his lips. "You always were a bleeding heart." His voice is full of gentle teasing.

His arm is pressed against mine, and the connection feeds some part of me I didn't realize was empty. "Remember how I wanted to help people who yearned for a different life than the one they were born into?" I whisper.

"I remember," he says. "Why didn't you?"

Why didn't I? Such a simple hard question. "Mom asked me to work for your father while they found a replacement, and then... I just never left." Not that I was doing much before I took the secretary job, which allowed my mother to retire. They were struggling to find a suitable candidate from the island, which was the only criteria the king gave my mother. Everyone who was interested in the job didn't have the right resume or didn't respond well to training.

At least, that's what my mother told me. Knowing what I know now about the king's condition, I wonder whether she suspected something was wrong with him a few years ago. It would be like her to manufacture his protection while appearing to do as he asked. My life became the collateral damage. Had she asked me, been upfront, I probably would have said yes anyway, so I can't be angry with her.

"Shame," Nick says, almost to himself. "You're one of the cleverest people I know."

Warmth floods my chest, and a reply of some sort is stuck in my throat when Koinet pops his head back into the schoolhouse.

"Ready to move on?" he asks.

"Yes," Nick says with a beleaguered smile. "On to the next."

We follow Koinet toward the makeshift tables set up with jewelry and trinkets run by the women. While I wander the stalls and chat with the women, Nick's words reverberate around my mind. Why does he believe being his father's secretary is a waste of my intelligence? It's actually a very challenging job with multiple moving pieces. Any complaints I might have about the position have nothing to do with being bored. In fact, it's quite the opposite. I'm often so busy looking after the king and his interests that I don't have much of a life beyond the royal family. My last relationship ended almost six months ago when he told me I was married to the job, and there wasn't enough room in my life for him. Not untrue, but the breakup definitely stung. This is the first 'vacation' I've taken in three years, and technically, I'm on the job right now.

I pick up a few trinkets for my younger sister, a few for my friends, and a Christmas tree ornament for my mother. At the last stall, I finally find a beaded bracelet that appeals to me, but when I dig into my wallet, I discover I've run out of cash on hand. I rummage around in the bottom of my bag hoping for some stray dollars, but nothing is appearing.

"Let me," Nick says. He passes the woman a few dollars around me and across the table.

"You don't have—" But when I glance up, there's a softness around his hazel eyes that I remember so well it stops my heart. The ache I thought I eased a long time ago with other friends and boyfriends bursts to life across my chest.

"This one's for you, yeah? Looks like something you'd pick." He fingers the bracelet before opening it to slip on my wrist.

We're standing so close, I catch the faintest whiff of his cologne. Not the one he used to wear when we were younger, but underneath is the familiar smell of him, and I long to rise onto my toes, bury my face in his neck, and take us back fourteen years. What would I change? I don't know. Something. Anything. Whatever I had to do so I could reclaim the comfort and security he once gave me. I've never found that depth of feeling with another man, but I've wanted to. So badly.

"We should return these clothes and get back to camp." Nick's voice is husky, and he clears his throat while stepping back.

When he turns to find Kafil in the crowd, I stare at his back like I've come out of a daze. Why am I the only one struggling with the mingling of our past and present? He's always so blithe, so easy, as though none of our interactions matters.

Maybe I never had that deep of a connection with him. Maybe his absence from my life made me give the relationship more importance than it deserved. We were something and then we were nothing. Happens all the time, right? I need to let the past, and my rosy memories, go.

NICHOLAS

There's a reason none of the charities I've started have anything to do with medical issues. No matter how rich you are, not everyone can be saved. So when we climb back into the Landcruiser, and Julia practically vibrates with the desire to butt into Kafil's family problems, I'm tempted to thwart her. From what I gathered of the conversation they were having in Swahili, there's a sick or injured child, and the family can't afford the medical intervention.

Did I lead Julia astray about the depth of my understanding? Sure. But I needed to get my head wrapped around how far I'm willing to go to offer aid. Reasonable and efficient. That's the help I can offer.

"Kafil," Julia says as soon as we're on the road. "What were you and those Maasai boys talking about? The bad news?"

"Nothing for you to be worried about. A personal matter." He scratches his head and glances at us in the rearview mirror.

"Can we help?" Julia prods. "We'd like to help if we can."

She'd like to help. I'd like to avoid the whole situation. Medical issues are not for me.

Kafil catches my gaze in the rearview mirror as though asking for permission. I take a deep breath and release it. The things Jensen gets me into.

"We'd like to help." I reiterate. He'll believe me since he knows what else I've been up to in his village. Hopefully, I can throw money at the problem and be done with it. Nothing too complicated.

"My relative, their child was born with a," he gestures to his leg, "wrong foot. She needs a surgery."

Julia draws out her phone from her pocket. A clubfoot is something that can be fixed, I'm sure, assuming I've understood him correctly.

"What have you got?" I nod at her phone.

Julia comes over to sit beside me, and shoulder to shoulder, we pour over articles, chatting easily about the information we find.

"Can we go see her?" Julia asks, glancing up.

Inside I brace myself for Kafil to deny her. It took me almost a week and laying out my plans in great detail to get him to take me.

"Yes," Kafil agrees. "If it's okay with His Royal Highness." He meets my gaze in the mirror.

"Call me Nick," I mutter. "Yes, it's fine." Is there anything a man won't do for a pretty woman? *A week.* It took me a week and a detailed plan to gain his confidence, and it's taken Julia two days and a few thoughtful questions.

While we drive, Julia and I search the web for more information. There's a program that performs the surgery for free in Tanzania, so I'm not sure why they're stressed about having the procedure done. When Julia and I read the article, our gazes connect, and the same question is in her eyes but neither of us voices it. I guess we'll find out.

When we arrive at the village, I try to see the place through Julia's eyes. Tiny houses, some made of brick, others of blocks of stone, some of mud and sticks like the Maasai community. The sun is setting in the distance as we make our way to one of the small brick houses. Kafil indicates for me and Julia to wait some distance away while he knocks on the door.

The woman who answers breaks into a wide grin at the sight of Kafil. They speak in hushed tones for a moment, and then he indicates to the two of us standing awkwardly.

"*Jambo*," Julia calls with a smile.

The woman steps back and ushers us into her home. I've been in the village houses before, so the open space, the beds on the floor, the small pot for cooking aren't a surprise. Near one of the windows is a makeshift wooden crib.

The woman begins to speak in rushed Swahili, and I'm catching every third or fourth word—not enough to piece together a narrative. I turn to Kafil. "Translate?"

He nods and begins to reel off the woman's welcome, offers of tea, a seat by the makeshift hearth.

"We just want to know how to help," Julia says, taking the lead. "We read in the vehicle on the way here that a clubfoot can be fixed for free in Tanzania. There's an organization that does it."

Kafil translates, and the baby in the crib stirs. I hold my breath, praying the kid doesn't burst into a flood of tears over the strange white people in her home.

The mother speaks again, but I'm focused on the crib. Can I walk over and look for myself? We're assuming clubfoot, and I'm not sure I'd know the difference if I saw it, but we could compare the foot to images on Jules's phone.

"The wait list for the procedure is two years," Kafil translates. "By then, she'll be almost four. The best time for the surgery according to the doctors is before eighteen months."

"How old is the baby now?" I ask before Jules can beat me to it.

"Seventeen months."

"Narrow window," Julia mutters.

"There aren't many doctors in Tanzania capable of doing the procedure." I glance at Kafil. "According to the internet, at least. I can make some calls."

"Can we do more than make calls?" Julia asks, giving me a hopeful look.

There isn't much I won't do for those blue-gray eyes when she sets her sights on me. It's been a minute since they were filled with such naked pleading directed at me. I'd quite like her to be *actually* naked and pleading. I take a deep breath and rub my face. Of all the times...

"We?" I raise my eyebrows at the implication she'll be doing anything and distract myself from all the inappropriate thoughts rising to the surface.

"I can help, somehow." She steps toward the crib. "Can we—are we able to see your daughter?"

Kafil translates, and the woman lifts her sleepy daughter from the crib. When the toddler sees us, her brown eyes widen. Perhaps I should have shaved or had a haircut. I'm well aware that I look like a sasquatch—according to Julia. Then she puts her arms out in my direction as though asking me to hold her, and her mother laughs, a quick string of Swahili following. I catch what she says, and heat rises to my face.

"What'd she say?" Julia examines me.

"Nothing important," I say. Not sure why the mother calling me handsome is so disarming.

The baby squirms in her mother's arms and reaches for me again. Reluctantly, I offer my hand, and the little girl practically crawls up my arm, and I'm forced to take her from the mother's outstretched hands. Her tiny fingers weave into my beard, and we make eye contact. She calls me pretty, and I chuckle. One of us is pretty, but I think it might be her with her wild curls and petite features.

"What happens if she doesn't get the surgery until later?" I ask, maintaining eye contact with the little bundle in my arms.

"Hard decisions will have to be made. She won't be able to walk," Kafil says. "She has it in both feet."

"Both?" I glance down, surprised. Sure enough, both of her little feet are turned at odd angles. "Can she stand up?"

When the mother answers, I don't need Kafil's translation, but he gives it anyway. "Not well."

"Nick," Julia whispers.

She doesn't need to worry. From the minute this little one clambered into my arms, I started mentally planning the steps to get her treatment.

"I may not be able to arrange the surgery in Tanzania. She may have to come to Bellerive or some other location." I make eye contact with the baby's mother. "Flights. Stays in the hospital. I'll cover it all, but I want to be sure she understands what might need to happen."

Kafil translates, and Julia breathes a sigh of relief. Her hand hovers near my bicep before sliding down my arm in a silent thank you. The contact makes me long to shift the baby to the other side, to wrap my arm around Julia and draw her against me.

We make arrangements for me to touch base with them again in a few days once Julia and I have had a chance to contact relevant people. I haven't touched my phone in weeks, so I'll have to charge it before I can do anything.

When we leave the house, it's almost nightfall, but I recognize one of the mothers in the street. She spots me and rushes over.

"*Asante, asante,*" she says.

"Why is she thanking you?" Julia's brow is furrowed. "How does she know what you're going to do already?"

The woman beckons to a little girl in a doorway in a school uniform. The girl comes over and does a twirl for me. Jesus, this is embarrassing. Feels like she's on display, and I don't need Julia asking questions.

"Why are you thanking him?" Julia asks.

"Uniform, for school." She points to the outfit her daughter is wearing.

Kafil clears his throat. "His Royal Highness started a foundation to sponsor school supplies for village girls. School is free, but all students must have a uniform and supplies to attend."

Julia glances at me, but I can't read her expression. Does she remember?

Instead, she focuses on the young girl in front of her, oohing and aahing over her uniform and congratulating her on being able to attend school. The young girl's mother basks in the attention, and I shift uncomfortably. This was a project I didn't want anyone to know about, least of all Jules.

"Will that be coming across my desk later?" Julia asks when we leave the woman and climb into the Landcruiser.

"No," I admit. "It's a private project." Not one I wanted shuffled across her desk, that's for sure.

On the ride to camp, Julia is silent beside me, and in my head, I'm making a list of all the phone calls I need to make. Back at camp, I head to our tent before Julia, who is still speaking to Kafil. When she arrives, she's unusually quiet while she gets ready for bed.

Once she slides under the covers beside me, I snap out the bedside lamp. A heaviness coats the air between us, and I can't read whatever emotion is emanating from her. I'm not going to ask what's on her mind because I'm not sure I want to know, but the weight of her emotions makes sleep impossible.

"I'm proud of you," she whispers.

In the pitch black, I turn toward her, surprised. Whatever I expected, that wasn't it. Tucking my hands under the pillow, I imagine her chestnut hair spread out against the pillowcase, blue-gray eyes brimming with kindness. My soft, sweet Jules. I'm not sure how to respond, but her words cause my chest to tighten almost unbearably. Proud of *me*?

"I don't know you anymore, and I think I've let my sadness, my bitterness over that truth color my opinion of you."

The anguish in her voice causes my throat to tighten. What have we done to each other? I don't even know how to respond, what to say to her. She might not know me anymore, but I've had my eye on the embers of her life for years. The flames flickering, getting as close as I dare without getting burned. Just another indication of how much I've cared and how little she has. She doesn't know me? I wish I could say the same.

"You should go home, Secretary Jensen. Clearly, I'm doing just fine without a babysitter."

She sucks in a sharp breath. "I extend an olive branch and you cut it in half?"

"Would you rather I broke it into quarters? I don't need your approval for who I am or the choices I make. I haven't for a long time."

The bed shifts as she rolls away from me. "You're insufferable. I don't know why I bothered to make an effort."

After a while, her breathing evens out into sleep, and I stare into the darkness, her words echoing in my head.

I'm proud of you.

Maybe I don't need her approval, but I still want it.

Jules

Fourteen years ago

Alex slithers his hand down my stomach toward the waist-band of my shorts. He traces the edge of the material, as though asking permission. We're lying on his bed, and the door is locked. Nick is at his Mandarin lesson, which is pretty much the only time Alex can get me alone. Our super-secret summer fling has been going on for a few weeks, and I keep waiting to get sucked in or under.

Alex is hot. Really freaking hot. Third-degree burns, five-alarm fire, hot. But there's just something wrong between us, no matter how hard I try to make it right. I should be very into this—into him. Maybe I need more time.

My stomach *does* flutter whenever Alex enters a room, but I'm not sure if that's the secret part playing tricks on me, or that

I can't believe, out of all the girls on the island, he's picked me. He could have anyone, and he's chosen me. That's pretty heady.

There is one, relatively large, problem.

I'm terrified Nick will find out or someone else will discover I've been messing around with Alex behind everyone's back. When we're alone together like right now, my mind can't stay focused in the room. Instead, I'm paranoid about what time it is, startle at the faintest creak in the floorboards in the hall, strain to listen to the ring of an internal phone in another room. Everything is a distraction.

Alex unsnaps the button on my shorts, and his hand slides underneath my panties, skimming my folds. One finger slips inside me, and I grip his biceps. His lips trail along my neck to my ear.

"I want you, Jules," he groans.

The alarm on my phone goes off, and I break the kiss, reaching for my device on his bedside table.

"Leave it," he mutters, his hand still in my shorts.

"I can't. Nick's done in five minutes. I need to go." When I try to sit up, he reluctantly removes his hand and then throws his arm over his face.

"We need to tell him."

"Uh, no, we don't. That's the opposite of what we need." I straighten my clothes on the edge of the bed.

"I want more than one-hour time slots with you in my room with the door locked." Alex lets out a huff of impatience. "I'm going to be the king of Bellerive. I shouldn't have to skulk around keeping the girl I like a secret. I shouldn't have to keep you a secret from anyone."

I stand up and turn to him. *The girl I like.* Those words leaving Alex, aimed at me, are truly stunning.

My face must be flushed, and I don't know exactly how to explain myself. No matter what, I can't risk my friendship with Nick. I won't. We've been too close for too long for me to let some make-out sessions with his brother ruin everything.

"This is a summer fling, right?" I say.

"Some fling," Alex grumbles. "You won't even sleep with me."

"I told you—"

"Yes." Alex glowers at me. "I've heard you several times. No need to repeat yourself. Gets a bit boring to hear the same thing over and over."

It's not that I haven't slept with someone before. The day after my sixteenth birthday I decided, like Nick, I was just going to get rid of my virginity. He didn't seem to care how or to who he lost his, so why should I care? The girl he slept with didn't even realize he was a virgin.

There was no need for sex to be something special or sacred for me either. Except, in my haste to get it over with, I didn't choose the guy very wisely. The experience was awkward, weird, and kinda painful. I wanted to do it, but I didn't expect sex to be quite so... blah.

So, I've vowed I won't do it again until I'm sure I'm comfortable and with someone who at least means *something* to me. The stakes are too high for me to make the same mistake with Alex, and I'm not sure I completely trust him. His little comments around Nick set me on edge. He wants me, but I don't understand why.

Besides, I still don't like the way he kisses, and we've been kissing a lot. The rhythm and pressure are wrong. My initial theory was that we might not be compatible at other things either. Though, that hypothesis hasn't proven true. He's *very* good with his hands, his fingers, and his mouth in other places. Sometimes being with him feels good *and* wrong, and I'm not sure what to do with my conflicted responses. If I was with anyone else, I'd ask Nick, but that's not an option.

He draws his knees up to his chest and dangles his arms over the top. "Look, I'm sorry, okay? I'm just in a pissy mood because you're always picking Nick over me."

"You're not competing for me." I cross my arms. Least of all because Nick doesn't even know there's a competition. "Nick is my best friend, and you're my... summer fling."

"Right. We fuck around for an hour in my bedroom three times a week—without actually fucking, I might add—and the rest of the time I pretend like I don't get a hardon the minute you walk into a room."

I gather my hair into a ponytail and use the elastic on my wrist to secure it. I crawl my way back to Alex on the bed. Even though I should go, there's something addictive about hearing him say I have such a big effect on him. He's been a mystery to me for years, still is in many ways. Whether or not I should, I enjoy being wanted.

"You get a hardon the minute I walk into a room?" I tease. "That must be... hard."

"Like a rock. Want me to grab your hand and press it to my dick next time as proof?" He takes my hand and runs it over his shorts, along his erection. "This is for you. Just for you."

I stare into his dark eyes, searching for something, but I don't know what. He wants to have sex with me. He's made that very clear many times. Part of me feels like a prude or a tease for holding out.

But at night, when I lie in bed, all the ways this fling can go wrong run on repeat through my head. Worst case scenario? Nick never speaks to me again. Best case scenario? Alex falls head over heels for me and asks me to marry him. The second thought makes me just as terrified as the first. I don't want to marry Alex, and when we're not in his bedroom wrapped around each other, I'm not even sure I want to be doing *this* with him. Which is ridiculous. Why wouldn't I want to be doing *this* with him?

"Don't you think it's better if we keep us casual?" I hedge. "My mother works for your father. I'm Nick's best friend. If things end badly, we'll have to see each other all the time."

"What if things don't end at all?" He kisses my neck and slides his hand under my shirt, lifting my bra to cup my breast. His thumb grazes my nipple.

"You don't mean that," I say.

He tugs me forward so I'm straddling him, showing me again how much he wants me while easing himself against my core. "Can you predict the future, Jules? That'd be a handy talent for a king."

He grinds against me, and I gasp. I circle my arms around his neck, and press my cheek to his, my breath quickening at the exquisite pleasure. He might not be much of a kisser, but he's definitely got other talents I haven't experienced before with a boy. I rock against him, and his grip on my hips tightens.

My phone rings, and he keeps me pressed against him, enticing me to stay with a rhythmic pressure.

"Stay with me. Don't answer it." His tone is almost a growl.

"I have to." I reach for my phone that's fallen out of my back pocket. Alex tries to draw me to him, kissing my exposed stomach. But I gently push him away. Climbing off him, I avoid making eye contact while I tuck the answered phone against my shoulder and adjust my clothes.

"Hey." Nick's voice streams down the phone line and warmth engulfs me.

All the tension inside me from a minute ago evaporates. There's so much tenderness in one word. A rush of pleasure causes all the hair on my arms to stand at attention.

"Hey." I keep my voice low. "All done?"

"You know it. Where are you? I've been on the hunt."

"Oh, um. Where have you looked?" I glance at Alex. He's flopped back on his bed, not even bothering to say goodbye.

With Nick on the phone, I can't say anything to him, either, so I crack the door and check the hallway.

Nick's bedroom is on this floor and given that we're not supposed to be in his room alone, he wouldn't have looked there. I shouldn't have stayed with Alex so long. *Stupid freaking hormones.*

While Nick lists off the places he tried to find me, I only half listen. Guilt eats at me because at any moment, he's going to ask me what I've been doing. When he does, I'll lie. We never lie to each other, but I've been doing it for weeks.

At first, keeping the secret was thrilling. Alex and Nick were mine in different ways. Who wouldn't want to be attached to both of them? Alex—older, darker, more mysterious. Nick—lighter, gentler. He's the keeper of my secrets and protector of my heart.

Now my fling with Alex is a burden. Partly because Alex is pushing for things I'm not sure I want to give him, and partly because Nick and I are closer than ever. Since he broke up with Vicky, our friendship is different, but I can't pinpoint how. It's a good change though. The kind that makes me want to stay wrapped around him rather than wrapping myself around Alex.

"Doesn't matter where you are," Nick says when I've clearly lost track of the conversation. "Meet me in the cinema downstairs, and we'll watch a movie. I'll make the popcorn. Weather is shit, anyway."

"Got anything in mind?" I take the stairs two at a time to get to the lower level where the cinema is located.

"*Final Destination 2*?" His tone is hopeful.

So many horror movies lately. I'm tempted to beg off and suggest something lighter. When I inevitably jump out of my skin, it'll give Nick a good laugh. "Ohh." I pretend enthusiasm. "Yes. Let's do it."

"Are you close?" Nick asks, and I can hear him starting the popcorn maker.

"Yeah," I say, and my heart expands in my chest at the thought of seeing him. "I'm making my way to you."

Julia

Things between Nick and me have been frosty but productive the last week since he snapped my olive branch in two... or rather fed it through the woodchipper. Each task to get Bahati, the mother, and Elena, her daughter, to Bellerive for the surgery and recovery is divided up and conquered individually. Every conversation we have is about them or our trips to the village to discuss developments with them.

Except for sharing a bed, we could be strangers.

At night when he turns off the bedside lamp, I stare at the ceiling, willing him to talk to me without a word leaving my mouth. The tit-for-tat we were engaged in has also ceased. I should be happy about that, but at least his attitude was playfully hostile before. Now? He's just... angry.

Frankly, his shitty attitude pisses me off. I might have to cater to the whims and moods of the king, but I do not have to bow to

Nick. I say I'm proud of him, and he morphs back into someone I barely recognize? Please. Get over yourself.

His behavior only drives home how little we know about each other anymore. At one time, I could have cajoled him out of his foul mood with a few well-placed compliments, an inside joke, or a reminder about some future event to take his mind off his sulk. Whenever I try to come up with something that might prod him to talk to me, I draw a blank.

We're not friends anymore. How do I know what to say?

Kafil waits by the Landcruiser when I exit my tent. Nick is already at the communications center trying to nail down a firm date for the first and second surgery. None of the medical professionals we've talked to wants to do both feet at the same time, which probably makes sense, but it's meant more coordination for us. Not one surgery and recovery, but two.

"Are you okay?" Kafil asks once we're roaring down the gravel road.

"Fine, yes." I stare out the window. We haven't been on any designated safari trips since we took up Elena's cause, and I wonder if that's also contributed to Nick's foul mood. He didn't come here to do work—he came here to relax.

Though I suppose that's not completely true since he's started the project he and I planned together years ago to buy girls uniforms and school supplies. Hearing what he's done is like being tackled through time. Not that Nick has told me anything, but I just might pepper Kafil with some questions. Curiosity is bubbling up inside me with no way to diffuse the tension.

It amazes me that Nick has taken the idea we organized with so much excitement, so much enthusiasm, and brought it to life with his own money. I gave up hope of ever seeing our idea developed when Alex won the not-so-friendly competition, especially when Nick suffered from a personality transplant shortly after that.

While I stare out the window at the passing scenery, I remember how we spent weeks delving into every detail and creating a tiered approach. We wanted to create something to allow women from poorer communities to flourish. At the time, I thought we'd spend years working on the project together. I couldn't imagine any other outcome. Of course Nick would win, and of course we'd build a charity empire together.

Then Alex took a throwaway comment I made about the twenty veterans on the island who needed accessible housing and swept the rug right out from underneath me and Nick. When I asked him, he said the disabled men and women were already on his radar and part of a tentative plan before I said a word. A *coincidence*. I chose to believe him because I was sixteen, he was nineteen, and what did I know? Rather than make waves, I swallowed his explanation. My entire teenage relationship with Alex can be summed up in those two sentences.

Besides, if I'd gone after Alex for using my idea, Nick would have found out about us. My worst nightmare. Our friendship ended up the same—in tatters—so maybe I should have told someone. At least then Alex would have been revealed as unoriginal.

"We're here," Kafil said, getting out of the car.

I follow him to the brick house, still lost in my own thoughts. "Who's running Nick's school initiative?"

"Running it?" Kafil asks with a frown. He's become less formal with me and Nick since we started working to help his cousin.

"Who's overseeing it? Nick or someone else?"

"Oh, well..." Kafil seems to consider how to answer. "Prince Nicholas held interviews for local men and women and then he asked my opinion on who to hire. He didn't want anyone who didn't treat women well, which is hard to be sure about in an interview. I did some interviewing too—less formal—but I gave the prince tips based on what I heard or learned."

"All locals?" My heart thumps in my chest.

A hint of a smile touches Kafil's lips. "He supplies the money and the financial structure, but he's leaving the decisions about who gets help to us to the individual villages. He's been very generous, and we've been trying to put good people in place."

The whole idea is so Nick of yesteryear that a chill goes through me, and I rub my arms.

"Cold?" Kafil nods at my arms as we approach Bahati's door.

"I think hell just froze over." That's what I told myself when he went through such a drastic change—it'd be a cold day in hell before Nick and I were friends again. Somewhere underneath his prickly exterior, *my* Nick still exists.

Kafil gives me a quizzical look but doesn't push me to explain. Inside, Bahati is alone with Elena, having just come in from working the fields with her husband. She carries Elena on her back in a sling seat fashioned from colorful material.

"Kafil says you have more updates?" She addresses me with Kafil's translation.

"Yes. Looks like she'll need two surgeries, a number of months apart. Prince Nicholas has agreed to pay all costs—transportation, housing, surgery, and recovery. We don't have an exact date for the first one, but we're trying to make sure it happens before she turns eighteen months. So, the process might be quick."

She nods along while Kafil translates in real time. Even though I speak three different languages, I'm not sure how he has one language go into his brain and another come out his mouth quite so seamlessly. He almost never stumbles to search for a word.

"She'll be able to walk after?" Bahati asks.

I purse my lips because I don't want to give any certainties when I'm not a medical professional. The doctors we're dealing with remotely for scheduling are making all their decisions based on photos and videos Nick and I have sent them. At no point has anyone indicated Elena's quality of life might not be good as a result of the surgeries, the opposite, actually.

"I believe so, yes," I say. "As with most surgeries, there might be some physical therapy to be done afterward. We don't know all the ins and outs yet, but we're working on securing all the details. The timeline is okay with you?"

She gives Kafil a look of triumph and rattles off something.

"What did she say?" I ask when he doesn't immediately translate.

"She says she was right to keep Elena even though her husband's mother didn't think she should." Kafil rubs his forehead.

I'm tempted to ask what they would have done with Elena if they hadn't kept her, but I'll wait to ask those questions in the vehicle.

"Bahati is okay with the arrangements?" I ask instead.

"Her husband relies on her to work the fields with him, but I am sure the village will pull together to help them out while she's in Bellerive."

Kafil already told me if Elena wasn't their first and only child, he wasn't sure Bahati would have been able to go to Bellerive, but since she is, her husband is okay with the trip. Here's hoping none of their other children have clubbed feet.

Once we're done relaying the newest piece of information, I follow Kafil back to the Landcruiser, lost in muddled thoughts about Nick and about what Bahati meant regarding her mother-in-law.

The radio at the front beside Kafil buzzes with chatter.

"An injured giraffe and a pride of lions, not far from us," he says. "Do you want to see it?"

I hesitate. Do I have the fortitude to watch an animal die? "Circle of life, right?"

"Yes. In action." He seems excited whether it's about watching the kill or securing me a rare sight, I'm not sure.

"Okay," I agree. *Carpe Diem.*

He tears out of the village, listening to the conversation on the radio.

"Kafil, what did Bahati mean about not keeping Elena?"

He hesitates and then turns down the radio. "They work a farm together. Their children will likely have to work a farm as well. Many, many people here are employed by farms or harvest their own food. If Elena could not walk, she could not live."

"You mean live *here*?" Or literally? My stomach clenches.

He meets my gaze in the mirror briefly. "Some give up their babies for adoption if they cannot care for them, some, like her mother-in-law, have other methods."

Oh, God. He did mean that literally. I swallow. "Is that—is that common?"

"Not so much, no." He shakes his head.

We drive in silence for a few more minutes, and then ahead, a large group of vehicles in a circular formation comes into view. The tall neck of the giraffe is visible, thrashing around, and everyone is glued to windows or leaning out of their popped-up roofs. My stomach rolls. I don't know if I've got it in me to watch this.

"Will the lions get the giraffe?" I ask.

"It's a hard kill," Kafil says as we approach. "But if the animal is injured enough, best to put it out of its misery. Feed the pride. Not much of a life if it's not going to get better."

"Has Nick seen a kill yet?" A debate we had in high school surfaces in my memory.

"No, no." Kafil shakes his head as we park the vehicle beside another. "Seeing a kill is not on his list." He looks over his shoulder and smiles. "Thankfully. Seeing an animal, you can almost guarantee, but watching an animal hunt? Unpredictable and much, much harder." He gestures to the calculated chaos happening in front of us. "This is special."

We observe in silence for a few minutes as the lionesses take turns attacking parts of the giraffe, and it thrashes and turns in circles to avoid the onslaught. One of the giraffe's legs is clearly lame, whether that happened before or during the attack is hard to say. The pride is relentless. They must sense they'll win.

The first time the giraffe turns its wild, panicked gaze my way, I'm done.

Perhaps watching an animal die is a privilege, but with all these vehicles and cameras, the event has veered into spectacle. My gut instinct is to intervene instead of letting nature run its course. I want to scream at the lions to stop rather than rejoicing in their ability to get a full meal.

Perhaps Nick is right—I was born with a bleeding heart.

"I think I'd like to go." A sudden sweep of vulnerability makes me almost weepy. I can't bear witness to this—I just can't.

"You don't want to watch the end?" Kafil asks. "They're close to getting it down. Once it's on the ground, the battle is over."

I shake my head. "No. It's getting late. I'd like to go back to camp."

Reluctantly, he starts the vehicle and reverses out of our prime spot and back onto the gravel road.

As though sensing my melancholy, Kafil says, "If the animal was injured and could not look after itself, it would have wasted away. A terrible death. Senseless. This way, the animal feeds the pride. It has a good death."

"Is there such a thing as a good death?" I'm not just thinking of the giraffe, but I'm also pondering what he said about Elena, about the king's terminal illness. Isn't death in any form bad?

He sighs and catches my gaze in the mirror. "Sometimes death is a kindness when the alternative is worse."

His words stay with me all the way back to camp.

NICHOLAS

When Julia comes back from visiting the village with Kafil, I can tell right away something isn't right. While we haven't exactly been best buddies the last week or so, she's had no trouble trading barbs with me about almost anything that comes out of my mouth.

Instead of asking Julia what's wrong, I seek out Kafil. There's no way I'm allowing myself to get dragged down any deeper into my feelings where she's concerned. I was sliding fast, and I've managed to throw on the brakes. Releasing them now is a mistake. But I can't help wondering why she seems, not just distant, but sad.

"Did something happen today with Julia?" I mix myself and Kafil coffees outside the common area. He's not allowed in the paying customer spaces, but I've talked him into a coffee at the doorway so I can get the scoop on Julia's mood.

Kafil sips his coffee after I hand it to him and sighs. "I took her to observe some lions bringing down a giraffe. I don't think she liked it."

"That's it? Nothing else?" I fiddle with my stir stick and consider his words.

"She seemed fine before that, so yes, I think that's it."

Another worker comes over to Kafil and pulls him aside. While they chat in hushed tones, I try to determine whether Jules would be that upset about seeing a giraffe die. Possibly. While we watched a lot of horror movies as kids, she enjoyed the ones that were more over the top, tending toward campy. I suppose that makes sense given that she never liked them at all. Still amazes me she sat through so many and never said a word.

The worker leaves, and Kafil comes back to my side. "We still haven't located a second bed for Secretary Jensen, but the camp is clearing out tonight. We will have an extra tent next week if you think she'd like her own space?"

My heart kicks at the thought of her being in a tent other than mine. A ridiculous reaction given the distance I've purposely put between us this last week. She'd likely enjoy being far away from me, able to ignore me as much as she wants.

"Actually, Secretary Jensen mentioned just last night that she's enjoying being in my tent. I don't think there's any need to inconvenience the staff with a move or a further search. She can continue to stay with me."

"Should I mention the second tent to Julia?" Kafil raises his eyebrows.

His use of her first name while he still calls me Prince Nicholas scrapes across my consciousness. She's easy to like, but it annoys me they've slipped into such an easy comradery.

"No," I say. "Julia is happy in my tent."

The minute the last word is out of my mouth, Robbie walks past us to take a cup from the self-serve coffee area. Lauren has been cozying with him when Julia and I have managed to tear ourselves away from the medical search in our tent to join them.

"You two certainly spend a lot of time alone together," Robbie comments while he pours cream into his coffee.

"She's my father's secretary," I say. "We have mutual projects." Answering him is pointless. He'll spread whatever lies he wants.

His grin around his coffee cup is knowing, as though he suspects *mutual projects* is a euphemism.

One of the meal tent staff comes over to our group and smiles at me. "Would you like your meal in the main tent or your tent this evening, Your Royal Highness?"

I suppress a sigh. Next time, I'm booking under an alias and keeping my mouth shut about my true identity. The last time there was a big changeover in guests, more staff got a break if I ate in my tent. They'll deliver as needed and leave me—us, now—alone.

"We'll eat in my tent," I say. "No need to go to any extra trouble. Something simple is fine."

"A feast, I'm sure," Robbie says not quite under his breath. He strolls to the edge of the tent where we're standing. "You must get immense satisfaction working so closely with Secretary Jensen. We've hardly seen the two of you."

"I didn't realize I came to this particular camp to entertain you. I apologize. I've been a terrible host." I peer at him. Did he luck into this camp at the same time as me or did someone tip him off?

"You used to be good for a story or two. Helped us pay our bills." Robbie muses.

"Never willingly," I mutter.

"I beg to differ. At the height of your modeling career, there was a new woman and a new story every week. If that's not willing, I don't know what is."

Half those stories were made up. All I had to do during those years was breathe next to a woman and there was a story in the tabloids. The problem with going to an American college—royalty is something they covet, even when they pretend they don't.

"Give me something, Nick, and then I don't have to use my wits."

"It's *Prince* Nicholas. And you've got wits? News to me. Perhaps you can write about that? Prince Nicholas stunned to find out tabloid reporter has two wits to rub together."

"All right," he says and holds up his hands, one of which still has a steaming cup of coffee. "I can take a hint. I can write what I want. Good to know." He winks at me and heads toward the communications tent.

I could chase after him, offer him the nugget that I've started a local foundation to support girls going to school, or that Jules and I have been holed up trying to get a toddler with two clubfeet speedy care. Instead, I let him walk away. There's nothing he can write about me that I haven't read before.

"The other reporter," I say to Kafil when Robbie is out of earshot. "The one who is supposed to be here next week, they've been moved to another tented camp?"

"Yes," Kafil confirms. "You don't need to worry."

While I might be used to the type of story Robbie is likely to print, Julia won't appreciate it. Guess I should give her some warning.

###

Julia emerges from the bathroom with her hair damp from the shower. On the little table where we eat are a charcuterie board, an oversized bottle of white wine, and some sparkling water. I didn't ask for the wine, so I'm wondering whether Kafil also thinks Julia and I are having sex. Maybe the whole staff does. We have spent most of our time together, and a lot of our time in this tent, since she arrived. There *is* only one bed.

I'm sure once Robbie is done writing his story, everyone who reads tabloids will think we're engaged in a torrid affair.

She eyes the charcuterie board, a hint of a smile playing at the edges of her lips. "Payback?"

"Hardly." I open the wine and wag the bottle at her. "Give me some credit for originality."

Behind her chair, she hesitates and then says, "What the hell. Pour me a glass." She slides into her chair and picks bits off the board, shooting furtive glances in my direction. "Why are we eating in here?"

"Changeover for the guests. New lot come in tomorrow. Rather than having all the staff cater to our whims in the large tent, I just asked for something simple."

"A changeover? Do they have an extra tent now? Or at least an extra bed?" She cracks the sparkling water and adds it to the wine I poured her.

Wine spritzer. Her favorite. Vindication!

"Nick?"

"Huh?" I take a sip of my wine and fill my plate.

"Do they have an extra bed or tent?"

"Oh, no. Sorry." I grimace. "All full again." Should I feel a pang of remorse or regret at lying? There's not even a whisper against my conscience.

"Really? Nothing?" She sighs.

"High season." I shake my head and avoid eye contact.

We eat in silence for a few minutes, but it's not the companionable silence we've had in the past. There's still something eating at her, and as much as I want to avoid digging under the surface, I can't tolerate her sadness.

"Kafil says you came across a kill on the way back?"

"We did, yeah." Her voice is quiet. "You're wondering if that's what's bothering me?"

I lean back in my chair and search her face. Startling how easily we slip back into old, familiar patterns. She was never one to beat around the bush, which is why the situation with Alex caught me so off guard. Why all of it caught me off guard. *My* Jules never hid anything.

"Yes," I admit.

"It's something Bahati said—about her mother-in-law. She said she suggested..." She seems to search for the right words. "Well, I'm pretty sure her mother-in-law suggested infanticide to Bahati when Elena was born with both clubbed feet."

"What?" I run my hands through my too-long hair. "Isn't that illegal everywhere now?"

"It is, yeah. Doesn't mean it doesn't happen." She breaks off a piece of bread. "I've just been thinking a lot about life and death since she said that, I guess. Is there a situation in which death is a kindness?"

"Why would anyone ever consider death a kindness?" I take a large gulp of my wine.

"That's what Kafil said to me about the giraffe. It was injured. He said it would have likely died a slow, painful death. He said a good death was preferable to a senseless one. You know, since the giraffe's death would sustain the pride."

I stare at the table, letting Julia's words circle in my mind. "I wouldn't have watched it either," I admit.

"I didn't think you would." Julia's voice is soft.

Maybe she does still know me, even if it's just a part of me, even if she doesn't realize it. "I can't believe any member of Elena's family would be okay with murdering her."

"From the way Kafil framed it, Elena's grandmother considered death a mercy."

I scoff. "A mercy? No. Her clubfeet aren't life-threatening. Even if her condition was life-threatening, family doesn't give up on one of their members."

She picks at the food on her plate, not eating anything, tearing several things apart. "That's a very privileged stance."

"You think the grandmother was right?" I can't keep the accusation out of my voice. Another reason none of my charities are medically based. Life and death decisions aren't for me, especially if there's even a *sliver* of hope. I'd pour my fortune down a black hole for a pinpoint of light.

Julia sips her spritzer and takes a while to answer. "No, I don't. But I also don't live here. This isn't my life, my culture, my survival. Do I think there are certain situations where death might be a mercy?" She meets my gaze. "Yes."

"Name one," I challenge.

She avoids my gaze and sips her wine, surveying the platter of food. "You know, I was really hoping for some of that rice pudding. I'll go ask about it."

Before I can gather my thoughts on her abrupt change in mood, she's unzipping the tent and slipping out the door. We've had the right to life debate before, and she's never backed down.

Slightly different arguments for different purposes, but I hand-ed her this discussion on a platter.

Then the real reason annoyance has been niggling at my brain since she unzipped the tent crystalizes—she didn't grab anything from the hooks by the door. She shouldn't be headed down the path alone at night.

"Julia!" I pluck a flashlight off a hook and duck out of the tent behind her.

But I'm barely out the door before I bump into her stiff back.

"Jules?" I ask when I register her trembling.

I follow her gaze, and my heart knocks against my chest. Realization dawns on me, and I fight the urge to sweep her into my arms and run.

Ahead of us, less than one hundred feet away, are a lioness and two cubs. The cubs are crouched low, but the lioness is clearly startled by our appearance. A mother and her cubs.

Jesus. This is not good.

"Nick." Her voice quivers. "I don't know what to do."

Nick

Fourteen years ago

Ever since I can remember, the last weekend of the summer has been dominated by my father's extravagant, country-wide, birthday party. A bottle of estate wine is delivered to every household on the island, and everyone is buoyed by the celebration. Other events are stressful, and perhaps for some people this one still is, but for us kids, it's a gravy weekend.

We dress up in our finest, but since my father keeps the guest list small—only a few hundred hand-selected people—we're able to be ourselves with less scrutiny. Everyone in attendance is trusted by the monarchy to run favorable stories, keep our stupidity out of the gossip circles, and enjoy themselves.

It's my favorite weekend of the year.

Last year and this year, it's doubly my favorite since Alex returns to *uni* on Monday. Can't come soon enough.

"What time is Jules arriving?" Alex asks while he peers into the mirror of our shared and expansive powder room. Attendants are still running around the three of us, but they aren't quite so sticky about perfect hair, straight bowties, and crisply pressed pants.

"You've become as bad as Nick." Brice runs a hand through his light brown hair, and Bea, who is normally in charge of final touches, winces at the disheveled mess he leaves behind.

Perhaps not everyone is as relaxed about our appearances as the three of us like to believe. But she doesn't rush to fix the disorder either. Seems like a win.

"I don't know what you mean." Alex sniffs.

"Where's Jules? Where's Jules?" Brice mocks, pretending to search the room frantically.

"He's not Jules's type," I mutter. Brice's comment stings. Even though I'd prefer to ignore Alex, he's made his interest in Jules about as subtle as a Mack truck plowing into a wall. Thankfully, she seems oblivious.

It must burn him that she'd rather be with me as a friend than with him in a relationship. This is the only time in my life where I'm certain I can't lose. In the past, whenever we've gone after the same thing, he's come out on top either legitimately or through devious means. The only fair play Alex is interested in is one that puts him on top. Drives me a little insane the façade he's constructed of being *such a good boy*. How many times have I heard that murmured comment to our mother or father at parties when Alex is holding court? People eat up his brand of bullshit like candy.

For my part, I've learned that competing with him is futile. He'll do anything to win—no matter who he tramples, no matter the cost. Whatever Alex wants, Alex gets.

As a result, I can't help feeling a bit smug he's become hung up on a person he'll never be able to get. Not that I'll have her, but at least he'll never have her either.

She's not interested.

Jules and I tell each other everything, and she's never hinted at any sort of crush on Alex. We both think he's annoying. Pompous, arrogant, and a thousand other unflattering adjectives.

"I'm everyone's type." Alex chuckles.

I snort, and Brice outright laughs.

"Jules and Nick are probably secreting banging behind everyone's backs anyway." Brice grabs a pack of gum off the table and shoves it into his pocket.

I flush, and Alex's jaw tightens at our brother's blithe comment.

"That's not what's going on between me and Jules," I say through clenched teeth.

"Don't feed me the line about being just friends. I see the way you look at her." Brice gives me a sly smile.

"They're just friends," Alex says.

He saves me the denial, but there's something about the vehement way he disputes Brice's claim that makes my gut twist, and a heaviness settles on my chest. Before I can question my unease, our mother waltzes into the room to survey the three of us.

"The guests are coming through the gates," she declares, and a genuine grin emerges. "Let's go celebrate your father."

I want to ask if the Jensens have arrived, but I hold back my question. Brice will laugh, and Alex will glower at me. He's come to hate how close Jules and I are. Of that, I'm sure.

We haven't seen each other all day, and I'm like an addict in need of a fix. A few text messages back and forth doesn't satisfy me anymore, and that realization is terrifying. The next boyfriend Jules has might ruin me, and every day I pray I can keep her close enough no one will be able to compete.

I should tell her how I feel, but I can't bring myself to risk rejection, risk our friendship to throw myself in the running for her heart.

If she doesn't return my feelings, can I handle it?

That unanswered question is the main reason I haven't done anything. Right now, I've got Jules. She's mine in almost every way that truly matters. But trying to talk myself out of longing for what I don't have is getting more and more difficult. I want to do things with her that have nothing to do with friendship.

We follow our mother out of the room and down the staircase to the front entrance. There, we form a second set of greeters after my father's centerstage position. I scan the ballroom, checking to see if Jules and her family arrived early, but it's still empty. When I turn back to the door, my breath catches.

There she is.

Her parents partially block my view of her, but as soon as they move past the king, my gaze locks on hers. Her deep red ball gown is strapless and hugs her curves before billowing down to the floor. I've seen her dressed up so many times, but my heart has never raced at the sight of her before.

Gorgeous. She's gorgeous. Warmth floods my body. True or not, it feels like she's mine.

She curtsies for my father with her sister and wishes him a happy birthday. When she gets to me, Brice, and Alex, she makes another curtsy, this one mocking in nature. She shoots me a playful smile, and her gaze slides over Brice and Alex, polite, but distant.

The tightness in my chest from Alex's earlier comment eases as she hustles away clutching Posey's hand and trailing her parents. I can't help turning to watch her go, and when I face forward again, I notice Alex also watched her go.

Doesn't matter. She wouldn't. She would *never*.

Once the guests have trickled in, we're free for the rest of the night to spend time with whomever we want. I search the crowd for Jules, but before I can locate her, Vicky catches sight of me. My parents invite her family every year, but they don't always attend. I hoped they'd be no-shows this year to avoid the awkward in-person conversation I've been sidestepping since I broke up with her.

No such luck.

I spot Jules in the crowd, and I start to make a beeline for her when Vicky steps in front of me.

"Can we talk somewhere?" she asks.

Her dress is short, low-cut, and a shimmery silver. Not really royal event appropriate. I'm surprised her parents let her get away with it, but I suppose most people aren't raised under an iron fist of decorum. Yet another reason Vicky wasn't a good fit for me. Is she hot? Sure. Sensible? Not a fucking chance.

"I, uh, actually." I gesture ahead of me as though I have somewhere important to go. But then the music in the ballroom slows, and Alex leads Jules into the middle of the floor where other couples are beginning to dance together.

Vicky is talking to me, but I'm not listening. I can't tear my gaze off Alex and Jules. His hands are all over her, and she's stiff as a board. She looks incredibly uncomfortable. I can't stop my jaw from tightening.

God, my brother *cannot* take a hint.

"Excuse me," I say to Vicky, sliding my hand along her upper arm as a condolence. "I have to rescue Jules, but we'll talk later, yeah?"

Her shoulders slump, and she follows my gaze to where Alex and Jules are slow dancing. "You promise?" she asks.

"I promise I'll find you later." Right now, I'd say anything if it meant escaping this discussion and breaking up Jules and Alex.

Leaving Vicky, I weave through the crowd until I get to them. When she sees me, her cheeks glow pink, and I wonder how much champagne she's already gotten into.

"May I cut in?" I tap Alex on the shoulder. He's a couple inches shorter than me—another thing I've won that he's got no control over.

"You may not." Alex's voice is sharp.

"Alex." Jules admonishes him. "You can cut in, Nick. Alex is just being... Alex." She shoots him a loaded glare.

He huffs out his annoyance and drops his hands from around her waist. "You owe me a dance later."

"She owes you nothing." Anger tinges my voice. The sooner he understands he and Jules will not be a thing, the better. He can't bulldoze his way into her life like he does everything else. He'd have to have a personality transplant before she'd give him a chance.

I sweep her into my arms, her dress swirling around us, and I waltz us away from him as though he was never even there.

Once we're in a rhythm, she relaxes against me, and a sigh escapes her. Exactly how I feel. All is right with the world when I've got Jules in my arms. My heart beats in time to the music, and I draw her a little closer.

After a few minutes, I twirl her around the room, and she laughs at my extravagant moves. Normally, I have to be conscious of making an ass of myself. Not tonight. Tonight, I can make her laugh and not worry the national papers will claim I'm drunk.

Drunk will happen later—it's inevitable. Too much unattended alcohol for me to resist. But for now, I'm soaking up Jules's company, her undivided attention.

A few times, I catch Alex watching us, and when I can't take his undisguised desire anymore, I lead Jules out of the ballroom by the hand, grabbing a bottle of champagne from the side table at the exit.

"Where are we going?" Jules laughs.

"Barn." I glance at her over my shoulder. "Fireworks should be starting soon. Perfect spot to watch."

"I won't argue with that." She wraps her free hand around my upper arm and leans into me.

I savor the feel of her pressed against me, and when we get to the barn, I gather our hidden stash of blankets, making our viewing area as comfortable as possible.

"You've really got this down to a science." Jules teases. "Have you memorized the layout of the blankets?"

"You'll thank me when your ass isn't sore later."

"If we drink that whole bottle of champagne, I'm not likely to remember I have an ass let alone worry about it being sore."

I, on the other hand, am unlikely to forget what's residing under her long dress. I rub my temples, and then I pop the champagne and chug from the bottle.

"What happened to ladies first?" She laughs.

"I didn't have to pack my manners tonight," I say with a grin. "Sorry about your luck."

She settles onto the blanket and then holds her hand up for the bottle. I pass it to her before taking my seat beside her. Tipping back the bubbly, she takes a gulp and then passes it to me. I swig from the bottle and stare out into the darkness.

Part of me wants to bring up Alex's obvious crush on her, but the other part of me doesn't want to draw any more attention to him than is absolutely necessary. She hasn't noticed, and I'd rather she ignored him.

"Last year of high school starts next week," Jules says, scanning the starry sky. "What clubs are you picking?"

"Debate. War Child. Island sustainability. You?"

"Debate for sure," Jules says and then taps her chin. "MUN, and I might do War Child, too, if I can fit it in. I know we're not going to get to do our project together, but War Child does good work, doesn't it?"

"They do," I say, and then we're off on a tangent about humanitarian work and aid in different countries while we get thoroughly drunk on champagne. Much of what Jules knows comes from spending so much time in the royal household and chatter around her own dinner table, but I get a lot of joy in planning fictitious future scenarios that have us at the forefront of charitable work around the world. The one piece of being a prince that I don't mind is my ability to do good.

Jules drains the last of the champagne just as the first firework lights up the sky. She leans across me to put the empty bottle beside my hip where the blankets stop. At the close contact, I suck in a sharp breath, and she raises her startled, drunk gaze to mine while still draped across me.

All logical thought vanishes, and I swoop down, sealing her lips with mine. There's the briefest moment where I'm not sure she's going to kiss me back, where I expect her to push me away and laugh, ask me what the hell I'm doing. Instead, she melts into me, and I pour all the frustration and longing I've been feeling for months into the kiss. She rises onto her knees and meets my kiss, pressing herself against me.

Fireworks go off inside me to rival the ones illuminating the sky. She hasn't just met my kiss—she's kissed me back.

Her blue-gray eyes are dreamy when she gazes at me with her arms loose around my neck, and then another firework pops in the sky, and her gaze widens.

"Oh shit. Oh, God. Oh, *no*." She pushes off me and gathers her skirts, rushing down the narrow ladder without her shoes.

"Jules!" It's the only word I can get out, and I sound desperate, deranged. One perfect, shining moment—gone.

Why would she rush off like that? Was the kiss that bad? I can take it back if I have to. Shove down my feelings.

I rub my face and stumble to my feet. My heart is weighed down by what I've just done, but I rush after her, determined to do everything to make us okay again. The kiss doesn't have to mean anything. It can mean nothing. A drunken mistake. I just—I can't lose her.

When I get outside the barn, I realize they've turned off all the lights on the estate. The fireworks are brilliant against the night sky. They're also the only things lighting the way back to the ballroom. It's so dark that I almost don't see them at first. But who can miss her red dress when the sky illuminates her? Not me. Though I'll wish every day after that I didn't catch that glimpse of red.

Alex has her pressed against the side of the building, kissing her. I rush forward, prepared to tell him to back off. But when the next firework goes off, he breaks away from her and strokes her cheek. Her expression isn't that of someone who's been kissed for the first time. I almost trip over my own feet, and I gape at the sight.

At the next flash in the sky, Alex spots me, and he smirks. Julia is talking, but with the conversations floating out of the ballroom, I'm too far to hear her. Her back is to me, but she smacks him in the chest to make him listen, a gesture so familiar to me. He breaks eye contact with me to stare down at her, and the realization of what's going on explodes in me.

Shrapnel embeds itself under my skin, behind my eyes, ensuring that every time I drift to sleep, I'll see this moment on replay.

They're together.

Jules and Alex.

My Jules and *Alex.*

Bile rises to the back of my throat, and I try to swallow it down. Alex glances in my direction, and he kisses Julia again, molding her to his body.

I can't watch this. I can't see this.

I can't believe this.

I turn on my heel, snatching another bottle of champagne from the table outside the ballroom. I unwrap the top and let the cork fly across the gravel pathway. Another firework bursts to life in the sky while I stumble down the laneway, away from the party, away from them.

How long do I wander, mind blank, heart heavy? Hours? Minutes? The bottle of champagne in my hand is empty, and I let it tumble to the ground with a thud.

The fireworks are over. The pathway lights are back on.

Ahead, I catch a shimmer of silver, a glimpse of blond hair stepping out of the barn entrance.

My heart pounds in my chest. *Alex and Jules.* Alex and Jules are a mantra at the edge of my consciousness. I keep pushing the images away, denying their existence, but nothing is banishing what I saw from my memory. I want to forget. Pretend none of it happened.

I never kissed Jules. I never saw them together.

Tomorrow, I'll wake up, and everything will be fine. No matter what, things between us have to be fine.

Except deep down, I realize nothing between Jules and I will ever be fine again. I kissed her, and she fled to Alex.

Alex.

I kissed her, and she chose Alex—has likely been choosing him for all these weeks when I've been so smug, so sure she'd never give him any opportunities to act.

So when Vicky calls my name from the barn door, I go to her, and I take what she's offering, even though I shouldn't, even though she's not who I've longed for.

Because now? Now all I want to do is forget.

JULIA

"Don't move, Jules. Not until I'm in front of you," Nick says.

At my back, I can sense him getting closer. "Don't come near me. Just tell me if I'm supposed to make myself bigger, shout and scream, back away—I just don't know what to do."

"I told you," Nick grits out and then he's beside me. "Stay still."

"This does not seem like a solid plan." Sweat pools in my armpits.

"Inch behind me and then slowly walk backward into the tent. Do not turn your back. Get the radio. Call for help. Get the airhorn and another flashlight. Only then come back out, slowly."

"I can't leave you out here alone. What if she attacks? Or one of the cubs attack? What if she's teaching them to hunt people?"

Since I stumbled out here and caught sight of them, my brain has been on overdrive.

"Jensen," Nick growls making himself big enough to obscure me behind him. He flicks on his flashlight, pointing it at the animals. "Follow my fucking instructions."

The lioness's tail swishes as I back up slowly. I almost fall into the tent, and when I tip in, I grab the walkie-talkie off the side table. We've hardly used it.

"Tent Twelve. Lions. Tent twelve. Lions." Whatever else I'm supposed to say dies on my lips at the sound of Nick's shouted curses and the erratic flashes of light streaming in the open entrance.

I snatch the airhorn off the wall, and I grab another flashlight. Taking a deep breath, I duck out of the tent and see the mother has moved closer. Nick's made himself big. He's waving his arms, the flashlight going haywire, and he's shouting at the top of his lungs.

Footsteps pound down the path, and between Nick's shouting, and the approaching gang from the camp, the cubs who have been crouched low, scamper away into the darkness beyond the edge of the tall grass.

It's only once the crowd becomes apparent to the lioness that she, too, bounds away.

"Holy shit," I breathe out.

Kafil is leading the charge with a hunting rifle. Others follow with spears, flashing lights, and various weapons.

"Where did they go?" Kafil asks, skidding to a stop in front of our tent. "How many?"

"That way." Nick points at the field beyond us. "A lioness and two cubs."

The men stand around conferring before forming a group and trudging into the long grasses, weapons drawn. Nick's hands rise to cover his face, and then he drags them back down to dangle at his sides.

My flashlight and the airhorn tumble out of my hands to the ground with a thud. Nick turns to look at me, and the tent door flaps in the breeze behind us. There are probably mosquitos storming the place. I catch myself on the thought. Could have been much worse things storming the tent, storming us.

Nick's stricken expression changes to one of determination, and he closes the distance between us in two quick strides. His hands slide into my damp hair, framing my face. The intensity of his stare is oddly soothing.

I'm washed out. Worn out. The fight or flight surge has vanished, and all I can think about is how pretty his hazel eyes still are, how much I've missed this feeling between us, this connection that goes beyond friendship, beyond sexual attraction. I'm loath to name it, but it's still there for me. An underground current, buried over, capped, waiting to be tapped again. An endless well of emotion and history.

"If anything happened to you—" His voice catches.

The same feeling is mirrored in me. How could he put himself in so much danger for me? How devastated would I be to lose him again—permanently this time? I'd never survive his absence. We may not be close anymore, but the notion of him not being in this world is devastating.

Our gazes are locked, and I wonder whether he can see my fear too.

"Nick, I—" The words die on my lips as his descend on mine.

His kiss is hungry, touching on frantic, but I meet it with my own freshly dissolved panic. Just like the last time, his kiss completely knocks all sense of time and place out of me. I'm so consumed by him, by the way he's kissing me that I don't realize we're back in the tent, making our way to the bed until my knees hit the edge of the mattress.

Even then, I don't care enough to stop this, to pause what's happening, to dissect why we're both insatiable.

But we are.

Our kisses barely break long enough to breathe before we dive back in. My hands tremble, and I slide them up under his shirt, reveling in his smooth skin, his firm muscles. After that brush with loss, I need to be as close to him as possible. Nothing else matters.

His shirt disappears over his head, and then his lips are back on mine, as though we're both afraid if we speak, the spell will be broken. We don't need to talk. I just want to feel.

We're on the bed, and when he rocks against me, a moan of pleasure escapes. I drag my nails along his back, and he shudders.

"Jules," he murmurs, and there's so much need in the way he says my name that my desire for him cranks into overdrive. I'm never going to want to hear my name said any other way.

My body is so switched on, and my brain so turned off that I don't understand why Nick stops kissing me and breaks away to half turn toward the door.

A throat clears again when I try to drag Nick back to me.

Oh shit. Someone else is here. I drop my hands from Nick and scramble back on the bed. My damp panties mock me. What was I about to do?

Kafil is at the entrance to the tent, just inside the door we didn't close, but his back is turned to us. "Sorry," Kafil says. "Very sorry to interrupt."

"It's fine. We should have zipped the door," Nick says, but his voice isn't quite back to normal.

We all know why we didn't zip the door.

Nick glances at me, and he tosses me his bunched-up shirt from beside him before turning his back to me, shielding my body from Kafil.

Confused by his shirt, I glance down and realize his shirt wasn't the only one that came off at some point. Oh my God. I'm in my bra. I didn't even realize he took off my shirt. What is wrong with me? I yank it over my head, and when I catch Nick's gaze over his shoulder, I can't read him. We just went after each other without a second thought, and I have no idea how he feels about what we just did.

Did I almost become a Crown Bunny?

I bury my face in my hands and take a deep breath. There is not a doubt in my mind I would have slept with him. The words *no* or *stop* or *we can't* weren't even at the edge of my consciousness. I wanted him. I raise my head to stare at his back. Oh, God. I still want him. My heart races.

"You can turn around now, Kafil." Nick sinks onto the edge of the bed in front of me, still keeping himself between me and our guide.

"I have to make sure there are no injuries, and I need to take a statement for our wild animal protocols." Kafil has a clipboard in his hand.

"How did the lioness get into the camp?" Nick's tone is sharp.

"We have protocols in place to deter wild animals. But we can never guarantee they won't get in." Kafil's pen is poised over the paper. "We have chased them off. Done some aggressive maneuvers to deter them from coming back. However, it is always dangerous to be outside your tent at night." He eyes Nick. "Which you know."

It appears our burgeoning friendship with Kafil has made him bold. He would never have said that to Nick a week ago. Nick tenses at the familiarity, and although he seeks friendly bonds with other people, he wasn't raised to be spoken to so casually.

"It's my fault," I say before Nick can defend himself or throw me to the figurative lioness. "I stepped out of the tent to speak to you or someone, and I forgot about the time. The whole thing is completely my fault."

Kafil gestures to the walkie-talkie he must have brought back in. "You realize you can call someone to come to you?"

Shame washes over me at my mistake. I could have cost Nick his life or one of the workers their life. Nick's challenge about situations where death might be preferable to life threw me off, and I stormed out without thinking. A few weeks ago, I had less of a problem keeping the king's illness from Nick. The closer we get, the more I worry about the king, about Nick, about how he'll take me not telling him.

But I made a promise to the king, and it's not the sort of promise someone like me can just opt out of keeping. He's my employer, but he's also like a second father to me. I can't tell Nick about the king's health problems when I've been expressly told not to.

"I do realize now that I should have used the walkie-talkie. I apologize," I say. "I was distracted. Trust me when I say I will *not* do that again."

Kafil maintains eye contact with me around Nick's shoulder, clearly trying to ensure I understand the gravity of the situation without pushing further with his words. He doesn't need to worry. Coming face to face with a lioness and her cubs without the barrier of a vehicle wasn't on my bucket list.

"What do you need from us?" Nick asks, his tone weary.

"I have incident statements that need to be completed. I can fill them out with your help, or I can leave them for you." He flashes the papers on the clipboard.

"Leave them," Nick says with a dismissive wave of his hand. "The secretary or I will get them to you in the morning."

"As you wish." Kafil slides the clipboard onto the side table and steps out the door, zipping it closed, without another word.

With him gone, Nick and I are silent for a few beats. Is he as stunned as I am about our make-out session?

"Are you still hungry?" Nick strolls over to the table and picks at what's left of the food as though he didn't just have his tongue in my mouth a few minutes ago.

We've hardly eaten, but it's not food I'm still longing for. "Not really."

He grabs the walkie-talkie, wagging it at me in a condescending way before calling for them to come take our food. He putters around the room without speaking to me, shirtless. It's a sight I've seen several times since we were forced to share a tent, but it's no less impressive. The memory of my hands on him lingers in my tingling fingertips.

I lift the neck of Nick's shirt to cover my mouth and nose, breathing in his familiar scent. My lips are sensitive from his kisses, from the scratch of his beard. My mind wakes up, and I catch myself smelling his shirt. I draw it down, hoping Nick didn't notice.

What is wrong with me? He's so casual, wandering around the tent like nothing happened between us, and I'm trying to bathe in his scent.

"Where is my shirt?" I can't see it anywhere obvious from my position on the bed.

"I tossed it with the rest of your mess." Nick points to the pile of clothes on the floor.

Clearly, I was the only one so into our make-out session I didn't realize I lost my shirt or where it went. He actually took the time to aim my top at my pile of dirty laundry, which admittedly, I've left there to annoy him more than anything. One of the workers even offered to take my clothes and wash them for me. Stubbornly, I declined.

Clambering off the bed, I switch out my shirt and throw Nick's back at him. He catches it with a smirk and tugs it over his head just before workers call to us from outside the tent.

Nick unzips the entrance, letting them in to clear our food. We watch them in eerie silence.

Am I supposed to mention the kiss? Such a freaking disaster last time something like this happened between us. Say something? Ignore it?

There's no point in making our working relationship awkward. We almost died. Our hormones were elevated. The whole thing doesn't need to go any further. We can stop right there. One of us just has to say something out loud.

When the zipper clicks closed and all the workers are gone, Nick avoids looking at me. Christ. He's going to make me say something first. Of course he is. The olive branch always has to be me. At least that hasn't changed.

"So," I say, drawing out the word. "Are we pretending we didn't just make out?"

"Is that what you want?" Nick peers at me over his shoulder with a narrowed gaze.

Okay, wow. Just like that he's flipped the decision back to me. How do I want to play this? Before I say anything, I gather my thoughts. Casual? Playful? Definitely not serious.

"I'm not sure," I admit. "As make-out sessions go, it was decent." Understatement. To this day, my first kiss with Nick is still the best kiss I've ever had. This one, tonight, is definitely rivaling it for the top spot. He got my shirt off, and I didn't even realize it. I've never had clothes leave my body while I was sober and *not* notice before.

"Decent?" Nick queries, prowling closer to where I'm standing at the edge of the bed.

"Above average?" I try again, a hint of a smile playing at my lips.

"Above average?" He's in front of me now, and his fingertips graze my cheek. "You *might* be willing to do it again?" He scans my face.

My breath catches at the naked desire in his hazel depths. Outside the tent, after the lioness disappeared, I'm not sure exactly what emotion was in his gaze, but it wasn't desire. The last time I saw him look at me like this, I was too drunk and too young to be sure until he was kissing me. With age comes wisdom and experience, and his desire is as bright as a full moon to me now. He wants me, which is sort of amazing.

"Would you rise to my standards if I raised the bar?" My voice is husky.

"I wouldn't just rise to the bar. I'd clear it and then set a new standard for anyone who dared to come after."

Our gazes meet, and the question in his is clear: *Are we doing this*? But I'm afraid to say yes. Once he's got me into bed, I'm not sure I'll ever want to crawl out again. Having him set a standard no one else can meet is not quite the brag or tease as he might think. Everything I've ever experienced with Nick from friendship to first kisses elevated my expectations for everyone who came after. Sex cannot become a disappointment as well once he's done with me.

I'm also not sure I trust this guy or any of the other versions of Nick I've witnessed on this trip. He's *my* Nick in some ways, but he's also a man I barely know.

My heart can't take being discarded by any version of him again.

"I think." I lick my lips, and his pupils flare. "We've had a really stressful experience and making big decisions right now is a mistake."

"Whether or not to sleep with me is a big decision?" He raises his eyebrows.

"Yes," I whisper. How can I explain without giving myself and my heart away? When he casts me aside, I'll be heartbroken. If I go down this path, I must be okay with us ending. I'm not there yet.

He searches my face and then he draws me to him to kiss my forehead. "All right, then," he says. There's no anger or frustration in his voice, but he does tug me into a hug.

When he kisses my temple before releasing me, his gesture almost undoes my resolve. "It's not that I don't want to," I try to explain.

He steps away from me, gathering his things for bedtime. "Truly, Jules. It's okay. One no doesn't mean *never,* the same way one yes doesn't mean *always.*"

It's a statement my Nick would have made had we ever got far enough with each other to have this discussion. His patience with me was often unending.

"I like that," I say with a partial smile.

"You should. You're the one who told me it. Don't you remember? When we were kids—you said you hated how boys always got so offended by a no and so grabby about a yes. Made me so angry at the time to think of someone treating you poorly." He stares into his drawer. "How could I ever do the same to anyone, least of all you?"

Before I can say anything in response, not that I could with my heart detonating in my chest, he slips into the bathroom.

To distract myself from the ache in my chest, I get ready for bed and consider all the contradictions of Prince Nicholas of Bellerive. One minute he shows me his gooey center, and the next minute he's granite, impenetrable.

When he comes out of the bathroom, I go in, and we pass each other in silence. We make eye contact, and it's not awkward like I might expect. It's as if we've both let down our guards a little and neither of us is keen to put them back up. *My* Nick is still in there, and every glimpse I catch of him makes me long for more.

We might be able to get *us* back.

We might not be completely lost to each other.

The realization is both terrifying and euphoric.

Nicholas

My alarm goes off, and I press the snooze button on the nightstand, trying not to disturb Jules who decided to cuddle with me in the middle of the night. She's pressed against my back, an arm thrown over my middle, and her hand dangles dangerously close to a morning surprise.

"Jules?" I murmur over my shoulder. "We've got to get up, or we'll be late to meet Kafil."

"Hmm." Her lips are pressed against my neck.

The contented noise causes my morning surprise to strain against my sleep pants. I want to roll over, pin her down, and kiss her awake. Bury my face in the crook of her neck, the dip between her breasts, the deliciousness between her thighs. Might be a few things I'd bury between her legs.

Last night when I kissed her, I made a leap, and I wasn't sure if I'd land on the other side or in the middle of a crater. Not sure I quite cleared the fall, but I'm not in the pit of despair either.

"I don't want to get up yet," Jules says against my back, and her cheek presses into my shoulder blade.

Instead of scooting away from me, which I feared when my alarm went off, she's only snuggled in more. I'm afraid speaking might give away how turned on I am by her proximity. A familiar story from every other morning I've woken up to the scent of her coating everything, but this time she might discover what I've been pretending doesn't exist—at least until last night. She definitely felt my existence last night.

"Prince Nicholas?" Kafil calls from the doorway.

Ah, right. Breakfast.

There's no way I can move right now. "Just give us a minute," I answer.

Julia moans and rolls away from me. "I really don't want to leave this bed this morning."

"There's a phone call in the communications tent for Julia," Kafil responds, still behind the tent flap.

When I rotate around, Julia is frowning.

"Boyfriend?" I ask. I've steered away from anything personal, and the Jules I once knew would never cheat on purpose. She turned me down last night, and while the rejection felt like a compliment, I should probably check she wasn't weighing her options. Her line—that being with me meant something to her—was a balm to my soul last night. Best to make sure it's not poisoned.

"A boyfriend? Hardly." She scoffs and gives me the side-eye. "I don't appreciate the implication I'm a cheater either. I didn't sleep with you, but I definitely wanted to."

"You did kiss me back," I remind her. My insides burst to life at her bold admission. Not only does she believe being with me will mean something, but she *wants* to be with me. It's like Christmas in this bed right now. What else can I get her to admit to?

"You kissed me first."

"Zero regrets on that." I tuck a stray strand of her hair behind her ear.

"Unlike last time?" She searches my face.

I suck in a sharp breath. Before I can formulate an answer, Kafil clears his throat outside the tent.

"I have your breakfast," he calls in an overly loud voice.

Julia sighs and climbs out of the bed, leaving our conversation unfinished. She heads for the bathroom while I stare at the ceiling wondering whether we really need to bring up the past. I'm content to keep it buried. Just the thought of discussing Alex and Julia, together, in any context, sours my mood.

"You can come in, Kafil." I keep my gaze on the ceiling when the tent door unzips.

He sets up the table and two chairs along with our covered dishes for breakfast. Julia's tea is there and my coffee.

She comes out of the bathroom dressed and gives Kafil a strained smile before slipping out the doorway for the communications tent.

"How are you feeling after your ordeal last night?" Kafil asks when I don't bother with my usual chatter.

I sigh and sit up, my feet landing on the floor beside the bed. "Probably as most people do after a near-death experience. Lucky and inclined to make potentially foolish choices."

"You mean you and Julia?"

"Not specifically, but yes." I glower at him.

He finishes setting the table and then meets my gaze. "You're well suited to each other. When you don't have your," he seems to search for the right word, "defenses up, you both appear happier."

"Do we?" I rub my face. "It's a complicated situation."

"I gather there's a lot of history between you."

"Almost too much," I say with a grimace. My happiness from earlier vanished at the mention of what happened all those years ago. Strangely, Kafil's comments aren't making me feel any better. Alex has wormed his way into my thoughts, and I can't seem to cut him out.

"I'll leave you to it." Kafil ducks out the tent and zips it up.

With a sigh, I rise from the bed. Julia's phone lights up on her nightstand. She has a different carrier than me, and if she puts her phone in just the right place, her texts eventually arrive. She discovered that last week. To say the signal is fickle and spotty is an understatement. The communications tent has been our only reliable way of keeping in touch with anyone. Not that I've bothered beyond the surgery details, but Julia has made a few calls to Posey.

Despite my better judgment, when her phone lights up a second time with the reminder of the message, I peer at the name.

Alex.

My lips twist in annoyance, and though I shouldn't, I press the screen to read the message preview. If I'm falling into something with Julia, and she's maintained a connection with Alex, I'm backing off.

Please tell me this is garbage gossip and you're not shagging my brother.

At the end of the message is the start of a linked article.

Robbie didn't wait long. Must have filed the story on the airplane.

I try to decipher Alex's tone, but other than his usual pompousness, I've got nothing. Does he still carry a torch for Julia? Do they still sleep together when they're both single? Does she still have feelings for him? That would be worse. Crushing, actually. An ache spiders across my chest.

Since I've avoided anything to do with Alex and Julia, I've got no idea how they began or ended. He name-dropped seeing her whenever he returned home during our final year of high school, and he visited her in America at our college.

After the visit during our freshman year, he never appeared again, and he started talking about other girls when he was home for his breaks.

So what happened?

If my father is truly stepping down, then Julia will be working for Alex by this time next year. They'll be together all the time. My stomach churns. The thought reminds me I haven't eaten this morning.

I plop into the breakfast chair, and I go through the motions of eating, but between Julia's comment and Alex's text message, my mood from first thing this morning has vanished.

When Julia comes back into the tent, she grabs the incident reports from the side table and passes me one. While we fill them out in silence, my curiosity over who phoned her gets the best of me.

"Was the call about Elena?" I ask.

"No," Julia says. She scribbles more details on her page.

I throw my pen onto the table with my final sentence and take a bite of toast. "So, who was it, then?" Not at all my business, but it's not like Julia to give an answer without ample explanation when the situation is straightforward.

'Your father. He'd like you to come home." She doesn't look up from her page until she finishes her final sentence.

"You must have told him that's not happening, correct?"

"Why wouldn't it be happening?" She gives me a sharp look and narrows her eyes. "We've done the safari thing. We've made the majority of the arrangements for Elena. The rest can be worked out at home and communicated with Kafil to pass on to Bahati."

"I still have another week and a bit here, and I have my trip to Vegas. I'm on vacation. The coronation isn't going to happen for months. I do not need to be there."

"He would like you home."

"Apparently, he knows the number to the camp now, so he can call me himself."

"He sent me here to bring you home."

"Which has never added up to me," I huff. "Can you honestly tell me his strategy makes sense to you? It's not like I was refusing his calls to the camp. He never called." Although her arrival almost two weeks ago pissed me off, I'm grateful for her appearance now. Having the snow thawing between us is a pleasant surprise even if I worry there might be another ice age in our future.

She squirms in her chair.

She left the tent tense, but otherwise in good spirits. As I eye her across the table, I realize what else has set me on edge other than the reminder of Alex's existence. She's back in royal business mode. First the incident reports, then the short answers, and now the haughty tone.

"What did he actually tell you on the phone?" Something isn't adding up, but I'm not sure what it is.

Julia meets my gaze, and there's an emotion in her depths I can't quite read. Regret? "Your father says if you don't return within the next seventy-two hours, he'll be on the hunt for an arranged marriage."

I slouch back in my chair, stunned. Whatever is going on at home must be serious. The arranged marriage schtick is an inside code my father and I agreed on when I started these royalty-free adventures. If my father ever threatened an arranged marriage, I needed to return home in the assigned time period. Something big is about to hit the fan.

"Seventy-two hours?" I clarify.

"Yes."

I sigh. "Book the tickets via Vegas."

"Nick, that makes no sense. We'd literally be flying in the wrong direction."

"Vegas first, for at least 24 hours, or I don't go home." She doesn't need to know I'll go home no matter what. My father enacting the code, even if it's through Julia, guarantees I'll turn up on time.

"Why?" she asks, mystified.

"I have my reasons. Make sure you book your ticket as well to join me." Once we're home, what will things be like between us? Last night and this morning gave me a glimpse of what we could be, and I'm not ready to let her go.

"I don't need to go to Vegas. I can just return to Bellerive."

I wag my finger. "You're here to escort me. Probably to keep me out of trouble. Secretary Jensen, you must come to Vegas. Also, Father will want some sort of security arrangement. I am not allowed to set foot on American soil unguarded."

Julia grabs some grapes off the table and goes to fetch her phone off the nightstand.

I watch her reaction carefully. The annoyance on her face deepens.

"Something wrong?" I ask.

"Alex. He sent me a link to a gossip story? Apparently, you and I are involved in some sort of long-term illicit love affair?"

I wish.

"Did you know about this?" she asks.

"Define *know*."

"Nick."

"Robbie heard me talking to Kafil the other day outside the meal tent. He made some conclusions that I couldn't tear down without revealing what we'd really been doing."

"Why wouldn't you want the press to know about the foundation for girls' education or the operation for Elena?" She raises her eyebrows. "That's good press. This," she waves her phone at me, "is not."

"It's not *bad* press, per se." Why wouldn't she want to be linked with me? Is an affair that farfetched? She just admitted this morning she wants to have sex with me. Granted, a long-term relationship is a significant stretch from a one-night stand. But she's making me feel like our conversation was all in my head.

"Sex sells. He would have gone with the more salacious story no matter what I told him."

"After this story, do you really think you and me in Vegas together is a good idea?" She purses her lips and closes her phone.

I stare at her for a beat, convinced she knows more about what's happening in Bellerive than she's telling me. Whatever it is, I'm sure I'll find out when I get home, assuming the gossip rags don't break the news first. That has to be the timeline—Father bought himself, probably quite literally, seventy-two hours to get me home before something significant hits social media.

"Yes," I say. "It's a good idea."

Once we're back in Bellerive, I worry this closeness we've managed to cobble together will disappear in a puff of royal protocol, official jobs, and an asshole brother.

The taste I got last night and this morning of Jules and me together isn't enough. I want more. So, I'll take my seventy-two hours, and I'll see if I can convince her we don't have to be the people who left Bellerive.

We can return as anyone we want.

JULES

Fourteen years ago

I lean across Nick to put the empty champagne bottle on the wooden floor beside him, and I realize exactly how drunk I've gotten. What is the alcohol percentage of champagne, anyway? High. Too high.

When I slide off Nick to my spot, he sucks in a sharp breath, and I glance up at him, wondering if I've somehow hurt him. Did I elbow him somewhere? The question dies on my lips at the expression on his face. Our gazes lock, and the air pulses with something I've never felt from him before.

God, I'm so drunk, but it feels like... it seems like...

Then he's kissing me, and from the moment his lips brush against mine, I'm lost. Gone. So consumed by him that all rational thought floats on the breeze around us. Nick's kissing me, and I'm kissing him, and nothing in my life has felt as right as this moment.

He tries to draw back, and I rise onto my knees, deepening the kiss, desperate for more. His lips slide against mine, pliable without being slobbery, and I'm a goner. It's not just a kiss. Every brush of his lips stamps his name deeper into my heart.

Nick. Nick. Nick.

Every time I look at him, I'll remember this kiss, and the feel of him pressed against me. I'm never going to let this moment go. My heart pounds in my ears, louder than the fireworks overhead.

When we finally separate, I stare into Nick's hazel eyes and wonder how I never saw him this way before. How did I miss *this*? My love for him is so painfully, so beautifully obvious. The kiss has left behind the crushing heaviness of desire, but more than that, I understand exactly what I've been searching for and failing to find, with Alex.

I'm not into Alex because I am *way, way* too into Nick.

I'm in love with Nick.

Holy crap.

I stiffen and draw away from him.

Alex.

Oh shit. Oh, God. Oh, no.

What am I doing?

I flee from Nick and lift my skirts to hustle down the ladder. I cannot be sitting on top of the barn making out with one brother while the other one thinks we're together. I'm not the girl who cheats, who betrays. I need to find Alex.

While I rush out of the barn, my life comes into a weird sort of focus. How did I not see that I'm in love with Nick? The idea swirls around my brain, the truest thing I've ever thought, and yet completely impossible.

I *love* Nick.

Not just that—that's normal—but I'm *in love* with him. The kind of love that movies, books, and TV shows describe but I never quite believed could be real. This sudden burst of feeling is every love song ever written. Stunning to realize how deep the emotion runs in me like it's always been there waiting to be uncorked.

Once I've broken things off with Alex, I'll go back to Nick. I'll tell him. I'll tell him I'm in love with him.

A spike of elation shoots through me from my toes to the top of my head. Nick and I are going to be together. Really together. Everyone will be shocked. I'm kind of shocked.

When I storm past the edge of the main building intent on finding Alex, someone snags my wrist, and my dress swirls around my legs. I'm spun into the shadows and swept into strong arms.

"What—"

The rest of my question is swallowed by Alex's lips hitting mine. My drunken brain takes a beat to realize what's happening. He can't just grab me and kiss me! Or maybe he can because that's what we've been doing.

But I don't want to do that anymore with him. I bite Alex's bottom lip when he ignores my mumbled protests.

He steps back on a chuckle, grabbing his lip between his fingers. "Feeling feisty, are you?"

I shift away from the wall, my back to the path, and I'm mortified that I've gone from kissing one brother to kissing the other. Who does that?

The only comfort is that I kissed Nick before I kissed Alex tonight.

God, if Nick knew my lips had touched his brother's, he'd murder me.

"I can't do this anymore, Alex," I say. He's not looking at me, focused on something over my shoulder. "Did you hear me?" I slap him in the chest. "I can't do this with you anymore."

He smirks, and glances down at me, tucking a stray strand of my hair behind my ear. I'm tempted to slap his hand away. This is another reason Alex and I would never work—he's lost in Alex-land and isn't paying attention to me at all. When I try to speak again, he sweeps me into another unwanted kiss.

Once again, he takes my drunken brain by surprise, and my reaction is a beat or two behind. He's completely ignoring what I want right now. I shove him, hard.

He staggers back on a chuckle. "Jules," he hisses, coming back to invade my personal space. "Don't be a fucking tease."

"I'm not joking, Alex. I can't—I don't want to do this anymore."

At the wounded expression on his face, my confidence falters. He doesn't actually care about me, does he? All he's ever tried to do is get in my pants. The number of real conversations we've had is few and far between.

But maybe that's my fault. When he tried to talk about anything important, I fluffed him off, especially after the homeless veterans debacle. Although I pretended like him using the idea didn't matter, I've never quite trusted him since.

Thoughts of Nick circle my consciousness, making it hard to concentrate on Alex's feelings, on the right words to use.

"I know I'm going back to uni on Monday, but this doesn't have to end." Alex runs a finger down my bare arm.

"I can't, Alex. I don't think—I'm not sure we have the right feelings for each other."

"What's that supposed to mean?"

"Well, it's just." I really wish I was sober right now. My thoughts are muddled, and all I want to spit out is: *Turns out, I'm in love with your brother. Surprise. Yeah, I'm shocked too. Sorry about that. See you around.* Except, you can't really say that to someone, can you? Drunk or not, that seems like a poor choice of phrasing. "I don't think *I* feel the right things for you." Who knows what he feels?

He chuckles and steps closer. "Didn't seem like you were struggling in my room to feel something all those times."

"That's just—it's just *sex*, Alex." I flush. "That's our connection. You know? You like sticking your hand down my pants, and I liked letting you for a little while. Hardly a love match."

Alex rears back as though I've slapped him.

Drunk me is a mess. Why did I say that? "Sorry," I say. "I'm sorry. I'm too drunk to be having this conversation, but it's important we have it tonight. Right now."

"I think it's probably more important we have it when you know what you want. You're definitely not sober. Where is this coming from?" His eyes narrow. "What's changed?"

Nothing. Everything.

"I can't be with you, Alex. I shouldn't have—I should never have let it go this far." Except I never suspected Nick might see me as anything more than a friend. I had no clue one kiss would send my heart spinning out of control. I'm drunk, but I've never been clearer on what I want.

Nick. I want Nick.

I'm giddy at the realization I could *have* Nick. In every way. He can be mine. He *wants* to be mine.

"You're breaking things off with me?" Alex's tone brims with disbelief. "Jules."

He tries to reach for me, but I sidestep him.

"Look, if this is about us having sex, I can wait, all right? I'll stop having a go at you about it."

I can't meet his gaze. Wouldn't it be so much easier if that was the problem? "That's not it. We're not right for each other. I wanted us to be right, but we're just not. I'm sorry." I glance over my shoulder, thinking of Nick in the barn. "I have to go." I rub my forehead.

God, I just walked out on Nick after he kissed me. What must he be thinking?

Before Alex can plead his case or get pissed off with me, which is probably more likely, I gather my dress and run back to the barn, oblivious to the rocks pricking my bare feet.

"Nick!" I climb the ladder and pop out onto the balcony area, prepared to apologize, kiss him again, declare my love for him. But it's empty except for my shoes.

I gaze out across the property, trying to think of where Nick might have gone. Will he be mad at me for leaving? Why didn't I stay?

A pit forms in my stomach. Strands of my hair that have come loose from my updo get caught by the wind, untethered.

I need to find him.

###

Time loses all meaning while I wander the property in the dark, and when the fireworks finish and the lights come back on, I keep looking.

Exhausted, and no longer on a high from our champagne feast and my newly discovered feelings, I head back to the barn. At some point, he'll return, right? I even checked his bedroom to see if he collapsed there trying to sleep off the alcohol.

When I get to the barn, there's a shaft of light streaming out of the cracked door. Strange. Nick and I haven't brought out the lanterns since the last time we tried the Ouija board and failed miserably.

Unsure, I push the door open with my fingertips. The light is dim, but it's enough—too much. There—sprawled on the blankets Nick and I sat on earlier to watch the fireworks, the blankets we've used for years to spend time together, the blankets he kissed me on—are Vicky and Nick. His shirt is gone, and his hand is up her very short skirt with his knee wedged between her legs.

My eyes sting, and I blink.

Am I drunk?

Is this a nightmare?

He's with Vicky?

"Nick?" I register the shock in my voice, and the fact I shouldn't be standing here staring at them, at the same time.

Vicky gasps, and she pushes Nick off her. "Nick, you didn't lock the door?"

He turns toward me, still lying on the ground, and his eyes are glassy with alcohol. He's so drunk I can't believe he's even capable of making out with Vicky. Definitely not in a *remember to lock the door* state of mind.

"Julia," he slurs.

Vicky straightens her clothes and kisses Nick's cheek. "Call me tomorrow?" she asks.

"For sure," Nick says, and he gives her a lazy smile.

She slips past me with her shoes in her hand.

I stare at Nick for a beat, and he stares back. As stunned as I was about him kissing me, I think I'm more stunned about finding him with Vicky. This empty barn is ours—his and mine—we've filled it with hours of conversation, drinking, and stupid games. Finding him here with her is a punch to the gut. Chills snake across my skin, and I give a violent shiver.

"Are you two back together?" My voice wavers.

He rubs the top of his head and avoids meeting my gaze. Then he sits up, his arms hanging over his knees. "Yeah."

"But you—" The words get stuck in my throat, and I don't know if I can say them without crying. "But you kissed *me.*"

He laces his fingers and puts them behind his neck, focused on the pile of blankets around him. When he meets my gaze, his expression is blank. "I wanted to see what it would be like. Now that I know, I don't ever have to do it again. It won't happen again."

His comments are arrows to my heart. They cut so deep and so quick, tears spring to my eyes. "What?" I whisper.

"I shouldn't have done it," Nick slurs. "I'm sorry. Can we just forget it? Can we just forget this night happened?"

"You want to forget it?" I have to squeeze out the words around the lump in my throat. The intensity of the ache festering in my chest makes it hard to breathe. I can't quite catch my breath. What is happening?

He rises and almost tips over when he tries to grab his shirt off the floor.

Normally I'd laugh at him, but I'm too stunned by his request. How do I reel in these feelings? The alcohol we drank together earlier is making this whole exchange surreal, dream-like.

Can I wake up now?

On his third attempt, he bunches his dress shirt into his hand, making a fist, and his jaw is tight with tension. Another discarded bottle of champagne lies on the floor beside the blankets.

"Nick?" I choke back a sob. Tiny cracks spider across my heart. This can't be happening.

"We just need to forget it." He glances at me over his shoulder, but when we make eye contact he doesn't even seem like the same person he was a few hours ago.

"Julia!" Posey calls for me out the door. "Julia! We're leaving."

"You should go, Julia." His gaze slides away from mine, and he stares at the bunched-up shirt in his hand.

"Nick." I try again, but I'm not sure what I want to say. My throat and chest are so tight, I don't know if I could get any more words out even if he wanted to hear them. I want to collapse in a puddle at his feet, beg him to tell me something different, to retract his words. He's back together with Vicky? Nothing makes sense to me.

Before I walked in here, everything made so much sense.

"Julia!" Posey pops her head into the barn. "We have to go. Are you coming home with us or is Nick—" Her eyes widen at the sight of him, disheveled and partially dressed. "Oh."

I clear my throat, but it's painful to move the lump. "Take me home." Turning on my heel, I loop my arm with hers and drag her out into the night.

"Oh, my God. You and Nick?" Posey says in a fierce whisper. "I always thought—"

"No." I shake my head. Unshed tears burn my throat. "He wasn't with me." The stupid lump that keeps rising appears again and strangles my voice.

When I get home, I'll curl on my bed and let the tears come. I just have to make it home. No one can ever know what happened, and then I can forget this night. We'll forget it.

My heart is cracking and cracking and cracking.

I press the heel of my hand into my chest. Why won't this stop hurting?

"He's not with me," I whisper.

He'll never be with me.

JULIA

Nick is sleeping beside me in our first-class seats at the tail end of our twenty-four-hour journey to reach Las Vegas. If I was smart, I would also be sleeping. When we arrive, he'll be refreshed, and I'll be bleary from lack of sleep. My judgment will be at my lowest while he'll be in peak party mode. It's been years since I've had a front-row seat to Nick on a binge, but I have a feeling I'll be bearing witness to that event in a few hours.

Then he'll be flying back to Bellerive with a hangover, and I'll be crossing my fingers no Nick scandals hit the media while we're in the air.

A hangover isn't exactly the prime condition to have the news outlets break his father's illness. King George told me on the phone he negotiated seventy-two hours to get all his kids back in Bellerive and tell them the terrible news before it's splashed across the internet. I wanted to have Nick on a plane home today instead of going to Las Vegas. Why cut the timeline close?

Instead, Nick took the timeframe as a personal challenge. What could he squeeze into three days?

At least he's not so grumpy since I agreed to his ridiculous terms. Of course, he had to agree to mine too. At the first stopover, I marched him into the airport spa where they cut his hair and trimmed his beard.

Truthfully, he's not the worst travel companion. During our layovers, he's gotten us access to ultra-first-class lounges. He's been witty and charming—his best self. If I wasn't already worried about my head and my heart around him, I'd be in full-on panic mode now. As it is, I think I've resigned myself to heartache as the best case, heartbreak as the worst-case scenario, once his interest in me vanishes again.

"Jensen," Nick says from beside me, one eye open. "You should get some sleep. You're not gonna get any once we arrive."

"I know they say it's the city that never sleeps, but do we really have to live the cliché?"

"Who is 'they' exactly? New York is actually the city that never sleeps." He stretches, and his T-shirt rides up to show a sliver of toned stomach. "Do you frequently hang around people who don't sleep?"

My fingers itch to slide along the waist of his jeans, up along his torso. Before he got the haircut and trimmed his beard, he was attractive but cleaned up, he's head-turning, panty-dropping, weak-in-the-knees gorgeous.

He wiggles, and the shirt rises higher, exposing more muscles. He chuckles.

I raise my startled gaze from his defined stomach muscles to his amused expression.

"I thought you might want more of a show." He smirks. "You're drooling, Jensen."

Before I can think about what he's said, I touch my mouth. His deep laughter sounds, and I slap his chest. "Teasing me about the fact you're incredibly physically attractive is immature. I didn't know you needed your ego stroked."

He lights up and rubs his hands together. "Oh, wow. Where do I start with that one? So many options." He pretends to think. "All right, I'll go easy on you." He gives me a seductive look. "You could stroke something else, if you want."

My cheeks are on fire. "Nicholas," I hiss. "We're on an airplane with other people."

"You don't have to stroke it right *now*."

I slap him again.

"The gossips have already outed our torrid affair. Just go with it, babe." He winks at me.

Even though I'm embarrassed and tongue-tied, my insides are melting at his overt flirting. When we were friends this didn't happen—ever. Though I witnessed him turn on the charm with other people, he never directed this brand of confidence at me.

Then as our friendship disintegrated, he became more and more aloof. This charismatic side of him, aimed at me, is like discovering a whole new person.

"I'm glad Kafil took our quick exit so well," I say in an effort to get us back on even ground.

"I'm sure the hefty tip coupled with all our contact information for Bahati and Elena helped. They should be on the island in the next couple of weeks for surgery number one."

A comfortable silence settles between us, and I can't decide if I want serious Nick or flirty Nick. Definitely don't want angry Nick. Suppose I should find out which version of him I'll get when the plane lands.

"So, what's the Vegas plan, then? Round up the crown bunnies? Get roaring drunk? Try to keep the exploits off social media?"

Nick scowls at me, all teasing vanishing. "I'm spending twenty-four hours with *you* in Vegas. That's what I'm doing. Just you."

My heart pounds, but I still manage a skeptical look on the outside. We're flying to Vegas so he can spend time with me? Seems extreme. We could have gone back to Bellerive and spent time together there.

A little voice in my head waves a red flag. Bellerive is fraught with potential conflict. What will it be like between us when we return? I can't imagine this rapport lasting when we're officially Prince Nicholas and Secretary Jensen. History will weigh so much heavier on us. A memory around every corner.

"And some alcohol. Perhaps quite a lot." He searches my face, and there's a poignant pause. "Just like old times. You, me, and some alcohol."

Now it's my turn to scowl. "Those good times led to some not-so-good times. Forgive me if I'm not keen to repeat them."

He slides a hand along my cheek and stares deep into my eyes. "What do you want to repeat?"

"Nick." His name sounds like a plea, and I'm melting under the heat of his attention. He's been flirty, and light, and fun, but he hasn't kissed me again. Part of me was starting to wonder whether he regretted last night like last time.

Luckily, he seems to understand what I'm pleading for, what I'm too proud to ask for.

He closes the distance between our chairs, framing my face, and drawing me into a deep kiss that chips away at another piece of my soul. Without realizing it, I've bunched a hand in his T-shirt, preventing him from drawing too far back when the kiss ends.

I won't survive whatever this turns out to be when he grows tired of me.

"What was that for?" I ask. My eyes stay closed to savor the moment.

He skims his lips across mine again before he answers me. "Can we make a deal?"

I open my eyes and scooch back, but my hand is still splayed against his chest. To push him away or to haul him back? The mention of a deal has my guard up. Any version of Nick is capable of making a deal with consequences I don't see coming.

"A deal?" I tip my head.

He closes the space between us again and plants a gentle kiss on my temple. When he inches away, we're staring into each other's eyes. "We've got twenty-four hours in Vegas before we return to whatever is going on at home. We throw caution to the wind, and we do whatever we want. Live in the moment."

"What exactly does that mean?" Sounds like an ideal way for me to have my heart crushed into a pulp.

"No talk of the past. No worrying about the future. We just exist, with each other."

"If this is your way of telling me," I glance around to make sure other people on the plane aren't paying attention to us, "this trip is an extended one-night-stand that means nothing, message received."

"Being with you is the exact opposite of *nothing*, Jules. I'm insulted you think I'd ever treat you that way." He slouches back in his seat and glowers at me.

Except he already has, in a way, over a kiss. Agreeing with him is madness. "You really think we can treat each other however we want, do whatever we want, and we'll be able to go back to the status quo on Bellerive?"

He stares out the window of the airplane and doesn't say anything for a minute. When he turns back to me, the light in him is gone. "What do you want, Jules?"

The wounded expression in his eyes makes me wish I could get inside his head and figure out what's caused this shift from euphoric to melancholy. Of course I want more of Nick brimming with joy, but I'm worried that on the other side of that lies a deep despair for me. "I don't want either of us to get hurt."

"Hurt is unavoidable." His grin is wry. "So, if that's our mantra—we'll be hurt no matter what—tell me how to make the hurt justified."

The answer to that is painfully obvious. I want Nick all to myself in any way and every way I can for twenty-four hours. I want to soak in his attention for when we go back to Bellerive, and he forgets I exist. That route is foolish, and I'm not normally a fool, but he's a temptation I've been forcing myself to resist and ignore all my life. He's handing himself to me on a platter, and I'm not strong enough to turn the experience down, even if it'll wreck me.

"You and me," I say barely loud enough for him to hear. "Twenty-four hours, no holds barred."

He comes to life again and leans toward me. "No holds barred?"

I purse my lips, but I manage a nod.

"All right, then." He grins and nods toward the bathroom ahead of us. "Mile high club?"

"Nick!" I laugh and shove his chest. "The whole thing starts once we land."

"Ah, I see." He invades my space again and twirls a lock of my hair around his index finger. "Is the airplane neutral, then?"

"Why?" Already I'm wondering if agreeing to this madness was a mistake but seeing him so happy causes an answering rush in me.

"Seal our deal with a kiss?" His forehead touches mine.

Instead of letting him come to me, this time I slide my hands around to the back of his neck, and I kiss him. Long and slow and deep, the kind of kiss that promises less clothes later. If we're throwing caution to the wind, then I'm going to treat Nick as though he's mine, as though no one can ever take him from me, as though it's possible he might love me just as desperately in return.

Carpe Diem.

Seize the day. I intend to seize every hour of the twenty-four I get with him.

NICHOLAS

I can't stop kissing her. Her lips are addictive. After years of denying myself this pleasure, I keep waiting for someone to step in between, tell me this is all an elaborate joke, or wake me from a dream.

She takes every ounce of my affection and then gives it right back in return.

The waitress goes past our poker table, and I grab another rum and coke off her tray. One of the best things about Vegas is the absence of time. When we got off the plane, Jules and I both set alarms on our phones for when we need to grab a taxi to the airport tomorrow.

Jules secured us a suite upstairs in this hotel—The Pearl Hut—the newest and most exclusive on the strip. There's no way I was letting jetlag get the best of us right away. Instead of going to our room, we went straight to the casino since it was midday.

We know our starting time, but otherwise, we've agreed not to check our phones or look at a clock. We're going dark. No one else but us for twenty-four hours.

We're an easy assignment for the four burly security agents who met us outside of customs and baggage claim along with two black SUVs.

I have no plans to go anywhere.

Casino. Hotel room.

Gamble. Live in the moment with Jules. Try not to get busted on social media. A simple plan, but I've had simpler ones topple sideways.

We've already had a few women from my previous trips to Vegas stop by to say hello and run their hands along my body. Normally their presence is welcome, but I'm politely peeling them off and introducing them to Jules. Every single one of them has mentioned the story Robbie wrote, and Julia's cheeks flame with embarrassment. Guess his article got wider circulation than I expected.

Ah well. If the stuffed cat's out of the bag, might as well turn it into a real one.

Hot royal office affair it is. The secretary and the prince.

The near-death experience seems to have turned the tide of Julia's feelings in my favor, but I can't be certain they'll last beyond our no boundaries deal.

Alex isn't here, but he'll be everywhere once we get home, especially if our father is ceding power to him. As soon as my brother enters my thoughts, I shove him out again. He's not here, and I'm not letting him ruin today. Whatever happened between him and Jules was a long time ago. It's a bit easier to let those old memories go when she's beside *me*.

Jules lays down her cards on the table and collects all the chips with a smirk. Her gaze drifts over my shoulder, and her pleased expression falters. Another woman must be zeroing in on me from behind. If we were at war, Jules would be an excellent scout for trouble.

We've got to get out of here, or I'll be in danger of ruining the day before it's even properly started. I stand up and take Julia's hand, dragging her against my side.

"Cash out and head upstairs?" I murmur into her hair.

"Already?" She glances up at me. "This doesn't seem like the famous Nick exploits of previous Vegas trips. I read about those on social media. I should get the full experience."

Is she teasing me or taking a swipe at the poor choices I've made in the past? "Ah," I say, and my lips tip up into an almost smile. "It's still early, Jensen. My best plans usually come after a bottle of tequila."

We cash out and make our way up to our room, but our progress is slow. We drag each other into corners or up against walls, our mouths breaking just long enough to catch our next breath. I have to say having Jules enjoy public make out sessions is a pleasant surprise. She was never one to flaunt her relationships, for which I was grateful. My mental health would have taken even more of a beating over the years if I'd had to watch her maul various other men. Once was enough.

By the time we get to our suite, I'm feeling bad for our bodyguards who've had to put up with our inability to keep our hands to ourselves.

Who am I kidding?

I don't feel bad at all.

Blindly, I wave the keycard over the box beside the door and listen for the unlock. I wrap an arm around Jules and lift her over the threshold of the door. She giggles in my ear, and it's a noise I haven't heard from her in years. Warmth floods my body at how happy she sounds.

She's not the only one.

The door clicks behind us, and I set her feet on the carpeted floor with the two-bedroom suite spread out behind her. Although I'm hoping we don't need two separate bedrooms at any point in the next twenty-four hours, I didn't say a word when Jules booked this.

"What's the plan?" she asks, breathless.

If it was up to me? My plan would involve worshipping her body in as many ways as possible before our phones go off. But she said last night she's not ready for that, and I won't be the guy who turns a *not yet* into a *never*.

"Room service. You hungry?" I kiss her temple and step around her to grab the hotel menu from the desk.

"We haven't eaten since New York. What have they got?" She wraps herself around my arm and peers at the menu beside me.

A comfortable silence settles between us as we read through the choices, but I'm hyperaware of her body pressed to mine. This whole day is turning into a dreamlike experience. I've wanted this—her—for so long. The reality is already better than anything I ever imagined.

When she gazes up at me, I drop a quick kiss on her lips. She rises on her toes, and her hand slides around my neck, drawing me into a deeper kiss. The menu falls to the floor with a thud, and I lift her onto the desk to step between her legs. Food can wait. I'll gladly starve and waste away to nothing if I can feast on her instead.

There's a knock on the door just as her hands slide up underneath my shirt.

"Ignore it," she murmurs against my lips, and then she tilts her head to draw me in deeper.

Sold. Not answering the door.

I tug her forward on the desk and lean into the kiss. There's still a surreal aspect to being with Jules, and I've got a lingering fear mingling with my happiness that I can't seem to quell. She's with me, but there's a ticking clock. One I set, sure. Doesn't change that it's there. There's also the wild card of Alex. Why would he send her that message about the gossip article? She didn't seem bothered about it, but I can't dismiss the exchange between them. Did she respond?

The doorbell to the suite rings, and I groan. "They're not going away."

Jules draws back and kisses my cheek. "I'll wait right here."

I back toward the door, and I don't take my gaze off Jules. She looks thoroughly kissed because of me. I did that.

Given that we're in America, I check the peephole. Even with guards, people keen to sell a story about me and my brothers have done some devious things. Outside is a hotel employee with a bottle, glasses, and a deck of cards.

When I open the door, the employee hands me the bottle of tequila, shot glasses, and cards. "Compliments of Prince Brice of Bellerive. He insisted it be hand-delivered."

I chuckle, turning the bottle of expensive tequila over in my hands. "Of course he did." While I might not be besties with Alex, Brice and I grew closer once Jules and I were no longer attached at the hip. If there's an upside to losing your best friend, it's developing a newfound appreciation for a brother. Only one of them though.

I pass the employee a tip and shut the door, still chuckling to myself.

"Tequila?" Jules takes the bottle from me when I reach the desk. "Who sent this?"

"Brice." I set the glasses beside her hip and take the bottle from her to unscrew the cap. Both shot glasses get filled almost to the brim.

"I haven't been drunk in years." Jules eyes them.

"Why not?" I pass her a shot.

"I sometimes get kinda sad, I guess? I'm not usually a happy drunk." She tips back the glass.

I frown and take my shot. "I don't remember you being like that when we were younger." In fact, she was often the life of the party. Wasn't she?

"If I become too depressing, just put me to bed." She shrugs and holds out her glass for another shot.

I suppress a smile. "I guarantee having me put you to bed would not be depressing."

"Nicholas Edward Summerset." She slaps my chest. "Why does everything have to become a sexual innuendo?"

"Julia Louise Jensen." I put a hand over my heart. "There's nothing sexual about me putting you to bed." I smirk. "Unless you want there to be."

She flushes and takes the card from my hand. "What are the cards for?"

"Probably for High Card. He knows I'm here with you, I'm assuming." I fill our shot glasses again.

"High Card?"

"A game he and I played when we grew bored of the Vegas scene and wanted to hole up in our hotel and get drunk. Whoever draws the high card gets to ask the other person a question. They can either answer or take a shot."

"Honest answers or silly answers?" She draws the cards out of their package.

"Honest. Brice sometimes calls it truth and tequila. That's what makes the game fun. You have to be willing to bare your soul or get drunk enough you bare it anyway."

"Bare my soul?" She quirks an eyebrow. "Wouldn't you rather I bared something else?"

"We can play strip poker if you want." I grin. "I was letting you win downstairs. The pot is more to my liking up here. I'll be happy to have you go all in." I trace the neckline of her shirt with my finger.

She blushes, and I brush my lips across hers. When I try to draw back, she bunches a hand in my T-shirt and keeps me close. "High Card."

"You're taking honesty over getting naked?" I ask. "Suppose either version of naked is fine with me." I grab the bottle of tequila, the two glasses, and her hand. At the couch, I line up the shot glasses on the coffee table, pouring a generous amount in each.

"I can shuffle." She tosses the box aside.

"Do I want to let you shuffle? You still remember how to do all those card tricks from when we were kids?" Voting for honesty and then stacking the deck isn't beneath her.

Her eyes light up and then a hint of a smile tugs at her lips. "I promise not to cheat."

"You realize if you go on any winning streaks, I'll suspect you."

She searches my face for a moment, and then she leans forward and kisses me softly. "If you catch me cheating, you can exact any kind of revenge you want."

"You're dangling a carrot you never intend to give me. *Catch* you cheating? I could never figure out how you did half those card tricks. *Suspect* you're cheating is a fairer deal."

"If you're not quick enough to catch me, you probably shouldn't get any reward." She drops the cards on the coffee table and then straddles me, resting her hands on my sides.

I brush the hair that's tumbled across her cheeks behind her ears and stare into her eyes. "It is wrong that I already feel like I've won?" When we were younger, part of me wondered if it would be weird to be with Jules like this. I got one drunken kiss and then our friendship disintegrated. The fact that we're already this good together is a prize in itself.

"You definitely know how to charm a girl." Her voice is soft, and there's no bite to the words.

Still, the implication I might say these things to any woman who's in my hotel room in Vegas is so far off the mark I don't even know where to start.

She reaches back and grabs the deck off the table and then presents it to me in the palm of her hand. "Draw a card?"

I slide one off the top and look at it. *Ace.* She's screwed. But I can't let my guard down. She might let me win a few before she turns the tide.

"Are you going to show me?" She tries to grab the card.

I chuckle and press it against my chest. "You draw yours and then we turn them at the same time."

She plucks her card off the top and flips it around for me to see. *Five.*

I show her my ace.

"Of course." She rolls her eyes. "You got any more aces shoved up your sleeves?"

"I'm wearing a T-shirt," I say. "But if you'd like to search me, I'll let you."

She walks one of her hands underneath my shirt. "Tempting. Very, very tempting."

"Are you ready for your question?" I ask.

"Technically that's a question. If I answer yes, am I off the hook?"

I lean forward and nip at her earlobe. The cards tumble to the couch, and her hands slide into my hair, her head tipping back to expose her neck. I nibble a line down to her collarbone.

"You need to drink as punishment for being a smartass," I say.

She chuckles but leans back and grabs the shot off the table, flicks it back like it's nothing, and then sets it down. "Why Vegas?"

"I thought it was my question?"

"It's like a proof of life question. Give me an honest answer, and I'll take the game more seriously."

"Far from Bellerive. Far from everything. There's always something to do." Superficial answers. She stares at me, unimpressed. That's not going to satisfy her. "Some of my best memories happened here—mostly with Brice but once with my dad. We were on this diplomatic adventure around the US. I was in college, and he, I don't know, let himself truly be my dad first for one night." I shrug as though that memory isn't sacred.

She gazes into my eyes for a beat and then she traces my hairline, thoughtful. "You pass the test," she whispers before kissing me softly. She scoots forward, closing the space between us so her chest rubs against mine as she deepens the kiss.

When we break apart, she reaches back and grabs us both another drink and then surveys the tangle of cards on the cushion and floor while we take our shots.

I reach around her to refill the glasses.

"High Card seems too messy. Maybe we should go old school?"

"And that would be?" I pass her another shot and take one of my own. If she hasn't drank in a while, this must already be going to her head.

"Truth or Dare."

"Seems like a way to get out of the truth, if you ask me." I tilt my head. "You afraid of the truth, Jules?" My bravado is false because I don't want it either. I never want to hear her tell me she once cared for Alex enough to cast me aside. Not in this lifetime or any other.

Why did I have to think of him right now?

Her cheeks are pink, and she downs her shot before giving me a haughty look. "I'll pick truth. I'm not afraid to tell you anything."

Oh, she's definitely drunk. I grin. "Favorite sexual position."

She peers at me for a beat, and her expression is serious instead of embarrassed. "With you?"

My heart booms in my chest, and my dick stands at attention at the thought of us together. I nod because my throat is drier than a desert in the middle of a drought. *Yeah, tell me that one, Jules.*

"Like this," she says, rocking her hips. "Me on top. Chest to chest. Face to face. As close as I can possibly get to you, so there's no question we're together."

"Jesus Jules." My voice is hoarse, and my heart swells while my dick becomes almost unbearably hard. Those words are better than any wet dream I've ever had. Never in my wildest dreams did I imagine her saying anything close to that to me.

I slide a hand into her hair. My other grips her ass, and then I kiss her. Her shot glass thuds to the floor. She meets my fervor by grinding against me while we tease and taunt each other. We barely come up for air before diving back in.

My breath catches, and I break the kiss to press my forehead to hers. She's gotta be drunk by now. This isn't a green light, and I need to get myself under control. The impulse to rip her clothes off and show us both how good it can be pulses inside me, ready to spring free.

"Truth or dare?" She's breathless.

A distraction. Just what I need. "Truth."

"What's your biggest fear?"

That I'll never get another moment like this again with you. That as soon as we're back on the island, the two of us will drift away from each other. I reach around her and grab the two shot glasses, buying myself some time. When I pass her one, she tips it back with a grimace.

"I'm getting really drunk." She giggles.

"You don't seem too sad to me yet." I take my own shot.

"I'm not too drunk to realize you didn't answer my question."

Then a solution to my fear comes to me, and my tequila brain latches on to it like a life preserver. Nothing ventured, nothing gained. "My biggest fear?"

She nods.

"That my father really will arrange a marriage for me."

"Nick, you know he doesn't mean it." She slaps my chest.

"He doesn't?" I raise my eyebrows. "So why are we on the way home?"

She flushes.

"He promised me he'd only ever use that threat if he meant it." That's true, but the context is warped.

"What's so wrong with marriage?"

"Nothing if it's to someone I want to marry. You once volunteered to fall on that sword, do you remember?" God, I hope she remembers.

"We were sixteen. I mean..." Her voice trails off, and our gazes connect. We stare at each other for a beat.

"Truth or dare?" My heart is in my throat, and no matter what she picks, I've got a question. The next minute could change my life forever.

"Dare," she whispers, and she runs her fingers through my hair.

I kiss her forehead, and then I frame her face to make sure she understands how much I mean what I'm about to say. "Marry me. Tonight."

Nick

Fourteen years ago

I tap my pen against my debate notebook and check the clock above the club supervisor, Ms. Kurusanather, again.

Julia is late—what else is new?

Since the semester started, Ms. Kurusanather has been picking our partners, and today is the first day we can select our own debate teammate. Normally, the rigid control over who we associate with pisses me off, but I've been grateful to avoid Julia. The teacher, like most people at school, assumes we're still best friends. As a result, we haven't been paired together at all.

Ms. Kurusanather crosses her arms at the front while she drones on about today's debate topic. Assisted suicide, which isn't legal in Bellerive. Could she have found a more depressing one? We've already done the death penalty this semester, and it was such a joy to realize all the people who've been put to death around the world who turned out to be innocent later. That's my theory on assisted suicide too—what if a cure for whatever ails a person is just around the corner?

Here's hoping I get the side I want to argue on the coin flip.

Julia texted me earlier about being a team, and I sidestepped the question by changing the subject to something else.

When it comes to Julia, I have to keep my options open.

Although I've tried to put what happened or is *currently* happening between her and Alex behind me, I can't find the ease we once had around each other. We don't fit anymore. The few times I've let circumstances align for us to be alone, our conversations have been stilted. A casual brush of the hand is fraught with tension, at least on my side.

I shouldn't want more with Jules, but I do. Nothing turns off that impulse yet. It's not that I haven't tried. I don't want to feel this way about her.

Vicky and I are still together, and when I'm not absorbed in royal business, I spend a stupid amount of time with guys from the soccer team—or football team—if you're Alex and arguing semantics. He and I have only drifted further apart, but Brice and I have formed a twosome against him. Lose one brother, gain another. Always a bright side, right?

Alex and I don't talk if I can avoid it. I don't want to know anything about what's happening between him and Julia. He knows I know, but neither of us has mentioned that night. When he makes comments about her now, I don't correct him. What can I say? Stay away from her? She made her choice.

The ever-present ache in my chest spreads, crawling underneath my skin like a disease, poisoning everything. The unanswered questions fester inside me.

Are they still a thing? How long have they been together? Are they fucking? Does she *love* him?

The last one is the most improbable. Julia in love with Alex? Come on. No way. But it's also the question that's wedged under my skin, a sliver on the brink of infection.

For the first time in our friendship, those sorts of questions are knives to my own heart. I can't ask them, and I don't want her to realize I saw them because she still hasn't told me.

She doesn't question me about Vicky either. Subjects that were never off-limits are now ones we tiptoe around like landmines. She's slipping through my fingers, and I don't know how we claw our way back to each other.

The worst part is that I'm not even sure I want to.

She didn't tell me.

She still hasn't told me.

Alex.

Of all the people in the world, she went for him. The realization burns through me.

We're drifting away from each other, but she's letting it happen too. The bullshit excuses I come up with not to spend time with her go unchallenged.

The teacher stops talking, and Julia still hasn't appeared. Releasing a sigh of annoyance, I scan the room for the next best person to partner with. If she can't be bothered to turn up on time, I'm not waiting around for her.

Becca is smart, and she's hot.

"Bex," I call to the East Asian girl in the corner with her two friends. They can't form a threesome, anyway, so one of them needs to leave. Or I join them for a foursome. The thought makes me smile. "Partners?"

"Oh," she says and straightens in her chair. "Aren't you partnering with Jules?"

"Julia isn't here." I shrug. "Yes or no?"

"Yes." She scoots back and scoops up her things from her friends.

They all exchange smirks and raised eyebrows as though one debate class is going to lead to something more. I'm still dating Vicky, even if it's more like, I'm still having *sex* with Vicky. Our conversations are superficial, but that's fine with me. My heart's under lock and key.

Bex settles in beside me, and the teacher starts writing names and assigning debate groups on the board just as Julia flies in the door.

She rushes over to me, tucking her long hair behind her ears. "Sorry I'm late."

I lean back in my chair and tap my pen on my notebook. "It's fine. I paired up with Bex."

"With Bex?" Julia rocks back on her heels and confusion mars her features.

"You weren't here." I raise my hand. "Ms. Kurusanather, is there someone who needs a partner? Julia doesn't have one."

She gapes at me, but I'm not changing my plans because she couldn't get here on time. Her last class of the day is literally two doors down. She had to actively dick around to be this late.

"Martin." The teacher gestures to one of my soccer teammates in the corner who is about as bright as a bag of rocks. Great guy to drink with but a terrible debate partner. His parents must have forced him to take this club. Half the time I'm not even sure he knows what's going on. As a general rule, he's stoned after lunch. She'll have to do all the work in that partnership. He's dead weight.

Julia shoots me a dirty look, but she hefts her messenger bag onto her shoulder and trudges over to Martin.

"Did you catch that, Nick?" Bex turns from the front of the room to me.

I've been busy watching Julia get settled with Martin, and I have no idea what Bex wishes I heard.

"Nope," I admit.

"We're against assisted suicide." She opens her laptop and connects to the school Wi-Fi. "We definitely got the harder side of this one."

I check the board and see we've been paired with Julia and Martin on the opposite side. *Awesome.* I rub my head and get down to work. We've got twenty minutes to construct our opening speeches, come up with questions to dismantle the opposition, and decide who's leading between the two of us.

When our time is up, Bex and I move over to the table where Julia and Martin are situated.

Julia gives her opening speech, and I write a flurry of notes to poke holes in her argument. All the groups are presenting at the same time since this is just practice, and the club is really only valuable toward the end of the school year when we travel to America and the UK for competitions. Until then, most of the debates are half-hearted.

When it's my turn to cross-examine her, instead of throwing her a few soft balls, I go after her, systematically dismantling her argument. It's an asshole move, and I can tell from Bex's tense silence and Julia's glare that I might have gone too far.

If she came late and then didn't prepare well enough for her opponents, that's not my fault.

At the end of the club period, Martin declares Bex and me the winners. Even he realizes his partner got crucified, and he wasn't much of an opponent in the first place. Satisfied, I toss everything into my bag and head for the exit without waiting for Julia.

"Nick," she calls from behind me, and her shoes flap against the hallway floor. "Wait up. Geez. Where's the fire?"

"I have practice," I toss over my shoulder.

"Come on. You can talk to me for five minutes. You flayed me in there. What was that about?"

"You weren't prepared. Not my fault." I don't stop walking, and I don't slow down.

She latches on to my arm and digs in her heels, making me slow to a stop.

"I'm going to be late." I don't hide my annoyance.

"So what?" Julia's face is tight with frustration.

"Unlike you, I can't always think of only myself. I understand that other people's time is just as valuable as mine."

"What?" All the color leaves her face.

"You heard me." I shake off her hand and step backward to head toward the exit.

A steel rod goes up her spine, and she stomps after me, keeping pace. "Your arguments were shitty today. If I had a better partner, we'd have won."

"You still wouldn't have been on the right side." I turn to propel the door open with my back so I can see her off. Even when I almost hate her, I can't help myself. "Bellerive will never approve assisted suicide as long as I've got something to say about. Which I will, of course."

"It was a hypothetical argument in a debate co-curricular. None of it means anything. When did you become such an asshole?" Julia practically vibrates with frustration.

"I didn't think you had a problem with assholes." I shrug. Then I'm out the door and headed down the path to the soccer fields.

Within seconds my phone pings in my pocket. I take it out and there's a text from Julia.

I'm sorry. Okay? I won't be late again for debate. Can we just, like, call a truce or whatever? I don't understand what's gotten into you.

I click reply and stare at the message, unsure what to write. A thousand different replies stream through my consciousness.

Truce? We're not fighting. It's fine.

You can't just do whatever you want and expect zero consequences.

You're fucking my brother behind my back, and I'm not sure I'll ever forgive you.

None of them properly convey the sucking wound in my chest. I close my phone and don't respond.

Maybe Julia is happy. Maybe being with Alex makes her happy. She certainly didn't seem *unhappy* pressed up against the wall. I don't want to hear her tell me she's sorry, but she's in love with my brother. I can't even pass that spot anymore without my stomach fluttering with anxiety. Hearing her say the truth out loud will ruin me. At least I can keep myself busy enough that my imagination can't run too wild.

But if she told me, if the words left her lips, I'd never be able to unhear them.

When I get to the locker rooms, I take my phone out of my pocket and stare at her message again. I take a deep breath.

We're cool, Jules. I'm just having a shitty day.

Her response is almost immediate. *I can come by later?*

I'm still staring at her response, part of me longing to say yes, and another part of me desperate to avoid her. How do I fix this? A second text from her rolls in.

I know you said we were going to forget about what happened in the barn, but we haven't been the same since. Maybe we just need to be honest with each other?

My heart pounds, and I can feel my jaw clench with tension. One of the other players comes past and claps me on the back. Honest with each other? That ship has sailed.

"You're gonna be late," he says to me before disappearing into the locker room.

I'm with Vicky. She's my girlfriend. I'm happy. If you've got something to say, go ahead. I'm not stopping you. As far as I'm concerned, we're fine.

I hit send in a rush of frustration and anger. Every word of my text is bullshit, and when I get out of practice to find Julia hasn't responded, I'm not even surprised.

Now we're both liars.

Julia

There's a chorus of bells in my dream. Church bells? No, that's not right. I crack one eye open, and my head pounds. When I try to sit up, the room sways.

"Oh God," I mumble. "I think I'm still drunk. Nick?"

He's on the bed beside me, dressed in the same T-shirt and jeans from yesterday, and he's not even under the covers.

There's a bandage on my finger, but I don't remember hurting myself last night. I stare into the distance. I actually don't remember much at all.

"Nick?" I shake him and try not to move my body. Every jarring action makes me wince.

My head throbs with each beat of my heart, and my mouth is like sandpaper. This isn't just a hangover. This is quite possibly the worst hangover I've ever had in my life. Why would I get *this* drunk?

The bells are still going off.

"Nick, what is that noise?"

"Huh?" He pries open one eye and squints at me. "Phone? Alarm?" He frowns but doesn't move.

"Oh, no." I scramble off the bed, and then I almost puke when the room spins. I clutch the bed and try to stay upright. "We have to get a taxi. We need to get to the airport."

"What time did we go to bed last night?" Nick sits up and rubs his face. "Did we do drugs? Jesus, what did we smoke or snort? I don't remember anything after..." His voice trails off. "That can't be right." He shakes his head and then grimaces. "I had some weird dreams last night. Really vivid though."

"I don't know what we did last night," I cry. Panic is zipping through me. We cannot be late getting back, which means we cannot miss our flight. Nick cannot find out about his father from some tabloid story.

I gather my stuff as quickly as I can without jostling myself too much. It's the hangover dance I haven't done in years. Move quickly while also barely moving.

Every time I turn my head to the side, the pounding intensifies, and I think I'm going to vomit. I'm still fully dressed, so I'm guessing we didn't have sex. Hopefully, I didn't collapse in a puddle of tears or confess my undying love for Nick or my barely repaired broken heart.

I groan. If I was drunk enough, I probably did all those things. Wouldn't be the first time I poured my heart out inappropriately. Thank the lord he also seems to have gotten blackout drunk. What were we thinking?

"You all right?" Nick is moving equally slowly around the room picking up his things. "I smell like a brothel."

"I really hope we didn't go to a brothel."

He chuckles. "The scandal. Can you imagine? If we did, I'm sure we had a fabulous time." His phone is still going off, and he silences it, and then he stares at his hand. "I hurt myself?"

"Me too." I flash my bandage at him.

"Doesn't hurt. I think I might still be drunk."

"What if they don't let us on the plane?" I press the heel of my hand into my forehead. If we didn't do drugs last night, I need them now. The whole twenty-four hours after we left the casino is a blur. How is that possible? I could have slept with Nick, and I would never remember it with this hangover. The thought makes me sad. I might never get to do it again. Why did I get so drunk?

We take turns teetering in and out of the bathroom, neither of us saying much. I down some aspirin I find stashed in the bottom of the toiletries bag, and then I offer some to Nick. He chews the aspirin, and I wince. His ability to do that has always baffled me.

Nick slings his bag over his shoulder and drags our rolling suitcases behind him. I don't have the energy or the balance to protest him taking my things for me.

"I can't remember the last time I felt this rotten," he admits.

"This is why I don't drink." I open the hotel room door.

"I thought you didn't drink because you get depressed?" He looks like he's trying to walk with his eyes barely open. The suitcase wheels rattle behind him. "I don't think I've ever been so grateful for first class. I'm sleeping all the way home."

The guards I hired flank us on the way to the elevator. They aren't the same ones from the casino, but I vaguely remember the agency telling me there'd be a shift change halfway through the night.

I can't even summon the energy to grill the guards on what Nick and I got up to once the alcohol and who knows what else took over.

At the airport, I'll check social media to see how much damage control I need to do. If we got this drunk, we must have done something dumb.

###

At the airport, we make it through security to the VIP lounge where Nick and I try every hangover cure he and the staff can remember. My head is too fuzzy, so I'm not checking my phone. If we did anything publicly stupid last night, I'll face it in a few hours after I've had more sleep. Alex hasn't texted me, and Bellerive is five hours ahead of Vegas. Whatever we got up to can't be that bad. He'd have raised hell if Nick or I embarrassed the country.

In first class, we recline our seats into the flat sleeping position, and just before I drift to sleep, Nick nudges me.

I pop open one eye in response.

"Thanks." His voice is brimming with sincerity.

"For what?" I mumble.

"Coming to Vegas with me. Getting roaring drunk. Probably giving me really great memories that are tucked away somewhere in the recesses of my brain."

"All great memories should be stored somewhere very deep for safekeeping." Unfortunately, the bad ones are often stored there too.

"We should do it again sometime." A hint of a smile plays on his lips.

I stroke his face and draw my thumb over his full lips and down his chin. "I'm never drinking again."

"Night, Jules." He chuckles.

"Night, Nick."

I fall into a deep sleep, the sort where you lose track of the day, time, and place where you're sleeping. My dreams are filled with drunken laughter, a whisp of material brushing my cheeks, and Nick's face alight with happiness. In my subconscious lies a drugged euphoria, and I gladly immerse myself.

Just before I wake up, I have a vivid dream about bees with metal stingers attacking my finger. I bolt upright, wide awake, and then rub my bandage. The dull ache causes me to wince, and I push back the strands of my hair that came free from my ponytail while I slept.

The pilot is announcing our descent into Bellerive. I slept for fourteen hours. *How did I just sleep for fourteen hours?* I don't even know what time we fell into bed last night. Obviously, my body needed the rest.

"Morning sunshine," Nick says from beside me. A frown mars his forehead before he peers out the window.

"Remember anything more?" I maneuver my seat into the upright position.

"Nothing that makes any sense. You?"

"Super weird dreams. I just dreamt a swarm of bees was attacking my finger." I flash my hand at him and give him a wry smile. "With a metal stinger. Guess I should make sure my tetanus shot is up to date."

"The last time I had that dream was when I got a..." His frown deepens, and he stares at his hand. "Jules have you looked under the bandage?"

"God no. I was too hungover when we woke up. I'm only starting to feel human now. I'm guessing we cut ourselves on something? Hopefully, the cut isn't deep, or we didn't make some sort of blood oath." I laugh, but I'm suddenly a bit uneasy. At least my headache is gone. Though I still feel like I ate cotton for dinner.

Gingerly, Nick peels the covering off his finger. "Yeah, you're gonna want to take that bandage off."

I try to peer at his hand, but he shields it.

"Do we need to go to the hospital when we get off the plane?" Were we so drunk we didn't realize we needed stitches?

I unwrap my finger and gasp. "Nick," I breathe.

That's his name, but it's also what's tattooed on my ring finger. Around the letters is an intricate pattern in the formation of an actual ring.

I have his name tattooed on my body.

In the place where a wedding ring would sit.

He flashes his hand at me. "Jules." His lips quirk up into an almost smile. "How cute."

His lines are thick and straightforward, but the design is definitely a wedding ring. I can't tear my focus from his finger. Is he freaking out like I am? I glance at him, but I can't read his expression. Why do I feel like I'm the only one freaking the fuck out?

My heart races, and I dig out my phone. There are unread notifications from when I switched my phone to airplane mode. I ignore them, and I keep airplane mode on while I click on my photos.

The gasp that escapes me comes from my toes. Oh, my word. We took so many photos last night. Why did we take so many pictures of our insanity?

"Check your camera roll," I whisper.

He digs his phone out of his pocket, and in silence, we scroll through our camera feeds. I can't speak until I've scrolled through the photos from the last twenty-four hours twice. Why didn't I think to check for evidence earlier?

We had a hell of a time.

There are a few snaps from earlier in the night when we were still in our hotel room that would make an excellent screensaver if Nick and I were really together. The later shots, though... glassy eyes, bright smiles, an ease between us we'd never be able to fake. They're exactly the sort of photos I could have taken with any of my boyfriends when we were on a night out togeth-er. Drunk and joyful. Happiness oozes out of us.

I wish I could remember.

He looks like my boyfriend.

If only we stopped there.

I close my eyes and take a deep breath.

I can't ignore the evidence on my phone, the tattoo on my finger. It appears we're also...

My mind stutters on the truth. I glance at Nick, but he's still thumbing through his phone with a crevice between his brows.

How did this happen? What must he be thinking? How did we get here?

I stare at his name scrawled across my finger. It resembles his handwriting, as though he autographed me. Why would I agree to have him *brand* me?

Maybe I've played a drunken prank on myself? Drunk me always thinks she's so funny when she's not bawling her eyes out.

I lick my finger and rub at the ink, but it doesn't come off.

When I glance at Nick again, he meets my gaze. I can't deci-pher his expression, and we just stare at each other for a beat. I search for some indication of exactly how upset I should be. How upset is he? I can't read him, and I can't get a handle on my warring emotions.

I think we're... I'm pretty sure we're...

"So, wife," Nick says. "I guess we showed my father. No arranged marriage for me."

All the blood drains from my face, and my stomach rolls. I fumble for the airsickness bag in the front pocket of the seat. I latch on to it and barely get it open before the contents of my stomach riot.

Nick and I are married.

Nick is my husband.

NICHOLAS

J ules is my *wife*. The thought plays on repeat through
my stunned brain while we collect our baggage, meet our
ground security, and climb into the backseat of the black Rolls
Royce.

Even flipping through the photos on the plane didn't bring
the night back in *enough* detail to make what's happened real.
We got matching *tattoos*.

If that doesn't spell commitment, I don't know what does.

And yet...

The last thing I remember is asking her to marry me. My
clearest memory is staring into those blue-gray eyes and hoping
she'd understand how serious I was.

What I can't remember is whether I had to convince her, or
she said yes willingly. My level of drunkenness suggests one of
two things.

The first could be that we were so happy and so in tune with our decision that I didn't need to worry about my alcohol consumption. Everything was great—who cared how much I drank?

The other option is that I drank to forget how hard I had to talk her into it, how reluctant she was to marry me, how I might have even resorted to a former-best-friend guilt trip.

Not one of those is beneath drunk me.

Drunk me is a classically bad decision maker. Epically poor.

Her reaction to discovering we got married last night is not easing my anxiety over which of those two scenarios is most likely. God knows I would have done *anything* to get her to say yes.

On top of that, I'm fairly confident we didn't consummate our marriage, which also makes me doubtful she was fully on board. Who gets married and doesn't have sex to seal the deal? She'll marry me, but she won't sleep with me? Makes zero sense.

Maybe I stopped things if she was too drunk, especially if I was that drunk too? I've wanted her for so long, I can't imagine the brakes were mine. But I would never want her to regret being with me. I'd want her to remember, and I would definitely want my memory clear or clearer too.

Memory loss sucks.

"I feel like we've slipped into an alternate dimension," Jules says without looking at me. She fishes her phone out of her purse.

Out of the corner of my eye, I watch her tense as she slides her phone from airport mode into eating up data. Immediately, her phone pings with a flood of notifications.

"Oh, no," she mutters.

"You should really turn off those push notifications." I gaze out the window and don't touch my phone. "Bad for your mental health to be connected so much."

"Oh," Jules says, her voice tight. "It's not the social media notifications that are the problem. Although someone leaked photos of us getting married. What happens in Vegas did not, in fact, stay in Vegas. So I guess we don't need to break that news to anyone." Her fingers fly across her keyboard in response to something or someone. "My 'oh, no' was related to your brother's ranting text messages."

My heart kicks. That gets my attention. I'm fine with the whole world knowing Jules and I got married in Vegas in some quickie ceremony that probably cost a couple hundred bucks. Robbie made sure anyone who cares about this sort of gossip already believed we were having an affair in Tanzania. An elopement is frugal. Responsible, even. Who needs all the pomp and circumstance when it's the right person?

Alex giving her a hard time is a whole other level of piss-me-off.

"Alex?" I hold out my hand. "Show me."

She passes me her phone and then stares out the window while I scroll through his irate messages, all about how she's let people down with such a massive breach of royal protocol, how irresponsible we've been, how we've derailed the coronation ride with a cheap Vegas wedding.

My blood boils, and I take out my own phone to see whether he's dared to send me the same messages.

Nothing.

Brice sent me an 'atta boy' complete with a gif from *Wedding Crashers* suggesting I 'lock it up' which would have made me laugh under different circumstances. His bottle of tequila and deck of cards is partially responsible for this mess.

Except, I don't regret what's happened, exactly. I just wish I remembered. It's hard to justify something you don't recall doing.

"I'll talk to him," I say through gritted teeth. He sure as shit won't be sending any more messages like this to my wife. Not a fucking chance.

Jules sighs. "You don't have to. He's right, isn't he? What were we thinking?"

Just wearing my heart on my sleeve again to have you shred it.

"Does he have any reason other than royal protocol to be *this* mad at you, Julia?" Asking her the question causes a piece of my heart to break and hover, ready to drift away or reattach.

"What?" The color drains from Julia's face. "No." She shakes her head, and when I cock mine in response, she doubles down. "No."

"Then he doesn't get to send messages like that to you. If you want to handle it, fine. But if not, I've got no problem defending you. We might not remember what happened, but we're adults.

You're my wife." I flash my tattoo of *Jules* in a swirling cursive at her. "Might as well be written in blood. He owes you more respect than those texts suggest."

We stare at each other, and I can't read her expression. Her phone vibrates in my hand, and I glance down to see a message from her mother.

"The former Secretary Jensen is on the rampage too," I mutter and pass Julia's phone back to her. That one I will not offer to handle. While the former Secretary Jensen doesn't intimidate me like she once did, I'm not keen to explain how I lured her daughter into yet another questionable decision after all these years.

The vehicle cruises through the massive palace gates, and soon we'll be at the main entrance.

"This will be a fun conversation given that I can't remember anything. Being drunk was never a good enough excuse for anything else. Tattoos and marriage aren't likely to go down well either."

"At least you waited until you were thirty to do both." I can't help a partial smile. "I mean, that's gotta count for something."

"With her?" Julia matches my half-smile. "Probably just that I *definitely* should have known better."

"We all make mistakes," I say in a glib tone, but swallowing what we've done as though it's a minor mistake tastes bitter.

She searches my face, a pinched expression on hers. "We should talk later, Nick. I just—I don't know what to make of this. Do you?"

I've got no regrets, but I'm not sure it's wise to say that when she seems so unsure. "Still processing." That's neutral, right?

The vehicle comes to a stop outside the main doors, and Julia's mother is the one to open the back door. She peers in at the two of us and makes a tsking noise.

"Julia," she barks. "With me. Prince Nicholas, your father would like a word."

I barely suppress my eye roll. Seriously, this is bullshit. We're not sixteen anymore. If we want to have a drunken wedding in Vegas that neither of us can remember, that should be no one's business but ours.

I grit my teeth. That's never been my life. I understood the risks last night as my heart pounded, waiting for her answer. Today in the harsh, hungover light of day, I realize this marriage is a massive fuck up for royal appearances, if nothing else. The wedding isn't a cost savings. We've denied the people of Bellerive the pomp and circumstance they feel entitled to since their taxes have historically paid for our lavish lifestyle. Royal weddings are an island-wide celebration, one that hasn't occurred in over thirty years.

As the second in line, chained to the royal title, I should have thought of all this.

Last night I didn't care.

I'm not sure I care this afternoon either.

Jules is *my wife*.

But if she wants out of this marriage, the marriage isn't just a *whoops*—we become a scandal.

Julia scoots out of the car, and she glances back at me. "Good luck."

I rub my face before following her out. By the time I get into the palace, Julia and her mother have disappeared somewhere. Their office, likely.

When I round the corner to my father's study, I almost run right into Alex who seems to be pacing the hallway.

"Ah, the man of the hour." Alex thrusts his hands into the pockets of his suit and shakes his head. "You know Dad's stepping down, right? Julia tell you? She never could keep a secret."

That's a lie, and we both know it. She kept the secret about the two of them far too well. Tension vibrates across my jaw, and I clench my fist. I haven't hit Alex since we were kids, and we had a nanny who couldn't keep us in line. There's a good chance I'm going to give him what he deserves today.

"You couldn't stand not having the focus on you and your ridiculous escapades? Had to suck up all the attention once again?" Alex accuses.

"Marrying Jules is hardly the scandal you're making it out to be. She's from Bellerive. She's the same age as me, and she's a long-time family friend."

"How'd you talk her into it? She's never wanted this life, the limelight and scrutiny we face." Alex stares at me for a beat. "How *drunk* did you have to get her, brother?"

His comment is a direct hit. I step up to him so we're practically chest-to-chest, but I've got the height advantage. "You want to be very careful about what you're suggesting here, *brother*."

"There may not be any divorce for the royal family," Alex spits out, "but once I'm king, I'll grant Jules an annulment if she wants it."

"You haven't even spoken to my wife," I growl. "How would you know what she wants or doesn't want?"

Alex flashes the home screen of his phone at me. There in bold is the unopened message from Jules, the one she must have written as she walked with her mother.

Drunken mistake. I'll fix this. Leave it with me.

All my confidence leaves me in a rush, and I step back from Alex. "Dying to play the night in shining armor, huh? Ride to her rescue from your wicked little brother?"

"She put what she wanted on the backburner for you for years."

"Bullshit," I scoff. "She's had fourteen years to put herself first. She's *still* not doing it. It's got nothing to do with me. That's just who Jules is, and the fact you don't know that isn't exactly shocking. You've got the emotional intelligence of a rock."

"So, she didn't put you first last night? You didn't talk her into marrying you?" He gives me an assessing look. "You didn't lead her to believe Father was going to rope you into an arranged marriage?" He cocks his head, and a smirk surfaces, probably at the surprise I forget to hide. "That's right—Father told me about your code. Who do you think delivered the message to

Jules the other day in Tanzania? Didn't realize you'd cart her off to Vegas for a quickie wedding, or I would have filled her in on the significance of the threat."

A flush rises to my cheeks. He might have the emotional intelligence of a rock, but he's not dumb. I didn't take her to Vegas to marry her, though I'm still not sorry about it. We went because so many of my best memories are tied to that city, and I wanted to tie a few more, with her, there.

The door to my father's office opens down the hall. "Nicholas?" he calls out into the hallway.

"Coming," I say, stepping around Alex. We both know I haven't explained or justified the wedding in any acceptable way. Did I trick Jules? Lie to her? I might have.

When I step into my father's office, I brace myself for another slew of questions I can't answer with any certainty.

JULES

Fourteen years ago

Alex is back from England for the weekend. How do I know? He's sent me approximately five hundred text messages. I think I've responded to three. It's a level of clingy and desperate I would never have suspected from someone like him.

If Nick and I were still attached at the hip, having my phone buzz every five minutes would have been hard to hide. Given that Nick has decided to suction cup himself to Vicky's vagina, I've got lots of time to ignore Alex. At school, I've even managed to make a few new friends on the swim team. Other girls aren't nearly as catty or crazy as Nick's friends led me to believe.

None of that changes the truth that runs under my life like water.

I miss Nick.

We see each other in debate club, around school, even sit near each other in one class. On the surface, we probably seem like good friends, but underneath us, the foundation has shifted. We can't seem to figure out how to wiggle ourselves back into alignment.

Truthfully, I hardly recognize him anymore. Between Vicky, the guys from the soccer team, and his royal duties, I'm lucky if I can grab lunch with him once a week. Even then, we're in a big group. Always surrounded by people, everywhere.

The gap between us is widening, and he's got no interest in closing it. The few times I've swallowed my pride and tried to talk to him about the kiss, he's brushed me off or been down-right rude.

The kiss has to be the issue. If I didn't know better, I'd think he was punishing me for something. For kissing him back? For rushing off? For not buying into his renewed interest in Vicky?

I've seen his face when she talks. She could be speaking Dutch backward for all he cares.

Tires crunch down the driveway, and I peer out my window. Although it never happens anymore, hasn't happened in months, whenever it's late at night, I still expect Nick to be the one sneaking onto the property.

When I realize it's a motorcycle, my heart kicks. Before I hustle down the back staircase to the side entrance, I double-check that everyone else's bedroom light is out. If he braved coming to see me so late, it must be important.

Nick.

I throw open the side door, my heart in my throat.

But it's not Nick sitting on the bike with a helmet in his hands. It's Alex.

My heart sinks, and I'm sure my expression gives away the sadness that settles over me.

"You're not happy to see me?" Alex's tone is teasing, but his eyes are watchful in the glare of my house's security lights.

"No, I—" But I can't finish my thought because I have no idea what to say. He's not the last person I want to see, but he certainly isn't the first. Annoyance zips through me. Didn't he understand my non-response to his repeated texts was a response in itself? Whatever happened between us this summer was a mistake.

"You were expecting Nick? He took off with Vicky to the barn right after dinner. I think they stole a bottle of wine from the cellar. You know how it is." He waggles his eyebrows suggestively.

Another knife to my heart.

"Right. Yeah. Of course. Yeah." I cross my arms over my chest and lean against the door jam. There's a crushing pressure over my heart. To think I once felt sorry for Vicky for coming second. My current misery should make me even more sympathetic to how she must have felt once, but the realization makes me angry. Dipping his dick has turned out to be far more important than our friendship.

All the times he told me nothing or no one would ever come between us and look at us now.

From his perspective, our kiss must have been pretty awful. I must be a bad kisser. Maybe the problem with kissing Alex was mine all along. *I'm* the shitty kisser.

I close my eyes and suck in a deep breath. There's a reason I've overscheduled myself this year. I blame Nick for the distance between us, but I've joined every available club, co-curricular, charity event, and community engagement initiative our elite private boarding school offers. Anything, *anything* to stop myself from thinking about Nick and Vicky fucking all over Bellerive.

"We have a diplomat dinner tomorrow night. Nick's bringing Vicky. Fancy being my date?" His tone is light, but the question weighs heavy in the air. He's on his bike, gauging my reaction.

He's taking Vicky? At one time, a plus-one at any event was always me.

I can't pretend I'm not tempted to accept Alex's offer. The last few months have been so lonely. Half the time when I text Nick it takes him days to get back to me rather than seconds, and his responses aren't sincere or clever anymore. They're riddled with blandness, as though he's responding out of obligation rather than friendship. It's easier not to text him than to experience the burning ache when he takes too long to respond or blows me off.

Showing up at the diplomat dinner with Alex would drive a stake between us, shattering any semblance of friendship. Nick's face would be a picture, that's for sure. Not a good one. I'm angry and frustrated and confused, but I can't do that to him. If he even suspected what went on between me and Alex this summer, he'd likely never speak to me again. The thought causes my temples to throb with the beginnings of a headache. We'd fight for sure if he ever found out I was with his brother. How do I even justify what went on between us? Stupidity? What was I thinking?

I wasn't. The aura of Alex put me in a fog. Everyone at school would have died of envy. What girl would say no to the first in line to the throne? At the time, I couldn't fathom saying no.

What girl would risk her most trusted friendship for a few mediocre make-out sessions?

Thank god Nick will never find out.

I'm clear-headed now.

Once he's done with Vicky, and we've had some time to put the barn incident behind us, maybe we can get back on even footing. I just have to hold on long enough to get there.

"I can't go with you, Alex. I'm sorry."

"Because of Nick? You realize he has a girlfriend?" His tone is biting.

"It's not—" I sigh. It's Nick, but it's not about my conflicted feelings for him. I've managed to bury those way down under my anger over our disintegrating friendship.

How do I tell Alex that Nick dislikes him so intensely that any association with him would detonate our friendship? Alex probably wouldn't believe me anyway given how I carried on with him. Back then I thought my friendship with Nick was strong enough to withstand anything. We were indestructible. I'm not so naïve anymore.

"I don't want you to get the wrong idea," I say.

"Consider me warned. Come with me."

I shake my head. "I've got a lot of homework. I volunteer at the homeless shelter tomorrow night serving dinner." Just what every sixteen-year-old longs to do. When my supervisor asked for volunteers, I didn't hesitate. *Operation Keep Jules Distracted*.

"I could join you. It'll be good publicity. We can go to the dinner late."

He's not going to give up, and a few months ago, I might have given in, taken a chance. But my friendship with Nick is so fragile now. Any outward show of support for his older brother will set fire to the remnants of our friendship. Of that, I'm sure.

"You're not going to win me over, Alex." I purse my lips.

"Doesn't feel like you've even given me a proper chance." He stares at his helmet and then glances at me.

Had I? Not really. From that first kiss, my heart and my head kept trying to tell me we weren't right for each other. But I bottled my uncertainty, smoothed over it in a haze of make-out sessions. I never let him have any of the parts of me Nick already unknowingly possessed. At the time, I couldn't have told Alex what was holding me back, and now that I can, telling him seems cruel and pointless. Nick and I will never be a thing. Pouring out my heart to Alex is yet another betrayal.

"Nick's a bloody fool to choose Vicky over you." Alex climbs off his bike and ventures closer.

"It's not like that between me and Nick. There was no choice to be made."

"No?" Alex searches my face in the light from the overhead lamp. "Not even the night you broke up with me?"

Heat creeps up my neck. I will take that kiss to my grave. "Not even then."

"Liar." A hint of a smile tinges the edges of Alex's lips.

"If Nick is happy, I'm happy for him. That's what friends do." I raise my chin. A true statement, but not in this case. Every time I see Nick, neither of us seems very happy anymore. Once he and Vicky break up, things will return to normal.

"If you ever need a Nick replacement—friend or otherwise—you've got my number." He scans my face for one more beat before tugging on his helmet and walking to his motorcycle.

The sound of his bike roaring out of our gates echoes in the still night.

A Nick replacement? Clearly, Alex doesn't understand how these things work.

No one will ever replace Nick.

Of all the realizations I've had the last few months, that truth is quite possibly the most heartbreaking. There'll never be another Nick, and I'm not sure I'll ever get *my* Nick back.

JULIA

My mother beat me into the office, and she's snagged my seat behind a desk that was hers for roughly thirty years. It's mine now, but you wouldn't know it from how comfortable she looks in my chair. I didn't redecorate when I took over her job, so she probably feels right at home.

Being the king's secretary was always supposed to be temporary. Doesn't feel so temporary anymore.

We're in a stare off, and for the first time since my glasses went unaccounted for, I miss them. They've become part of my armor, and my contacts don't give me the same sense of wisdom and protection.

My mother hasn't mentioned the wedding, our drunken photos, or the rather extensive gossip article Robbie from Tanzania published and posted. Instead, she kindly printed it out for me to read, and the pages are neatly laid out on the edge of the desk.

The old grandfather clock to the right of us ticks a steady beat.

Stubbornly, I haven't touched a single page or read anything other than the glaring and large headline: *Angling for a Promotion? King's secretary and Prince Nicholas in hot Tanzanian affair.* Whatever is in the article is a bunch of lies, and I'm not making excuses for someone's imagination. Though it turns out Robbie must be psychic because I have, somehow, been promoted to *wife*.

My hands are folded in my lap, carefully concealing the bold tattoo with Nick's name. Should I have put the bandage back on it? The skin is so red, and I know nothing about tattoos. If I need to have the intricate design removed, it's going to hurt.

"You've got nothing to say for yourself?" My mother finally cracks, easing her ramrod spine into the back of my chair.

I wish I pushed her out of the way at the entry to the office. At thirty, I'd rather not be getting a lecture from my mother about my behavior. I didn't even know this sort of conversation was still a possibility. Naïve, really. With my mother, it's always possible.

"I believe, actually, that I might outrank you now. So, I'm not sure I technically *have* to explain myself," I say.

Her eyebrows get lost in the sweep of her fringe. There are streaks of silver lacing her chestnut hair, but she's never bothered to hide them. Vanity does not live in my mother. "Outrank me?"

There's disbelief in her tone, and I wonder if my stubbornness is going to make this conversation worse than it needs to be. "That's correct," I say. In for a penny, in for a pound.

She splays her hands on the massive desk and takes a deep breath. "I was hoping we could have this conversation as mother and daughter. But if you want me to play the king's secretary to your nonsense, I can do that as well." She eyes my folded hands.

She was never going to let me have an even playing field. But drawing the mother card this early is surprising. "What do you want me to say?"

"I'd like to know how you went to Tanzania with the objective of keeping Nicholas out of trouble, and he's landed in elephant dung up to his neck instead."

"Marrying me is elephant dung? Such flattery."

"Don't pretend you don't understand. I find it hard to believe you woke up this morning and thought: *My decision-making skills are top-notch. Well done to me.* You've been exemplary as my replacement the last three years. Whether or not you want to, you understand what a bloody PR nightmare this elopement is. The fact that the two of you look incredibly drunk in the photos is a problem on top of a problem." She makes a heaping motion with her hand.

I rub my face and breathe out a sigh.

My mother gasps.

I freeze and close my eyes. The tattoo. *Whoops. Man, I suck at secrets.*

"You got a tattoo!" The pitch of her voice hits my ears, and I wince.

I draw my hands down and give her a sheepish look. "At least they can remove those, right?"

"You don't *want* to be married to him?" Now it's her turn to bury her face in her hands. "Oh, Julia. What were you thinking?"

"I didn't say that!"

She glances up. "Then what's with the talk of having the tattoo removed? The biggest crisis here is that I have to arrange a proper royal wedding on top of a coronation. If you and Nicholas don't intend to stay married, that's—that's—" She shakes her head.

I swallow. I guess this is the moment where I come clean. "So." I take a deep breath and twirl a strand of my hair around my index finger. "Neither Nick or I technically *remember* getting married."

"Oh, God. Oh, Lord. Julia Louise Jensen, you have got to be kidding me." She stands up and starts pacing behind my desk.

In the car, I realized this situation was bad, but sitting in her office now, I'm starting to see how much worse it could be. Funny, Nick's usually great with worst-case scenarios, and he didn't lay any of them out in the car on the way here. Or perhaps not funny. I could really use someone to help me sort out the mess we made last night.

"Nicholas wants to end the marriage as well?"

I twist my mouth, really wishing I could somehow avoid this conversation. Yes, she's giving me a hard time, and although I'd never say it out loud, her frustration is justified. "So." I take a deep breath. "We haven't actually discussed that yet."

"What? You had fourteen hours on the plane. *Fourteen hours*. That's a lifetime in a situation like this. More than enough time for the two of you to have a plan."

"We were hungover. Neither of us was even awake." I toss up my hands. She can't expect me to magically solve a problem I didn't know existed. "Also, we didn't discover we were married until the plane was descending to Bellerive."

"This is unbelievable, you understand this, right? I feel like I'm trapped in one of your ridiculous stories from when you were sixteen. You and Nicholas used to get into all sorts of sticky situations."

"Trivial rebellion. Not one of those led to a scandal."

"Until now."

"Maybe we can..." My brain is working overtime now. "Maybe we can stay married for a bit and then quietly get divorced?"

"Divorced?" She scoffs. "Have you forgotten who Prince Nicholas is? Bellerive Royals can't get divorced. Your only option would be for the king, either George or Alexander, to annul the marriage."

The clock ticks, and I sit in the armchair, anxiety and helplessness warring in me. Why did I agree to marry Nick in Vegas? We hardly know each other anymore.

My mother comes around the desk and perches in the chair across from me. She takes my hands in hers and stares at me until I return her look.

"When you were sixteen, you and Nicholas were closer than I've ever seen two teenagers who weren't dating. I've never asked what happened, but something must have. Perhaps I should have asked. His bike accident was proof enough that something was seriously wrong." She scans my face and releases a deep sigh. "Leaving Prince Nicholas's opinion out of this, what do you want? Would you want to be married to him?"

A chill of indecision snakes down my spine. Both resolutions are so complicated. At my core, I don't think there's any way, drunk or not, I would have married Nick without good reason. I definitely wouldn't have agreed to this ridiculous tattoo idea—most likely Nick's terrible influence—if I didn't believe in what we were doing. Last night, I'm sure I *wanted* this marriage. I just don't understand *why*.

The last thing I recall is playing a silly card game with Nick in the hotel room. I don't even remember who asked who to get married.

"That's a really complicated question," I admit. "We've drifted so far apart, and while we obviously became closer in Tanzania..." I toy with the knuckle of my tattooed finger. "I'm just not sure." My voice catches, and I try to force the burning in my throat to go away. "I don't know what I would do when he grew tired of me again? If our marriage became an arrangement and not real." Goosebumps rise across my arms. "I doubt I would handle it well."

My mother's whole body softens. "Oh, sweetheart," she murmurs. "Whatever happened between you and Nicholas back then, it had nothing to do with him growing *tired* of you. That poor boy was miserable for months." She seems to think about it for a minute. "Years."

"Not over me," I say with a small shake of my head. Back then, I was the one crushed by his behavior, by the way he discarded me and our friendship. "You're *my* mother. What about *my* misery?" I cry.

She squeezes my hand. "I asked you what was going on between you two. You never wanted to talk about it. You kept saying Nicholas was preoccupied with his girlfriend, and once they broke up everything would go back to normal. But the two of you never did."

We definitely did not. In fact, when Vicky was no longer in the picture, Nick went from gluing himself to one vagina to sampling as many as he could, including my freshman roommate. Thoroughly disgusting. The memory makes my stomach dip.

When he came out of my dorm room and said what he said, the last shred of our friendship vanished. Distanced politeness ensued on both our parts. For the longest time after that, whenever we were in the same room, I couldn't even look at him.

I was in love with someone who didn't exist.

I suppose in some ways believing that made it so much easier to let him go. I'd been clinging so hard, hoping so much, and then all of that just... evaporated. But the pain lingered, for years.

"We're not sixteen anymore, and there's so much muddy water between us. I just... but I wouldn't have done this," I say and flash my ring finger, "if at least part of me wasn't completely sure. Even drunk me has a modicum of common sense."

My mother's lips twitch, but she doesn't correct me. She holds my face between her palms and maintains eye contact. "You and Nicholas need to speak honestly to each other and be realistic about this marriage. Do you want it? Can you make it work? There is no divorce, and an annulment will only make sense for so long. Do you understand what I am telling you?"

"I'm not still drunk, Mom. Also, I would normally be the one giving this speech." I sigh and draw back from her embrace.

"You also need to get that tattoo properly tended to. Isn't it supposed to have a bandage on it? I'll call Dr. Bennett, the royal's doctor."

"Seems like overkill," I mutter as I rise to my feet. While my mother is right that Nick and I need to have an honest conversation about the choices we've made so far, I'm not looking forward to it. There's no way to have that discussion without revealing all the various ways he's hurt me over the years as well as the fears I have about remaining married to him now.

"Is Nicholas also branded?" she asks, peering at me over the desk where she's dialed the doctor's direct line.

My lips quirk up in a partial smile. "My name—right there," I admit.

"As I would expect. Only Alex would get his own name tattooed there instead." She winks at me.

Relief surges through me, and I even manage a brief laugh. She might not agree with the storm we've unleashed, but at least she's not still angry.

She arranges for the doctor to meet Nick and me in his wing of the palace within the hour. I gather my purse from the floor, and I head for the door. Then I remember I should be taking back my role as secretary.

"Are you going to catch me up on what I've missed?" I ask.

There's the slightest stiffening of my mother's shoulders before she meets my gaze. "King George and I have decided to divide your duties until we're certain you'll be continuing in your role."

"Oh," I say. Is it disappointment or relief I'm feeling? "So which half do I have?"

"I'm taking all the political commitments. You can manage his coronation calendar."

That's not a fair division. She'll end up with far more work than me, at least right now. "Are you sure?"

"Alex knows about the coronation, and Brice was told this morning before you arrived. You told Nick in Tanzania, but the king was speaking to him as soon as you arrived. So, you can start with organizing coronation details, and I'll keep everything else chugging along."

I stare at her for an extra beat because there's something niggling at the back of my brain, and I can't pinpoint what's bothering me. "Are you sure? You've managed a coronation before. It might be easier for you to take point there."

"No, no." She waves me off. "I'll be here to support you, but otherwise, you might as well learn on the job."

"Is there something you're not telling me? I'm getting a weird vibe."

"Something I'm not telling you? You mean like running off to Vegas to get married, complete with matching tattoos? Nothing like that happening on my end." She's teasing, but there's still an underlying bite to it. As long as she's occupying my desk, she'll be straddling her duty to The Crown with being my mother.

A rock and a hard place I'm also wedged into now that I'm Nick's wife and keeping the king's health a secret.

"I'll come see you tomorrow to figure out first steps," I say.

"Excellent." Her smile is genuine. "I look forward to putting you to work."

"Don't get too comfortable." I open my office door. "It's still my name on the door." I slide my finger underneath the Julia Jensen nameplate.

"I'm just here to ensure a smooth transition, for old time's sake." Her smile falls a little. "A personal favor to the king."

"He's lucky to have you." My mom and King George work together like a well-oiled machine, and I'm sure with his illness he'll be grateful for someone who understands his role and responsibilities sometimes even better than he does.

"If you love Nicholas or if you think you *could* love him, you need to tell him. Life's too short not to risk a little heartache."

I give her a sad smile. "It's the heart*break* I'm worried about."

"We're mortal," she says. "At some point, we all break. Embrace the joy, Julia. Embrace it with all you've got." Her voice is full of emotion, and she plucks a tissue from the box on her desk. "Now get out of here and work out some path forward with your husband."

I'm tempted to hug her and give her a chance to let down her tough façade. No doubt hearing the king's diagnosis rattled her, even if she might have suspected it earlier.

When she waves me off again, I tug the door shut behind me, and I wonder when marital labels get less weird.

Nick is my husband.

Nicholas

Being in my father's office inspires a strange mix of trepidation and awe. The room is brimming with the history of all the men and women who've come before us. It's the most impressive room in the palace. In every corner lies a story, an artifact, a piece of our family history, which is, in fact, the history of the island itself. The full weight of the monarchy sits on my shoulders whenever I enter.

Rarely have I been called in here for anything routine. Instead, I've been scolded, told to step up, or commanded to take on a role I wasn't sure I wanted. Which of those will it be today?

On his desk is the front page of the Bellerive National. I'd make a joke about anyone still buying physical papers, but we're royals, the last bastions of the status quo and tradition. It would be weird if we didn't buy papers, wouldn't it?

"I see you've caught a glimpse of the happy news," I say, tapping a finger on the photo of Jules and me on the front page. Not sure he'll be delighted to hear I'm the one who leaked this particular story. I recognize the photo from my camera roll, and the guy who wrote it is an old friend from high school. Since none of that will weigh in my favor, and I can't remember why I would have thought a social media onslaught was the best way to announce our startling decision, I'm going to keep quiet.

"Ah, yes. The happy news. Shame I didn't hear about it from my son or my secretary." He eyes me across the desk, and the older I get the more I see myself in him. He's giving me his best unimpressed look.

"Sometimes you just can't keep a good story down. You know how it is." I shrug. Inside anxiety swirls. This conversation could go so many ways, I've lost count of them all. Will he insist on an annulment? A statement about how Jules and I made a foolish mistake? *We* haven't even talked about whether we made a foolish mistake.

My father huffs in exasperation. "You can always keep a good story down. I've done it several times." He pauses for maximum weight, and our gazes lock. "For you."

I swallow. There are few things I dislike more than disappointing my father. For a while, I didn't care who I let down, but I got over myself around the time I exited college. Me with wild American girls was the lead on the gossip sites every year of my degree in international politics. On top of the college girls, a few equally famous actresses and models were thrown in for good measure. Variety and poor decisions were the spices of my life. I'm surprised Bellerive didn't disown me.

As Robbie so kindly pointed out in Tanzania, I put food on writers' tables. Would my father be proud to know I've done it again? Supporting the local economy. I'll count it as a win—silently.

"Didn't you go to high school with this boy?" He points to the byline.

Busted.

"Take any photos of your shotgun wedding?" He tips his head at my phone.

Fuck.

Well, he's nailed me to the wall, hasn't he?

Whether or not Jules wanted to marry me, I've got no regrets. Doesn't change the truth of our marriage, though, and I squirm in discomfort. This may not go well. "I'd really like to say I can explain this, but I actually can't remember any of it."

We stare at each other in silence.

"None of it?"

"The last thing I remember is asking Jules to marry me. Why we got married, who paid for it, who attended, what we did either before or after?" I wave a hand around the top of my head. "Either the alcohol ate those brain cells, or the memories are buried so deep I'll never find them."

"The blank spaces where memories should be can be disconcerting. Are you—" He seems to fumble or search for the right way to phrase what's coming next. The hesitation goes on so long, I'm not sure he'll continue. "Dealing with the loss all right?"

I want to laugh and tell him it's hardly the first time I've gotten blackout drunk, but I'm oddly touched by his concern. Most parents would be furious I can't remember my own ill-timed and ill-advised Vegas wedding to a woman who probably doesn't want to be married to me. My father has always led with kindness though. How he and my mother ended up with Alex as a child is a mystery.

"I am slightly concerned about how Jules is going to react when I see her again. She's off talking to the former Secretary Jensen." I examine the tattoo on my finger.

"You say you asked her to marry you, so I'm assuming the two of you mended some fences in Tanzania?"

"Mended fences?" I give him a sharp look, and then I narrow my eyes.

"No one who lives in this house or works for me is an idiot. I don't know the details, and after this long, I don't need them if you two have managed to work out whatever caused your rift."

As far as I remember, Julia and I worked out nothing—not even our sexual tension. I run a hand down my face and don't meet his gaze. "Let's just say, for argument's sake, Julia and I did *not* work out our differences. What are the options?"

The king's eyebrows snap together. "There's only one. An annulment. The sooner the better, quite frankly. That would be an embarrassment on a grand scale, but I suppose it's better than the two of you being miserable."

"Right."

"Should you decide to stay married," the king says, "we'll plan a lavish ceremony for the people of Bellerive and the press. Everyone loves to celebrate love." He rises from behind his desk as though our conversation is over.

I rise with him, but unlike him, I'm not done. There are a million other things I could say about me and Jules, but I don't even know how she's feeling right now. Discovering our marriage didn't produce much enthusiasm in her, and I doubt that's changed. Her text to Alex could be interpreted in a thousand different ways, and despite how Alex wanted me to take it, I'll put on my big boy pants and ask Jules later. If our marriage was a drunken mistake, best to rectify it before I'm too invested.

The king and I are alone, and I can't leave the room without bringing up the other elephant in the room. "Are you going to tell me personally about the coronation?"

He starts as though I've delivered a surprise blow. "Yes, well, yes. As I believe Secretary Jensen told you, I've decided to retire from royal life. Alex is ready to take on the weight of The Crown."

"Is he?" The man I just met in the hall isn't someone I'd want to represent me. Smug bastard. I grab a peppermint from the candy jar my father keeps on the corner of his desk.

"I'm not going to pretend he doesn't have more to learn. While you've always worn your heart on your sleeve, Alex has kept his almost too carefully guarded." He sighs. "I'm confident I'm making the right decision."

"What's really going on, Father?"

"I've spent my whole life bowing to the needs of Bellerive. That's all." He squeezes my shoulder and leads us to the door. "Best to bring in some fresh blood."

Lies, and not even particularly good ones. To keep from calling him on them, I pop the peppermint into my mouth. We're going to talk about this again soon, but right now I need to find my wife.

"Let me know what you and Julia decide—the sooner the better." He grimaces. "Memory is a funny thing, isn't it? How some events are so sticky and others..." He makes a fluttering motion with his fingers. "Vanish, sometimes without you even realizing it."

"I love you, Dad." On impulse, I hug him at the door. "Thanks for not hating me for the PR nightmare I set off."

"Whether or not this is a PR nightmare is yet to be determined." He chuckles and gives me a wry smile.

My stomach rolls at the truth of his statement, and I exit his office.

###

I'm almost to my wing of the palace when I catch sight of Brice headed toward me down the wide hallway. A grin stretches across his face, and I can't help my own in response.

"Tequila and cards have led many places, but to a chapel?" Brice crows from a distance.

I chuckle and stuff my hands in the pockets of my jeans. My tattoo stings, but I don't need Brice giving me a hard time about that as well until I know what Jules is thinking.

"Does this mean I can blame you for my shotgun wedding?"

"Blame?" Brice stops just before me. "You mean, *thank*, right? It's Jules. She's every wet dream you've ever had."

I glance around to make sure no one else just heard him publicly declare my love for... my wife? Wow. That's still weird. I'll spend all day getting used to the title only to find out she doesn't want it.

"She sent Alex a text saying our marriage was a *drunken mistake*." Though I've been trying hard to tamp down the spike of anxiety those words caused me, Brice has heard it all. Many, many times.

"Can't dispute the drunk part. I wouldn't put too much weight behind a text she sent to Alex." He laughs. "The glassy-eyed photos you leaked to Dimitri at the Bellerive National paper weren't your classiest move."

"Do you think Jules has put that together yet?"

Brice raises his eyebrows.

Suddenly, I'm not so keen to talk about Jules and our potentially epic fail of a marriage. "Where were you when you got called home?"

"Macao. Gambling. Shame we didn't get to meet in Vegas like we planned."

"Definitely wouldn't have married you," I mutter.

Brice laughs. "Only because that would be illegal." Then he shakes his head. "Alex as king. Somehow, I never really thought it would happen. Dad's always felt like he'd live forever."

"Has he told you why he's stepping down?" I peer at my younger brother.

"Wants to enjoy his retirement or some bullshit like that. Is that what he fed you?"

"With a silver spoon." I frown. "Something doesn't add up. Many things, actually. Why send Jules to Tanzania? Why enact the seventy-two hours if I already knew about the coronation? Why bring us both home months before anything is actually happening?"

"Mid-life crisis?" Brice jokes, and then his smile fades to a serious expression. "If there's more to it, he'll tell us when he's ready. You and Julia clear the air before you did the deed?"

"Some things are better left buried."

Brice stares at me for a beat. "You know, I've never said anything, but you've avoided competing against Alex out of some sort of misguided belief you wouldn't measure up. Most of the time, you're better than Alex. It's just that Alex will do anything to win. Life lesson number one, right? Alex always wins."

The thought of him winning Julia again sours my stomach. If his outburst in the hallway wasn't misplaced jealousy, I don't know what that was about. Maybe they were together long after I realize.

"You're better than him, you've just never wanted something," he tries to catch my gaze, "or *someone* badly enough to fight him for it."

Was that the problem when I was sixteen? I didn't want Jules enough? No. No. Julia wanted Alex. She ran away from me and straight into his arms. What good would fighting have done? It wasn't a fight I could win.

"What's your point, Brice? Alex and Julia aren't together." I flash my tattoo, and Brice lights up. "She married me." We marked each other, and the realization does bring me a strange comfort.

"A tattoo? You got a fucken tattoo with her name on it?" He bends at the waist with laughter. "I legit wish I'd been there. How did I miss this?" When he catches his breath, he grabs my hand and stares at Julia's name—well, *Jules*, really. "You dumb fuck. This is amazing!" He drops my hand and squeezes my shoulder. "Seriously. Talk to her about whatever happened with Alex. You might not think it matters now, but she wasn't the one who listened to your drunken whining ass in Vegas for years. Those scars run deep, man. Let 'em heal."

I flex my hands at my sides. He's not wrong about how deep that particular scar runs.

"She got a tattoo too?" he asks, and his lips twitch with amusement.

"Nick in bold." Though talk of an annulment, the text she sent Alex, and her vomiting at the realization we're married don't bode well for her keeping it. My euphoria from earlier has vanished. The cold, hard reality is that she might not have wanted to marry me. She might have been too drunk, or perhaps I tricked her into it. We might never know the sequence of events that led us down the aisle.

"Get out of your feelings, man, and get into your head." He punches me in the shoulder. "I've known Julia all my life. A tattoo? Drunk or not, she doesn't do that unless she wants to." He hesitates for a second. "Not even for you. Not even back then."

"It's been fourteen years, and I still don't want to hear her say it." I run a hand through my hair.

His expression softens. He might give me a hard time and make fun of me, but he also knows exactly what I mean. "If you don't ask, you will *always* wonder."

He's right. Of course he's right. Though I've tried my best to put the past behind us the last few weeks as we've grown closer, it's still underneath every interaction.

"I gotta go talk to Mom," Brice says stepping around me. "Think about it this way—if the shoe was on the other foot, would you want to be punished for your teenage mistakes forever? None of us got out of those years without a few scars." He cocks an eyebrow and runs his middle finger over a faint scar on his forehead. "'Cause you were a real dick."

"You're a beacon of wisdom." I roll my eyes and shove my hands back inside my pockets.

He puts a hand to his ear, walking backward. "Bacon? Did you say something about bacon? Excellent idea. I'll go talk to Joyce in the kitchen."

Then he's gone, and I'm left alone in the hallway, a short distance from my wing of the palace. I need to gather my thoughts in my room, and then I'll track down Jules.

My gut clenches. So many things could go wrong with our conversation.

But for now—right now—she's my wife, and that's something I never thought I'd be able to say. For just a few more minutes, I'll let that be true in case it's a title she'd prefer not to keep.

My stomach dips. There's no greater torture than seeing everything you want within your grasp and having it slide through your fingers, a mirage.

Nick

Fourteen years ago

Even in the dead of winter, Bellerive rarely gets snow. Frost, maybe. A slick coating on the roads if it rains and the temperature drops fast. Having been to Canada around the Christmas season, I appreciate how snow enhances the beauty of garish decorations.

Since we can't do much about the weather, Bellerive's tradition is to coat the courthouse square with manmade snow, ice sculptures, winter activities, and an abundance of decorations. The air has a crisp texture to it while we wait for the opening ceremony to conclude, and the scent of deep-fried pastries wafts toward me. The dessert constructed in the shape of a Bellerive rose is coated in local honey when it comes out of the frier. A sticky highlight every year.

In about thirty minutes, once the sun has set, we'll flip the comically big switch in front of us, and all of Tucker's Town will light up for the Christmas season.

Other cities and towns around the island turn on their lights earlier, but the Christmas Festival of Tucker's Town always takes place a handful of days before Christmas, and it's a command performance for us kids. Other years I haven't minded. As soon as we were done the royal part, Julia and I would toboggan down the constructed hills, skate on the ice rink, and throw snowballs at each other. We scrawled our names in the snow using donated paint, coating the lawn with whatever catchphrase was currently our favorite. And we laughed—we laughed so much.

This year, I don't even know if she's coming.

Actually, that's a lie. She texted me, but since Alex is home, I'm assuming she's coming to see him and using me as a cover. No thanks.

Vicky is in the crowd somewhere, and she's promised to put her warm lips and wet tongue all over my dick when this is over. It's not hills, rinks, and snowballs, but getting a blowjob isn't nothing either. Watching her blond head bob is one of the few things that seems to give me even a moment of happiness anymore, so I'm not turning *that* down.

The mayor of Tucker's Town says her usual spiel about the Christmas season, being thankful for where we live, so on and so forth. Then she turns to us, and my grandmother, the queen of

Bellerive, uses both hands to draw down the lever, illuminating the city in a burst of color.

A surprised and pleased murmur travels through the crowd.

I have to admit, it's impressive.

After we've schmoozed with important politicians and wealthy Bellerivians, I search for a familiar blond head. My job is done, and now I get my reward.

"Looking for me?" Julia asks from behind me.

I whip around, surprised she snuck up on me. Her long chestnut hair falls around her shoulders in gentle waves, and I'm struck for the millionth time by how pretty she is. An ache blooms across my chest. "Uh, Vicky, actually. We're supposed to hang out."

"Oh." The smile on her face slips. "I texted you. You didn't get it?"

"Haven't checked my phone in hours." I shrug. I'd feel bad lying if she wasn't living one too.

"Oh. Well. Maybe we can take a few runs down the hill before you have to disappear? It looks like they put moguls on it this year. My ass will be so sore tomorrow." She grins at me and pats her backside.

Why does she have to mention her ass? I shift on my feet, trying to keep my dick in check. Letting myself think about her like that doesn't help any of us.

"There you are." Vicky loops her arm through mine and bumps my hip.

Perfect timing. I'm not sure I could have watched Julia's smile slip off her face a second time without someone else being responsible.

"Are you ready to go? I've got big plans for you." Vicky rises on her toes and kisses the corner of my mouth.

"You're leaving now? You're not staying at all?" Julia's tone is bewildered.

"My parents are away for the weekend." Vicky's tone implies Julia should be able to deduce what that means.

Julia flushes and presses her mittened hands to her cheeks. "Shame you still have to deal with security."

"Oh, it's not so bad," Vicky says. "They sweep the house and then leave us alone. Right, Nicky?"

Julia cringes and half turns away.

"They know how to make themselves scarce," I agree. But the expression on Julia's face is wrenching my heartstrings. If I didn't know she was with Alex, I'd wonder if I've read her all wrong. Is she bothered by the idea of me having sex? Or the idea of me having sex with Vicky? She never cared before.

Vicky tugs me away, and reluctantly, I follow.

We've only gone a few steps, and the emotion on Julia's face lingers at the forefront of my mind. Am I being an asshole? Should I have stuck around for a bit? Gone down the hill a few times for old times' sake?

I turn back to tell her I'll text her later, but when I do, Alex is in front of her, and he's got her hand clasped in both of his.

There's a hint of a smile on her face, and the words die in my throat.

She doesn't care that I've left after all. Perhaps she got what she's wanted all along. My throat closes up, and I clear it, trying to banish the sensation. Feels like I'm drowning. My lungs are full, and I can't quite inhale a full breath.

"I can't wait to get you alone," Vicky squeals when one of the security guards with us opens the rear door to the car.

Turns out Vicky really means that. She belts herself into the middle seat, and as the car drives out of the parking lot, she's unzipping my pants.

Instead of stopping her or being embarrassed that security will get a clear view of her giving me head, I thread my fingers through her silky hair and close my eyes. As warm wetness envelopes me, I don't allow my mind to drift back to the sadness I saw mirrored in Jules.

###

Christmas Eve dinner is one of the few times during the season when it's just us around the oversized table in the formal dining room. Grandmother, grandfather, my parents, Brice, Alex, and me. Tomorrow, dinner extends to the rest of the family both near and far, but tonight, it's just us. The quiet before the storm.

Julia texted me earlier about exchanging Christmas presents right after dinner. We've done it for years, Christmas Eve in the barn, just the two of us. I have something for her, but I had it made months ago—too long ago—and it didn't occur to me to change it until it was too late.

I had our Tanzania school plans bound with an inscription at the front that reads, *When you're ready for this, let me know,* which feels entirely too personal now. Even the name of the organization is ill-advised. Foolish and presumptuous and stupid.

I would have realized earlier that my present for Julia was inappropriate if I hadn't been so stressed about what to get Vicky. Finding something that says, *I enjoy having sex with you, and you give fabulous head, but we're done at the end of senior year,* was harder than I expected. Any other Christmas, Jules and I would have had that frank conversation, and she would have made fun of me and then helped me navigate the intricacies of a gift.

But I couldn't bring myself to ask her. I can't bring myself to talk to her about much of anything anymore, and when my life slows down enough, I sink into intense loneliness. Every time I have a problem, or something strange happens or even something funny, I pick up my phone to call her or text her. Then this wash of sadness rushes over me so completely that I put my phone down. What are we to each other anymore? Something has died between us, and I don't know how to revive it.

I haven't even texted her back about the exchange because I don't know what to give her. Re-gift something? I've gotten lots of useless gifts from diplomatic trips over the years. Perhaps I can find something funny or clever in the loft.

I'm not giving her the bound Tanzania plans.

Grandmother has led the conversation through most of the main course, and I've let it drift around me. Honestly, I don't feel like talking to anyone about anything.

As dessert is served, my mother turns to the three of us. She's been so busy the last few months with royal commitments here and abroad that we haven't seen her much. We're all used to the ebb and flow of our family unit.

"Alex, you said you have somewhere to be after dinner tonight?" My mother dips her spoon into her crème brûlée.

"Meeting up late tonight with a friend to exchange gifts."

"Oh, that's lovely," my mother says. "Take security. I didn't realize you exchanged presents with anyone local. Nick always exchanges with Jules, but you've never really done that." She eyes him expectantly.

"Well," he says and slides his gaze in my direction. "She's not so much a friend as someone on the island I'm seeing. I didn't want to say anything. It's early days, but she's a great girl. Perfect, actually."

My stomach rolls, and I stir the custard mixture in my little bowl, but I don't take a bite. The girl is Julia. Has to be.

"An island girl." My mother sits up straighter. She hesitates for a beat before continuing. "I'm sure I don't need to tell you because you've been so discreet so far, but if the press catches wind—"

"You don't need to worry." A sly smile slides across his face before he takes a sip of his water. "She's trustworthy. A good girl. Very, very good at keeping secrets. You've got nothing to worry about. Our relationship won't get out unless we want it to."

My mother's shoulders relax. "Oh, well, I'm happy for you, Alex. She sounds lovely. I hope we get to meet her someday."

Little do they know. My heart is contracting in my chest, and I'm struggling to get a full breath. Alex and Jules keep playing in my mind. *Alex and Julia.*

What will he give her? I don't want to think about it.

"What about you, Nick? You seem to be spending an awful lot of time with Vicky lately. Is that getting serious?"

They've never cared as much about who I was with compared to Alex's girlfriends. With him, they're keenly aware, as is the rest of the country, that Alex's tastes will help lead the country. My girlfriends are gossip, nothing more.

"Not overly," I mutter.

"Does she realize you aren't overly serious?" My mother frowns.

I catch my grandmother's gaze across the table, and there's a frown creasing her brow. Her silvery hair is pinned into a neat updo, and despite her age, she's never seemed old to me. Strong and fierce, that's my gran.

"I'm actually not feeling well." I set down my spoon. "May I be excused?" I direct the question at my grandmother since she's the one who runs the Christmas Eve table and any other table she sits at.

"You may." She picks up her own fork, and I can feel her eyes on me as I exit the room.

When I reach my family's suite, I collapse on my bed and stare at the ceiling. Julia sends me another text with a series of question marks. I turn off my phone.

I don't know how long I lay there trying to fight off the edges of panic gnawing at my insides, but by the time I get up, it's dark, and the house is quiet.

I wander down to the kitchen and search for leftovers, but there isn't anything I can stomach. Julia and Alex circle in my head, and I hate it, but I don't know how to push them out.

A ride. A fast ride down some dark, winding streets will clear my head. When I'm busy or distracted, the dragging, aching sadness doesn't overwhelm me.

On the way out the door, I grab my keys and leather jacket. I throw it on without zipping it up. There's a bite to the air tonight, and it feels like rain.

When I get to the garage, Alex's motorcycle is missing. I stare at the empty space for a minute. My heart sinks. He'll be with Julia somewhere. In her room? Are they together right now? Do they ride around the island like she and I used to? Her pressed against his back with her arms wrapped around his middle. The thought causes my gut to clench.

I haven't had the nerve to turn my phone back on, but I do that now. Other than the question marks, she hasn't sent another message. Busy, probably.

I hit the button to raise the garage door and swing my leg over my bike. For a moment, I don't switch on the ignition. Whenever I sit still, there's a deep canyon that opens up in me. Sometimes I think it'll swallow me whole.

Before I can second-guess my escape in the middle of the night from my life, I turn on my motorcycle and roar down the long laneway toward the gates.

On instinct, I take the roads that lead me to Julia. They're the ones I know best in the dead of night. Rain drizzles down from the sky. With each exhale, my breath puffs out and is carried away by the breeze.

The faster I go, the stronger the wind is against my chest. The pressure feels good, and I accelerate more, daring the speedometer to tick up higher and higher.

I'm so focused on the freedom, the absence of the aching pain in my chest that I forget about the blind corner at the top of Julia's road.

Stupid. So stupid.

I squeeze the brakes with all my might, but the road is slick from the rain. The motorcycle slips to the side underneath me and careens toward a tree. My last thought before I slam into the tree is Julia.

JULIA

When Nick strolls into his room, he freezes at the entry to the sitting room portion of the suite where I'm seated in an armchair while Dr. Bennett inspects my tattoo. A frown creases his brow, and my heart kicks at the concern etching his face. The tenderness in his gaze is familiar, but it's also foreign. When was the last time he showed such open affection and concern? My stomach flutters. I didn't even realize how much I missed having him look at me that way.

"Are you okay?" He comes to peer over the doctor's shoulder.

"Mother's orders." I flash my hand. "Can't let the royal ring get tarnished."

Amusement tinges Nick's hazel eyes. "Not so easy to polish." He takes the seat next to me. "Suppose I should look after mine as well. Or rather," he says, gesturing to Dr. Bennett. "The good doctor can earn his keep."

"I believe I've earned my keep several times over with you, Your Highness," Dr. Bennett says without removing his focus from my finger. "It's actually quite a pretty design." He finishes with me and pats the back of my hand.

"That's true. As far as drunken mistakes are concerned, I've got good taste." My gaze slides to Nick, and he raises his eyebrows but doesn't say anything.

The doctor plucks some salve from his kit and bends over Nick's hand next. "You must have directed the show, Secretary Jensen. Otherwise, I believe Prince Nicholas would have been more creative with where he put his tribute to you." When he peers over at me, the doctor's eyes glint with good humor.

"You know him well, I see." I tease.

"Yes, clearly Jules has the market cornered on common sense. If you're getting a tattoo, get the best tattoo—my name," Nick says.

The doctor laughs, and I can't help following along. This situation shouldn't be anything close to funny, and yet with Nick sitting beside me, it doesn't feel dire anymore either. He finishes Nick's finger and gives us a few tips on how to care for the tattoo in the coming days since neither of us can remember where we got it done. We'll have to check our bank accounts and credit cards later to make sure we didn't go to some back-alley place with poor hygiene.

"It's not my first tattoo," Nick says with a hint of a smile when the doctor borders on a lecture.

Although Nick's declaration is news to me, I don't say anything. How strange is it to be married to him and to know less than I did at sixteen? At one time I was intimately familiar with almost every square inch of him. I could have drawn him with incredible detail from memory and told anyone exactly what Nick would think before he realized he thought it. Such a privilege to understand someone so well.

Dr. Bennett bids his goodbyes and leaves with his little medical bag that makes me think we're in a 1950s sitcom, or maybe drama, depending on what comes next for me and Nick.

Nick heaves out a big sigh and sits forward, running his hands down his face. "What did your mother say?"

"That I needed to put on my big girl pants and speak to you like an adult instead of avoiding a confrontation." Might as well jump to the point. If I stick to the facts and keep my feelings out of it, this conversation will be easier. Honest, to the point of bluntness, and I can't dwell on any of his answers. That's my strategy. All of his answers can skim across me as though I'm ice, and none of them will hurt me.

"Not too far off my conversations with Brice and my father." He huffs out a laugh and glances over at me.

"Brice?" His father isn't a surprise, but Brice is rarely serious. He's a crowd-pleaser, but he's not the one anyone goes to for helpful advice.

"You know you've slid pretty far down the reasonable scale when *Brice* is the voice of reason." Nick jokes.

We stare at each other, and I wonder whether he's struggling to do up those adult pants like I am. While we must talk about what's happened, I can't wrap my head around how I feel about our marriage, let alone what I want him to say in response.

"Did we fuck up?" he whispers.

"I have no idea," I admit.

"Was your mother upset?"

A good avoidance strategy. Let's talk about how other people feel before we pick at our own wounds. "Not really. Just... she wondered how I felt about the whole thing. King George?"

"Not angry, surprisingly." Nick flops back in his chair and stares at the ceiling. "Asked me the same question."

"We hardly know each other," I say. Staying married to him doesn't make sense given we've only been speaking properly for a few weeks. Before Tanzania, our exchanges were stilted politeness. Despite what the world believes, there's been no torrid affair, not even the consummation of our marriage.

"Anymore." Nick amends. "At one time, you knew me better than anyone."

The honest declaration causes such a sharp ache that tears spring to my eyes. At one time we told each other everything without inhibition, with no worries about hurt feelings or misunderstandings. We both seemed to understand each other's limits, the places a best friend didn't go. We were deeply, utterly *connected*.

That sort of no holds barred friendship is rare, and I didn't appreciate it enough until Nick was giving other people all the pieces I used to get. In fourteen years, we've drifted so far. How do we come back from that?

"What do you want to do?" I brace myself for the obvious choice. We annul the marriage and handle the fallout. If we don't do it now, the embarrassment if we failed would be worse, wouldn't it? We can't build a marriage on the non-relationship we have right now.

"I want to rewind time to have a few less drinks." He turns his head toward me, and our gazes connect. "We got tattoos, Jules. The only other tattoo I have, I got because it *meant* something to me. Despite what you might think," he holds up his finger, "I wouldn't have done this on a whim—not even drunk. Trust me, I've had lots of opportunities with Brice to get meaningless tattoos in Vegas. Hasn't happened once."

His reasoning is exactly my own. The wedding I *might* have agreed to thinking we were so clever and funny. An arranged marriage? Not likely if he's already married! Aren't we hilarious?

But the tattoo? There isn't enough alcohol in the world to erode my common sense that much.

"What are you saying?" I run my hands along my thighs to get rid of the sweat pooling across my palms. The implication is clear, but I need him to say it.

"I realize an annulment is, perhaps, the tidier solution to what we've done..." He catches my gaze. "I don't want to do that."

"Oh," I breathe out, and my skin prickles with nerves. My internal pact to keep my emotions out of whatever Nick said to me has been shot down by this unexpected turn of events.

Sober Nick used to be practical with a hint of rebellion when the constraints of royal life got a bit too tight. A marriage is a restraint I never thought Nick would willingly take on. One woman, forever? Impossible, right?

Except he seems to be suggesting that one woman could be me.

He chuckles, but there's no humor in the sound. "Not an enthusiastic 'me either,' which I guess is what I was expecting." He sighs. "If you want the annulment, I won't fight you."

My heart drops. "What if I don't want it either?" If Nick could be mine... if Nick *wants* to be mine... the brokenhearted sixteen-year-old girl surfaces at the thought.

"You *want* to try this?" He gives me a skeptical look, which would have slain me had he not already told me he's willing to try.

"I think—I think what you said is true. I can't remember what happened, but I know I wouldn't have gotten this tattoo if I didn't believe in being married to you. I just... I just wish I remembered what led to this, you know?" I flush and shake my head. "I don't think—I mean, we didn't even..."

A genuine chuckle escapes him. "Jules, come on. Say it."

"We didn't sleep together, did we?"

"Sleep? More like passed out."

Now he's teasing me, and I suppress a smile. "You know what I mean."

"I do." He smirks. "Trust me, if we'd had sex, your memory would be technicolor and clear. You'd want to write my name in the stars for all the world to see." He draws his hand across the air in front of us as though he's headlining a movie.

Now I laugh. "Oh? You've got some sort of magical mojo that can bring a girl back from blackout drunk?"

He meets my gaze, all trace of humor gone. "Not quite. There's no way in hell I would have had sex with you if you were that drunk. That's not how our first time together goes—married or not."

He says it with so much sincerity and confidence I'm momentarily light-headed. Has he thought about it? I haven't let my mind wander there in a long time. Sex with Nick? The outline of that thought died in college. But I still remember what I imagined being with him would be like.

"How would our first time be?" My voice is husky.

"I'm tempted to give you a line," he says with a hint of a smile.

"Don't give me something you'd give anyone else." It's a plea and a command.

He searches my face, and his smile fades. Without saying a word, he leans over and kisses me, a brush of his lips against mine that makes me yearn for more. When he draws back and my eyes open, he's still close enough to touch, for his breath to stir the tendrils of my hair framing my face.

"Sex with me would be the most connected, emotional experience of your life." His voice is rough with desire.

I suck in a sharp breath, and then I bridge the gap between us, looping my hand around his neck, drawing him into another kiss. He responds without hesitation, as though he's been waiting for permission to cross this threshold again.

Connected and *emotional* should be a line, phrasing he uses to win over a woman—me—into his bed. But the sentiment is true, as though he's already slipped inside me and knows the very darkest secrets of my heart. Whenever I pictured being with Nick, that's exactly how I thought it would be. Deep and meaningful—the kind of sex that breaks your heart and heals it all at the same time.

He draws me out of my chair over to his, and he tugs me onto his lap, his lips finding mine again. We shouldn't be kissing. We should be talking. My brain is waging a losing battle against my body.

After that night in the barn, I convinced myself Nick didn't want me, couldn't want me like this. To realize he might—that he does—is exhilarating and terrifying.

He frames my face and softens the kiss. "What do you say, Jensen? Want to stay married to me?"

Does he love me? Could he love me? The bud of love has lain dormant in me, but with care, it'll blossom and bloom. Scary, but true. If we do this, my heart will be invested, even if his isn't. Can I live with that?

"Marriages should probably be based on more than the possibility of good sex," I say. It's the closest I can come to asking him how he feels about me.

A hint of a smile touches his lips. "Royal marriages have been built on less, I'd wager."

"What if it doesn't work out?" I bite my lip.

"That's a risk in any marriage, isn't it? No matter the intention, desires can change." His tone is blithe, easy, as though breaking up a royal marriage is as simple as ordering a second dessert off the menu.

I take a deep breath because this next question is going to hurt, but I have to ask. Depending on his answer, there's no point in trying to make us work. "What happens if you get tired of me?"

No matter what my mother believes, that's how sixteen-year-old me interpreted that night in the barn. He kissed me, deemed me unworthy, and then traded me in for a series of other people who amused him more.

In the end, he didn't drop me for Vicky, he dropped me for everyone—from the soccer team to his younger brother and anyone in between. In college, when I thought things might finally get better between us, they only got worse. I couldn't draw him back, but I couldn't figure out how to cut the threads of our friendship either.

I missed him. Longed for him. Spent hours pining for something I understood I'd never have again, but I couldn't help wishing for anyway.

My first sixteen years were colored with the miracle of Nick's unyielding friendship, and the last fourteen were tainted by the stain of his indifference. The only thing that's changed is that he's decided to notice me again. Or was forced to since King George sent me to Tanzania, and we had to share a tent.

Nick sucks in a deep breath. "Oh, Jules. I never grew tired of you." His hazel depths are marred with pain. "Not sure I ever could."

I climb off his lap and go back to my chair. I bring my knees into my chest. Now *that* sounds like a line. "You kissed me, and then you cut me out of your life, one step at a time. How do you explain that if it wasn't because you got tired of me?"

He puts his head in his hands and takes a few unsteady breaths. "God, I've avoided this conversation for years. I've never wanted to have it."

"Whatever happened was a long time ago." His agonized words make me think I don't want to hear his explanation. Maybe it'll be more hurtful than what I already believe. "Forget I brought it up." Losing his friendship was like having my axis removed, but maybe we can move beyond the past without dissecting what was lost.

Silence settles between us, and I try to decipher why he'd want to stay married to me. The drunken marriage is in line with an ill-advised prank, but to stick with it instead of doing the obvious mea culpa to the public is surprising.

"We're not in love with each other." The words are tart on my tongue. "If you think we can make a marriage work, I guess I need to understand *why* you think that?"

"You don't think we could?" He leans back in his chair and eyes me.

"We couldn't even make a friendship work."

"Our friendship didn't work because we started keeping secrets from each other." He stares across the room, and a muscle in his jaw tenses. "A marriage probably wouldn't survive that either."

"Keeping secrets?" I cock my head, my mind grappling for what he's talking about.

He turns to me, and resignation settles over his features. "Why didn't you tell me about Alex?"

"What?" All the blood rushes around my body in a flurry of confusion, and I press a hand to my forehead to steady myself. Oh, my God. *Alex.*

"I followed you that night, Jules. I saw you with him." His voice cracks. "I saw you, and it broke my fucking heart."

Nicholas

We're on the cusp of the confrontation I've never wanted to have, the one I've avoided at all costs, and instead of feeling queasy, a weight is lifting off my shoulders. The wedge I've allowed to sit between us will either be rooted out or widened beyond repair. We're either meant to be together, or we'll go our separate ways forever. Our hasty marriage is forcing us to get real with each other in a way we haven't been in years.

Tears fill Julia's eyes while she stares at me, shock registering on her face. "You saw me with Alex?" The words are garbled as though her throat is closing up.

"Imagine my surprise." I grimace and lean my elbows on my knees and then I focus on the colorful rug under my feet. Watching her cry prompts an answering surge in me. She's the only person on Earth whose tears inspire my own. But I'm not going to cry my way through this conversation. I did it once, years ago, and I vowed I'd never shed another tear.

"I don't know what to say," she whispers. "I can't believe this never occurred to me."

"How long?" My voice is thick, and I glance at her. "How long were you with him?"

"Whatever you think—" She shakes her head.

"I've thought a lot of things." I give a harsh laugh. "Too many things. There's nothing you can tell me that I haven't already considered."

"We were together a few weeks that summer. Just a few weeks." She sniffs and wipes a stray tear. "Is this why you—is this why you froze me out?"

A few weeks? That's impossible. All sense of sadness dries up in me, replaced by a wave of frustration. "It was a long time ago, Julia. You don't need to lie about it to spare my feelings anymore."

"Lie about it?" She gives me a bewildered look. "I'm not lying."

"Alex talked about you all the time after I saw you two together the night of my father's birthday. He visited you in California at Stanford. At *our* college." Opening this line of questioning slices new wounds, but I'm not leaving this room without the truth. For too long I've avoided it.

"He was in San Francisco on some diplomatic trip, and he stopped off at campus. We had lunch." A frown creases her brow. "I don't know why he'd talk about me all the time. We weren't together."

"I saw him coming out of your room the next morning. Unless lunch led to dinner led to..." That's not a thought I'm willing to finish. Catching sight of him leaving her room was enough to make me want to lash out, do stupid things.

She raises her eyebrows and wipes a last tear from her cheek before her gaze hardens. "My room? I guess I don't have to think too hard about what you were doing in my dorm that early in the morning."

Back then, I was eaten alive with jealousy and grief. Whatever I could find to mask those emotions, I latched on to it. Women, alcohol, drugs, modeling—nothing productive—not during those years. Numb seemed pretty good to me.

The handful of years between the end of college and Julia starting to work for my father were my sanest. The promise and temptation of seeing her around every corner vanished when she stayed in America while I returned to Bellerive to be put to work. And work I did. Every opportunity I came across that took me far away from Bellerive or California, I grasped it with both hands.

Then she came back, and we saw each other too much and not nearly enough. It was easier not to see her at all, and it was definitely easier not to see her with Alex. A casual brush of her hand on his sleeve made my gut clench, and I had to excuse myself from whatever discussion was happening. Each time my heart cracked open, a fresh wound. So I ran from the feeling. I've been running since that night.

I'm tired of wondering and imagining what the monster under the bed looks like. The worst has already happened. When she had a choice, she chose him.

"Can you just tell me the truth? The one thing I can't stand—will not tolerate—is being lied to." I spit out.

"I'm telling you the truth," she cries.

"Not the whole truth." I shake my head and glare at her. "This can't be the whole truth."

"The wheels are turning now." Her finger circles her temple. "I'm starting to wonder if you've been punishing me for being with Alex for fourteen years."

"Well, if I've been punishing you, trust me, I've been punishing myself as well. Not a very clever punishment if it hurt me as much as you." I can't keep the bitterness and injury out of my voice. She has no idea what it did to me to see her with him like that. The person I trusted most in the whole world with the person I trusted the least.

Her shoulders slump, and all the anger deflates out of her. "I never meant to hurt you. Honestly Nick. I didn't even know I could. I was a stupid sixteen-year-old kid who was flattered by nineteen-year-old Alex's attention." She sighs. "Then I tried to force myself to feel things for him that I just," her voice catches again, "I didn't feel."

None of this fits with the narrative that's lived in my head. Some of it I could have invented, for sure, but other bits were either planted or encouraged by Alex. "The night I kissed you..." I clear my throat when it threatens to close around the raised scar of the truth. "You ran to Alex."

She draws her legs up to her chest and rests her chin on them. "I guess it would have looked that way. But I went to find Alex to tell him what we'd been doing—hanging out behind your back—had to stop. I told him I didn't want to be with him like that anymore."

"But I saw you kissing." The red dress, her pressed against him, the smug look on his face when he realized I saw them. They're images that have haunted me when I've allowed them to get a foothold. I close my eyes at the memory, but it lives behind my eyelids no matter how tightly I shut them.

"He kissed me before I could say or do anything to stop him. I didn't want him to kiss me." Our gazes connect. "I didn't choose Alex over you, not knowingly." Her voice is heavy with tears again.

"Why didn't you ever tell me?" My throat tightens.

"I thought you'd be angry with me. Think I was dumb or something. It was *Alex*. I understood what that meant." She closes her eyes, and a tear slides down her cheek. "Or I thought I did, and I did it anyway." She sniffs and brushes her tears away. "Why didn't you ever ask?"

It takes me a moment to gather my courage, and I run my fingers through my beard in rough movements to distract myself from the sadness expanding in me. "I didn't want to hear you tell me he meant more to you than I did." My voice is rough, and I turn toward her. "Because there was no one who meant more to me than you."

"Oh, Nick." She breathes out the words in a rush. "Oh, Nick. No." She climbs out of her chair and pushes me back into my armchair. She straddles me. "Never. I never would have said that." She frames my face and stares into my eyes. "I was young and stupid. I thought if you ever found out about Alex, you'd yell at me. I never, not in a million years, thought... I never thought it would *break* us." Her chin trembles, and her breath hitches on a sob.

I scoop up her tears with my thumb, and then I lean forward and kiss each of her cheeks. Her lashes flutter closed, and she breathes out a shuddering sigh. Even all puffy from crying, she's lovely. The loveliest.

"I tried to find you after I talked to Alex and"—she breaks eye contact to look over my shoulder—"boy, did I find you."

I clench my jaw. After I saw her with Alex, the rest of the night became a blur. Vicky. The barn. Jules walking in on us. Me asking her to forget everything. Her fleeing with Posey.

"My greatest forms of self-defense: women and alcohol." When it seemed clear she didn't want me how I wanted her, I needed a way to get us on even footing. Vicky was a perfect barrier. It's not like I could spend my whole senior year drunk—though that happened a lot too.

"I thought we were..." She swallows. "We were going to be together."

Tears are rolling down her cheeks again, and the ache spreads across my chest and down into my arms and legs. I hate to see her hurting, but I can't ignore the hurt she caused in me either.

She frames my face with her thumbs on my cheeks, and she puts her lips close to my ear. "I was choosing you, Nick. I wanted you."

I dig my fingers into her hips and tug her tighter against me. My breath is ragged. Only a few times have I let myself even consider the conversation going in this direction. All the evidence pointed to the opposite. She didn't want me. I shouldn't have kissed her. I ruined everything. Hearing her say those words is like submerging a searing burn in cool water. Painful and soothing.

Her lips skim my earlobe, and goosebumps rise across my skin. God, I want her. When she draws back, my lips catch hers, and she sinks into me. She digs her hands into my hair and presses her chest against mine.

"Say it again," I rasp, and trail my lips along her exposed neck.

"I wanted you. Just you."

When I rise from the chair with her in my arms, she clings to my neck and wraps her legs around my waist. Finding her mouth again, I keep half an eye on the route to the bed while sneaking a hand up the back of her shirt. With a flick of my fingers, the clasp of her bra releases.

She laughs into my mouth. "I'm not sure I've ever had a guy do that quite so smoothly."

"I tell you," I say, nuzzling her ear before laying her down on the bed. "You'll be writing my name across the stars."

When I glance down at her, she's biting her lip.

"You're not sure." I try to back off her, but she clutches my forearm.

"I'm sure I want you," she whispers.

"So what aren't you sure about?" I stretch out beside her and ease my hand along her stomach.

"There's still a voice in my head that worries we'll screw this up."

I put my hand over my heart. "For my part, I'm in this. I'm in. I'm not backing out." The words I want to say rise into my throat. After only a few weeks, I can't tell her I'm in love with her. *Still* in love with her. "I know how I felt about you at sixteen, and I'm confident I can feel that again." *Because I never stopped*.

I'm not worried about myself at all. Am I worried about her? As long as we're honest with each other from now on, I can't see how this can go wrong. We're married. We're a team. The roar of the crowd doesn't matter if we've got each other to keep us steady.

She traces the curve of my jaw. "I think I can feel that way again too."

"Then we've got nothing to worry about." I smooth her hair and stare into her eyes that I love so much. "Trust me?"

"More than anyone else in the world."

Julia

They're the words we once used to comfort and encourage each other, and they feel right in this moment, but I'm not sure they're true yet. How can they be? We've only started being real with each other. No matter what he says, there's a lingering doubt in me. Alex was a mistake, and it cost me dearly, but I can't help feeling like Nick shoved me aside too. I disappointed him, and he cut me out. What happens the next time I don't measure up?

There's a glassy sheen to his pretty hazel eyes, and he strokes my cheek with his thumb. "Jesus, what'd we do to each other, Jules?"

My heart squeezes at the regret in his deep voice. The question cuts to the quick. For the first time since our friendship broke apart, I've realized I wasn't the only one breaking. We really did shatter each other, and we're finally gluing the pieces back together.

I hope this glue holds.

Instead of answering him, I sink my fingers into the back of his hair and draw his mouth down to mine. If there's one thing I've learned about Nick's kisses, it's that they are capable of making me lose all sense of time and place. Right now, I don't want to think or dwell on the decisions we need to make.

He's my husband, and I've been silently battling a fierce vein of protectiveness since we discovered our blunder on the plane. How can I claim something I don't remember doing? But I'm done fighting my instincts.

Nick is *mine*. He's mine in a way I never thought I'd achieve—not even when we were as close as two friends could get. If we re-cement our bond, turn it into concrete, no one else will ever get a look in, no one else will ever know him again the way that I will. It's a heady sensation to realize the boy I once loved so fiercely can be the man I get to love forever.

I just hope he ends up loving me enough in return.

When he seems hesitant to go further, I draw his shirt over his head and toss it on the floor. He watches it land and then meets my gaze, the question in his eyes.

My stomach flutters in anticipation. He's not going to push for anything I don't want to give. All signs point to yes, but he wants to hear it. Just a few days ago, I told him I couldn't be with him like this, but now I don't know how I've resisted. Every inch of my body wants every inch of his.

"Are you going to ice this cake?" I tease, and I pop the top button of my jeans.

"Ice the cake?" He raises his eyebrows, and his index finger skims across my waistband.

A shiver of anticipation races through me. I bite the inside of my cheek. "Or eat it."

"You know," he says, sliding my shirt over my head and then tossing my loose bra with it. "I never got to taste my wedding cake."

"That you remember." I correct.

He suppresses a smile and traces a finger around my breast. "Oh, I think I'd remember *this* cake even if I don't remember the wedding." He lowers his head and flicks his tongue against my nipple and then swirls it around, drawing it into his mouth.

Desire zips down my center to my core. I dig my fingers into his hair, and I arch my back with the need to get closer. Will we ever be close enough?

"Beautiful and delicious," he murmurs.

His body slides over mine, and he leaves a trail of hot kisses up to my lips. When we're back face to face, he cups my chin and angles his mouth over my lips. His tongue brushes against mine, bringing with it the taste of peppermint. That's all it takes for the haze of sensations to sweep me away. I'm lost. There's nothing quite like having Nick, *my* Nick, setting my body on fire.

How did I go this long without this burning passion? I caught a glimpse of it the night he kissed me on top of the barn and again in Tanzania, but I never realized he could barely touch me and make me weak in the knees. Nothing in my life has prepared me for how good this could be between us.

Nick presses his mouth against my exposed skin on the way to the zipper on my jeans, and he peels them down my body. He slides his hands up my leg and then he kisses my inner thighs.

I grip the sheets to stop myself from wiggling closer, urging him on.

"My wife," he murmurs against my thigh. He slips his index fingers into the edges of my panties and drags them down my thighs.

Warmth floods my core at the possessive taint to his voice, at the way his lips are worshiping my body as though he can't get enough of me. When he drags one finger along my entrance, I raise my hips, wordlessly begging for more.

"You're so wet," he rasps. "You're so wet for me."

"I want you, Nick." I run one hand along his shoulder. In so many ways, I want him.

He gazes at me greedily with hooded eyes. "I need a taste." He parts my legs to lick up my center.

I squirm with wanton desire. Will I ever be satisfied, or will I always crave more with him?

He groans, and he glances up at me. "I knew one taste would never be enough." He closes his mouth over me, and his tongue flicks along my core, circling my clit with exquisite pressure.

Just like when we were young, Nick seems able to read every movement, sigh, and caress of my hand as though I've spoken aloud. Other men have needed directions, a manual, but he knows my body, understands me. We've already got a rhythm like we've been doing this for years.

God, we could have been doing this for years.

His hands are under my ass, tilting me forward to give him better access. Tension coils in my belly, but I don't want to come like this. I want to come with him inside me, as close as we can possibly get to each other. I want to look into his eyes when he achieves his own release and to know I'm the one who gave it to him.

"Nick," I murmur. "Nick, please."

"Tell me what you want, Jules." His words vibrate against my core, and I shudder with pleasure.

"I want you inside me," I say, dragging him up my body.

He moves back from the bed. His jeans and briefs hit the floor, and he opens the drawer of his nightstand, extracting a foil packet. I rise onto my knees and take it from his hand. Before I open it, I stroke the silky length of him, and he closes his eyes. His face is tight with pleasure, and then he swoops down to kiss me, deep and long. His hands are under my thighs, and he lifts me off the bed, so I'm clinging on to him.

I laugh with the packet still clutched in my hand. "What are you doing?"

"Making sure you get your favorite position." His lips quirk up. "Not all of Vegas is a blur." He gives me a quick kiss as he climbs onto the bed, hauling me with him until we're near the headboard.

I trail a line of kisses along his jaw. "Not all of Vegas is a blur?"

"I remember up until I asked you to marry me." His voice roughens when my hand finds him again, stroking up and down in a leisurely rhythm.

"You asked me?" Most of me thought it was likely him in a bid to get out of his father's arranged marriage threat. But given the familiar ease that sprung up between us, I wasn't sure if I might have suggested it jokingly, and we went a little too far.

A short burst of laughter escapes him. "That was in question?"

"I remember playing cards in the hotel room and drinking tequila. I don't remember a proposal whether it was serious or silly." My last memory is a blurry mess of cards spilled across the couch and onto the floor.

"I saw an opportunity." He frames my face and kisses me deeply.

"To best your father?"

"To repair something between us that never should have been broken."

When his gaze meets mine, the sincerity in his expression causes my breath to catch. I want to tell him that I love him, that part of me has probably loved him since that night in the barn, even before that. I've loved him my whole life, in one way or another. But I don't want to jinx what's starting. We were inseparable once, and I want that back before I tell him he's got my heart.

As familiar as he feels to me, there are so many things we no longer know about each other. Even though I have a better understanding of what went wrong between us, loving Nick still feels impossibly risky. Bungy jumping without being entirely certain the cord will hold.

None of that changes what I want right now, what part of me wants forever already.

Ripping the foil package open, I work it down the length of him. He braces his shoulders against the headboard, and then he crooks his finger and smirks.

I straddle his hips, and he settles his hands on my waist, guiding me down. As I sink onto him, my breasts brush against his chest, and he bites his lip. We stare at each other for a beat, adjusting to this new reality. There's no backtracking from this moment between us. For the rest of my life, no matter what happens between us, I'll remember what it feels like to have Nick as close to me as humanly possible.

There's a weight to the air around us, and I'm overcome with the desire to show him how deeply ingrained he is in my heart, even if I've just vowed I wouldn't yet.

He threads his hands through my hair. "You're so beautiful, Jules. I don't think I've ever told you how beautiful you are."

My heart contracts in my chest, and I kiss him. We've told each other all sorts of things before—true and not—but I've never considered how he sees me. To have him think I'm beautiful is a gift I never knew I wanted.

One of his hands stays in my hair, maintaining our smoldering kiss while the other settles on my hip again, urging me into a rhythm.

When our mouths break apart, our foreheads rest against each other, and our breathing is labored.

"You have no idea how many times I thought of us like this," he murmurs against my ear.

I wish I could say the same. But I wouldn't let myself go down this route. Once his opinion of me fell so low, I couldn't let myself imagine this ever happening. It was too painful. So instead of answering—the truth, which would break the mood, or a lie that would soothe him and hurt me—I kiss him again, holding him close, pouring everything I can't say into him.

"Can you come like this?" Nick's voice is strained. "Because if you can't—"

I swallow his words, and warmth floods my body. Not everyone cares enough to ask. "I can." I press my cheek to his and savor the rise and fall of our bodies against each other. The cologne he wears has a hint of cinnamon, and it's subtle enough I can only catch a whiff when we're this close. "Just like this." I grind against him. "Don't stop."

"Don't worry." He nips my earlobe. "I've got you, Jules."

He eases his arms up my back, drawing me even tighter against him. The heat between us is almost unbearable, but I don't want to give up even one inch of contact. The slip and slide of our bodies in sync is the most delicious sensation. I throw back my head and moan as I chase the sensation building in my core again.

Then my orgasm is there, plowing through me with full force. I jerk toward him, my head falling onto his shoulder. His name is on my lips while I clutch the back of his neck. "Holy shit," I whisper. My inner muscles squeeze around his length, and I want to stay here with him forever.

He kisses my temple, and then he picks up the pace beneath me, chasing his own release. "Fuck, Jules," he groans as he thrusts up one more time before he stills and pulses inside me.

When our gazes connect, I realize I've never felt more in tune with someone. I stroke the side of his face, and he kisses me softly. All this time we've missed together.

"Want to write my name across the stars?" His tone is playful.

"Screw the stars," I say, nuzzling his neck. "I'm getting your name tattooed all over my body."

"Seems extreme, but since you're my wife, can we put *Property of* before my name? There wasn't enough room on your finger. Your body would make an exceptional canvas."

I give him a light smack on his chest, but every time he calls me his wife, my heart kicks. If anyone had told me this would happen when I left for Tanzania, I'd have told them it was more likely Nick and I would kill each other than get married. There was always so much unresolved tension between us, and I couldn't figure out how to bridge the gap. Then I stopped trying.

Knowing that *this* is what lay on the other side of our gap, I'm a fool for not trying harder. With other boyfriends, I kept searching for something I could never find. Each relationship ultimately ended in disappointment. With Nick, the intangible is just here between us. No more searching. I have arrived.

"Do you think," I say, "if things hadn't gotten so screwed up between us that it would have been like this then too?"

He searches my face and tucks a stray strand of my hair behind my ear. "Probably not tattoo your body with my name amazing, no." A hint of a smile tugs at the corners of his lips before he grows serious again. "But I know I would have loved figuring this all out with you." He shifts away from me and gives me a kiss on the forehead. "I'll be right back."

He disappears into the en suite, and I tug the covers out to slip underneath them. Despite what just happened between us, I can't help the melancholy seeping in. We've wasted so many years.

Nick comes out of the bathroom and stops to stare at me for a minute.

"What?" I ask, and a smile works its way onto my face.

"Taking a mental snapshot." He climbs onto the bed, and once he's underneath the covers, he draws me to him. "When are you moving all your stuff in?"

"Moving in?" I freeze in his arms.

"I can't live in your tiny apartment in the center of Tucker's Town. Security would be a nightmare. We can move into one of the vacant houses on the property, if you want. Or keep this wing of the house. Whatever you'd prefer. I can talk to my father."

"I guess I hadn't really thought about exactly what staying married means." The logistics of the whole 'being married' hasn't been on my radar. Up to now, I was worried about whether Nick wanted to be married to me at all, and if he didn't, the scandal we'd create by getting an annulment.

"Have you changed your mind?" Nick tenses.

"No." I run my hand along his chest and throw my leg across his for good measure. "No." He's mine. Really mine. After fourteen years of believing something—that he discarded me and couldn't care less—it's hard to switch off my caution. "We can create a list of the major decisions we need to make and then we can go from there, okay?"

He runs a finger down my arm and seems lost in thought. Maybe he doesn't like my list idea? I love lists. There's so much gratification in checking something off.

"Do you think," he says, his voice soft, "I tricked you into marrying me?"

"What?" I prop myself up on an elbow. "No. Why?"

"The arranged marriage schtick. That was a code my father and I worked out so I'd know to take a request to return home seriously. He would never have arranged a marriage for me. But I'm fairly certain I wouldn't have told you that."

"Oh," I breathe out and sink back down into his arms. "You think you made me feel guilty? Manipulated me? Used our old pact against me?" Sixteen-year-old me might have been sucked in by a sense of obligation, but thirty-year-old me wouldn't have, not even with a ton of alcohol.

"Yeah." His voice is raw with emotion.

I rise onto my elbow again so I can make eye contact with him. His obvious concern breaks my heart a little. "Whatever happened between us, I wouldn't have married you if I didn't want to. That much I know for sure."

He doesn't say anything while he moves more strands of my hair away from my face.

When he stays silent, I can't fight the urge to say more. "I think we hurt each other a lot, even though we didn't mean to. It's going to take both of us some time to get past that. But I think we can. I wouldn't be here with you right now if I didn't think we could."

"I loved you so much back then." His voice cracks. "You have no idea how much I loved you."

I do because I loved him with the same intensity. My heart bled the same way his did. I kiss him, and he rolls us, so I'm pinned underneath him. I arch into him, and then I'm lost in a haze of sensation. I empty everything I can't or won't say into the movement of our bodies, and I pray that Nick never cuts me out of his life again.

JULES

Fourteen years ago

When I wake on Christmas Day, the house is eerily quiet and there's a chill in the air. Though Posey and I are both beyond the excited squeals over toys and trinkets at the crack of dawn, I can't believe everyone let me sleep this late. It's almost noon.

I throw on a robe and check the bedrooms. Everyone else is up. So strange.

"Merry Christmas!" I shout as I come down the main staircase.

Posey is conked out on the couch, and there's no sign of my parents. I check the kitchen and the bathrooms, but the house is so silent. Even Posey sleeping on the couch is weird.

I wiggle her shoulder to wake her up. "Where are Mom and Dad?"

She squints at me and rubs the drool off the corner of her mouth. She props herself onto an elbow. "They went to the hospital."

"The hospital?" A swell of panic rushes across my chest. "Is one of them sick?"

Posey shakes her head and then glances at me. She bites her lip as though she's not sure she should say anything.

"What?" I ask. "Why did they go to the hospital?"

"Nick was in a bike accident." Her brown eyes are tinged with sympathy. "A bad one. They didn't want to wake you until they knew more."

All the blood rushes from my body, and I collapse into the couch beside Posey. "A bike accident?" My heart kicks, and there's a queasiness in my stomach that makes me glance around for a garbage can. I think I might be sick.

"On our road," she murmurs. "Security found him in a ditch by tracking his phone."

"Oh, my God," I breathe out. She might not know the answer to my next question, but I have to ask it. "Is he alive?"

"Yeah," Posey says, and she squeezes my hand. "Apparently, he's really banged up. I mean, obviously. He was unconscious in a ditch."

"On our road." Was he coming to see me? He never texted me back about exchanging gifts. "I have to get to the hospital."

"Mom said she'd call us when he could have visitors." Posey follows me from the room as I hustle to my bedroom to get dressed.

"It's Nick." I shouldn't have to explain to her of all people why I need to get to him. She's the only person who even has an inkling of what's going on between us.

Posey stands in my doorway as I throw on sweats and sweep my hair into a ponytail. Hastily, I brush my teeth in the en suite. She trails me to the front door and hesitates for a second, still in her pajamas.

"Are you sure you should go without Mom calling? It's Christmas Day."

The reminder sends me back to my room to grab Nick's gift. I stare at the envelope in my hand. I purchased it months ago and wrote the inscription as soon as it arrived. Back then, I still had hope things would go back to normal between Nick and me with enough effort on both our parts. Except, only one of us has been trying.

If I don't give it to him, it feels like I'm giving up on us, and I'm not ready to do that yet. Once he's done with Vicky, we can salvage something or rebuild it, maybe. So, I fold the envelope and tuck it into the pocket of my coat. Might not look amazing when he gets it, but the sentiment is the same.

I pass Posey in the front entrance without saying a word. The air outside is crisp, and there's a thin sheen of ice on the road from the night before. I imagine Nick, driving too fast down familiar roads, and ditching his bike. Maybe my mother was right months ago that his solo trips around the island were an accident waiting to happen.

###

My mother is the first person I see when I get to the hospital. She's pacing in the waiting room, and my father is sitting to the side reading a magazine. When she catches sight of me, she stops and glances in my father's direction.

"Julia," she says. "What are you doing here?"

"Posey said Nick's hurt. Why didn't anyone wake me up?" There's a touch of anger in my voice.

She releases a deep sigh and draws me into one of the family conference rooms off to the side. As soon as the door is closed tight, she motions for me to have a seat on one of the faux leather chairs.

"I'm not sitting down," I say. "I want to see Nick."

"He's sleeping. His parents and brothers are with him."

"Why didn't anyone wake me up? It's *Nick*." I clench my hands at my sides. "Is he going to be all right?"

"Bad concussion. Broken ribs. Broken collarbone. He's lucky his phone was switched on and security, which he should have had with him in the first place, were able to track him." She smooths strands of her hair behind her ear.

I ease into the chair across from her and put my head in my hands. "Was he coming to see me?"

My mother doesn't answer, and when I glance up, her face is pinched. Whatever is going on, she doesn't want to tell me.

"Was Vicky with him?"

"No." My mother shakes her head. "He was alone."

"But he wasn't coming to see me?" That's the only logical explanation for the look on her face. There has to be more though.

"No, he wasn't. He said he was just out for a ride."

I nod. Okay, well, I don't know what to make of that, but at least he's okay.

"Can I see him?" I ask.

"Maybe when his family is done in the room." She purses her lips.

"Maybe?" I cry. "Mom, I need to see him."

She takes a deep breath and releases it. "It's my understanding that he's asked that only family... and Vicky are allowed in the room. I haven't even seen him."

Her words are a one-two punch to the gut. How many times had Nick told me he was closer to me than anyone else in his family? How many times had he proclaimed that no one would ever interfere in our friendship?

"He doesn't want to see me?" I whisper. Tears spring to my eyes.

"Sweetheart, has something happened between you two?"

"He's just so consumed with Vicky. I just—I didn't see it coming." I frame my face with my hands and stare at the white tiles on the floor.

"Is that all?" Her voice is gentle.

"Yeah." I wipe away my tears and glance up. "Yeah. Once they break up, I think things will go back to normal."

"If this is the way he's going to behave when he has a girl-friend..." My mother runs a hand along my shoulder in comfort.

The words, *he might do this to you again* float between us, but she doesn't voice them, and I won't let them land. What's happening between us right now is temporary.

"Will you give his Christmas present to him for me? Or ask someone to give it to him?" I draw the envelope out of my pocket. Maybe it's better this way. While I want him to have it, to be reminded of how close we once were, I'm not sure I can take him tossing it aside as though my heart isn't attached to it.

"You don't want to stay? He might change his mind about visitors once his head clears." My mother sinks into the chair beside me and tugs me into her side into a half-hug.

My throat closes, and I can't say anything, but I shake my head. If Nick doesn't want me here, I don't want to be here. He's going to be okay, and that's the most important thing. As long as he's okay, we can retighten the bond that's loosened between us. Patience. I just have to be patient and hold on.

"Just make sure he gets it." My voice is garbled by unshed tears.

"Oh, sweetheart," she mutters into the top of my head. She kisses my temple and squeezes me tight.

I close my eyes and let her affection provide a barrier, however thin, against Nick's careless abandonment. This isn't going to be forever. Maybe someday we'll laugh about this—remember that time you ditched me? And then we'll laugh and laugh.

But right now, all I want to do is cry.

I leave the hospital in a daze, and when I get home, Posey and I watch Christmas movies and drink too much hot chocolate.

My parents arrive home late in the day, and I ask if Nick got my present.

"He did," she says, but she doesn't meet my gaze.

Did he open it? The words stick in my throat, unasked.

For the rest of the day while we open our family presents and eat our meal, I check my phone, hoping for a message. A *thanks* or a *come see me* or anything that makes the void between us seem less deep and wide.

Not a single word arrives. When night falls, I turn off my phone and cry myself to sleep.

Nicholas

Taking a shift in the soup kitchen in the middle of Tucker's Town, the capital of Bellerive, is a PR move my father has employed multiple times over the years. Whenever we've dropped our royal butts in the shitter, he's used local outreach to drag us out. Given the lineup out the door and around the corner, I fear he might have utilized this place one time too many.

"I feel like I'm in a receiving line at a wedding," Brice says as another person comes through and congratulates me on 'making an honest woman out of Secretary Jensen.' I didn't even know people still used that expression. If Jules were here, she'd be horrified or amused. Bit of a tossup, actually.

"Should have made my wife come." I suppress my laughter at the notion of 'making' Jules do anything. Another person murmurs congratulations as they take their bowl from me, and I give them a grin. "Fabulous news, isn't it? We're looking forward to celebrating with the whole island soon."

"What's Julia been doing since you two lovebirds returned?" Brice asks while he scoops another bowl.

Me. On every conceivable surface in any spare moment we've got. We're on a sex binge, and I'm not even a little bit mad about it. Might even have a growing addiction to the feel of her naked body pressed to mine. God, I should not be thinking about her naked body right now. *Bad idea, Nick. Bad, bad idea.*

"She's working on coronation stuff," I say while offering the bowl to a well-wisher and subtly adjusting my pants with my free hand. It's a good thing I'm actually happy about who I married while too drunk to remember or this mock receiving line would be torture. "The movers are hauling all her things to my wing of the palace tonight. We're also supposed to be figuring out when we're making our marriage Bellerive official."

"All the pomp and circumstance?" Brice raises his eyebrows and fills another bowl.

Some drips over the edge, and I wipe it with a cloth before handing it over the counter. The last week since Jules and I got home has been a whirlwind of island outreach. Father wants to make sure the people of Bellerive aren't too upset about my hasty marriage, and these informal social engagements give me a chance to spread the word that there will be a royal wedding soon.

"Apparently," I say. "Have to give the people what they want."

"So you two are solid?" Brice takes a moment to banter with one of the employees about the dwindling soup and excessive line outside.

I consider his question while I ladle more liquid into bowls. "We're figuring it out."

"Traditionally, that's done *before* the wedding," he says dryly when he turns back to me.

I resist the urge to punch him in the arm since we're in public. Dad frowns on those public displays of affection. Any displays of public affection, actually. When we're out in society representing him, we're more figureheads than people.

"Alex has been in a foul mood since you announced at the royal family meeting that you're seeing this marriage through."

I ignore his comment about Alex because his feelings on my marriage aren't my problem. Whatever happened with them before is nothing compared to what will be happening between Jules and me for the rest of our lives. Perhaps that should make me more charitable. I've been him. But I'm convinced he deliberately drove a deep wedge between me and Jules. Alex and I haven't spoken since Jules and I returned last week and he caught me outside our father's office. I'm not even sure Jules has spoken to him, but with the coronation planning, she's bound to have things to discuss with him. I really wish they'd divided the secretary duties in the run-up to the coronation differently.

"I thought when the royal strategy meeting was called, we might be told the real reason Father is stepping down," I say.

"You think Julia knows?" A frown creases Brice's forehead for a beat before he looks up to grin at another customer.

"No." I answer on instinct. "She'd have told me." Maybe not at first, but the barriers between us have been coming down, brick by brick. If we're going to make this work, we have to put each other first.

When I expressed surprise my father didn't reveal the real reason he was stepping down at the meeting, Jules said that maybe he really did want to enjoy his golden years in peace. A perfect opening for her to tell me more, and she didn't. There wasn't a hint of uncertainty in her voice.

"She's still Dad's employee," Brice reminds me.

"Not for much longer."

"You're going to ask her to quit?"

"I'm not having her work for Alex," I mutter. "Besides, as my wife, she'll be engaging in charity work, community outreach, all the things we do." Every time I say 'wife', a shot of adrenaline zips through me. Marriage was never a serious consideration before Julia inserted herself back into my life. Now, *wife* is my favorite word.

"Suppose you could loop her into the foundation in Tanzania. Heard you two were flying a woman and her child over for some surgeries?"

"Elena and Bahati, yeah," I say. The line is finally starting to dwindle, and I breathe a sigh of relief. My face hurts from pasting on this fake smile each time I deliver another bowl.

We serve the last customer, and one of the workers flips the sign from open to closed. Brice and I help tidy up the kitchen and do the dishes while our security detail prowls the front. Neither of us is the type to rush away as soon as the public aspect is done.

Brice opens the dishwasher and steps back as steam pours out. "What's the deal with the surgery?"

"Two clubfeet. The waiting list for the surgery would have been two years."

"Wow." Brice shakes his head. "How old is the baby?"

"Just shy of eighteen months." I finish drying a dish, and since we've been here so many times, I slot the item back into the right place. Gus, the man who runs this place, gives me a nod of approval.

"She would have gotten the surgery eventually. I suppose that's good." He shakes out his hand when he tries to pick up a dish that's still too hot from the washing tray.

"The mother-in-law suggested to Bahati that Elena might be better off not existing at all."

"Infanticide?" Brice leans against the counter and crosses his arms. "Illegal, but I don't doubt it still happens some places."

"People break laws all the time."

"Desperation. Backed into a corner." He sighs and runs a hand through his short brown hair. "The older I get, the more I appreciate how life is rarely black or white. We live in the gray areas."

We finish the cleanup in silence and then shake Gus's hand before following our security out the front door.

"I can't imagine feeling such despair that ending a life is the right choice—especially the life of a family member," Brice says once we're in the back of the car. "Makes me want to save them all. If only we could."

"Luckily," I say, "Bahati didn't follow the mother-in-law's advice, and Julia's bleeding heart led us right to them."

"When do they arrive?"

"Next week. Kafil, my guide from Tanzania, is coming to act as a translator. Seemed the easiest way to make sure everyone felt comfortable and safe." Julia suggested Kafil when we were struggling to find a proficient translator on the island. What was one more plane ticket?

"Maybe you should expand your Bellerive foundation there to encompass some of these surgeries with long wait lists."

"The idea has crossed my mind. I was going to ask Jules if she wanted to help run it."

Brice chuckles. "Why not? She's already an integral member. Considering the idea was originally hers, I can't imagine she'd turn the opportunity down."

"I'm not entirely sure how attached she is to the secretary position." In Tanzania, she implied she fell into the job and never left. But watching her organize and plan the coronation has made me appreciate how good she is. Just because she didn't intend to do the job forever doesn't mean she isn't invested in the work.

"Yet another thing to figure out," Brice teases.

The list does seem substantial and never-ending at the moment. Why wouldn't it? Julia and I have only been back in each other's lives for a few weeks. We went from barely speaking to married. Bound to be some adjustments. Nothing to worry about.

"We'll be fine," I say. "As long as we're honest with each other, we'll be fine."

###

Julia is doing what she does best—directing the chaos. Movers are streaming in with suitcases of her clothes, personal items, and a few pieces of furniture. Most of what she owns is going into one of the royal storage facilities until we decide whether we're staying here or inhabiting one of the vacant houses on the estate. My vote is for a fresh start on the property after a quick reno. Julia has been more reluctant to commit, and I'm trying not to let her lack of enthusiasm bother me.

She agreed to stay married to me, and she can't keep her hands off me when we're alone. I can't expect everything to fall into place with a snap of my fingers.

Although I always thought I was the only one hurt the night of my father's birthday, I've realized we both bear those scars. Fighting my attraction and trying to snuff out my love for Julia burned us both. Our fire blazed too hot to be contained.

So many stupid mistakes.

I'm not making any more. So if she needs time to adjust to this whirlwind we've spun ourselves into, I'm not going to let uncertainty get a foothold in me. She said what she once felt for me can be recovered. Stay the course. I know what I want, and right now I've got it. Don't fuck up. Simple.

"Is it all too much?" Jules comes to stand beside me. She crosses her arms and bites her lip as more suitcases flow into the walk-in closet. Her silky shirt, which is begging for me to touch it, is distracting. What's underneath her pencil skirt? I'm torn between hoping for commando and realizing my mental health is in trouble if she's not wearing anything.

As for her stuff, she could literally back the moving truck up here and dump it all. I wouldn't blink an eye as long as there was a surface to perch her ass on or bend her over while I find way number five to make her come so hard and fast she takes God's name in vain. Just the thought makes me hard.

"No, I don't see a problem," I say with a hint of a smile as I peruse her from head to toe. Definitely panties. She's been working.

"Get your mind out of the gutter." She smacks me in the chest.

"How do you know it's in the gutter?" I eye her with amusement.

She slides in front of me and pretends to observe the movers while her other hand reaches around her back to stroke me through my jeans.

She's swept her hair into a ponytail at some point today, and her neck is exposed. Licking my way up might be a tad obvious with an audience. She's likely to squeal. Instead, I lean down and scrape my teeth along her earlobe. Goosebumps rise on her arms.

The soft sigh she releases is barely audible, but I know exactly what's going on underneath her clothes. Pert nipples. Dampness between her thighs.

When she turns in my arms, and I see the heat in her gaze, I could care less about movers or furniture or any of her things. *Naked.* She needs to be naked. I'm going to help her climb a mountain and then observe, fascinated, as she topples over it. Watching Jules come is my favorite pastime.

I nuzzle her nose with mine and hover my lips a hair's breadth from hers. When she tries to tug me into a kiss, I sidestep her.

"Tease," she mutters.

"Thank you very much, gentlemen," I say, striding toward the movers. "Shouldn't be too much more. You can leave the rest in the hallway. My wife and I will bring it in later."

When the four movers exchange skeptical glances, I say, "We have some very urgent royal business to discuss."

One of the movers smirks, but he doesn't say anything except offer me a salute and send an appraising glance Julia's way. Suppose I'll have to get used to other people thinking my wife is hot. Can't decide if that'll suck or not. Thank God she literally has my name tattooed on her body.

As the last one shuffles out, I snap the locks into place. When I turn to face Jules, there's a wicked glint to her expression. I love it.

"Urgent royal business to discuss?" Jules widens her eyes in mock concern. "Did something come up?"

"There's a rising concern." I prowl toward her.

"Will it be hard to navigate?" She traces the ridge of my erection and gazes up at me.

"We've got to get some rocks off. You can handle that, can't you?" I kiss her temple and feather kisses along her hairline. Her silky shirt floats around my hands, and I slip it over her head and toss it toward a chair.

"Mmm." She undoes the button on my jeans and unzips my fly. "Probably needs my full attention to satisfy all parties."

"The party is just a little lower," I say when she traces the edge of my boxer briefs. I unsnap her bra and send it sailing toward her shirt.

She leans back to make eye contact. "The party is in your pants? That's the best you could do?"

I lift her up and carry her to the bed, tossing her into the middle. "It's a very fun party."

She giggles and crawls back toward me on her hands and knees.

Fucking hell. My brain better be recording this in high resolution for later. I toss my shirt over my head, and when she meets me at the edge of the bed on her knees, I frame her face and kiss her. After being home with her for a week and getting to do this every spare moment, it's still surreal. The dream has become the reality.

I'm a lucky fucker.

"I was worried," Jules says, her voice breathless, "that the party might need some resuscitation."

My lips quirk into a partial smile. Her comment could be offensive or lead into something else I'm definitely not turning down. "A little mouth to mouth might be in order." I kiss her again.

"Mouth to mouth?" she murmurs.

"Mouth to dick might breed more success."

She laughs and pushes my pants and boxers to the floor. "Mouth to dick? Could get explosive."

"Here's hoping."

She's still laughing when she eases me between her luscious lips, and within a few swirls of her tongue, neither of us is in a talking mood anymore. I'm grateful to her ponytail for the second time while I watch her slide up and down my shaft. The clear visual coupled with her rhythmic hand, mouth, and tongue, and I'm in danger of having a very short fuse today. As much as I love this, there's nothing better than sinking into her and hearing her moan of satisfaction.

Then there's the way she looks at me as though she's exactly where she wants to be—under me, on top of me, backed up against me—her expression soothes the lingering ache I try to pretend isn't there. Can't spend fourteen years believing something and get over it in a week.

"Jules," I hiss when she rolls her tongue along my tip. "If you keep doing that, I'm not going to last."

"Isn't that the point," she murmurs before licking up my shaft.

I chuckle. "I think the party has moved to your pussy."

"A pussy party?" Jules strokes me and kisses her way up my body and along my neck to my earlobe. "Sounds juicy."

"Let's find out, shall we?" I push her back on the bed and make quick work of her skirt only to discover that she wasn't wearing underwear. "Jules," I groan and run my lips across her hip bones. "I'll be walking around the palace with a permanent hardon if there's a chance you're panty-less under your skirts."

"Perhaps we'll run into each other in empty corridors a little more often," she breathes out while her fingers dig into my hair.

She knows what's coming, and I bet anticipation has made her soaking wet with need. I run a finger up her center and suck in a sharp breath. So wet.

"Please, Nick." She squirms under my hands.

"How do you want it?" I rasp, and my lips are inches from her clit.

"Make me beg for it."

I grin just before I cover her with my mouth. My favorite.

Julia

Nick is my drug, and I am an addict. There's no other explanation for the sex haze I've been walking around in for the last two weeks. Fourteen years of pent-up sexual frustration have been released on the world. Or at least all over Nick's wing of the palace.

I can't even remember the last relationship I was in where we had this much sex.

Never.

I think never is the answer.

Which is great, right? We're sexually compatible. From our first kiss, there wasn't much of a doubt in my mind, but it's good to have it confirmed—over and over and over again.

Except, we've been so busy mapping each other's bodies that we haven't set a wedding date, haven't talked about Alex in any more depth, haven't delved into jobs or kids or any of the practical things most married couples should discuss *before* the wedding. We're married, but I'm not sure we're *ready* to be married. We're in the honeymoon stage of the honeymoon stage.

The minute Nick steps into a room, my brain short circuits, and all I can think about is him. Actually, my brain might be losing the plot in general. He takes up at least 85% of my mental capacity on any given day whether or not he's within my line of sight.

But when we're not together, I remember all the things we haven't decided, and anxiety creeps in. Then there's his father's illness. Initially, I didn't loathe keeping King George's secret because Nick and I weren't close. My allegiance, my loyalty, lay with the king. But now? I have no idea what the right path is. Keeping the secret from Nick is wrong, but I don't know why the king hasn't told his children. Multiple times in the last few weeks I've anticipated a family meeting and a reveal, and each time he's given us something trivial or obvious instead of addressing the elephant in the room.

The press caught wind of the coronation itself but the reason, the real reason, is still buried. For how long? Since he consulted multiple doctors, it seems impossible that one nosey, driven reporter won't root out the truth.

I haven't had a chance to speak to the king alone either. There's always someone else in the room, and I'm never sure how much other people know. If I haven't blurted the truth out to Nick, I can't be careless with other family and staff.

To keep my mind off everything else, I've been going through the coronation to-do list to set things in motion, but I definitely haven't been at the top of my game. So many things are distracting me from my job, which never used to happen.

Also, I've been avoiding Alex.

Every time he appears in a corridor or a room I'm in, I duck in somewhere else or claim a commitment elsewhere. It's not just that Nick wouldn't like me confiding or confessing to Alex, it's also that Alex is likely to be upset with me. Whether he's hurt or furious, I don't want to face it.

I'm hustling past the door to his office on the way to a meeting when his door pops open. He stands in the entrance for a second, staring at me. While I'm tempted to hide my face and keep walking, that's not exactly the most mature response.

"Are you going to talk to me now?" He scowls.

"I have a meeting."

"It's not for an hour." He opens the door to his office wider. "I'm going to the same meeting."

Of course he is since it's about royal protocol leading up to the coronation. We're supposed to be figuring out an appropriate time to slide in a royal wedding ahead of the coronation. King George thinks the optics look better if we marry before Alex takes over as king.

But that's not the meeting I was rushing to. I booked myself in for a private conversation with the king. Telling Alex that will open a whole other line of questioning I'm not prepared to answer. A quick meeting with Alex, and I won't be too late to meet with King George. He's often running behind anyway.

With a sigh, I step into Alex's office, but I don't take a seat. This conversation could go about a million ways, but every single one of them will probably feel like being put through a meatgrinder.

He slides behind his desk into his leather chair and eyes me for a minute.

He's making me feel like I'm in the principal's office.

"You've been avoiding me," Alex drawls.

"I've been busy. Being gone for a few weeks left a lot on my plate."

"Seems like you're calling your mother incompetent. Wasn't she looking after all your duties while you were off playing the tourist with my brother?"

I purse my lips.

"I know my father said you and Nick had decided to ride out your marital blunder, but if you're being pressured by him or by Nick to stay married, I can annul it as soon as I'm king. We can delay this whole date-setting idiocy today. I've got no problem cutting that off." He taps a pen on his desk and stares me down.

Annoyance and sympathy war in me. While he hasn't said a word to me in years about wanting to marry me, I've been aware of what he'd like to see happen. When he visited me in college, I made it clear I didn't want what he was offering. But as I know all too well, the heart can't be reasoned with.

We *have* been friends with varying levels of closeness over the years, which is why I'll entertain at least a bit of this conversation.

"I don't want an annulment, Alex."

"Are you being pressured to stay married to him?" He leans forward and gestures to one of the chairs.

I'm not sitting. This conversation isn't going to be a long one. Nick would hate that I'm in here. "I'm not. This is my choice."

"You've been speaking to him for a few weeks and that's enough to build a marriage on? I remember when you told me you'd never get married. And in the unlikely event you did, you'd never marry into the royal family because you didn't want the social pressures, the scrutiny."

"I was eighteen. People are allowed to change their minds." At the time, I was angry with Nick, and I didn't think gaining his love was even possible. I already knew I didn't want Alex's attention, at least not in that way. Telling him anything different, even at eighteen, felt dangerous. He was pinning expectations on me that I didn't want. He still is.

Alex stands up and shoves his hands into the pockets of his suit pants and stares out the window. "I've been hoping you'd change your mind, but this wasn't what I expected."

"I've been very honest with you, haven't I?" Maybe I led him on that summer, but I tried so hard to keep boundaries between us after that. Yes, we've been friends, but I never accepted any of his romantic overtures.

"Do you love him?" He turns to face me.

Yes. There's not a single doubt in my mind, but I haven't even said the words to Nick, so I definitely can't give them to Alex.

Besides, Alex will probably laugh at me. In love with Nick after such a short time? He'd label it lust or unlikely, as though I'm still some naïve schoolgirl.

This isn't my first experience with love. I've loved other men or thought I did, but never with the depth I once loved Nick. Nick's been in my heart, dormant, for years. What's happening between us now is a reawakening. My heart is coming out of hibernation after a long winter. It feels good to embrace the sun. We knew each other so completely. I want that back with him, and I think we can get it. He hurt me. He hurt me so badly. But the pain is receding, and the scars are fading.

"Nick wouldn't be okay with us having this conversation. There are things that I can't share with you. We can't be each other's confidants anymore."

"So you marry Nick and stop being my friend?" He squints at me in disbelief.

I can't tell him Nick doesn't like him. Alex has told me he regrets they aren't close, and he doesn't understand why Nick prefers Brice. Becoming their go-between won't help any of us.

A different tactic is needed and given all the pieces to the puzzle I've slotted into place since Nick and I started to talk things through, I've got some questions of my own.

"The night of your father's birthday, the summer we were together, did you see Nick? Did you know Nick saw us?" The way Alex kissed me the second time never felt right to me, but I couldn't pinpoint why.

He turns back to the window and doesn't say anything for a beat. "It was dark. I have no idea what he saw or didn't see."

That's as close to a confirmation as I'll ever get from Alex.

"I need to go." I head for the door. Alex must have suspected that second kiss is what blew Nick and me apart, and he never said a word to me. Never even hinted at Nick discovering our aborted affair.

He follows me, hot on my heels. When I throw open the door, he grabs my elbow. "That's it?"

"He saw us," I hiss. "And you knew. You saw me absolutely gutted, bewildered at the loss of Nick's friendship, and you didn't say a word." I wrench my arm free. "I'm not sure we were ever friends. I think you've been biding your time, hoping I'd change my mind. But I haven't. I won't."

"You and Nick didn't work then. You're not going to work now either." His expression is a mixture of anger and frustration.

"We never had a chance," I say. "You made sure of that."

I take a step away from him, determined to put this conversation behind me.

"No." He reaches for me again, spinning me toward him almost into his arms. "No, the outcome wasn't my fault. I took advantage of an opening, but it existed because you two weren't honest with each other. Just like neither of you were honest with me. Don't lay your foolish behavior at my feet."

I grit my teeth to keep from lashing out at him. "We're not the same people."

"No?" He searches my face. "You've told Nick *everything* you know?"

When I flush, he shakes his head. Does that mean Alex knows about his father's illness? If that's true, why isn't the king telling Nick and Brice?

"You're still keeping secrets." He scoffs.

"She doesn't need to share her secrets with you," Nick says, and I jump at the sound of his voice down the hallway.

How much did he hear? My pulse thunders in my ears. How do I explain Alex's comment?

"Apparently, she doesn't need to share them with anyone," Alex says, raising his eyebrows, but he doesn't let go of my forearm.

"Do we need to have a talk about how you treat a woman?" Nick's voice is deceptively quiet as he prowls closer. "About how you treat my *wife*?"

"You do love throwing that word around." Alex releases my arm. "You always claimed possessive men turned you off," he says to me while straightening the sleeves of his suit jacket.

"His emphasis was on the title, not the possession." When I leave Alex's side to stride over to Nick, he loops an arm around my waist and kisses my temple. He must not have heard the whole conversation or I'm sure I'd sense some tension in him. His lips linger on my skin, and my stomach flutters.

"Should we go back to our wing of the house?" Nick bends to murmur against my ear.

He's acting like this mostly because of Alex. Despite what I said, Nick *is* being possessive. But I don't mind since I feel equally possessive of him. Either way, I can't be their favorite toy to fight over for the next months or years or however long this animosity lasts.

"I have to be somewhere," I say, drawing away from Nick. "I'll see you at the scheduling meeting in an hour. Maybe you should take this time to speak to Alex? Clear the air?" I keep my voice low because if Nick turns down the idea, I don't need to add more fuel to their sibling fire.

"I don't see why I would. It's smog. There's no clarity to be found." He laces his fingers with mine, but he doesn't meet my gaze.

"Can you try?" I give him a hopeful look and go on my toes to kiss his cheek. His jaw is clenched, and I run my hand along the bearded edge. "You're brothers, and we're going to exist in the same family forever."

"Forever, huh?" He peers down at me, and a hint of amusement undercuts his obvious anger at Alex.

"Please," I say again.

Nick glances over my shoulder, and then he gives a curt nod. "I think it's pointless, but I'll do it."

I grasp his face and give him a quick kiss before dashing down the hall to meet with the king. My heart is beating erratically. While I need them to get over their one-upmanship for the sake of the whole royal family, I'm terrified Alex will tell Nick about their father before I have a chance to speak to the king.

I've known the king is dying for weeks, and I haven't told Nick. Alex has a point—I'm still keeping secrets with dire consequences.

Nick

Fourteen years ago

After being in the hospital since sometime early this morning, I thought I'd be used to the antiseptic smell. The assault on my senses only seems to be getting worse now that I'm finally alone, and my stomach rolls with renewed anxiety.

Of course, it's been rolling since I woke up in here. The actual accident is a blank space. The last thing I remember is leaving the royal property on my motorcycle.

Shortly after I regained consciousness, Vicky showed up smelling as though she showered in perfume. Alex called her, apparently. She threw herself across me to sob about how I could have died, and she's just so grateful I'm alive.

She cried more than my mother and Gran combined. I would have preferred she not come at all.

I'm starting to worry the scales between us have tipped, and she's way more invested than I am. How that can be, I'm not sure. We barely speak to each other about anything beyond school. She doesn't know me. Nothing important, anyway.

It's that last thought that's been on repeat in my head for months now. No one knows me.

While I'm always surrounded by people—workers, cling-ons, media, staff, family, friends—I've never felt particularly close to more than a handful of them. The lack of authentic connections didn't bother me before because I had Jules.

But I haven't had her, not really, for months. I'm spiraling, sinking, drowning in a loneliness so deep that I'm worried I won't be able to crawl out. There's a constant, aching heaviness, and sometimes it's so solid, I almost can't breathe.

"Nicholas?" My gran, the queen of Bellerive, calls from the doorway.

I glance up and give her a hint of a smile. "Still here," I say.

She steps into the room, immaculately dressed in her typical blazer and skirt even though she was woken in the dead of night, and she closes the door. Alex inherited her midnight eyes and black hair. Though her hair has gone silver with age, her eyes are just as sharp.

"I wanted a chance to speak to you alone without all the fuss of other people."

I'm certain she means Vicky, and another wave of sadness washes over me. Gran has always liked Julia. I'm sure she'd be delighted to realize Julia and Alex are together. The thought turns my stomach.

She comes close to the edge of my bed and pats the spot where my knee lies under the blankets. My legs got off fairly well, all things considered. Some bruises, but no breaks.

Her gaze bores into me. "You haven't seemed like yourself for quite a while now."

I flush, and my pulse pounds in my skull. A headache sits at the edges, waiting to take over. There's nothing honest I can say in return to ease her mind. I haven't been myself. No one knows me, and I don't even know myself.

"We've all been very busy this fall and winter season with diplomatic trips, but you haven't gone unnoticed. It seems to me that something has happened between you and Julia. While the two of you were once like twin souls, she's hardly around anymore. Is that your choice or hers?"

Trust my gran to cut to the quick. She's spent her whole life reading people and navigating their moods.

"We've just drifted apart." My voice is rough from ill use. Everyone has been so busy talking about their own feelings since I woke up that I've hardly had to say a word.

Her expression turns assessing. "Perhaps." She lets out a sigh. "And perhaps it was always meant to go this way. That sort of closeness is often reserved for romantic relationships as we grow older. You have been spending more time with that Vicky girl."

Does she realize how close she is to drilling into the truth?

When I don't respond, she puts the back of her hand to my forehead. "Cool, perhaps a bit too cold," she says, drawing her hand away. "Alex is our granite, and Brice is our putty. You've always fallen somewhere in between. Hard on the outside, but soft on the inside, like a walnut. It's okay to let the softness show, Nicholas. Sometimes it leaks out of us, even when we don't want it to."

Tears flood my vision, but I can't look at her. Instead, I focus on my hands folded on top of the white hospital sheets.

"It's nothing," I say.

"Oh, on the contrary, your poor heart is breaking about something. Talk to me, Nicholas. I see you. Talk to me." She strokes my hair and then squeezes my hand. "Give your gran your problems. Might lighten your load."

I sniff and run the heels of my hands under my eyes. Crying solves nothing. "It's not Vicky," I say. "Julia is dating someone I don't approve of."

"Have you told Jules this?"

"If she's happy, it's none of my business. She doesn't need my approval."

She takes in a long, deep breath. "I suppose in many ways, that's true. You don't like hearing about her boyfriend?"

"That's not it," I say. Though that might be the problem if Julia ever told me about Alex in the first place. "We're just." I clear my throat when it threatens to close. "We're growing further and further apart, and I don't know how to stop it."

"You miss her friendship," Gran says.

She's so close to guessing what I haven't told anyone. So, I meet her gaze, and I hold it. She searches my tear-stained face, and her expression softens.

"Oh," she says. "I see."

Goosebumps rise across my skin, and I break eye contact to stare at my lap again. "Yeah."

"Does she know?" Gran asks.

"Yeah," I say. "That's not what she wants."

"That certainly explains how cool you are with Vicky."

Am I? Distant, maybe. "I know you don't like her."

"On the contrary, I like her just fine. I've never been completely convinced *you* like her."

I flush. Her observation causes shame to rise in me. There's nothing wrong with Vicky, and I hate that she might feel used when this is over between us. But I *am* using her, and I can't bring myself to stop just yet.

"It's that obvious," I say.

"Maybe not to some. Doesn't seem obvious to her. Which also might be a concern." She straightens my covers with a little tug. "You and Julia have always glowed around each other, and being in a room with the two of you was like being a step behind, one inside joke short of the punchline. Are you absolutely certain that Julia doesn't return your feelings?"

Alex sweeping Julia into his arms a second time flashes in front of my eyes. Her saying, 'Oh, shit. Oh, God. Oh, no' when we stopped kissing still rings in my ears. Obviously, the kiss was terrible, or she didn't want it. She ran, literally ran, to Alex.

The smell of champagne makes me nauseous, and I haven't been up to the roof of the barn or even inside it since that night. When I walk past the building, I can't even look at it. A place that once brought me so much joy is tarnished beyond repair.

It's not even that she's chosen someone else, though that would be bad on its own.

Alex.

Anger and frustration well up in me. Of all the people on the island she could have chosen, she picked him. On top of that, she hasn't even had the guts to tell me. Every day that passes, the pressure in my chest grows. Tick. Tick. Tick. Like a bomb. When will it explode?

"Yeah," I say. "I'm sure."

She cups my cheek. "If you ever need to sit or just let the sadness show, you come see me. My door is always open to you, Nicholas." She fixes a stray strand of my hair. "The first time your heart breaks, it can feel a bit like dying."

Jules and I used to make fun of characters in books and movies and TV shows whose heartbreak seemed over the top. Neither of us could believe that a simple breakup could wreck someone. I'm not laughing anymore, and breakups don't seem so simple.

"Thanks, Gran," I say.

From the purse hanging off her arm, she takes out a folded envelope. "Secretary Jensen said Julia wanted you to have this, and she wanted to wish you Merry Christmas as well. Would you like me to stay while you open it?"

"Jules was here?"

"Her younger sister informed her about your accident." Gran purses her lips.

"No one told me she was here." My voice is gruff.

"Would you have wanted to see her?"

A simple question with such a complex answer. More than anyone. Even right now, I want to see her face more than I want to see anyone's. If someone had told me she came, I wouldn't have been able to resist.

But things aren't the same between us, and every time we're together, our new reality hardens from cement into concrete. Unless I can stop wishing for things that'll never happen, we can't go back to the way we were. There has to be a way to get over her.

I try to shrug and wince at the pain.

"Would you like me to stay while you open it?" she asks again.

I shake my head. No words will move past my lips for the lump in my throat. My name in Jules's swirling cursive is scrawled across the front. She'll never know about what I intended to give her, and I'm not sure what to replace it with.

The door to my room clicks closed with my gran's departure. I wipe the tears that won't stop spilling from my eyes, and I slide my index finger under the envelope flap. Slowly, I peel it back.

A bright pamphlet in pinks and browns falls out, and there's a square card too.

Warmth spreads across my chest at what she's done. Jules sponsored a girl in Tanzania for a year under the name J.N.

Bellerive. It's not an international organization but one based in Dodoma, the capital of Tanzania. She must have spent quite a bit of time researching just the right charity to use. The loss of her as a friend, a confidant, settles deeper inside me.

The square card is folded, and I flip it open, taking in Julia's neat handwriting without focusing on the words.

Nick,

I feel like I write the same thing every year. What do you get for the guy who's got everything? So, I'm going a little sappy, but meaningful, I hope.

We gotta start somewhere, right? One girl this year in Tanzania, and someday hundreds or maybe thousands of people will benefit from your open heart. I've got dibs on a front-row seat. You're going to be amazing.

Merry Christmas!

Love, Jules

I read the note over and over, and the words swim around the card. The tone is so lighthearted, so easy, as though we'll always be the best of friends. When did she write this? We haven't felt like these people in months, at least not to me.

She wrote *love*, but it's not the kind of love I want from her. Whatever switch flipped inside me, I have to find it and smash it.

We can't go on like this, can we? It's killing me.

I want my best friend back.

I don't want to care that she's screwing Alex.

I want her to be honest with me.

I never want to hear her say she's in love with Alex.

I want her to love me the way I love her.

The last thought breaks me, and the sob I've been holding in for hours, days, *months* rushes out and into the quiet of the hospital room. I curl into myself, the card clutched in my hand.

If she has a front seat to my life, it'll most likely be in a chair beside Alex. My heart, which is already cracked, shatters at the thought.

Alex will never let her go. Why would he ever let her go?

Nicholas

Julia's heels click down the tiled hall, and while I'd normally watch her go—one of my favorite views—turning my back on Alex feels more dangerous than normal.

"You don't have anywhere to be?" Alex asks. "Your wife isn't so keen on you amusing yourself with crown bunnies, I suspect."

Ah, my favorite term back in play. Alex wouldn't have come up with that on his own. It's a Julia expression, which means they've talked about me before. The idea of them sharing confidences makes me irrationally angry.

Every scrap she gave Alex should have been mine.

"I've always done more than galivant around the world, despite what you might think."

"Yes, I heard about your latest venture in Tanzania. Cute name for your foundation, by the way."

I can't tell if it's rage or a hint of embarrassment that causes my chest to heat. I'd love to fire whoever fed Alex the information on my charity and what I named it.

How can I have such an intense dislike for my brother? Isn't there supposed to be some hero worship at play? TV shows, movies, and books always make the younger sibling look up to the older one. If I ever did, I don't remember it.

"Was there something you wanted to discuss?" Alex asks, gesturing toward his office. "Or are we done here?"

I rub my temples and think of Jules. She's right. We can't keep on this way, but I'm afraid if I go into that office, Alex and I will come to blows. What's worse? Veiled dislike or open hostility?

I step around him into his office, but I don't sit down. At least I'll be able to tell her I honestly tried.

"You and Jules seem to have an aversion to chairs today," Alex says as he takes his seat behind his desk. "They're perfectly comfortable, I assure you."

"She was in here?" The question escapes before I can reign it in. The two of them alone with the door closed grates on me.

"Yes." Alex meets my gaze but doesn't say anything more.

He's probably counting on my imagination and insecurity running wild where Jules is concerned. I hate that both are flaring to life inside me. She doesn't want him—never has.

"Jules and I are married now. We're staying married. We have a meeting in less than an hour to set our public wedding date." I glare at him. "You can't win her around anymore. She's been won and not by you."

"Does she know you talk about her like an object?"

I clench my jaw. He's not dragging me into some feminist argument he probably doesn't even care about. He'll say anything to gain the upper hand. "She's going to be part of this family as my wife. Whatever feelings you're harboring for her, you need to let them go."

"You know Jules never wanted to get married. Said the idea of marriage was an antiqued institution meant to dominate women."

My instinct is to become defensive. Instead, I take a deep breath. That sounds like college Jules. I might not have been particularly close to her, but I hovered enough around the edges to see the changes in her. That was her bitter and disenfranchised phase. She hated marriage, and she hated me. Flipped that on its head, didn't I?

"Guess she changed her mind. People do that." I shrug and then hold up a finger as I reconsider. "Some people do that. You've been the same asshole for years."

"*I'm* the asshole?" Alex splays a hand over his chest. "Me? The one upholding every single commitment in Bellerive and abroad for years? The one who's never had even an inch of the freedom you have? You and Brice team up against me, go on trips together, have inside jokes, mock me openly—despite the two of you dragging Bellerive's name through the mud—I'm the asshole?" He rises and leans across the broad desk. "I'm not the asshole here."

"Nobody gives a shit about any of that except for you," I huff.

"Right. Because I have to. What choice do I have? Once Dad's gone, I'm the one in charge. I don't have the luxury of fucking off or fucking up. Whereas you can run off to the Serengeti this year, Nepal last year, and the middle of Australia the year before. Gone for weeks, and none of us dare to contact you. You get away with it because Mom and Dad feel sorry for you. Poor Nicky born into wealth and privilege. Must be so hard for him." His gaze bores into me. "You go to Vegas and get married on a whim and no one bats an eye." Alex lets out a frustrated grunt.

"You wouldn't care, either, except that I happened to get married to Jules."

"*Happened* to get married to her? Even the way you talk about your wedding is careless." He circles the desk so it's no longer between us. "Neither of you even remembers getting married. It's a farce. A sham. I bet I know her just as well if not better than you do."

His comment stings. Is he right?

"What do you know about her anymore? Next to nothing, I bet." Alex mocks.

"If it wasn't for you, I'd never have stopped knowing her," I grit out. He's wrong. Just because I wasn't at her side doesn't mean I stopped noticing her. I never stopped noticing her, tracking her in a room, and listening for any snippet of news on her life.

"That's my fault? How do you figure?" Alex snatches a pen off his desk and twirls it around his fingers. "I asked you and her point-blank, several times, if there was anything going on between you. If you want to know what she told me, all you have to do is think back to what *you* told me. The two of you swore up and down you were 'best friends' and any romantic connection was ludicrous." He shakes his head. "How do I become the villain in that scenario? I certainly didn't chain Jules to my bed all those long afternoons. She *came* willingly."

My hand is already clenched at my side, and when he glances at me, the implication of his words is solidified. Yeah, he's fucking talking about bringing my wife to orgasm. *Motherfucker.*

So, I hit him. Hard. My fist rams into his jaw and cheek. There's a satisfying crunch, and he stumbles back.

His hand covers his cheek, and he eyes me from farther away. He wipes his face, and a hint of a smirk plays at the edge of his lips. He works his jaw. I hope a massive bruise blooms for everyone to see and for him to explain in meetings and in front of the press. Every time he's forced to explain, he'll remember I'm the one who put it there.

"You're better at that than when we were kids," he says.

"Been in a few bar fights with all that freedom I've gotten." Also trended on social media for having a mean right hook.

"How could I forget? I was probably off at some diplomatic event while you were getting drunk in a bar." He stares at me for a beat. "You can hate what happened between me and Jules, but you can't change it."

"You should take your own advice." I tip my chin at him. "She chose me."

"Was it a real choice when she was drunk and didn't know any better? Somehow, I don't think so."

"Why can't you just let it go?" I burst out.

"Because I've been the one *here* with her for the last fourteen years while you've been off doing whatever and whoever."

"Don't pretend like you don't know the things I do for Bellerive and for our diplomatic relationships. It's literally my job, just like you." I throw out my hands. "You act like you don't want the responsibility of being first in line when you've been rubbing it in my face and Brice's face since you were old enough to talk."

"I offered her an annulment." He gives me a bland look.

He's put the desk between us again, which is smart because he just keeps ratcheting up my anger. "Why? Do you think if she gets an annulment from me she'll consider an offer from you? I have a feeling she's already rejected all those propositions." I let out a mocking chuckle. "Talk about a scandal."

A muscle in Alex's jaw tics. "Deep down, she doesn't want what you're offering the same way she didn't want what I offered. She's banking on old memories and a lost connection. At some point, neither of those will be enough to satisfy her."

"Oh, trust me, she's *completely* satisfied."

Alex grimaces before turning away from me. "For now. One of you is going to fuck this up." He slides me a glance over his shoulder. "I'll wait."

I shake my head in disbelief. "You'd rather betray me than support me? Is that really where we've landed?"

"Have we ever supported each other?" He faces me, frustration spilling out of him. "The only person who has consistently been there for me is Julia. For years. You and Brice have fucked off at every opportunity and never gave a shit how I felt about anything."

"You haven't exactly made it easy to give a shit about you. Case in point—right now, you're threatening to steal my wife. That's fucked up, Alex. Even for you."

"I imagine I see the same qualities in her that you do. She understands this"—he gestures around himself—"lifestyle. On top of that, she's loyal, trustworthy, clever, gorgeous—"

"And also *my* wife."

"I notice the emphasis is on a different word this time."

"Yeah, because you're not getting it. Any minute now I expect you to sputter 'fake news' every time I say 'my wife' as though this is some kind of political maneuver instead of our lives."

"Our lives *are* a series of political maneuvers." Alex lets out a frustrated huff. "You've just never been particularly good at political strategy. But this isn't a strategy. With such a public declaration of your drunken marriage, I won't be with Jules."

My level of frustration with him keeps rising. Why can't he understand she doesn't want him?

"You're going to hurt her," Alex says. "She doesn't deserve that."

"I'm not going to hurt her," I rail. "I love her. I would never hurt her." The words are out before I can even consider whether I should have told Alex. I haven't even had the guts to tell Jules.

"We'll see." Alex eyes me. "You've never been very good at forgiveness."

My phone beeps with the reminder of the meeting to set the date for our wedding. I shake my head and stare at him. What I'm about to say has nothing to do with Jules, and I hope he hears me. He might be my brother, but he'll never be my friend.

"Sometimes," I say, "there's just too much to forgive."

Julia

While I make my way down the corridor to the king's office, I pray that Nick and Alex can put to rest some of their animosity toward each other. If I understood all the consequences of being with Alex all those years ago, I never would have done it. The wedge between Nick and me wasn't the only one that grew exponentially. Alex and Nick are very different, but I wonder if I've become the reason they don't get along. The thought turns my stomach.

The king's door is partially ajar when I arrive, and I run my knuckles along the wood lightly to signal my arrival. He glances up from the papers on his desk and smiles.

"Julia! Come in. Come in."

All the awkwardness of 'Surprise! I married your son' faded once Nick and I confirmed we would stay married. The king is more forgiving when a massive royal scandal becomes a minor blip in the history books. Our Las Vegas wedding might even make for a funny story someday… not sure who'll be telling it since neither of us has produced a clear memory. We do have lots of very poorly taken photos on camera phones though. Always a bright side.

Except right now.

Is there a bright side to trying to force the king to reveal his terminal illness to his kids? I can't see one.

After I've closed the door tight behind me, I slide into the leather chair across from him, a seat I've grown familiar with over the last few years. While I was sometimes the bearer of bad news, I've never had to confront the king about anything. He's always been logical and reasonable in his approach to governing and his role in the monarchy.

"What are we discussing today?" He draws out his calendar, expecting more notes on coronation business.

Already, I can sense he's not going to take this well.

"I was hoping we could discuss your illness."

"My illness?" He raises his eyebrows in surprise.

We haven't said one word to each other about it since I returned. If he thought I forgot, he's mistaken. Talking about it openly feels like a betrayal of Nick's trust in me. So, I've been avoiding it, pretending it's not true since we returned. Just like he has.

But I can't keep doing that because my clandestine dalliance with Alex ruined us once, and I won't let a second monstrous secret destroy what we're rebuilding.

"Yes," I say. Do I have the guts to push this as far and hard as I might need to?

"Do you have a question about the diagnosis?" He laces his fingers together on his desk.

"No." I take a deep breath and slowly exhale. "Does Alex know?"

"Why?" His hazel eyes, so much like Nick's narrow.

"A comment he made to me."

The king doesn't say anything.

He's not going to make this easy for me. "I think if Alex knows, which is the reason you gave for not telling your boys, that Nick and Brice should be told as well."

"They will be," he says with a wave of his hand.

"When?"

"In good time." He leans back in his chair and runs a hand down his face. "Now is not the time. The wedding. The coronation."

"With all due respect—"

"Is that all you came for?" He rises and gestures toward the closed door.

"King George—"

"I do not need your counsel, Secretary Jensen. This is not your place."

"It is my place. It's become my place. Nick is my husband now. I can't—I won't lie to him."

"I haven't asked you to lie." King George scoffs. "I've simply asked you not to tell him."

"He'll see it as a lie. Trust me. Believe me. He will not forgive me for this."

"Of course he will." King George comes around the desk to stand beside me. "He loves you. It's been written all over that boy's face for years. Every time he looks at you, it leaks out of him. He'd forgive you anything."

Since I'm not about to get into what happened with Alex, I can't directly disprove him. Despite how good things have been between me and Nick, I'm not sure he *has* forgiven me for Alex. Piling this lie about his father on top will set fire to us.

"He shouldn't have to forgive me for this," I burst out. "They need to know. You can't hide this forever."

"I know that!" King George matches my raised voice.

Normally, I'd back down and try to placate him. He's not someone prone to yelling, but his booming voice only drives me to continue. "If you don't tell them, someone else will."

"Not you, my girl, not you!"

"If not me, then someone else. Social media, one of the doctors you consulted, a reporter—it only takes one leak for this to come crashing down."

"You will not tell them. I forbid it. If anyone tells them, it will be me."

"When?" I grab his hand and try to get him to look at me. He's been avoiding eye contact. "Why not now? If Alex knows, the coronation argument is void. I know, and I'm telling you if I know and Nick doesn't, he'll never forgive me."

He withdraws his hand from mine, but his anger seems to have dissipated. "I'll tell them when I'm ready." His voice is quiet as he ushers me toward his door.

"King George," I plead.

"I'm not ready," he insists.

When he gets to the door, he places his hand on it, whether to open it or keep it closed I'm not sure. I haven't followed him to the door, but I go to him now, and I put my hand on his shoulder.

"I don't want to tell them," he whispers, and when he meets my gaze, there are tears in his eyes. "Once I tell them, the clock will start ticking."

I can already hear it. Those words are impossibly cruel, and no matter how much I want him to tell Nick and Brice, I'm not capable of slicing him open.

"Once I tell them, we all change, don't we?" He chokes out the words. "I'm afraid, Julia. I've never been so afraid."

There's nothing I can say. So instead, I wrap my arms around him, and I hold him while he cries.

###

I only have ten minutes left until I'm supposed to meet the scheduling team at the table to look at possible wedding dates. While the wedding doesn't fall under my mother's umbrella, she's coming for moral and calendar support. She has the best understanding of how long, realistically, big events take to plan and schedule. If she wasn't being diplomatic, she probably would have picked my wedding date and decreed it to everyone.

The last thirty years of her life have been dominated by diplomacy and royal protocol, so I don't expect her to change now.

I'm still reeling from the king's tears and the reality that he's unlikely to tell Nick or Brice anytime soon. He didn't even fully admit that Alex knows.

My mother will have the full picture, so I go to her office.

"Can I have five minutes?" I ask from the doorway.

She glances at the prominent clock on our wall and sighs. "That's about all I have unless we're going to the meeting late. I make it a point to be on time."

"Me too… now."

"Teenage rebellion," she says. "My least favorite years."

Mine, too, but probably not for the same reasons. "Quick chat?"

"It's your office." She points to my nameplate. "As you've reminded me more than once."

Pretty much every chance I get. My rebellion against my mother takes different forms now. Despite that, she's still been, through the years, the most level-headed voice of reason. We may not always see eye-to-eye, but I trust her to tell me the truth and her honest opinion.

I take the seat across from the desk after closing the door. "I just finished speaking to the king. I tried to push him to tell Nick and Brice about his illness. I take it Alex knows."

"Helen told him. I'm not sure if she told him the entire truth, but she told him enough for him to understand the true reason his father was stepping down. Alex refused to go through with the coronation until he understood why the coronation was happening."

Sounds about right. Alex can be relentless. "Why hasn't Helen told Nick and Brice?"

"King George felt his relationship with Alex changed too much once he knew, so he asked Helen to wait until he was ready to tell Nick and Brice himself."

"When do you think that'll be?"

"Your guess is as good as mine." My mother raises her shoulders in an exaggerated shrug. "He's definitely not ready yet. I slide it into conversation weekly."

I take a deep breath before testing the waters. "I'm going to tell Nick."

"No." My mother's voice is clipped. "It's not your place."

"I'm his wife," I say.

"Julia, I mean this in the most loving way, but you and Nick got married on a whim. You're getting to know each other again after years of disconnect. You were told about the king's illness as his employee, not as his daughter-in-law."

"Nick won't see it that way."

"Of course he won't."

"I cannot keep this secret from Nick."

"You can and you will. If you tell Nick he'll feel angry and betrayed by his dying father. His *dying* father."

My instinct is to bite back, but instead, I take a deep, steadying breath before I respond. "Nick will never forgive me for knowing and not telling him."

"He will." Her gaze softens. "He will in time. That's the luxury you have. Time. King George doesn't have that. If you tell Nick, their relationship might not recover before it's too late."

Will my relationship with Nick recover at all if I don't tell him? King George and my mother have a confidence I don't possess. They don't know that a secret, one I should have told him, drove us apart fourteen years ago.

My mother rises from behind our desk and ushers me out the door to the meeting. The whole way there, I can't stop the spiral of thoughts.

What's the right thing to do? Betray King George, and at this point, my mother? Or betray Nick? Would he ever understand why I didn't tell him?

At the meeting room, my mother raps on the door before opening it.

"If he asks me, I'm not lying," I say in a rush.

She raises her eyebrows but doesn't respond. I can't tell whether she thinks my declaration is wise or idiotic. She strides into the room, and an aura of control oozes out of her.

Around a large table are all the people we need to consult, and they have various day planners and calendars open around them. While we all use electronics to remind us of events and activities, the master calendars are for big events and are always scheduled on paper first.

Alex and Nick are on opposite sides of the table, and both are brandishing ice packs. Alex has one gingerly pressed to his cheek, and Nick has one across his knuckles. Both of them are scowling, and the room is so quiet that the steady drip from the ice water machine is noticeable in the room.

Guess Nick decided he'd rather smash the fences than mend them.

JULES

Twelve years ago

There are guards coming down the hall of my dorm, and at first, I expect the boy sandwiched in the middle of the four-man crew to be Nick. My heart kicks in my chest. No matter how often I scold myself, I can't stop hope from blooming at the sight of him around campus. We barely speak at college, but we seem to have fallen into a similar extended circle.

I see Nick both more than I need and less than I want. The memory of our friendship hovers and lingers in the air around us whenever we share a space.

During our first few weeks here, I tried to regain our friendship footing by popping over to his dorm to see him. He and Vicky broke up before we hopped on a plane to California. No girlfriend, no problem, right?

After the third time I caught him, almost literally, with his pants down and some crown chasing bunny polishing his pole in his room, I stopped making an effort. He's fallen into a sex hole, and there's no dragging him out.

So when I realize it's actually Alex coming down the hall toward me, I'm relieved and disappointed at the same time. I should have known. Nick never travels with that much security, and they never wear suits.

"Alex!" I exclaim, and then I notice everyone is staring at him.

"My favorite Bellerivian." His lips twitch.

I can't help a small laugh. The gossip he's going to inspire with a comment like that in an all-girls dorm is unreal.

Security sweeps my room. My roommate went home for the weekend, so I'm the only one in the small space. It takes them all of ten seconds to verify there's no one hiding inside waiting to kill or kidnap Alex.

"Come in." I usher him into my room. "What are you doing here?"

Alex doesn't answer me right away. Instead, he takes in my space, the photos on my wall, and the pictures littering my roommate's space. "Nice place."

"It's a shoebox."

"You don't have classes, right?" Alex asks.

"It's Saturday, so no." I'm still trying to figure out what he's doing here dressed in jeans and a T-shirt like he's hanging out at home.

"Fancy some lunch?" He raises his dark eyebrows in question.

"Where do you want to go?" I grab my purse off my desk chair.

"Somewhere on campus is fine." Alex runs a finger along the top of my desk.

"You're going to maximize the campus gossip. For any particular reason?" I loop my purse over my arm and open the door for him to exit.

"Feeling a bit down, to be honest. Looking for normalcy—whatever that's like." Alex sighs and runs a hand through his hair as the guards lead us toward the food court.

"What's going on?"

"I texted Nick, but he didn't respond." Alex avoids my gaze.

"He probably has a different number now. Did you check with your dad? I've heard rumors he switches his number almost as often as he switches women."

"No bitterness there, I see." Alex smirks.

"I'm done chasing after Nick's friendship. He'll come around when he's ready." I don't try to hide my continued resentment. "I spent sixteen years trailing after him doing whatever he wanted. It's nice to be independent. Free of him."

"If that's not actually how you feel—"

"It *is* how I feel." I throw back my shoulders. "It's really freeing to not have to wonder what Nick will think or feel about whatever I'm doing. I do what I want, when I want."

Alex throws an arm around my shoulders and kisses the top of my head. "Miss independent."

"I'm being serious, Alex." I shrug him off and shoot him an annoyed look.

"Yes, I can see that." He makes a mock serious face.

I shove his shoulder, and he laughs.

We're in the food court, and people are staring. Whether the guards draw the attention or if it's Alex himself, it's hard to tell. Nick travels with two guards, and they're always dressed in casual clothes to blend in. Alex's guards are dressed like federal agents. There's no blending with them.

"So, this is what it's like to be famous," I say. I've been on the edges of it before in Bellerive with the royal family, but I've never felt like everyone was staring at me quite so intensely before.

"How do you like it?" Alex scans the list of places to eat.

For a beat, I consider my response while I take in a few people's questioning looks when they pass. "I have zero desire to bring this much scrutiny and pressure into my life." That feels true.

"What if the person you marry is famous?" He doesn't ask me what I want but instead heads toward one of the storefronts. "You're in model and acting land around here."

Here being California. Nick has already sampled his fair share of both, according to the gossip around campus.

"Nope. Not happening. A—I'm not getting married. And B—even if I did get married, which is incredibly unlikely—I'd never agree to marry a famous person. I don't want your life or a life with anyone else remotely like yours."

"You never seemed to mind being famous adjacent with Nick." Alex scans the menu of the Chinese food place in front of us.

"You're proving my point for me." I read the menu and decide on chicken balls and rice. Chinese isn't my favorite, but it's not worth getting into a debate with Alex. He's going to insist on paying, and I'm not dragging him to multiple places. "I know exactly what famous by association is like, and I can say I don't want it with confidence."

He gives me an assessing look before rattling off his order to the person behind the counter. The girl's eyes widen at the sight of him, and his faint British accent. The two pieces together—his attractiveness coupled with his accent are definite panty droppers for at least fifty percent of my school's population—possibly more. He's also a prince, which if she realizes who he is, automatically elevates his hotness beyond the level of mere mortals.

"If you ever change your mind," Alex says. "I'd be happy to make you my queen."

"Yes, because I'd love to become your property." I roll my eyes. "That's all marriage is. Some archaic institution put in place to keep women down. If I ever say I'm getting married, question my sanity." Even as I say the words, I'm not sure I believe them. But I know beyond a doubt I'll never marry Alex. We get along better as friends, and he's been surprisingly kind about my collapsed friendship with Nick.

"We tolerate each other well enough, and you know what the royal lifestyle entails," Alex says, paying for our food.

I grab my tray and lead him to a table on the fringes of the crowd. There is no need to draw even more attention to ourselves. Most of the people on campus seem to have gotten used to Nick and his bodyguards, and I'm certain it's the way Alex's are dressed that's drawing people to us like bees to a honeypot.

"I do know what the lifestyle entails." I lean across the table so other people can't overhear us. "Which is why I'm saying a big fat no, Alex." I pick up my fork and spear a meatball. "Besides, I'm eighteen, you're twenty-one. Neither of us is in a position to get married to anyone."

"At some point, I'll be expected to marry. It's surprisingly difficult to get anyone to take me seriously." Alex cuts into a piece of beef.

"If you're going around asking multiple people to consider marrying you, that's your problem right there." I narrow my eyes.

"This is why I like talking to you. You don't give a shit that I'm next in line to the Bellerive throne." Alex chuckles and takes a bite.

At one time, it was impressive, but at some point during our make-out sessions, he became less of a mystery and more of a boy. Just a boy like any other boy.

"For the record, I am not going around proposing marriage to multiple teenage girls."

"Ah. So you're aiming for women then, instead?" I cock my head and take another bite.

"I'm not aiming for anyone. I suppose I'm cursing my level of fame a bit lately. Not nearly as famous as Nick, at this point. He seems to be making it his mission to be on every gossip magazine in every country."

The mention of Nick drops the smile off my face, and I stir my rice and sauce without looking at Alex. I clear my throat and square my shoulders.

Forget about Nick. He's forgotten about you.

"Is that why you've been feeling down lately?" I ask, glancing up.

"It's hard to make genuine friends sometimes." Alex shakes his head and then gazes around the food court.

"What are you doing this afternoon?" I'm supposed to meet up with some friends, but I could bail on them if Alex needs some normalcy. Nick used to crave those genuine connections too.

"I've got a thing in San Francisco for the rest of the day and evening. Was hoping to see you and possibly grab a beer with Nick. It'd be nice if we got on a bit better, being brothers. Wishful thinking on my part, I suppose."

I shake my head and take a sip of my drink. "His schedule is probably jam-packed for the weekend now, anyway." Nick won't want to see him, and I'm sure his crown bunnies are taking up the majority of his spare minutes. The days of me having the fast-track to Nick's ear are long gone.

"I fly back out tomorrow mid-day. Do you fancy breakfast?"

Two meals at the school might be too much for the gossips. Especially if the second one is so early in the morning.

"I can bring breakfast to your dorm, if you don't want the spectacle. It would just be nice to be myself for a bit before I fly back to uni and everything there."

His request sits between us, and I'm hesitant because of optics, but that's silly. Why do I care if gossips on my floor assume Alex and I slept together? They all know I'm on the fringes of the royal circle anyway. Several of them have asked me to introduce them to Nick, which is an automatic *no fucking way* every single time.

"Sure," I say. "And Alex, I'm positive there's someone out there who will treat you exactly how you want to be treated."

"Ah," Alex says, sitting back in his chair. "You're a closet romantic, are you? Not me. I'm a realist. Too practical for all that happily ever after, soulmate crap. The chances of me forming a genuine connection with someone once I've left university are slim. On Bellerive, I will always be the next in line to the throne." He shrugs like it doesn't matter and picks up his napkin to wipe his mouth.

Part of me wonders if *that's* what's bothering him. He's in his final year of uni in England, and apart from a few brief affairs, he hasn't dated anyone seriously. He's cautious, which I understand, but I think that cautiousness is beginning to breed loneliness. My heart softens a little at the realization he and Nick aren't so different. It's a shame they aren't able to lean on each other.

"Do you talk to Brice much?" I ask.

"We text a lot," Alex says. "But with the five-year age gap, he doesn't comprehend the pressures I face. He's the youngest. I'm the oldest. Parental expectations are vastly different."

When we chat, he often mentions the disparity in expectations and standards for him versus his younger brothers. Alex talks a good game about being the heir, but sometimes I wonder whether that's all it is—talk. Nick saw his attitude as bragging and arrogance, but it's more like he's buoying himself up. He knows his place and he's accepted it, but I'm not convinced he enjoys it. False bravado at its best.

"So, what should I bring you for breakfast in the morning?" Alex asks.

"Anything but eggs benedict. Hollandaise sauce is disgusting."

"Noted." Alex grins.

"I'm glad you came." I return his smile.

"Me too." Alex's smile fades, and he scans my face. "Me too."

Nicholas

The icepack lies across my knuckles, and I check the clock over the door. Jules is late, but I shouldn't expect any different at this point. Some things never change.

When the door opens, I *am* surprised her mother walks through first. Was that the meeting she had to go to? Why she left me alone with Alex to try to sort out problems that can't be solved with words?

"Your chat didn't go well," Jules states in a low voice as she takes a seat beside me.

The room is so quiet, her whisper might as well be a shout. I'm not lowering my voice. "He got the message he needed to receive." Alex and I lock eyes across the table.

Yeah, we're not coming back from this. I doubt he's upset about it. I know I'm not.

She skims her fingers over my knuckles, and the tension eases out of me. No matter what he thinks, she's sitting beside *me*. We're here to discuss our wedding. He's deluded if he thinks he's still got any avenue to being with her. I scoop her hand up and bring the back of it to my lips. I let the contact linger, and anger sparks again in Alex's eyes.

Julia sighs and leans into me, and when I break eye contact with Alex, she's staring up at me. She doesn't look pleased.

A flare of annoyance flashes. She hasn't seen him for who he truly is for years. I clench my jaw again in frustration. Why would she bother to give him the benefit of the doubt? He sowed the seeds of division between me and Jules, and then he watered them, let them bloom in me until I couldn't tell the difference between a weed and a flower. Plucked out all the wrong things.

Her mother calls the room to order, and instinctually, everyone sits straighter in their chair, turning to their calendars. Desmond, the secretary I share with Alex and Brice, takes us through all the normal commitments on the calendar and suggests a few dates months down the line.

The conversation continues around me, and Jules runs her hand along my leg, occasionally chipping in additional information about items not yet on the king's calendar or Alex's that might complicate a particular timeline.

When all is said and done, a Sunday three months from now is locked in.

Everyone grabs their calendars and phones, but Desmond and Julia's mother linger. Alex is the last one out, and he tries to catch Julia's gaze, but she doesn't notice. Finally, he draws the door closed behind him.

I release a deep sigh. We need to move out of the main palace so I see him less often, and I'll have to talk to Jules about stepping down as the king's secretary when Alex takes over. Maybe we can promote Desmond, and Julia and I can hire someone else.

"Nicholas and Julia. Desmond and I were hoping you'd be open to hiring a wedding planner from the island. She has excellent references and has even done a few events in England, America, and Canada. I can provide you with her portfolio if you want. With the coronation planning as well, there just aren't enough people to oversee all the important details. We can't skimp on a royal wedding," Julia's mother says.

Rather than answering her, I turn to Julia. I got what I wanted—she's my wife. The royal bit doesn't mean much to me. "Are you okay with that?" I ask.

"As long as I get to choose my dress, the rest of the details are neither here nor there to me." Julia shrugs. "Are you okay with that? I don't know. Is there anything about a wedding you've dreamed about?"

My lips tip up into a half-smile, and I raise the back of her hand to my mouth. "I got my dream wedding scenario."

"Drunk in Vegas?" Her eyes light up with amusement.

I search her face. "You." At this point, how can she not know? While I haven't said the words to her, they feel written large behind every interaction, impossible to ignore. I've never loved anyone the way I love her, and I never will. "Hire the wedding planner," I say keeping my gaze trained on Julia. "Let's show the world that a drunken wedding isn't always a mistake."

###

I've been in our bedroom suite stewing since the meeting. Alex's words, no matter how much I try to pretend they don't matter, keep reverberating around my skull.

Jules comes in the suite door and hangs her keys on the rack. "Let me see your knuckles. Did you really hit him?"

"He deserved it. Has had it coming for years," I mutter, but the sight of her bowed over my hand softens the rough edges lingering in me.

"I didn't ask you to talk to him so you could work your differences out with your fists." She gazes up at me, and my heart kicks.

The air between us crackles with sexual tension like it does every time we're this close. Normally, I sink into it without a second thought.

"He says he knows you better than I do." Nothing else he said landed quite like that proclamation.

She blinks and looks away. "Oh." She twists her hands and goes to the sidebar.

At first, I think she's going to pour herself a vodka, but it's water in her glass.

"Does he know you better than I do?" I ask, my voice husky.

"We drifted apart, Nick. For better or worse, Alex stuck to me like glue for the fourteen years you spent pushing me away. Does he know me better than you? I don't know. How would we even determine that? I'm not keen to set up some sort of Julia quiz for the two of you to try to best each other. No one wins in that scenario."

"I'd win. You'd rig it for me, wouldn't you? Weight the questions from the ages of zero to sixteen more heavily? I *am* your husband."

She shakes her head, but there's amusement in the twist of her lips. As she sips her water, she touches my name on her finger. "I'm in this with you, Nick," she says when she lowers the glass. "The two of you rub each other the wrong way, but no matter what Alex might say or do, we'll be okay as long as we're honest with each other."

Her complexion pales, and I wander over to run the back of my hand down her cheek. "Are you feeling okay?"

"I haven't eaten much today." Jules doesn't meet my gaze.

"Too busy?" I move to the internal phone on the wall near the door. It's a direct link to security, the kitchen, and almost any other room in the house I could ever wish to speak to. The system is ancient, but it works, so none of us complain. When the sous chef picks up, I rattle off a few of Julia's favorites and request we have dinner in our suite.

Once I'm off the phone, I rearrange the two armchairs near the fireplace so they're facing each other. We could do this on the bed, but I don't trust myself to talk instead of act. I've justified the last few weeks of us living in a sex haze as fine since we have a lifetime to get to know each other in other ways again.

But Julia has claimed many times we don't know each other at all anymore. At first, her assertion bothered me. I still knew her because I cared to notice. Given that our actual conversations have been few and far between, my 'knowing' isn't the same as understanding. If Alex can drive a knife into my heart with a throwaway comment he might not even believe, I need to eliminate that weakness sooner rather than later. It'll fester in me, and we'll be rotten before we have a chance to ripen.

Thoughts of Alex and Julia, in any context, are poison.

"What are you doing?" Julia asks. "We've already had sex on both of those."

I chuckle and observe my handiwork. Sitting opposite each other and not touching is probably the safest bet. "I'm considering a sex ban."

"Absolutely not." Julia sets down her glass and comes over to run her hands underneath my T-shirt and up my back.

I frame her face and brush my lips against hers, the briefest taste, and I realize my mistake. Even that small contact is enough gasoline for the fire that rages between us. She deepens the kiss, and my shirt goes over my head before I can think to protest. I'm hard and ready in an instant.

It would be so easy to keep stoking this fire.

"You really want to spend our time together talking," she murmurs against my lips.

"We must talk today about important things." I lift her shirt and unsnap her bra. This can't happen. I've got to get myself under control. A sex ban. We need a sex ban.

She kisses me again, her tongue dancing with mine. Her hair streams over her shoulders in silky waves and brushes against my hands cradling her back. Her partially naked body is her rebuttal. She doesn't need words.

"We need to speak soon about important things." I drag the zipper of her skirt down. Talk first, and then have more sex. That's the order this should be happening in. My brain knows this, but my dick is first chair in this debate.

"Hmm," Jules agrees, and she trails kisses across my chest. Such a strong cross-examination. Who could resist?

"We should." I swallow when her fingertips skim along the edge of my jeans. How is it possible after having sex so many ways and so many times for the simplest touch to skyrocket my desire? I want to throw her onto the bed, sink into her, and drive us both to the brink of insanity. "We should talk at some point about important things," I mutter.

"How about now?" Her voice is breathy.

Somehow she's undone my pants without me realizing it, and she's got my dick in her hand. She strokes from the base to the tip in a leisurely manner with just the right firmness.

Just like that, any thought of debate is over. There's no fucking way we're talking right now. It's not a sex ban, it's a discussion ban.

"Not now," I manage to get out. Her skirt and panties drop to the floor with a little push from me.

"Are you sure?" She steps out.

I sweep her into my arms, and she laughs as I cart her to the bed, tossing her into the middle. She raises herself on her elbows to watch me discard the rest of my clothes. I crawl up her body.

"We'll talk over dinner." I circle her clit with my thumb, and she clutches my bicep, a low moan slipping out between her lips. "The only words I want to hear right now are you taking the lord's name in vain. Or my name. I'm okay with my name too." With a kiss, I increase the pressure of my hand the way she likes, and then I get my wish.

"Oh, God," she breathes, arching her back. "Please, Nick."

I slip inside of her, and coherent conversation vanishes.

###

We're in bathrobes, which is dangerously easy access for round two, but we're on opposite sides of the food cart delivered about ten minutes ago. My willpower where she's concerned is in the red zone.

"What did you do before you took on the secretary job? I know you were in California." I cut into the chicken breast stuffed with brie and cranberry. Julia has excellent taste. "We should have this at our wedding." I motion to the plate.

"We really should." She takes a bite and closes her eyes, savoring the taste. "So good." Once she's wiped her mouth with the napkin, she shifts deeper into the armchair. "I worked for a tech company in their global outreach division. It wasn't anything like I thought it would be, so when Mom called and said she wanted to retire, I figured I could take the job temporarily."

"And almost three years later," I say.

"I know." She groans. "I like the work well enough, I guess. But I always saw myself doing something more impactful. Well." She gives me a small smile. "You know."

I let the silence sit between us for a few minutes while I gather my courage. "When Alex becomes king, do you want to work for him?"

"I don't think I can," Julia says. "For so many reasons." She picks up an asparagus stalk and takes a bite. "The two of you don't get along. Alex has never quite gotten the memo it's not going to happen between us. I'd like to work with you more on things we care about."

"Yeah?" The idea sends a wash of warmth across my chest.

"Yeah." She meets my gaze. "We make a good team. We always did."

"You'd be okay with," I struggle to put the role into words without making her sound like a royal sidekick, "partnering with me on all my charities, patronages, and foundations?"

She beams at me. "Yes." She takes an audible breath. "It's actually sort of been my dream since we were teenagers." Her smile turns sheepish. "Given how far we drifted apart, that probably sounds far-fetched."

"To know I'm currently making all your dreams come true?" I smirk, but inside my heart thuds heavy and happy.

"Well, when you put it like that." Julia's cheeks pinken.

I reach across the table and run my thumb along her cheek, and then I can't resist dropping a kiss on her lips. She slants her mouth to deepen it, and I chuckle, withdrawing.

"Nope. You're not sucking me in a second time."

"Got it." Her eyes twinkle. "No sucking."

I hold up a hand. "Let's not get hasty. No sucking *right now*." I wink at her.

She tucks a strand of hair behind her ear, and she searches my face. "I don't think I've ever been happier."

"Who knew my father sending you to Tanzania would work out so well." She stiffens slightly, and I lean across the table to kiss her. "For both of us. I hope that didn't come out the wrong way."

"It didn't." Her voice is husky. "Tell me your dreams, Nick. You're giving me mine. How can I help you get yours?"

God, I love her. She's exactly the Jules I remember but better because instead of me pining after her, feeling like a lovesick fool, it seems like we're both in this together this time. I don't doubt that she feels *something* for me, even if we haven't named it yet. In the Las Vegas pictures on my phone, there's a vibe between us that can't be faked. But the few times we've been photographed in public since we returned has only solidified that sense of mutual adoration. She looks at me like I'm the most important person in any room, and I hope she sees the same thing reflected in me.

"Brice has this theory about relationships. He thinks he should only be in one where the other person loves him more."

I've never understood it. Seems like a breeding ground for insecurities and resentment.

A frown forms across her brow. "Sounds like a recipe for disaster. Exactly the kind of thing Brice, when he was younger, would have said. I thought he was growing up?" Jules picks up her wine glass and takes a sip. "Love shouldn't feel like a competition, should it? I love you more. You love me less. Nobody wins."

Hearing her say 'love' so many times in a row is doing strange things to my chest.

"Dessert?" I set my fork and knife across my plate. "I can call the kitchen for a Bellerive flower pastry."

She groans. "So tempting, but unlike you, I don't have workouts scheduled into my business day. If I keep gorging on pastries with you every night, I'm in trouble."

"Hardly." I take my own wine glass off the table. "It's not like we don't work off those calories." Many of those desserts end up smeared on Julia's body, and I make it my mission to get her all clean.

"You didn't answer my question earlier, is that because you don't know what you want or you're afraid to say?" Her voice is gentle.

"I'm not afraid to say." I sip my wine. "You, our own house on the property, some kids. In terms of work for the monarchy..." I think of Elena and Bahati who will be on the island very soon for the first surgery. "I'd like to expand what I started in Tanzania, with your help, if you're up for it."

"Yes," she breathes out, and a smile blooms on her face. "One hundred percent yes. After it took you three days to thank me for the donation in your name when we were teenagers, I figured I'd never get the chance."

I suck in a sharp breath. The memory of that Christmas rises to the surface. "I'm sorry I was such a dick back then."

She shrugs, but some of the playfulness has gone out of her. A quick subject change is in order.

"Kids?" I ask.

"How many do you want?"

"As few or as many as you want. I'm open to whatever makes sense for you and for us." Before Tanzania, kids were an abstract idea. I figured I'd have a child someday, but I'd never longed for a family. But since we returned to Bellerive when I see pregnant women or parents with their children, my mind strays to Jules, to what we could build together.

She stands up and holds out her hand, her expression soft. "Come here."

I set down my wine glass and take her hand. She leads me over to the bed, and while I'm tempted to throw on the brakes, I've got no willpower. She glances at me over her shoulder. "I just want to lie with you," she says.

I chuckle when she slides her robe off at the side of the bed. "Is *lie with you* a euphemism?" Cause if it's not, she's in for a surprise when my robe falls.

She undoes the belt and pushes the material off my shoulders. It pools around my ankles.

When she gazes up at me, there's no hint of teasing in her depths. "Does this feel surreal to you?"

"You and me?" My voice is gentle.

She scans my face. "Sometimes I look at you, when we're out somewhere or just now, and it's like... it's like I'll never get enough." A thin sheen of tears coats her blue-gray eyes. "I've missed you, this you, so much. I missed *us* so much."

Those words and her tears make my heart feel too big for my chest, and it's more than ample to break my fragile willpower.

"There is no enough." My voice is husky. "I'm always going to want more of everything with you."

There's nothing playful about what happens between us next. The intimacy is real, soul shatteringly real. We're so connected my chest aches, as though I'm missing her, even while I'm swallowing her soft sighs with my kisses, burying myself so deep inside her it's impossible to remember a time we weren't like this. We can't possibly get any closer, and it's not enough.

Later when we're lying facing each other, not saying anything, just tracing each other's bodies in wonder, Jules circles the inscription on the outside of my upper thigh.

"Is this for your gran?" Her voice is quiet in the semi-dark room.

"How'd you guess?" I brush a loose strand of her hair back behind her shoulder.

"The two of you seemed to become really close leading up to her death." She follows the two lines, which are almost too small to read. "My heart broke for you at the funeral. I wanted to talk to you so badly. So badly," she murmurs.

Jules and I made eye contact for the briefest moment at the family graveside service late in the day, after all the public mourning was done. Then Alex moved to stand beside her, which made my losses so much worse. Her tear-stained face coupled with his presence was too much with my own heartbreak. Even though I longed to go to her, I spent the rest of the day avoiding her at every turn.

"Why here?" she asks. Her fingers are light against my skin.

"It's just for me. Hard for the paparazzi to get a pic of it there. I've never told anyone who it was for or why I got it."

"Maybe I shouldn't have asked?" Jules lets out a soft laugh.

I lace my fingers with hers, and she meets my gaze. "I'm glad you asked. I don't want to hide anything from you."

Her expression is stricken for a moment, and then she kisses me. When she draws back, she searches my face for a beat, her hesitation obvious.

"What is it?" I ask.

"I love you." Her voice brims with sincerity and conviction. "I love you so much."

A searing warmth blazes across my chest, and I place my forehead against hers, nuzzling our noses together. "I love you too." My voice cracks. "I can't remember a time when I didn't love you."

"Oh, Nick," she breathes. She presses her body against mine and kisses me deeply.

Then we're getting lost in each other again, so lost I'm not sure I'll ever find my way back. Doesn't matter because I never want to.

434

Julia

I told Nick I loved him last night because I couldn't help myself. I've been holding the words back since we returned to Bellerive. Whatever happened between us in Las Vegas before we got married shifted something inside me. What changed? I'm not sure, but I'm not quite as afraid Nick will grow tired of me or that we're not strong enough to withstand whatever storms blow our way. Maybe we will be okay. He hasn't given me any reason to doubt his love, but old habits die hard.

We had so much faith in each other once, and we ruined it.

There's a chance I'll ruin it again by dividing my loyalty between the king and Nick.

"What do you think?" Merida's afro bounces, and one clearly defined spiral curl falls across her forehead.

"Sorry," I say with a shake of my head. She's going to think I'm a total flake. I haven't been able to focus for more than five minutes on any of the royal wedding details. My phone keeps buzzing with coronation details, Nick is in my head, and I'm worried about when the king will finally tell Nick and Brice the truth. The last thing I want to be doing right now is planning a wedding. Not an acceptable response when a wedding planner, a very expensive wedding planner, is standing in front of you.

"The only thing I really care about is the dress." I give her a sheepish grin. "Do you know who can pull it off in the timeline we've got?" I have a few Bellerive designers I love, but so many of the bigger names work months or years in advance.

"Nandi Lawson and Kira Mensah are keen to present designs."

"Both of them?" I can't help the shock in my voice.

Merida grins. "It *is* a royal wedding. The first the island has seen in over thirty years." She flicks through things on her phone. "Your husband is popular around the world."

"Yes," I say dryly. "I'm aware of Nick's international appeal." He's left few countries unmarked by his behavior, but he's so charming that even the most scandalous stories have tended to include a pinch of humor.

"Not just him, I suppose," Merida says, glancing up. "There's something for everyone between those three men." She winks.

I can't help my chuckle. When my mother produced Merida this morning without a scheduled appointment in my calendar, I wasn't sure how I was going to feel. We just discussed hiring her yesterday. My mother doesn't like to waste time when big events are looming.

"The three of them are very different," I agree.

"You'd like design ideas from Nandi and Kira?" Merida steers us back on course.

"Yes," I say. "That would be amazing. Is there anyone else you'd recommend?"

"Philip Squire isn't technically a native Bellerivian, but he does have a holiday home here. I can approach him, if you think that'll be acceptable?"

I bite my lip. Philip Squire would be amazing, but he dresses mostly American and British celebrities. "Do you think he'd even be interested?"

"I think you're underestimating the importance of your wedding. Have you been on social media since the royal family announced the date last night?" She raises her carefully arched eyebrows.

I didn't even realize we announced the date last night since we only set it yesterday afternoon. A small frisson of unease darts through me. It's all happening so fast.

"No," I say in a quiet voice. "I've been busy this morning."

"Yeah, I guess," Merida says. "Secretary Jensen mentioned the family is preparing for a referendum or something? The political maneuvering on that must be quite a task."

I frown, and then I try to smooth out my features. Referendum? What in the world would require an island-wide vote? Alex didn't mention anything the other day. My mother's insistence on taking the political load makes more sense now. Are they planning this behind my back? Why wouldn't anyone tell me? Or Nick?

Does Nick know? He'd tell me, wouldn't he?

But I haven't told him about his father.

"I feel like I've said something wrong." A wisp of a smile crosses Merida's face. "I don't know what the referendum is about, if it's supposed to be top secret. Actually, now that I think about it, your mother glossed over it fairly quickly."

I bet she did. But why?

"Yes," I agree. "It's top secret. Until it's announced to the public and we're sure we're moving ahead, there's no need to engage in public debate."

"Makes sense." Merida passes me her phone. "I was thinking something like this for the dress. Do you have any inspirations I can give to the designers as references?" She settles into the seat around the conference table, opening her laptop.

Then we're down a rabbit hole of dresses and styles, royal protocol, and other timeless considerations. Before I realize it, we've been talking about dresses for an hour, and Merida has a list of notes and photos saved on her computer.

"It's a good start." She gathers all her materials. "I have a team working with me, so you might hear from someone else. If you're not sure they work for me, the code word is Arusha."

"The Tanzanian city?" A small smile blooms.

"I always try to pick something that's significant to the couple getting married but that would take a lot of guesswork on the part of the public or press."

"I'll let Nick know." Nick's weekly schedule is relatively consistent. Today is his correspondence and signature day. He told me this morning when he left to play tennis that he only needed to know where to show up for the wedding. In some ways a typical, and in other ways a surprising, response.

Once Merida is gone, I try to track down my mother via text and good old-fashioned footwork. But she's either ignoring me, or she's too busy to respond. I don't tell her Merida spilled the referendum beans in case she is trying to hide the subject from me.

Then I'm drawn back into royal business when the cleaning company that specializes in limestone calls me back. Since the last coronation and this one are going to take place uncharacteristically close, I'm not even sure the outside of the church needs another cleaning. But I've been instructed to spare no reasonable expense, so I might as well get some quotes. If it fits in the budget, I guess I'll book it.

At least the coronation date is a year away. While some details will take months of advance planning, others, by necessity, will be more last minute.

I've just finished speaking to the secretary at Limrock's Limestone Cleaning about having a quote sent over when Alex's office door opens ahead of me. Without meaning to, I slow my pace as a bunch of politicians file out.

Usually, they meet at the Great Hall in the center of Tucker's Town, not the palace.

Part of me wants to confront Alex about the referendum, but I don't have the right to use our friendship as leverage anymore to get answers. Nick and Alex got into a physical fight yesterday. From where I'm standing, the blueish hue of a bruise on Alex's cheek is visible while he watches the group of politicians leave.

Before I can duck into another room, make myself scarce, or pretend to be on an important phone call again, Alex sees me.

I can't talk to him. I shouldn't. Nick wouldn't be happy to hear I went to Alex for information. Maybe Nick does know about the referendum and assumes I know too. I'll speak to Nick, and we'll go from there.

I waltz past Alex on my way to my own office. The heat of his laser focus sears me, and I make the left hand turn away from him and my curiosity, and toward my own desk.

Maybe my mother will be there, and I can ask her.

When I get to my office, I don't bother to close my door, but my mother isn't there either. I check my phone again to see whether she's responded, and when I verify the information in our joint secretary calendar, I see her whole day has now been coated with the light green. She's with the king. That wasn't there before.

I rub my face in frustration. My gut is telling me they're keeping something big from me. I can't ask Alex. Nick. I'll talk it through with Nick.

With a renewed sense of determination, I spin on my heel and head for the door, focused on my phone.

I plow into a firm chest, and my phone clatters to the rug. Thankfully it didn't hit the tiled floor, or I'd need a new one.

"You all right?" Alex's voice is gruff.

"Fine," I grit out. I rise and straighten my fitted dress.

He eyes me warily, and I return the look.

"Nice bruise," I say.

His expression softens a touch. "Nick is right this time—I probably deserved it."

"Were you fighting over me?" I can't dance around the truth if we're all going to co-exist.

"Is there someone else we'd fight about?" Alex leans against the bookshelf, and his hot gaze runs over me.

I hate when he examines me like that. Can I claim sexual harassment from a look? "Why would you fight at all? You and I are friends, and you're sort of my boss. He's my husband. Those are the facts. Nothing to fight about."

"In the hallway just now, it seemed like you wanted to ask me something." He crosses his arms and ignores my assertion.

I freeze and search his face. For all the talk of Alex being poor at reading people, he often reads me better than I'd like. Another reason why I don't understand his refusal to accept Nick and I are together, staying together. How can he not see Nick is who I want?

"What's the referendum about?" I ask. Maybe Nick knows, but I'm positive Alex does.

"Who told you?" His eyes narrow.

"Doesn't matter. I caught wind of it. I can't believe I haven't caught wind of it before. Are you all trying to hide it from me?"

He runs his fingers through his hair and then shoves his hands in the pockets of his suit pants. "Not you so much as Nick and Brice. Your mother thought you'd want to tell Nick if you knew. So, we've opted to keep it from you as well."

"Will you tell me?" I hedge.

"You can't discuss it with Nick until the topic is out in the public."

I hold up a hand. Another secret between Nick and me is two too many. "Don't tell me. I don't want to know."

"You might as well know, Jules. You can't plead ignorance at this point. You realize there's something big coming. What are you going to tell him? I knew, but I didn't know?" He stares me down. "He'll call bullshit. He'll want to know why you didn't tell him either way."

"Maybe I will tell him." I raise my chin.

"Yes, I'm sure. You're being so truthful about everything else you know." His tone is biting.

"Your father asked me—my mother asked me—"

"They come before my brother?"

"It's not that simple and you know that. You of all people understand the weight of duty versus doing whatever you want." My voice thickens at how black and white Alex is painting everything. The gut-wrenching part is that Nick will paint my choice in these colors too.

"The referendum is on assisted suicide. The king would like to legalize it." He lets the bomb drop and then he studies my reaction.

"What?" I whisper. "No. No. No." Legalizing assisted suicide? He's trying to sign his own death warrant. Not that his condition can be reversed, but... tears spring to my eyes in earnest, and I close the distance between me and Alex. "Because of what's happening to him?"

"You can't even say it?" Alex's voice is low, and he stares down at me with a mixture of tenderness and frustration.

My mind turns over the revelation. Nick and I haven't spoken about the issue for years, maybe since the debate club, but he wasn't in favor of assisted suicide then. Given his reaction to Bahati and Elena, I can't imagine he'll be on the pro side now either. He'll fight The Crown in their efforts to ram this through.

"Nick will be—"

"Which is why you can't tell him," Alex says.

"Alex," I breathe out, a tear slipping down my cheek. "Nick and Brice deserve to know what's at stake. If the king isn't going to tell them, you need to. Or Queen Helen needs to. Or I will." My chest tightens unbearably, and I press the heel of my hand to my breastbone.

"I'm in favor of legalizing it, Jules. I'm on my father's side." His gaze is tender and pained. "Brice might come around, but I agree with you. I'm not sure Nick will."

"I won't have Nick finding out about his father's illness when the referendum is announced. I can't do that to him. I won't.

He'd never forgive me. Either you tell him, or you get one of your parents to tell him or—or—I'll tell him."

Tears stream down my face, and there's a creeping desperation in me now. Before when I was keeping the king's illness from him, that was bad. But this? Knowing the king intends to use legislation he's running through the court of public opinion without telling Nick and Brice? It's unacceptable. How can the king's judgment be so impaired? Why is everyone enabling this?

"I'll talk to him," Alex says. His thumb grazes my cheek, catching a tear. "Give me twenty-four hours. If our father won't tell them," Alex takes a deep breath, "I will."

"Oh, thank God," I murmur. Without thinking, I throw my arms around Alex in a desperate hug. "Thank you. Thank you."

He squeezes me tight and sighs against my hair. "Jules," he murmurs.

"Jules!" Nick calls from the hallway.

I draw away from Alex and run my fingers underneath my eyes, averting my gaze from Nick when he appears in the doorway.

"Everything all right?" Nick's tone is wary.

If I look at him, he'll know I'm crying.

"Fine." Alex steps away from me, all business again. "Jules, call me if you need help with anything else."

Trust Alex to simultaneously offer help and drop me into a pile of unexplainable dung.

When Alex tries to shoulder past Nick, he doesn't move from the doorway.

"What did you say to her? Why is my wife crying?"

"Ask *your wife* yourself." Alex doesn't hide his annoyance and then he's gone.

A heavy silence coats the air between me and Nick, and when I turn to look at him, I plaster a fake smile on my face. I just have to make it through the next twenty-four hours and then there will be no more secrets between me and Nick.

"Are you okay?" Nick draws me into his chest, and he runs his hand along my back. "Was Alex being an ass to you? Do I need to give him matching cheeks?"

The soothing touch and protective stance are almost enough to set off another crying jag. I just hope he'll understand why I couldn't tell him when the truth comes out. "Can we talk about what's upset me tomorrow? I just need a bit of time to process."

"Yeah." He searches my face and then nods. "Sure. As long as you're okay. We've got all the time in the world." Then he feathers a line of kisses from my temple to my chin before planting a quick kiss on my lips.

I breathe out a sigh of contentment and relief. Tomorrow Nick will know, and everything will be okay.

"Lunch?" Nick asks. "I'm starving."

JULES

Twelve years ago

My roommate, Dru, has dragged me out to the bar with a bunch of the other girls from our dorm. I have an essay due on Monday, so I'm not drinking, but I did agree to come out.

Already, I'm regretting it.

At the bar in the center of the building, Prince Nicholas is holding court, surrounded by a bus of crown bunnies, and my roommate is angling to become one of them.

"I'm not introducing you," I say for the hundredth time. "Just walk over and join the crowd. I guarantee he won't mind."

"Come on, Julia. Why are you so resistant to hooking me up? You went to high school with him. Your mom is the king's secretary. You must know him well enough to walk over and introduce me." Dru flicks her long dark hair over her shoulder.

"I don't know him well enough," I say with a shrug. *Not anymore, anyway.* So far Dru and I have gotten along, but if she keeps trying to wrangle an introduction to Prince Nicholas, we'll develop a rift. In high school, I didn't tolerate anyone using me to get to Nick, and I won't tolerate anyone using me to get to Prince Nicholas either.

Sometimes being fame adjacent sucks.

Dru releases a huff of annoyance, but then she flags down some guys she recognizes from the soccer team, and all is forgiven. We dance, and they drink, and by the end of the night, I'm probably the only sober person in the whole place.

Prince Nicholas has stuck his tongue down at least three girls' throats. Is that how you get oral herpes? I'll have to look it up later. Really, I'm doing Dru a favor by keeping him away from her.

"Dance?" A tall, broad soccer player I've caught giving me the once over a few times has his hand extended to me. He sways slightly on his feet.

He's cute. I'm bored. The night is drawing to a close, and the dance tracks have switched to slow songs to encourage people to hook up here before hooking up elsewhere. We won't be hooking up—one-night-stands with drunk guys have yet to satisfy me—but I'm not opposed to an end-of-the-night make-out session on the dance floor if he plays his cards right.

On the dance floor, he draws me into his arms, and when I try to keep a little distance between our bodies, he tightens his grip. I shift uncomfortably, but I don't say anything. I've learned drunk guys are better to appease than to fight most of the time.

"You look so fucking hot in that tiny skirt." His bitter breath stirs my hair, and the stench of beer swirls around me.

One of his hands snakes up my leg, and I bat him away with a laugh. Some guys have a sense of humor, and they'll laugh with me, make a joke about trying their luck. Not this guy. It appears I've fallen down a hot, humorless hole.

The next time his hand comes back, it's firmer, more insistent. I stall his hand and try to make eye contact with him so he'll know I'm serious. But he doesn't allow any space between our bodies, and I'm as rigid as a board, much like the boner in his pants.

"You cannot wear a skirt like that and be a frigid bitch," he mutters. "Should be illegal."

"My clothing isn't illegal." My voice is tight. "You trying to touch me when I don't want you to, is."

A hand lands on my dancing partner's shoulder. "Go fuck off somewhere else, Cam."

I raise startled eyes to Nick, and I can't decide if I'm breathing a sigh of relief or trepidation. We haven't spoken in months.

"Come on, Prince Nicholas. You can't get all the hot chicks," Cam says.

"Julia is not some *hot chick*. Her mother works for my father. Get your hands off her or I'll gladly remove them. And learn to read some fucking body language." Nick yanks him off me. "When a girl is uncomfortable, you leave them the hell alone."

Rather than squaring up to Cam when he stumbles back, Nick nods over his shoulder to the two plainclothes security people who follow him everywhere. One of the men leads a drunk Cam toward the exit.

"Must be handy to have your own bouncers," I say.

Without a word, Nick tugs me into his arms so we're dancing. "No need to thank me, Jensen. It's nothing. Don't mention it."

I'm not sure I could mention anything else even if I wanted to. At the close contact, my heart thuds an unsteady beat in my ears. He still smells the same—a tangy freshness that takes me back to starry nights, and dark movie theaters.

Why wouldn't he smell the same? It only feels like we haven't been friends for decades.

He gathers me close, and I can't help sinking into him, soft and pliable as though he could do anything to me, and I'd let him. My body is betraying me, but I don't have the will to stop myself. It feels *so good* to be close to him again.

We don't talk, we just dance. One song bleeds into another, and he doesn't move away, and neither do I. No discussion. We just—don't. Dancing with him inspires a riot of emotions, a weird sense of calm along with this incredible recognition of his body. Every tiny movement shoots awareness through me, and the air around us is thick with tension. I want to murder him for destroying our friendship, and I want him to kiss me again. And then again, and again, and again.

I've almost worked up the courage to say something to him, to try one last time to draw us back together when Dru stumbles over.

"You said you didn't know him that well." Her voice is shrill and accusing at my shoulder.

With a sigh, I step back, and for the briefest moment, Nick's fingers tighten before he releases me.

"She told you we don't know each other?" Prince Nicholas arches his eyebrows in my direction. "We know each other very well, actually." He turns to my roommate. "And you are?"

"Dru," she purrs and sidles up next to him. She glances around before pulling a flask out of her purse. "Drink?"

He eyes her with amusement before taking the flask and tipping it back.

It's quite possible the very act of him drinking Dru's flask is causing her to have a spontaneous orgasm. The expression on her face would be priceless if Nick's subtle flirting wasn't putting another crack in my heart.

The two of them fall into a flirty conversation, and all the warmth that had flooded my consciousness while Nick and I danced evaporates.

This is who we are now. The realization stings. For a minute there, I half-convinced myself of something different.

When the crush of rowdy boys Prince Nicholas arrived with swirls around us, we head back to the dorms as a big group. Dru and the prince share the flask and talk in exaggerated movements ahead of me.

"Yes!" Dru practically shouts. She's got her drunk voice out. "She said she knew Prince Alexander but not you. I didn't believe her. Prince Alexander comes to visit her in our dorm, and she doesn't know you? Unlikely."

A rock of realization drops into the pit of my stomach, but he doesn't turn around to look for me, to verify Dru's statement. She's never believed me that Alex and I aren't hooking up. Everyone on our floor discussed Alex's appearance for weeks. I can only imagine how the gossip circulated around campus.

As I listen to her go on and on to the prince, I realize our tentative roommate friendship is over. I can't forgive this outright betrayal. She's twisting things she knows nothing about.

He takes a longer drink from the flask and then grins at her. Maybe he doesn't care that I said I know Alex better? Old Nick would have, but I don't know this guy walking ahead of me, whoever he is. Maybe our crumbled friendship is a blip in his life, a speedbump in an otherwise smooth road. It's been a crater in mine.

I'm tempted to run ahead to catch up with them and explain myself. What do I say? At this point, I *do* know Alex better than I know Nick. Telling Nick why I said those things to Dru isn't a simple explanation, and it's definitely not one I'm confident he'd follow when he's clearly decided to go beyond the buzzed he seemed to be when he stepped in between me and Cam to stumbling drunk.

Behind me, Prince Nicholas's friends are taking bets on whether Nick sleeps with Dru. It's entirely possible my head will leave my shoulders, spin around, and screw back on sideways if that happens. I'm headed back to the dorms with them right now. Dru wouldn't, would she?

I slow my pace as the realization seeps in that I'll probably end up in the hallway listening to them fuck while his security guards pretend to be busy on their phones or manning the external doors or something equally useful.

Sure enough, when I get back to our dorm room, Dru has stuck the *Do Not Disturb* door hanger she stole from the hotel her parents stayed at when they dropped her off.

"Excuse me, Miss," a guard calls from down the hall. He starts walking in my direction. They must be double-checking the area. "I'll have to ask you—oh, hey Julia. What are you doing here?"

"That's my room." I point to the door in front of me.

"You were the girl Prince Nicholas almost got in a fight over at the bar?" Rocky, the guard, looks me over.

"If that's what that was." *Almost got in a fight over* seems like a stretch.

"But he came back with your..."

"Roommate, yeah. He's such a stellar guy, isn't he?" I roll my eyes and turn on my heel. Maybe the common space is empty.

But it's not. Too many drunk, horny people on my floor tonight. All the usual hideouts are taken.

I head back to my room and sink to the floor across from my doorway.

"Happen a lot?" Rocky asks from his spot a little way down the hall.

"Yeah, actually," I admit. Dru enjoys sex with a variety of partners. It's not my thing, but I've never judged her before. I'm definitely judging her tonight. "How about you?" I raise my eyebrows and give him a knowing look.

He chuckles but doesn't admit or deny what Prince Nicholas has been doing since he landed on campus. The answer is *everyone*. Of that, I'm sure.

It's not enough for Nick to be a man-whore around campus, but now he's literally doing it in my dorm room. On impulse, I send a text to Alex to let him know Nick is fucking my roommate. He's probably sleeping with the time change, but my phone lights up right away in response. We text back and forth, and I'm grateful for the lifeline because my roommate is not quiet by any stretch of the imagination, and if I let myself dwell on what's going on in there, I'll never be able to look Nick or Dru in the eyes again. As it is, I'm not sure how I'll be civil to Dru after this.

When Prince Nicholas emerges from the room half an hour later looking disheveled and still drunk, I can't hide my disgust.

He doesn't say anything to me, he just signals to his guards to follow him, and one starts down the hall, while Rocky pops off the wall to bring up the rear.

Except, I can't let this go.

I should. I should roll my eyes and pretend like Prince Nicholas's behavior doesn't bother me. But it kills me to see him like this. His carelessness is murdering my soul. He's become the opposite of everything I loved about him.

Instead of staying in my place and waiting for the anger to pass, I tuck my phone in my pocket and chase after him.

"What happened to you?"

"Isn't it obvious what just happened to me?" He chuckles but doesn't look at me.

"No, I don't mean in there. Eww. That's disgusting."

I grab his arm to force him to stop walking down the hall, but he shrugs me off and pushes through the dorm exit.

"Leave it, Julia." His voice is tight.

"Fuck you, Nick." I follow him out the door and this time when I grab his arm, I haul him to a stop. "What happened to the guy I used to know? I don't even recognize you anymore."

He looks up at the sky and takes a deep breath. Then he levels his gaze at me. "Whatever guy you're referring to never existed, Julia. He's been a figment of your imagination this entire time."

It's hyperbole, but at the core is a truth I've been trying hard not to recognize, even as we drifted further apart, even as his behavior became more erratic. I've wanted him to be someone he's not. I clench my jaw and stare at him for a beat. "I guess I'll just stop imagining he'll come back then."

"You're already telling people you don't know me, so just don't fucking know me. Okay? We shouldn't talk anymore."

"Pretty easy since we're not talking now. We haven't spoken to each other about anything important in almost two years."

There's so much bitterness in my voice I can taste it, but I don't care.

A muscle in his jaw tics, and I think maybe he'll actually say something, anything to change where we're headed.

"Excellent. Fan-fucking-tastic." He throws his hands out. "Have a good life, Julia." He storms away, and the guards jog to keep up with him.

I stare after him, and the last tethers of our friendship snap, snap, snap, but instead of being consumed by sadness, all I feel is numb. I'm in love with a person who no longer exists, and I can't keep clinging on to someone who's long gone.

As he fades into the night, flanked by his guards, I finally realize he's never coming back. "Goodbye, Nick."

NICHOLAS

All day, I've tried to put the scene in Julia's office out of my mind, but it's playing on a loop. Hard to banish it from my brain when I'm engaged in mindless tasks—signing memorabilia and replying to royal correspondence.

What did I see? My crying wife being comforted by my asshole older brother. My asshole older brother who believes he can undermine and delegitimize my marriage. My blood has been simmering all day.

Under any circumstances what I saw between them would bother me, but her avoidance of whatever happened only makes the situation harder to dismiss.

With other women, I'd let the encounter slide. My relationships have been fleeting, and the word 'love' hasn't entered into any of them. If those women wanted to cry on my brother's shoulder, what did I care?

But this is Jules, and we've already let one massive misunderstanding ruin our lives for fourteen years. I'm not letting us build our marriage on top of sand.

She loves me, and I love her. That realization, so new and fresh, stopped me in my tracks a few times as I went about my day. The way we feel about each other isn't changeable or moveable. Had we not exchanged those words last night, I'm not sure how I'd have taken the scene between them. Not well or nearly so calmly, that's for sure.

Alex doesn't figure into my marriage equation. He's the odd man out. Whatever happened between him and Jules today can't happen again. Maybe he used to be a confidante or someone she turned to, but I want to—need to—fill that role now.

After lunch, I put a bottle of wine in the mini-fridge to chill, and I've got sparkling water and ice cubes as well. Cold wine, hot bath, uncomfortable conversation.

There's already a band of discomfort around my chest at the thought of discussing anything to do with Alex. Although I have a better understanding of what happened all those years ago, my imagination ran rampant at even the hint of something going on between them. And Alex dropped a lot of hints. While I know they weren't together for very long at all, that most of what I believed was manipulation and imagination, there's a part of me deep inside that still feels like they were intimately connected for years.

My stupid fucking brain that can't remember getting married—likely the happiest I've ever been—but can vividly remember all sorts of terrible and sordid imaginary scenarios I dreamed up about Alex and Jules. They've played on repeat so many times, whether or not I called them up, that the pretend has become the real.

No matter what I refuse to let my incompetent brain ruin what my heart has been begging for since that night in the barn. I've got her, and I won't let some unresolved insecurities tear us apart. I might not have been better than that then, but I am now.

Since Julia texted she'd be back to our suite of rooms soon, I've started the bathwater. She likes it hot, deep, and bubbly. Or at least I hope she still does. The last time she had a bubble bath in my deep jacuzzi tub was after the Bellerive Charity Half-Marathon when we were fifteen.

So many memories.

So many years wasted being upset about smoke and mirrors, nothing of substance.

"What's this all about?" Julia asks from the doorway of the en suite.

When I glance in her direction, she's already shedding clothes, an amused expression on her face.

"A bubble bath built for two?" I suggest.

"Wine spritzers and a bubble bath." She places her hands on her curvy naked hips.

All of a sudden, I'm feeling overdressed. Easy enough to solve. I grab the back of my shirt and tug it over my head.

Naked, she wanders over and places a gentle kiss on my lips. She stills my hands on the waistband of my gray sweats.

"Allow me," she murmurs.

"If I allow you, we might not even make it into the bathtub," I say. This time, I'm not letting anything but my brain lead. Willpower is a thing I will possess. Today. Right now.

She slides her hand along the front of my sweatpants, and when she glances up at me, I snag her lips in a searing kiss.

Fucking willpower. Who needs it?

My pants and underwear hit the floor, and when I lift her up, she wraps her legs around my waist. I step out of my tangle of clothes and press her against the door.

She kisses me deeply, and then her fingers graze the hair just above my ear. "I love you Nicholas Edward Summerset."

There's tenderness in the depths of her blue-gray eyes, and it's a look that reminds me of ones I received from her a long time ago. Deep love and friendship are a lot more connected than I ever would have believed at sixteen.

"I've never loved anyone else the way I love you," I say gruffly.

She wiggles, and my erection lands at her entrance. Her gaze lights up with desire and a trace of teasing humor. "Say it again once you're inside me."

No need to ask me twice. I thrust into her, and she tightens her legs around me.

"I'll never love anyone else the way I love you," I murmur against her ear.

"Oh, Nick," she gasps, digging her hands into my hair and drawing my mouth back to hers.

We're kissing, tongues tangling, and her body is so warm, so soft. It's the first time in my life I've had true empathy for addicts. I cannot get enough of Jules. Quitting her would kill me.

###

Jules sweeps her wine glass off the sideboard and settles against my chest, bubbles foaming around us. I take a sip from my own glass, working up the nerve to mention Alex. Somehow in the sex haze, I almost convinced myself we didn't need to discuss him. If I see them together like that again, I might lose my shit.

"How long did you say you and Alex were together that summer?" I try to keep my voice light, unassuming.

She tenses against me. "A few weeks. Maybe a month or two? It was—it was quite a bit of the summer."

"And the night of my father's birthday—"

"I broke up with him after you kissed me." She sets down her glass and turns in the bath so we're face to face. "I want you to see me when I say this, and I'll say it as many times as you need me to, okay? I realized when you kissed me that I loved you." Her gaze shifts over my shoulder in a faraway expression. "There was always something missing or not quite right between me and Alex, but I couldn't figure out what. And then you kissed me, and it was the biggest lightbulb moment of my life. I didn't feel what Alex wanted me to feel because I already felt it for you."

Not gonna lie—her explanation floods my body with warmth. But I can't get stuck on the past because, although that still bothers me, it's what's happening right now that's the real problem.

"And now?" I ask. "Are you two friends? Best buds? Acquaintances? Employer and employee?"

"Is this because of today?" Jules asks, averting her gaze to pick up her wine again.

"I wasn't thrilled to discover my wife crying in my older brother's arms."

"Yeah, I can understand why that would bother you."

I tip my wine glass up for a long drink. "You and I spent fourteen years dancing around each other. But from my perspective, every time I turned around, you and Alex were huddled together. For years. I need to understand or put what I saw today in perspective. It'll drive me insane otherwise." It already has, several times over, but she doesn't need to realize that.

She takes a deep breath and seems lost in thought for a minute while she sips her wine. "I'm not sure you're going to like what I have to say."

"Hit me with it." The heavy band around my chest reappears.

"Alex is a very lonely and isolated man, and he was a very guarded teenager too."

Not exactly the terrible declaration I braced for. "That's because he's an asshole. No one wants to be friends with an asshole."

"I said you wouldn't like it."

"What does his self-imposed isolation have to do with you?" I don't bother hiding my annoyance.

"After we stopped being friends, I was lonely too." She meets my gaze.

"Are you trying to tell me you've had sex with my brother?" An irrational spike of jealousy emerges from its very brief slumber. I knew it was a possibility, but I never intended to ask.

"No. I've never slept with Alex." She slaps my chest and water sloshes over the edges.

"And you never will. That's the second half of that sentence."

"That's a given. If I haven't yet, it's not going to happen at all."

"Damn right." I slide forward and plant a kiss on her lips.

She twists around in the bath and settles her back against my chest again. With her free hand, she links her fingers with mine. "I just meant that, in the absence of *our* friendship, I became closer to him, I guess. Never the same way we were." She slides her fingers along mine.

"I'm not following." Or maybe I don't want to follow because it sounds a bit like Alex replaced me in a way.

"We're friends. Alex often uses me as a sounding board or confidante, I guess? If he needs help with a situation, he'll call me."

"You're the one responsible for him being an asshole?" I'm teasing, sort of.

She reaches back and pinches my nipple.

"Oww."

"Deserved it. I'm trying to be honest, and you're poking fun." She half turns to meet my eyes. "I've been careful not to let our friendship creep into anything resembling a relationship." She gives a rueful smile. "I'm guessing I know Alex as well as he's ever let anyone know him."

"So not particularly well." It's a snarky comment, and I let out a deep breath. "Whatever friendship you've had with him, I'm not okay with what I saw today."

"I get that. I'm sorry." She squeezes my hand. "If I was in your shoes, I wouldn't have handled it nearly as well as you did, as you still are. He caught me at a bad moment when I was feeling low."

"I want to be the person who lifts you up when you're feeling low. I want that back," I say gruffly.

"Oh, Nick." She sets down her wine and turns in the tub to straddle me. She cradles my face and stares deep into my eyes. "You are the first person I think of whenever something bad happens. You *are* the person I want to talk to most in the world. He just happened to be there today. But I promise you I will be more conscious of how I am with Alex in the future. It won't happen again. I promise."

Her expression is so open and sincere I find myself nodding.

"Okay," I say, and I plant a soft kiss on her lips. "Okay."

###

For some reason, I turn on the local news the next morning. Normally, I don't watch any news stations. The world is a depressing place, and anything relevant for my diplomatic missions, my secretary will fill me in. Since Jules climbed out of the bed at the butt crack of dawn to head to the airport, I haven't been able to sleep. She headed off to collect Kafil, Bahati, and Elena to take them to their hotel.

Brice and I are booked at the local women's shelter to give out gifts to all the children with birthdays this month. We tried to move the event so I could go with Jules to the airport, but it became a scheduling nightmare.

The banner flashes across the bottom with a 'breaking news' scroll. I take a bite of my oatmeal and chew slowly.

Bellerive Advisory Council in conjunction with the Royal Family announces upcoming referendum on legalizing assisted suicide.

My spoon clatters into my bowl. The Royal Family announces? What the hell is this? Last I checked, I was the face of that family too. Tossing my napkin on the table, I grab my phone from the bedside and text Brice to meet me at Dad's office before we head to the shelter.

He texts back almost right away with a question mark.

Did you know Dad and Alex are pushing for a referendum on legalizing assisted suicide?

My phone rings.

"Had no idea," Brice says before I can even say hello. "You're going to find out what the deal is from Dad?"

"I'm not going to Alex. Who else would I ask? Julia's mom?" Though I am sure the former Secretary Jensen would know since she's been handling the political side of the secretary job while Jules has been coordinating the coronation.

"You don't think Julia knows?"

"She's been too busy with wedding and coronation stuff." My brain ticks through how distracted the two of us have been kept since we returned. "Almost feels like they've hidden this from us deliberately, doesn't it?"

"I don't know, man. Shit is getting weird. I'll meet you at Dad's office in ten."

Since I don't know how long our chat with Dad will last, I dress in the clothes I intend to wear to the shelter and then head toward his office. On my way there, I become more and more convinced that everyone has been keeping this news from me, Brice, and Jules.

Brice and I meet at the juncture to the royal offices from our private wings of the palace.

"I've got a bad feeling about this," Brice admits as we walk to the office door. He rolls his shoulders in his suit jacket and adjusts the cuffs.

"You mean that they deliberately hid the referendum from us?" I ask. I've never made my feelings on this topic, and many others, a secret when they've come up during policy meetings.

"I'm not sure you've quite followed the logic steps yet," Brice says as he knocks on our father's door. "I hope I'm wrong."

Our father opens the office door looking haggard. "Did we have an appointment?" Our father rarely pulls any punches, which is why his subterfuge here is surprising. No topic has ever been too difficult for a family discussion or an informal debate in the middle of a corridor. Though since I've returned from Tanzania, I've noticed changes in him I didn't see before, particularly in his ability to focus and remember recent conversations.

"Nick saw the referendum news this morning," Brice says, stepping past my father into the room.

I'm still at the doorway, putting together Brice's words. My gaze runs over my father. Is he sick? My stomach churns with anxiety. Is that what Brice thinks he's put together?

Instead of saying anything, I follow Brice to the seats across from my father's wide desk. At the door, my father hesitates for a moment before pushing it closed and locking it.

Another frisson of unease snakes down my spine. When he settles into the third seat on our side of his desk, I'm convinced Brice has put the plot together faster than me. My instincts are usually better than his, but I've been so distracted with Julia, Alex, and the wedding. How did I miss this?

"What's going on?" My voice has a gravelly texture. There's a ball of anxiety rolling around my stomach.

"Alexander and I, along with the Advisory Council, have opted to hold a referendum on legalizing assisted suicide. I had hoped to speak to both of you before it became public, but we must have sprung a leak."

"It's a hot button issue," Brice says.

"Is it?" Our father asks, his eyebrows rising.

He must know it is, or he wouldn't be pushing for a referendum instead of ramming it through the Advisory Council.

"At least in our family," Brice says, sliding a glance in my direction.

We haven't had a referendum since the Advisory Council opted to make the royal family the deciding vote in any split decisions. As far as I can remember from my royal history, that was a couple hundred years ago.

"The Advisory Council is split?" I ask.

"They are." His gaze shifts between me and Brice.

"Why can't you be the deciding vote?" I ask the logical question, but I suspect the answer is obvious.

"You're sick." Brice sucks in a sharp breath. "That's why you're stepping down early. Holy shit." He rubs his cheeks. "That's it, isn't it?"

Our father pales, but he remains ramrod straight in his chair. "I didn't feel it was right for me to cast the deciding vote on legislation I might employ one day."

Although I expected it, my heart still stutters to a stop. "What's wrong with you?" I whisper.

He stares at us for a beat, and his jaw works as though he's grinding his teeth.

"Dad?" Brice's voice cracks.

"I've been diagnosed with Alzheimer's. I am in the very early stages, but as I'm sure you're both aware, there is no cure." Our father swallows.

"How long have you known?" I bury my face in my hands and lean my elbows on my knees.

"I've gone to three experts over the course of the last year, and I got the final confirmation a few months ago." His tone is weary.

"What stage are you in?" Brice asks. One of his patronages is Bellerive's Alzheimer's Society. Of course he'd think to ask that, and it only makes his exclusion from the news stranger. Of all of us, Brice would understand the most what this diagnosis means.

"Stage Two. Very mild cognitive decline. Stepping down now seemed like the right thing to do before it gets worse. I can't be in charge of making major decisions. Finances, dates, word finding—I struggle."

He'd still be a better decision maker than Alex. My gut is spasming, clenching and releasing as though it's not sure if it wants to keep my breakfast or release it.

"Who else knows?" He knew before he sent Jules to Tanzania. Does she know? I click through all my memories where my father came up. If she knew, and she didn't tell me...

"Your mother, Alexander, the Advisory Council, Secretary Jensen..."

My stomach heaves, but he might mean her mother. I hope he means her mother.

"Both of them," he clarifies, gently.

I close my eyes and slouch deeper into the chair. Julia knew. She's known all along. There are so many emotions racing through me, I don't even know which one to latch on to. Anger, fear, betrayal, sorrow.

"You told the Advisory Council before you told us?" Brice's tone is scathing.

Our father stands up and paces around to his desk, but he doesn't sit down.

"I felt it was only fair to tell them since I refused to be the deciding vote. Telling you boys... I didn't even tell Alexander. That was your mother."

"But she didn't tell us!" I shoot up from my chair. "If you're having a referendum on a measure you wish to use, the public deserves to know what they're voting on. What they're giving their blessing to."

"I'm hoping the people of Bellerive will vote for compassion." He's staring out the window, not looking at either of us.

"It's not compassion," I seethe. "It's murder. New medical developments are happening all the time." I whirl around to Brice. "Right?"

He looks as stunned as I feel, but there's a grimness to the set of his mouth. "It's a horrible disease, Nick."

"Of course it's horrible," I say. "There are no good illnesses or diseases." I give my father a hard stare. "I will not allow the people of Bellerive to vote in favor of this."

He releases a deep sigh, his hands thrust into the pockets of his suit pants. "I can't stop you. But I hope you'll come to understand how this looks and feels from my perspective. I don't want to die, Nicholas. I'd love to see my children settled and happy. I'd love to have grandchildren bouncing on my knee. Would love to see Bellerive flourish on an international scale.

Perhaps some of that I *will* get to see. But when the time comes, and I am no longer myself, I want the option to bow out gracefully."

I huff out a breath of frustration.

"We put animals out of their misery when their suffering becomes too great. Why are we, as humans, above the same kindness? The same empathy?" My father's voice is commanding and persuasive, a tone that always made me proud to call him my father when he stood at a podium.

Not today. I refuse to let any of his words be absorbed. There's too much anger in me at him, at Jules, at everyone else who knew and didn't tell me. He's known for almost a year this was possible. Jules has known for months. *Months.*

My phone beeps with the alert to head to the shelter. Brice hoists himself out of his chair, but his movements are sluggish.

Before we leave the office, I stare at my father. "You need to tell the people before the referendum. They need to understand they're voting to kill you." My voice grows rough at the end, but it's not sadness, it's rage. With that parting shot, I draw the door to his office closed.

"Nick," Brice says once we're out of earshot.

"No." I give a sharp shake of my head. "We're not talking about this right now. I can't. We throw on our royal faces at the shelter, and then I need to speak to my wife."

"Don't be mad at Jules. Dad should have been the one to tell us. Or Mom. Telling you wasn't Julia's job."

"She's my fucking wife. *My wife.* If they couldn't or wouldn't tell me, she should have." I slice a hand through the air as we get to the main entrance where the car is waiting. "I don't want to talk. We do our duty, and we get the fuck out of there."

"She's been your wife for five minutes," Brice mutters. "Give her a fucking break."

I can't cut her any slack because my mind has zeroed in on something else. Yesterday's tableau in Julia's office is playing on repeat with a new meaning behind it. Alex, squeezing her tight, Julia in tears. This must have been what they were talking about. That more than anything is a knife to the gut.

Just like last time, Alex and Jules conspired to keep the truth from me.

JULIA

The news of the referendum breaks in the SUV on my way to the hotel with Bahati, Kafil, and Elena. The three of them are filled with joyful exclamations on the beauty of the Bellerive coastline, the size of the island from the plane, the lush greenery they've never seen before. Meanwhile, my stomach is rioting, convinced that I'll return home to a shit storm.

Did Alex leak the referendum? Could have been anyone if Merida knew yesterday, but someone at the palace would have confirmed it. Does Nick know yet that his father is sick?

God, it's all such a mess. I've texted Nick, but I haven't received a response. There's no delivery notification, either, so his phone must be off. Maybe he doesn't know about the referendum. Seems like it broke around the time he would have needed to get to the shelter. Maybe I'll get home, and he won't know yet.

That's magical thinking, and I know it.

"Are you okay?" Kafil asks, drawing me out of my thoughts.

"Yes," I say. "Something came up that Nick won't be happy about, and I can't reach him."

"We can get ourselves settled at the hotel if you need to get home. We can see you at the hospital tomorrow." Kafil rapid-fire translates for Bahati, and she nods in agreement.

"Are you sure?" I feel terrible dropping them off at the hotel and abandoning them. "I've asked for a stroller to be in your room, so you can walk around Tucker's Town if you like. Nick also arranged credit at a bunch of restaurants in the area. The front desk will provide you with a list of options when you check in."

"Thank you." Bahati squeezes my hand and gives me a kind smile.

"Oh, we're happy to do it. In fact, Nick and I—" But the rest of the words die in my throat. I'm not sure what Nick and I will be doing if he finds out I knew about the king's illness and the referendum. "That's not important right now." I give a tight smile. "We're happy to help."

Kafil gives me a questioning look, but he doesn't pry. We've been in constant contact over the phone, and we've become quite friendly. I even told him the other day I was going to wrangle him an invite to our royal wedding.

"Tomorrow," Kafil says.

"I'll meet you at the hospital before the surgery, and then I'll be there after, too, just in case anything comes up." I give a nod of reassurance as our driver pulls into the front entrance of the hotel. "Are you sure you don't want me to go in?"

"We'll be fine." Kafil smiles. "We're grateful for what you have done already."

The driver gets the suitcases out of the back and piles them onto a trolley for Kafil to maneuver into the hotel. Bahati carries Elena on her hip, and I'm glad my mother suggested the stroller for their room.

On the way back to the palace, I come up with a thousand different outcomes to my impending conversation with Nick. In at least fifty percent of them he's so angry he suggests we annul our marriage.

Tears are pricking at my eyes, but I'm not going to cry. The other fifty percent of my scenarios have him not mad at all, understanding, reasonable.

Except Nick's feelings around medical issues and assisted suicide have been set in stone for years. He had those beliefs when the stakes were much lower than they are now—hypothetical, philosophical—this referendum will hit him right in his home, in his heart. Despite Nick's sometimes outwardly prickly appearance, his heart is buttery soft.

When we get to the palace I hustle through the main entrance and follow the corridors back to our wing. Will Nick be there, and if so, what will I find? I'm half-hoping to run into someone who might offer a clue to Nick's mental state, but the palace is uncharacteristically quiet. At the door to our suite, I take a deep breath.

He'll either be in there, and we'll hash it out, or he won't be, and I'll need to track him down. I'm not sure which is worse.

I open the door, and Nick has his elbows on his knees, a glass of clear liquid balanced in his fingertips. He glances up at me, and his gaze is clear. Whatever is in the glass isn't alcohol, thank God. But his usual flirty, happy to see me smile is absent as well.

I can already tell which scenario of the two I crafted in the car is most likely. The air is thick with tension.

"You're home," I whisper.

"You got Kafil, Bahati, and Elena to the hotel without any problems?"

"I did." I take a step into the room and shut the door behind me.

He doesn't get up, and he doesn't say anything else.

"We should probably talk," I suggest.

"Should we?" He squints at me. "Honesty seems to have become your least favorite quality. It's a shame—used to be the one I relied on the most."

"I haven't lied to you."

"I imagine if I went back to every conversation we've had, there's a lie rooted in there somewhere. Or a half-truth, an evasion of the truth. It's all the same."

I try a different tactic because I can't remember every conversation we've had over the last couple months. There's a whole swath of time in Las Vegas that I don't remember at all. The line I've been forced to walk hasn't always been clear. The duties of an employee, a wife, and a friend have been muddled along the way.

"Have you spoken to your father?"

"You mean, did he tell me he has Alzheimer's? Yes. Did he tell me you knew? Yes. Am I pretty fucking furious?" He stands up, and water spills out of his glass. "Yes, again."

My hand is trembling when I tuck a stray strand of hair behind my ear. "He asked me not to tell you." At his look of disbelief, a lump forms in my throat. "*Ordered* me not to tell you."

"So what?" He practically throws his glass on a side table and runs a frustrated hand through his hair. "You're *my wife*."

"I know. But I wasn't then."

"Okay, fine. Let's say in Tanzania, your loyalty belonged to my father. We've been home for weeks. Fucking weeks. You've heard me muse about what might be going on with my father beyond the obvious and you knew. You knew and you didn't tell me."

"I went to King George, and I asked him to tell you. But he refused. Said he wasn't ready. He cried in my arms, Nick." My shoulders sag at the memory. "He broke down in my arms. How do I betray him after that?"

"So you betray me instead?" Nick scoffs.

He's too angry. We're not going to get anywhere with this conversation. Even though I know it, I can't help trying again. "I hoped you'd understand the difficult position I was in."

"The real kicker," Nick says, moving to put more space between us. "Is that I've realized that's likely what you were speaking to Alex about yesterday. Am I right?"

I swallow down another ball of fear. "Yes," I whisper.

"You and Alex, keeping another massive secret from me."

"Alex agreed to make sure you were told today."

"You know what you could have done? You could have fucking told me yourself."

"I made a promise." I'm pleading now. Worry about where we're headed is eating away at any rational thoughts in me too. Confiding in Alex about the referendum might be the tipping point.

"You made a promise to me," Nick roars. He points at his tattooed finger. "To me. We put each other first. That's what this means. We don't let other people wiggle their way between us. That's what this means."

"I'm sorry." Tears stream down my face. "Please, Nick." I step toward him, but he takes a step back.

"I can't do this." His tone is resigned. "I can't have you here."

"Nick." His name is garbled coming out of my mouth.

"Please, Jules. Just go." His voice cracks. "I can't take your fucking tears on top of everything else. Just go."

"Does this mean..." I can't say the words, and my throat is so clogged with tears it's hard to breathe. The last time I disappointed him, he snapped our friendship in half. Will he do that to our marriage too?

"Doesn't mean anything," Nick mutters, but he won't meet my gaze. "I don't want you here right now. I can't have you here right now." His gaze connects with mine briefly. "I still love you. I just don't know how to trust you."

His comment stings, and I'm too stunned to defend myself. Can I defend myself? What do I say? His father is dying, and I didn't tell him.

"Okay." The word is strangled coming out of my lips. "Okay." All I want to do is cling to him, hug him so tight he's got no choice but to feel my regret. But there's enough of the old Nick still in him for me to understand that his anger won't be gone anytime soon. As much as I don't want to give him the space, crowding him will only lead to more fights. Worse fights.

In the walk-in closet, I toss things into an overnight bag blindly. If I have to come back for more, I'll do it when he's not here.

At the door, I take a deep breath. Maybe he doesn't want to hear it or acknowledge it, but I need to say it anyway. "I love you, Nick. I'm so sorry I hurt you."

I don't wait for a response because I'm sure one isn't coming. Instead, I close the door and try to figure out where I'm going now.

###

Posey opens the door to her modest, but beautifully decorated, apartment in Tucker's Town and steps back to let me enter. We texted while Kane, one of Alex's guards, drove me to her house.

"He kicked you out?" Posey shakes her head and leads the way into the living room. "I already texted Brice to get him on Nick's case. This is bullshit."

As an interior designer, she has an eye for color schemes and pretty things that I do not possess. I drop my bag in the center of the room. "I lied to him."

"He's taking unreasonable to new lows if he doesn't understand why you didn't tell him."

"He's upset, and he's blaming me, and while I don't like it, I understand it." I use the palms of my hands to wipe the tears that won't stop falling. Nick's anger is understandable, I'm terrified we won't come back from what he sees as a giant betrayal.

"You are a better person than me. If Brent kicked me out of anywhere, he'd be dead to me." Posey holds up an open bottle of wine from the kitchen doorway. "Drink?"

"Better not. Maybe he'll call and change his mind."

Posey snorts. "He should arrive here begging for you to forgive him for overreacting. But Nick is stubborn, so that's not happening tonight. Might as well drink." She pours me a glass.

I toy with my ring finger and trace the lines of Nick's name. "At least we're married. He can't really just get rid of me that easily."

She lets out a sigh and passes me the wine before sitting down with her own glass. "He's not going to get rid of you."

A shaky breath escapes me. "I loved him and then I hated him and then I was indifferent to him. Or I thought I was. Maybe I never quite escaped the love-hate paradigm." I rub my face, and exhaustion settles over me. "Things have been so good between us. So good. I dreaded the truth coming out, but I hoped he'd understand I was stuck in an impossible situation."

"He didn't cancel the wedding, right?"

"Do I keep planning it when he's so angry with me? Who wants to plan a wedding when you're worried your spouse hates you?"

"Julia," Posey says. "Whatever he said, he doesn't *hate* you. He's mad. Mad Nick has been a force since we were kids. Big emotions get away from him so, so easily. Aren't you the one who told me that?"

"I don't know what to do. I don't know what to do." My voice hitches on a sob. "He's so angry with me, and I don't know how to fix it."

Posey puts down her wine and comes over to tug me into her arms. "Oh, Jules. You'll figure it out. If there's one thing I know about you—you don't give up easily."

But it's not me giving up this time, and you can't force someone to fight for you, to fight for a relationship.

"Ask him about the wedding tomorrow," Posey says. "I'm sure he'll say it's still on. He's just angry, but it'll pass."

I'm not so sure. She didn't see his face, and the memory makes me curl into her on another sob.

Nicholas

I didn't let myself drink last night, but it still feels like I've been on a bender. When Jules told me she loved me just before leaving, my heart cracked in two. I wish she told me the truth. I wish I didn't care so much about her closeness with Alex. I wish my father wasn't dying.

My emotions are jumbled together, and I can't separate any of them into something that makes sense.

Despite how shitty my life feels right now, the one thing I've learned as a royal is that the world doesn't stop for my personal crisis. At least this time what I need to be present for is a result of my own doing. Today is Elena's first surgery.

I texted Jules to let her know I'd be there, and she didn't respond. I hope the implication is that she shouldn't attend, but since she didn't ask, and I couldn't bring myself to spell it out without prompting, I'm not sure if she'll be at the hospital or not.

No matter how angry I am with her, just like last time, my desperate love for her runs underneath like a deep, untapped reservoir.

For now, our wedding is still on. Part of me isn't sure it should be—clearly, we've got a lot of issues to work on, but another part of me can't stand the idea of an annulment. It's got nothing to do with public embarrassment either. If I really didn't want to be with her, I'd gladly stand in front of the entire country and declare our marriage a drunken mistake.

Every time I glimpse the tattoo on my finger, I realize how serious I must have been the night we got married. I thought we could make a lifelong commitment work, and abandoning our marriage would let down the faith drunken Nick must have had in sober Nick to persevere.

Kafil and Bahati come out to the waiting room, and the stress of the surgery is written all over Bahati's face. I'd be a wreck if Jules was the one undergoing surgery. I can't imagine how I'd feel about a child.

"Thank you, again." Kafil shakes my hand and grins at me.

"It's been our pleasure to arrange this for Elena." An answering smile rises on my face automatically. I've been trained well.

"Where's Julia?" Kafil looks around.

"I'm here," Julia says, coming in the waiting room door. "Sorry. I got caught up in something else." She hugs Bahati and Kafil, but her gaze doesn't stray to me.

Was she standing outside the waiting room door gathering her courage? Or just late like always?

She comes close enough that I can catch a hint of the coconut shampoo she uses, but she keeps her focus trained on Bahati and Kafil, as though I'm not here. The tension in her shoulders tells me how aware she is of me, of her proximity to me. For my part, I can't keep my gaze off her. You'd think I hadn't seen her in years the way I'm eating up every detail of her appearance. Skirt, flowery shirt, blazer, heels, and her hair is loose. So fucking pretty my whole body aches with longing.

The gulf that's opened up between us is almost palpable.

Kafil asks me a question, and I don't catch it because Jules has slowly tilted her gaze to meet mine, and it's like the whole world fades away. There are dark smudges under her eyes, and I wonder if she didn't sleep very well either. I've gotten so used to having her body pressed against mine that the bed was hollow last night, a deep void of nothingness in the space beside me.

"Nick?" Kafil prompts.

I tear my gaze from Julia's and let out a deep sigh. "Sorry. My brain is filled with royal business today. What did you ask?"

Julia stiffens beside me.

"If you'd care to go for a walk to find some breakfast? We were up so early we haven't had a chance to eat. Bahati wants to stay here, so we'd need to get something to go."

When I hesitate, Kafil says, "Julia already mentioned she can't come. So, if you also have royal things to take care of, not to worry."

My shoulders ease at the realization Julia can't join us, but my gut tightens. The constant push-pull where she is concerned is back in full force. I long to both be around her and stay far away from her at the same time.

"I can walk with you to get some takeout." I check my phone. "Then I'll have to duck out for a while, but I'll be back for when the doctor gives you and Bahati the rundown on the surgery."

Kafil's gaze shifts between me and Julia. "Okay, good."

"Can I talk to you for a minute?" Julia turns her blue-gray eyes up at me, and my chest constricts. "In the corridor."

"Yep." I lead the way out, not keen on a scene in front of Kafil. My heart knocks against my chest.

Julia comes out and runs a hand through her hair. "I'm supposed to be meeting with the wedding planner today. I just—" She glances at me before her gaze slides away. "I wasn't sure if I should press pause on that or keep pushing ahead."

The question hits me with more force than I'd expect. "Pause is a good plan." The response tumbles out before I can properly consider it.

She takes a shaky breath, and her chin trembles. "Okay." Without waiting for anything else from me, she removes her phone from a pocket as she strides down the hallway.

I'm a fucking asshole. Why did I say that?

Before I can run after her, Kafil is clapping me on the shoulder. "Breakfast?"

For a beat, I stare after Julia's diminishing figure in the hallway. What would I say if I went after her? I don't even know. My father is dying, and my wife didn't tell me. Can I ever be okay with that?

"Yeah," I agree. "Breakfast."

###

We're flanked with security when we leave the hospital, but I'm so used to their presence, I hardly notice it. They're helpful to have right now given the referendum storm that kicked off yesterday. While we walk down the street, random citizens call out their opinions to me, but I don't respond.

"Seems the referendum news is popular," Kafil comments.

"Everyone loves a debate." Or at least I used to. The stakes have never been so personal before.

"I don't even understand why it's a question." Kafil shakes his head.

"Me either," I mutter.

"Who would ever wish to see someone or something suffer?"

"You're in favor of it?" I'm not sure why I assumed he wouldn't be. Maybe because we always think other people should fall on the side we believe in.

Kafil takes a deep breath. "I fall on the side of empathy."

"I fall on the side of hope," I counter.

A brief smile blooms on Kafil's face. "Empathy is where the head and the heart meet. There is nothing more that can be done to cure someone. That's the head. The suffering someone I love is experiencing can be ended. That's the heart."

"A solution might be found right after someone chooses to die."

"That's the heart masquerading as the head." Kafil touches his chest, and then he touches his temple. "Sometimes we lead with the heart. Sometimes we lead with the head."

"I can't get behind this," I admit. "Doesn't feel right to me." The thought of sitting at my father's bedside, knowing he's dying settles a crushing weight across my lungs.

"Life is about figuring out when to cling on and when to let go. We all reach those conclusions in our own time. But denying someone else the right to make that conclusion for themselves will never be right."

I'm quiet while we walk, absorbing his words. Is that what I'd be doing? Denying my father the option to make one final choice in his life?

"Are you and Julia arguing about this?" Kafil asks.

"What makes you say that?" I peer at him.

"The tension between the two of you in the waiting room almost choked me."

"We're not seeing eye-to-eye on a few things." I shove my hands into the pockets of my pants.

"The first time I saw you look at her, I knew there was more to your story. Probably why that reporter latched on to it so quickly."

Curiosity sparks in me. "How do I look at her?"

"Like she is the sun." He grins. "Who wouldn't want to bask in its glow?"

Having him mention basking in Julia's glow brings forth a spark of jealousy. Ridiculous. Why would I be jealous of

Kafil? My annoyance at myself grows. I need to get my head on straight. All these stupid, unproductive thoughts.

"To love someone that deeply is truly a gift," Kafil adds as we get to the door of the takeout breakfast diner.

Since his powers of observation seem to be so keen, I don't hold back my question. "And Julia? How does she look at me?"

"Ah." Kafil grins and steps through the door my security guard opens. "Exactly the same way—as though the two of you are locked in your own little solar system."

Orbiting around each other.

For the first time since I sat in my father's office yesterday, a small ball of comfort forms inside of me. Is repelling Jules really the best way forward?

Julia

I'm killing time in Posey's downtown apartment making calls for the coronation because my brain isn't capable of focusing on anything other than Nick. The calls are ones that could be made any day at any time because they're details that aren't pressing or important. Mindless work for a mind that won't cooperate.

"You seem really sad. Probably like how I felt when Brent and I broke up," Posey says from the couch where she's drinking a cup of tea.

She told her work at the most prestigious interior design company in Bellerive that she wouldn't be in today, and she cleared her schedule to be with me. The obstacle she faced with Brent wasn't insurmountable. A terrible ex-girlfriend isn't heaps of lies and miscommunication. They're not on the same scale.

"Considering I had to tell my wedding planner I was hitting pause on a royal wedding that's set to take place in less than three months because my current husband isn't sure he wants to be married to me, I suppose I have a right to be a little sad."

"That wasn't a criticism," Posey says. "I just haven't seen you care about anything enough to be sad about it for years. You rebound from disappointment and heartbreak like a champ. I expected you to have a plan and be firing on all cylinders."

"His name is tattooed on my body." But it's the tattoo on my heart I'm more concerned about. It's not going to be as easy to erase.

"He'll come around," Posey says. "Do you want me to call up a photo collage of all the pictures that have been snapped of the two of you the last few months? He looks at you like you're the center of his universe. He's not going to throw that way."

"I was the center of his universe fourteen years ago. That's how long it took him to get over my last betrayal. *Fourteen years.*"

"That's because neither of you understood what went wrong, and you were young and stupid. But you're both aware of the issues this time, and I have faith you can talk them out like reasonable people. Or you can, at least. You're reasonable." She releases a deep sigh. "Please tell me you're not giving up after one fight."

"I'm not giving up, but I can't be the only one fighting for us. I did that last time when we were kids. At every turn, I was there trying to get us back to where we'd been, and I pushed him further away."

"You love him. He loves you. The only way this doesn't work is if both of you give up."

I pick at the blankets on the bed and don't respond. There's nothing I can do that'll make Nick see reason.

"You're married. Have you never listened to Mom and Dad go at it when one of them is pissed about something?"

"Dad always backs down," I say.

"Sure. Someone needs to calm the rough waters. Mom does it all day for her job, and I think she'd had enough by the time she came home." She sets her teacup down. "You're missing the point. You're going to fight. Brent and I disagree sometimes, but we figure it out. You're not always going to see eye-to-eye, especially as members of the royal family, a royal family entrenched in the political system of this country."

"I lied to him."

"Because you're currently trapped between two roles—wife and employee—but that's not going to last forever. You're not going to become Alex's secretary. That's a recipe for disaster."

"Yes, well, we already agreed I can't work for Alex." I take a deep breath. "We were making plans to expand Nick's foundation in Tanzania."

"Good. I hope you go to Tanzania for a while. Leave all this bullshit behind and get to know each other better again. You and Alex actually need a break, or he needs a girlfriend. He's too laser-focused on something he'll never have with you."

"Do you think I've led him on?" It's the question I've been afraid to ask anyone else but besides Posey or Brice, I'm not sure who I'd ask. There are very few people close enough to Alex to get a sense of what's going on behind the mask.

"No." Her refusal is emphatic. "For whatever reason, he's been fixated on you for years. I tried to ask him once when I was drunk. He just glared at me."

"Sounds about right."

Posey laughs. "Forget about Alex. We need to set up *Operation Get Nick Back* so we can shove this royal wedding on the track. I really want to be a bridesmaid."

"Yes, I should get married so you can be a bridesmaid," I say dryly. If I dwell on the idea of the wedding not happening, I find it hard to breathe. The alternative is an annulment, and I don't want that. Nick said he was in this with me. A knot forms in my stomach at how quickly we fell apart.

"I'm sure people have gotten married for worse reasons," she says.

My phone pings with an alert from the hospital. Elena is out of surgery, and the doctor will be speaking to Kafil and Bahati within the hour.

"I've got to go." I grab my blazer off the back of Posey's kitchen chair. "Elena is out of surgery."

"Good luck!" Posey calls. "Tell Nick I said hello."

I roll my eyes at how blithe she's being about the potential dissolution of my marriage. "Get right on that," I mutter on my way out the door.

###

My driver drops me off at the front entrance, and I hustle my way through to the room Kafil texted me a few minutes ago.

I breathe a sigh of relief when I reach the room and Nick isn't anywhere in sight. Maybe I can get in and get out before he appears. Despite Posey's suggestion about *Operation Get Nick Back*, I'm not sure he wants to be back with me. Not yet. Maybe not ever. Seeing him makes my heart hurt.

While I make idle chit-chat with Kafil, my gaze keeps wandering to the door of the hospital room.

"Nick's not coming today," Kafil says when my attention slides back to him again.

"No?" I frown.

"Said something came up unexpectedly, and he'll stop around later tonight or tomorrow."

"Oh, well..." The sinking sensation in my stomach is unexpected. Even if my head wasn't sure seeing him was a good idea, my heart clearly had other ideas.

Bahati appears at my side and runs a comforting hand down my arm. Her gaze is tender as she looks at me and then says a whole bunch of Swahili I can't follow. But I catch Nick's name a few times.

With a furrowed brow, I nudge Kafil. "I caught about five words, and three of those were Nick."

"She thinks Nick will come around about whatever you're fighting about," Kafil says.

"How does she know we're fighting?" My cheeks heat.

"Nick mentioned this morning that the two of you weren't seeing…" He seems to flounder for a moment. "Eye-to-eye."

I'm surprised Nick said anything to Kafil, but none of us are acting exactly as we might normally. My world, at least, has been turned on its head.

"Is that all she said?" While I don't speak the language, it seemed like she said a lot more than he translated.

"Hmm." Kafil rubs the back of his neck. "She thinks he'll get over the argument because of what he named his foundation."

"His foundation in Tanzania?" Now I'm really confused. "He calls all his foundations a version of the same thing. N.E Summerset-Bellerive Tanzania is probably this one, right? The country at the end changes, but the rest is the same."

"You really don't know?" Kafil chuckles.

"I guess not?" I search his face. "What's the one in Tanzania called?"

"The J.J. Bellerive Foundation."

"What?" I press a hand to my chest, and I gape at Kafil.

Bahati grins, and another stream of Swahili flows out faster than I can pick up.

"She said everyone asked him who J.J was, but the first time she saw you two in her home, even before she knew you were Julia Jensen, she knew you were J.J." Kafil's pleased grin matches Bahati's.

Nick named the Tanzanian foundation we planned as kids after me. He named it for me before I appeared in Tanzania, before we shared a tent, and before we got married. I'm stunned, but there's a strange warmth emerging in my chest. Even when we weren't speaking, even with fourteen years between us, Nick loved me enough to stick my name on something he intended to do alone, without my knowledge. He loved me enough to include me even when he couldn't figure out how to draw me back into his life. The realization is amazing and frustrating at the same time. So many wasted years.

Just then the doctor enters to give us a rundown on the successful surgery. I listen and answer any relevant questions, but my brain is already at the palace, hunting down Nick, telling him that *pause* doesn't work for me.

As soon as the doctor leaves, I make my excuses to Kafil and Bahati and meet my driver out front again. We zip to the palace, and my stomach flutters with excitement and a hint of unease.

The car has barely come to a stop before I'm ducking out the door and almost skipping to the front entrance. Maybe Nick won't want to see me, but I need him to admit we're not a lost cause, that we can make things work, even if we still have our issues.

I'm almost through the main entrance when Alex calls out to me. The temptation to ignore him and keep going is incredibly strong.

"He's not here," he calls after me when I don't slow my pace. "And I know you're not staying there right now."

I whirl around. "Did you leak the referendum?"

"Yes," Alex admits, his voice tight. "I couldn't talk sense into Father. He wasn't going to tell them. So, I forced his hand."

"And dropped a bomb in mine." I huff. "A little warning would have been nice."

"You asked me to get King George to tell them. I got King George to tell them." Alex shrugs. "I could have told you Nick wouldn't take it well no matter who dropped the truth in his lap. You could have told him, and he still would have raged about you not telling him earlier. If you told him in Tanzania, he would have been pissed you weren't loyal to Dad. That's Nick. Sensitive, hard to please, Nick."

"Neither of you reads each other very well." I shake my head.

"Or maybe you don't read either of us well," Alex suggests.

I suck my teeth and cross my arms. "Where is Nick?"

"Not sure. But not here." Alex comes closer.

I let out a sigh and mull over my options. Wait for him. Leave and hope he seeks me out later.

"I made some inquiries into your wedding in Las Vegas."

"What?" I ask, unable to hide my surprise. "Why?"

"Call it curiosity." Alex crosses his arms. "Did you know there's no State of Nevada marriage license for you and Nick?"

I can feel the color drain from my face, and I press my fingers into my forehead, lightheaded. "What?"

"Despite the tattoos," Alex says with a nod at my hand. "You and Nick aren't legally married."

Holy shit.

The one thing I've been counting on while Nick and I sort out our relationship is that we're married. The fancy royal wedding was a bonus, not a necessity. If we're not really married, what will that mean for us?

Nicholas

Instead of going back to my own suite of rooms at the end of our various public commitments today, I went to Brice's wing. The truth is my wing of the house is a stark reminder of what I had with Jules just two days ago. Every nook, cranny, and piece of furniture has a memory of her attached to it. I want to embrace it all or burn it all to the ground. There're no half-measures in my thinking.

"Take a drink." Brice pours two more shots.

"You can't keep asking me the same question." I tip back the shot.

"Actually, I can. It's not in the rules anywhere that I can't keep asking the question until you answer." Brice draws a card and smirks.

I draw a card and curse. This is my third two. We've only drawn six cards. When we turn them around to face each other, Brice chuckles.

"You going to drink now, or do you want me to ask the question first?"

"Don't ask the same fucking question. It's obnoxious and counter to the whole game."

"When are you going to take your wife back?" All hint of teasing drops off his face.

I take the shot and glare at him.

"There's a death train that's chugging toward us, and you don't want to face that without her," Brice says. "Trust me."

"She lied to me."

"Did she? Really? Dad asked her to keep his secret. She works for Dad. You know who you should be mad at? You know who I'm pissed at? Dad." He takes a deep breath. "And Alex, but that's like any day ending in Y."

I shake my head and take another shot. I resisted getting drunk last night, but I'm not strong enough to resist tonight. This day has been the longest of my life.

"Fuck the cards." Brice tosses the deck on the table, and they scatter everywhere. "You're not mad she lied to you. You're smart enough to understand the conflict she faced. So what are you really mad about?" He tries to catch my gaze. "Is it because you think she knew, and Alex knew, and therefore in your simpleton brain, they hid the truth from you together?"

"Wouldn't be the first time," I mutter.

"She only found out Alex knew the other day."

"How do you know?" I cock my head and pass him a shot. If we're having a heart-to-heart, he's not allowed to be sober for it either.

"Because, unlike you, I actually talk to Alex. We speak quite often." Brice takes the shot and smacks his lips. "God, I love the taste of truth and tequila."

"You believe him?"

"He's got no reason to lie to me. It's just the two of you who are constantly engaged in a giant pissing match. Been like that since we were kids. Never understood it." He leans forward and slaps my knee. "Would you want Alex's life?"

"Not a chance." The answer is automatic, but I might have enjoyed the attention and praise he received so often when we were kids. Alex could never do anything wrong. Maybe I would have gotten over my insecurity earlier, but his insistence on rubbing his relationship with Julia in my face didn't make it easy to let go of my animosity.

"I'm not sure how much Alex wants it half the time. Gonna throw this out there—but maybe cut him just a tiny bit of slack?" Brice sighs. "Anyway, enough about him. My point is, you've been in love with Jules since your dick was capable of getting hard. Right? So forgive her. Go back to being happy. She forgave you for being a fool as a teenager."

He has a point—a very good point—about Julia's ability to forgive. She hasn't held any of my past behavior against me. A lot of it was likely very hurtful. I'm not sure I could be so gracious if the situation was reversed. She's always been better at forgiveness than me.

"What about the referendum?" I stare into my empty shot glass.

"What about it?"

"You agree with it?" I peer at him.

Brice takes a deep breath and pours himself another shot. "Either way, we're going to watch our dad die. I don't want to lose him a day earlier than I have to, but that's not how this disease works, Nick. It's going to be fucking painful, but I think he deserves to dictate when enough is enough."

"What if he dies and there's a breakthrough?" I slide my glass onto the coffee table.

"Sure, that's a risk. But here's what I know. Breakthroughs for something like this aren't often a cure. More time. A delay. It's not a stay of execution."

I run my hands through my hair in frustration. "In summary, you think I'm wrong about everything."

"Pretty much," he says.

"I can forgive Jules for not telling me. I'm mad, but I also understand her position." I glance at him. "I don't know how I get over my obsession with her and Alex."

Brice slouches into his chair. "Time, man. You need time. You spent fourteen years thinking the two of them engaged in some hot, illicit affair, and that's so far from the truth. It was a couple weeks one summer when we were young. It's nothing. A blip.

She dated other people way longer than that, and you're not losing your shit over those."

Right now. I lost my mind over those as they were happening. If I had to face one of her ex-boyfriends day in and day out, I might lose a whole lot of something over that too.

"It's just hard 'cause she works here, and he's our brother," Brice says. "That feeling in you will fade. Give it time."

"He still carries a torch for her."

"Does he? He's so hard to read. He's never told me that. Either way, she doesn't carry one for him. If he does love her, you should feel sorry for the bastard. You've been on the other side of that. You and Jules are so into each other, it's actually gross. Vomit inducing. Like I want to throw up every time I see the two of you together."

I reach across the coffee table and punch him in the shoulder.

"Ow," he says, rubbing his bicep. "Ease off on the violence. I'm calling it like I see it. And I see a lot of it. All over the freaking palace on the daily."

I make a snort of annoyance just as there's a knock on the door to Brice's suite.

"Should I assume it's not an armed murderer who's managed to get past all security and tell them it's open? Or should I go check?" Brice muses.

"Tell them it's open," I say. "Probably the only person who'd like to murder me right now is Jules."

"It's open," Brice calls.

The door creaks as it swings inward, and Jules is standing in the doorway. My heart squeezes in my chest.

"Have you got a gun?" Brice calls out.

Julia's brow furrows in confusion. "Personal gun ownership is illegal in Bellerive."

"Guess that's a no, then. You looking for your husband? He's drowning his sorrows in a bottle of tequila. I believe you're familiar with the concept." Brice gestures toward me across the table from him.

Since the minute she appeared in the doorway, I haven't been able to speak. Our brief conversation earlier this morning wasn't nearly enough. She's changed into leggings, and her hair is in a ponytail. Somehow, she's managed to find her glasses, and they're perched on her nose. Those fucking glasses. It's like she's preparing for battle.

"Can I—" Julia's gaze shifts between me and Brice. "Can I talk to you alone?"

I pour myself another shot and take it quickly before following Julia out of Brice's room and across the hall into another one. When she said she wanted to speak to me alone, I sort of assumed we'd end up back in our wing, but I guess not.

"You want to talk here?" I scratch my neck and sink into a very uncomfortable couch.

"How much have you had to drink?" Julia asks before she starts pacing.

"I don't know. A bit." I throw an arm over the back of the antique couch and glue my attention to the sway of her hips. How can I be so angry and so turned on at the same time?

"I don't even know how to say this," Jules mutters.

"Another secret?"

"One we kept together." She shoots me an agonized glance, and I furrow my brow at how upset she seems. "Not that we realized we were keeping it."

"Out with it, Jules. The suspense is killing me." The other thing killing me is having her so far away.

"We're not legally married," she says in a rush. "We never got a marriage license in the State of Nevada."

"That can't be right." I rub my face and squint at her. "We got tattoos. There were photos. The press reported on it."

"The 'press' being you. You leaked the story and the photos. I put that together almost right away." She perches on the couch beside me. "We're not married, Nick." Her voice is thick.

I'm glad for the drinks I had with Brice or else my heart might be clogging my throat. "We're not married?" I manage to squeeze the words out.

"I just found out," she whispers. "And then I made some calls to confirm."

"Who told you?" I stare at the tattoo on my ring finger. *Jules.* There's a chance I *am* drunk. This is starting to feel like a hallucination or a nightmare.

She takes a deep breath and when she doesn't say anything right away, I raise my head to meet her gaze.

"Alex."

"Of course he did." I run a hand through my hair and collapse back on the couch. "Did he then propose to you himself?"

"Nick," Jules breathes out my name. "I love you. Alex doesn't love me. He thinks I'm a good fit for a job I don't want."

"Queen?" I raise my eyebrows.

"I don't want the job. Marriage shouldn't be a job." A pretty pink rises to Julia's cheeks.

"Should it be easy?" Brice's words are floating around my head, but I can't figure out whether these differences Julia and I are having should sink us. I don't want them to, but that's my heart talking.

"I would never call my parents' marriage easy, but I know they'd both say it was worth it. What do you think your parents would say?"

Truthfully, I have no idea. They've always made it a point not to get into big fights around us, but I've realized from the silences at various dinners that they *do* happen. Maybe seeing their arguments explode and resolve would have helped me now.

"There's no divorce for royals," I say. "This is our chance to be sure we want to be married right now."

Julia sucks in a shaky breath. "You're not sure about us?" Her voice breaks at the end, and a sheen of tears glosses over her eyes.

I stare at her for a beat and try to be completely honest with myself. The tequila I just drank makes my tongue looser than normal. "That's not what I said, and it's not what I meant either. I love you more than I've ever loved anyone. But a grenade went off in my lap the other day. My father is sick. He's dying." My voice catches on that reality. "My country is holding a referendum on a topic I feel very strongly about. My wife—sorry, I mean, *you*—kept a lot from me."

It breaks my fucking heart to see her so sad. The last thing I want to do is hurt her, but I don't know how to put all these intense negative emotions aside either. Not yet. Maybe Brice was right about at least one thing.

"I need a bit of time to sort through my feelings. We toppled headlong into this, didn't we?

"We did," she agrees. "But it doesn't mean we were wrong." There's a hint of pleading in her voice.

"Just give me a little bit of time and then we'll talk it through, I promise." I drag her into my arms and kiss her forehead.

"I'm not giving up on us." She wraps her arms around me and breathes me in.

We stay like that, relaxed and holding each other while my eyelids grow heavy.

When I wake up, she's gone, and the hollowness in my chest is back.

Julia

I've spent the last two days in Posey's guestroom reading through the four-hundred-page document that makes up coronation protocol and avoiding the outside world. My highlighter is beside me, and I'm making notes on my laptop of all the things that are legally binding for the coronation as well as things that are no longer viable because of changes in technology, tradition, or the materials no longer exist.

Someone needs to condense and update this protocol for modern times. Perhaps I'll suggest it to whoever takes over as Alex's secretary once the coronation is over.

On top of my own personal drama, news of the king's illness broke late last night, and I'm sure the palace is in a frenzy. Who leaked it? Could have been Alex, could have been Nick... could have been any of the people who overheard one of us talking about it the last few days.

I should get dressed and head over to the palace to help manage the fallout, but I can't bring myself to leave my bed.

Posey knocks on the doorframe to my room. "I'm leaving for work. Remember we're ordering sushi tonight. Tomorrow, Brent arrives." She eyes my mountain of blankets. "Are you going to get dressed today?"

"Not sure why I would," I mutter while I make another note on my laptop. Listening to Brent and Posey make up for their long distance over the next few days is not my idea of a good time. Maybe I'll need noise-canceling headphones.

"If you don't get dressed today, I'm calling Mom."

I laugh, but it doesn't hold any humor. "Mom is too busy to come to your rescue. You're stuck with me squatting in your spare room, dirty and miserable."

"Fine. I'll call Nick."

That gets my attention. I glare at her and try my best to shoot fire out of my eyes. "You wouldn't dare." Since I haven't gotten out of bed for two days, I have safely avoided any run-ins with him. Last time I saw him, he was sleeping peacefully on an uncomfortable couch in Brice's suite.

"If I called and told him you needed him, he'd come."

"I'm not playing dirty. He said he needed space, and I'm giving him space." Staying away has sent me into a spiral, and I can't deny that. Part of me wants to storm the estate and tell Nick he's ridiculous, and part of me is terrified that pushing too hard again will send him further away.

"Don't worry, I'll play dirty for you." Posey winks and juts out a hip. She turns in the doorway and sails down the hall. "If you're not out of bed when I get back, game on!"

I growl and sink lower into the plush bedding. She won't do it.

Picking up my highlighter again, I turn the page in the manual and check the newest batch of things the incoming king must possess. My hand stalls on line ten, and my blood runs cold.

Prior to the coronation, the heir apparent must be wed.

I read the line over and over. Must already be wed? As in, must have a spouse? I stare at the wall across from me and try to imagine Alex married. Who would marry him on such short notice? He's never invested more than a passing interest in a romantic relationship.

His longest one was probably Anna Samuels, if you could even call it a relationship. Fuck buddy, maybe? They exchanged gifts at Christmas and had, according to her at a party years later, a lot of sex. But he made her keep the whole thing super hush-hush. Not exactly a love match, but I know he did that *and her* for at least three Christmases. Maybe when he was home on school breaks too. She must have been good at keeping secrets because I never caught wind of it at the time.

Who do I call about this marriage clause? My mother is the logical choice, but I know she'll be supporting the king in the aftermath of his diagnosis coming out. There's supposed to be a press conference this afternoon.

Then it comes to me—exactly who to call. I throw back my covers and follow the one request my sister made. I'm getting out of bed.

###

Nick opens the door to his suite on the first knock. He's dressed in gray sweatpants and a fitted navy-blue T-shirt, and my heart thumps in my chest. Normal clothes, messy hair, and a smile tinged with wariness. My body liquefies at the sight of him.

I've never loved anyone more.

He drinks me in with the same intensity, as though we haven't laid eyes on each other in years. I scan him from head to toe, absorbing every detail, comparing each piece to the one in my memory and discovering it didn't do him justice. Recollections of him will never be enough to sustain me. I need him in my life as much as any other essential. He's so deep in my heart not even fourteen years of separation could completely root him out.

Seeing him in the flesh spikes my fever for him even higher. There is no viral load that makes me immune to Nick.

Please let this turn things around with Nick.

"You said it was important?" He steps back to let me into the suite where most of my stuff still lives.

It's strange to be a visitor in my own home, and maybe I don't have any legal right to this place or to him, but my heart clings to my old reality. My home. My husband. I can drown in sadness, or I can fix our problem. I've never been one to sink when I could swim. While I might have come about something else, I'm hoping my visit restores us as well.

"I needed to tell someone what I discovered," I say, and I shove the coronation manual into Nick's hands.

"You came to me for help?" He doesn't look at the manual. Instead, he's busy scanning my face.

"Yeah." I search the room for anything that might have changed in the few days since I was last here before meeting his gaze. "Is that okay?" The expression on his face tells me I was right to come to him first, that this show of faith in him and in us will do more good than anything else I could have said or done. I'm trusting him first. Confiding in him first. He's the one I come to when I need help.

Can Nick discover some woman for Alex to marry? Unlikely. Am I guaranteeing Nick isn't the last one to find out? Absolutely.

He gives a curt nod and riffles through the manual. "What page?"

"Three-o-two." I ease into one of the armchairs. "I highlighted it."

"I see that." Nick sinks into the armchair across from me. "Alex needs a wife."

"Know anyone willing to marry him?" I ask in a light tone.

"Not a friggin' clue. Do you?" Nick chuckles.

"Did you ever catch wind of him and Anna Samuels? They exchanged gifts for a few Christmases and had, apparently, a whole lot of sex. I think he might have seen her for a few summers too. I don't know all the details. She was drunk at a party when I first started as the secretary, and secrets started spilling along with her cocktail. Maybe her? Or maybe not her? She might be married by now. I haven't checked."

"Anna Samuels?" Nick's frown deepens. "She was in our class, went to all the same parties as us."

"I know. I'm surprised it never got out. Not sure how Alex convinced her to keep them such a secret, but..." The thought trails off when I realize what I've said. Heat rises to my cheeks, and I shrug.

"Wait." Nick holds up his hand, and his shoulders grow tense. "When did he start up with Anna?"

"She said Alex was at her house when he got the phone call about your bike accident."

Nick winces. "Jesus." He closes his eyes. "I thought he went to see *you* that night."

"Me?" I laugh. "Why would he come see me? I was sitting at home waiting for you to text me back. You were such an asshole back then." My words are light, but there's a renewed heaviness in my chest at the memory.

"The levels of my idiocy just do not end. There's no bottom, is there?" Nick drops the manual onto the floor to bury his face in his hands.

"What are you talking about?" I frown and sweep the manual off the floor. I'm going to need that to prove to someone that Alex has to find a wife, pronto.

"I let myself get crushed by assumptions back then. Just... flattened." He glances up at me. "You're right. I was a really big asshole."

"I made mistakes, too, Nick. I should have told you about Alex, or maybe I should have tried harder to get you to talk to me. Or, given how things have gone between Alex and me in the intervening years, I shouldn't have gone in that direction in the first place. We can't fix the past. But we do have to find a way to move beyond it—whether or not you decide you want to be with me. For your own good, you've gotta let your animosity toward Alex go."

"Brice told me something similar... for the last three days." Nick gives a rueful smile. "Gotta admire his persistence."

I'm not sure what to say to that. It seems while I wasn't looking, Brice grew up.

"I need to get out of my own way," Nick says, and he stands up. "I'm a fucking mess, Jules. I treated you so badly back then. I ruined everything. Would you even *want* to be married to me?"

"Are you kidding me?" I let out a quick laugh. "I haven't been the one asking for time and space. I didn't want to hit pause at all. Yes, you hurt me back then, but it was fourteen years ago."

I let out a huff of frustration and decide to lay everything out. "I learned to let that hurt go. I accepted that you became someone I didn't know. But in Tanzania I realized, underneath it all, the Nick who used to be my best friend is still there. The asshole you worked so hard to present wasn't really you." I give him a hard, determined stare. "But you need to deal with your relationship with Alex. Did he play a *small* part in what happened between us back then? Yes. But he's not a villain."

He nods and runs both his hands through his hair until he's cupping the back of his neck. His shirt rides up, revealing his taut stomach, and my gut twists with raw desire. I went months without having sex, and it didn't bother me in the slightest. Three days without Nick has been agony. I should not be thinking about sex right now, but maybe it's the closeness I'm craving more than the physical act. We were happy, and we can be happy again.

"You're right. I have things I have to sort out. You're right," he says. "I want this to work between us, Jules."

His response surprises me. "What are you saying?" I search his face. "Are we unpausing?"

"It means a lot that you came to me first today. Even though I couldn't solve the marriage problem, I want to be the person you turn to whenever you've got any kind of issue. I think, in a lot of ways, that's what's been most hurtful this time and the most last time. I believed I *was* that person for you. I thought we told each other everything. I want us to tell each other everything. However hard marriage is, the only person I'd ever want to do it with is you."

"From the time I wake up until I go to sleep, you're on my mind. I spend a tremendous amount of my brainpower thinking about you," I admit.

He's staring at me so intently, I might melt under the force of his gaze. He wants to be married to me. That's what he said, right?

"From now on, if I know something, you'll know it too. There are no more secrets." Hope is flooding my body.

"I don't know if I had a right to be mad at you or not about my dad, about the referendum, about Alex. But I was. I was really fucking mad." He takes a deep, shuddering breath. "More than that, though, I love you." He presses the heel of his hand to his chest. "Deep in my soul—you're never coming out of there—love you."

I catapult myself out of the chair and into his arms. He chuckles as he catches me and squeezes me tight.

"Oh shit," I breathe out. "You didn't answer me. Are we unpausing?"

"We're hitting play," he says against my hair. "I don't want to do any of this without you."

I close my eyes and hold him tight. The knot in my stomach releases, and I realize a part of me, one I didn't want to acknowledge, was worried he'd never forgive me. Or that it would take another bazillion years for the stars to align again.

"Brice is taking me to the Alzheimer's wing at an old age home tomorrow. Can you—do you think you can come?"

When I try to draw back, he splays his hands across my back, keeping me close.

"If you want me there, I'm there. Is this because... you're still not sure about the referendum?"

He presses his lips to my temple, and they linger there. "I've had some conversations with people the last few days that are making me reconsider my stance. Before I say anything publicly, I need to be sure where I'm at."

"Makes sense," I whisper. "Just tell me what time tomorrow, and I'll clear my calendar." Not that there's much on it. Once my mother found out Nick and I were on the rocks because of her terrible advice, she kept taking commitments off my calendar and plopping them into hers. Normally, that would have started an argument, but I couldn't bring myself to care enough to say a word.

"Three o'clock," Nick says, and he lets me draw away. "Are you coming back here tonight?"

I consider the mess I've left in Posey's spare room, along with this coronation marriage I need to sort out. Tonight is sushi with Posey. Something on my face must give me away because Nick chuckles.

"If you've got other plans, just move your stuff back in tomorrow." His forehead brushes mine, and he drops a quick kiss on my lips. "I never should have asked you to leave. I'm so sorry."

"I want to come back, it's just—I haven't been super tidy at Posey's house—"

"You? Not tidy?" He gives me a mock baffled look.

I slap him in the chest. "And she'll kill me if I leave it like that. We're having sushi for dinner tonight. But I also need to alert people to this coronation complication. And then your dad is having the press conference today..."

Nick runs a hand down my back and kisses my temple again. "It's okay, Jules. I've got meetings tomorrow, and a few things of my own to work out." He smooths my stray hairs. "Tomorrow night—I'm planning dinner for us. You and me. Deal?"

I rise on my toes and give him a quick kiss. "Deal," I murmur just before he deepens the kiss, and I slide my hands under his shirt and along his abs.

"I have to get ready for that press conference you mentioned." He groans. "The whole family is supposed to be there in a show of support. Do you want to come?"

I bite my lip and then shake my head. My mother told me I didn't need to go if I wasn't up to it, and whatever has just happened between Nick and me is too fresh to take out into the public.

He rubs my ring finger and drops another quick kiss on my lips. His heated gaze meets mine. "Tomorrow night."

"Tomorrow night," I agree. "I can't wait."

NICHOLAS

There are two conversations I've been avoiding. Since Jules revealed yesterday that the local girl Alex was seeing all those years ago was actually Anna Samuels, I've been rethinking every interaction my older brother and I have ever had since I saw him kiss Jules at our father's birthday party.

Each time he mentioned a local girl, I assumed she was Jules. He never once named Jules, and he never said Anna either. But my sixteen-year-old brain couldn't fathom a world in which Alex would give Jules up. Or a reality where she didn't pick him over me.

When he started naming women not long after I saw him at the college coming out of Julia's room, I assumed they'd finally broken up. It never once occurred to me they hadn't been together all that time.

Brice is right—so much rage and so much hurt for what amounted to a blip on Julia's dating radar. Next to nothing. Who made their interactions into something? *I did.*

Every fucking time.

Assumed. Assumed. Assumed.

When Alex answers the door to his office, I take a deep breath. "I think I owe you about fourteen years' worth of apologies."

A spark of surprise lights up Alex's dark eyes. "Well, if we're going to start from that place, you can come on in."

"You and Julia lasted, what?" I move past him into his office, but I'm too wound up to take a seat. "A few weeks?"

"Maybe eight weeks. I don't know." Alex grimaces and gives a small shake of his head. "Most of that summer, probably."

"Are you in love with her?" I've assumed the answer for years, but I'm done living from that place. Julia says he doesn't love her, but I can't imagine anyone being so close to her and not being in love with her. This conversation is all about digging down into the dirt, getting to the truth.

"No." Alex sighs. "I feel..." He runs a finger along the surface of his desk, which he continues to stand beside rather than taking a seat.

Maybe he thinks I'm going to hit him again. Part of me expects a snide comment, but he surprises me.

"Protective of her. Would I have married her if she'd said yes any of the times I asked? Of course. She's an amazing woman, and I admire every quality she possesses."

Hearing him talk about her like this isn't helping my long history of insecurity. Instead of blocking out what he's saying, I force myself to hear every word.

"Our marriage wouldn't have been about love. She's a good fit for the roles we need to play. I don't think I'm cut out for love. Not the romantic kind. Not the kind she seems to want." He lets out a deep breath. "I've never been sure you deserved her. You saw me kiss her once, and you tossed her aside."

"I thought you two were in a *relationship*. A relationship you both kept from me." I can't keep the edge out of my voice.

"We were—up until that night." Alex glances at me, his annoyance clear. "I really, genuinely liked her—still do. At the time, I asked both of you repeatedly if there was something more than friendship happening, and you both swore up and down there wasn't. I didn't understand your friendship with her, but since the answer never changed, I figured I'd shoot my shot." He slides into his chair behind his desk. "Out of curiosity, who confirmed we were together after Dad's birthday? Must have been someone for you to be so sure. Did she?" He eyes me, and I let my gaze slip away from his. "Yeah, I didn't think so. She's not one to play games. And I *know* you never asked *me*."

I stare at him in silence.

"You know what I did see, though? You, parading around town with that blond chick glued to your dick. Julia saw it, too, and because I'm *not* an asshole, I tried to comfort her whenever I could."

"Your comfort looked like a closeness I couldn't tolerate." Which makes me sound like an asshole. Couldn't tolerate, didn't understand, didn't want to face.

"Because you never asked."

"I'm—" I rub my face and then draw my hands through my hair. "I'm seeing that now."

"I'm pretending I'm blameless, and I'm not." Alex takes a deep breath and lets it out. "I knew you saw us, and I never told her. You were back with blondie by the end of the night, and I tried to get Jules to take me back. Why not? You weren't an option. At first, I thought it was better if she didn't know you saw us. Later, I didn't think you deserved her. She was better off without you."

Better off without me. That cuts deep. I swallow down my biting retort because this conversation isn't about who's right, it's about figuring out what went wrong. "You must have seen how upset we both were?"

"I knew she was upset because she'd let something slip once in a while. But we stopped talking—you and me. How was I to know she wasn't the only one upset? I wasn't home much, and when I was, we were both busy."

Do I buy that? Does it matter? The reality is that my assumptions sank me and Jules back then. I wasn't able to talk to her about things that mattered. I held a grudge, and I let her slip through my fingers. Maybe that's the truth I needed to discover, to reconcile, so I never let it happen again.

"You're on board for this referendum?" I ask. Brice's stance is clear. If our father chooses to go down this path, assuming it's approved by the Bellerive population, he'll support him.

Alex's expression softens. "I'm not ready, for any of it, but I love him too much to deny him the ending he wants. The whole thing is, honestly, a bit terrifying."

I can't even remember the last time Alex and I had such a refreshingly honest conversation. Brice and I have joked for years about Alex being an asshole, but I'm starting to see that Brice was truly joking, in the way brothers do, and I was serious. Deadly serious. Another thing I might have been wrong about.

"Maybe you were right when we had that argument over who the asshole in the family is," I say.

"You were probably right—it's likely me. I'm quick to anger, and when I get angry, I don't hold back. It's the quality our father finds most disappointing in me, I think. Honesty over diplomacy every time."

"Julia mentioned you were with Anna Samuels for a while."

A brief smile tugs at the edges of Alex's lips. "I thought you knew, actually. She told me she got drunk and told you she was 'fucking your brother' at a party one time. I said if she ever spoke another word to anyone else, she wouldn't be doing that for long."

I slide my hands behind my neck. Had she told me that? Honestly, in high school girls got drunk all the time and told me they 'wanted to fuck my brother'. Listening wasn't my finest skill when I'd had too many drinks, and I drank a lot our senior year of high school. Far too much.

"I didn't know," I admit. "If she told me that, I didn't hear her."

"Thought you knew." Alex shrugs. "As soon as it was clear Jules wasn't interested, I found someone else." He meets my gaze for a minute. "I never gave up hope Julia would change her mind. Royal marriages have been built on weaker foundations than friendship. She was the most logical choice for me, and she's got all the qualities I already mentioned once or twice." He gives me a rueful smile.

"I think it's probably better if you stop telling me about how great my wife is." The moniker slips out before I can correct myself.

"You haven't spoken to Jules yet?" He raises his eyebrows.

"No, she told me. Slip of the tongue."

"I heard from Merida that you were 'hitting pause' on the wedding plans. Is that still where you're at or..."

I brush off my annoyance at him for speaking to our wedding planner. Alex is becoming the king, and just like my father, he'll have his fingers in every royal family transaction. I'll have to live with that.

"No, we're—we're moving ahead." I meet his gaze and hold it. "You still might not think I deserve her, and maybe past me didn't, but I've loved her forever. From the moment she set foot in the camp in Tanzania, I've been crawling my way back to her.

And I'm there—and I just want you to stop trying to fuck it up on me."

"The speed of the whole thing has taken me by surprise." He runs a hand through the side of his dark hair. "I couldn't fathom that Jules could fall that deep that quick. And you? Historically indifferent about the women you dated. For the two of you to form a lasting relationship in a matter of weeks was impossible to comprehend. How is it even possible? And maybe it's not. Maybe the truth is that she could never pick me because she'd already chosen you."

Hearing him say it, admit it, sends a shot of warmth through my chest. His words are similar to ones Jules has used, but it feels like a strange kind of approval coming from Alex.

"As long as she's happy, I won't interfere," he says.

"I swear I will leave no stone unturned in seeking out her happiness."

"Then we won't have a problem." Alex reaches across his desk to extend his hand.

Instead, I rise and hold out my arms. "I think we should hug it out."

"For old times' sake." Alex chuckles but meets me around the desk.

"For new beginnings where assumptions have no place."

"I'll hug to that," Alex says, and he draws me in tight.

###

I left my meeting with my father until after Julia, Brice, and I went to see the Alzheimer's patients at the local old age home.

Julia walks with me from the car to my father's office door.

Brice was a gem at the facility, and everyone there, unsurprisingly, loves him. But man, it was fucking hard to see people in various states of cognitive decline.

Then Brice arranged, unbeknownst to me, a series of meetings with caregivers and relatives of those in the facility. Another spike to my heart was pounded in while I listened to them talk about their loved ones or the patients they care for. Every time he gently brought up the referendum, every single person said they hoped the legalization went through. Not because they wanted their loved ones to die but because they wanted a choice about how the end came.

Julia squeezes my arm and clings to my hand outside my father's office door. "Do you want me to go in with you?" she asks.

Tears prick at my eyes, and I shake my head. We haven't talked much since leaving the home, but this conversation with my father is one I need to have on my own.

"When we're done, I'll come get you for dinner," I say.

"I've got faith in you." She rises on her toes and kisses my cheek.

"Even when no one else does." I give a hoarse chuckle.

She squeezes my hand one last time, and then she heads down the corridor to our suite of rooms.

Before I can lose my nerve, I knock on his door.

"Come in," he calls.

I'm in his calendar, so he must know it's me. When I open the door, he grins at me behind his desk. Despite the poor way we left things a few days ago, he's happy to see me.

For a moment, I stand in the doorway and soak up the expression on his face, the tenderness in his gaze. The people I saw and talked to today showed me these moments are ticking away. What I'm about to tell him makes me feel like I'm part of the clock.

"I've been thinking about you a lot," my father says, gesturing to the chair across from his desk. "Come in and tell me how you're doing."

And that's my father in a nutshell. Staring down his mortality, the demise of his consciousness, and he's worried about me. Since I've decided to live my life devoid of assumptions, I'm going to start with something I've been wondering about but haven't asked. Coincidentally, it's a much easier topic than what I really need to say.

I slide into the seat across from him and rub my hands along the thighs of my jeans. Since the visit to the home was informal, we all dressed in regular attire. My father wears a suit everywhere. There is no dressing down for him, and now that I think about it, Alex is rarely without an immaculate suit as well.

From across the desk, I meet his gaze. "Why did you send Jules to Tanzania?"

My father takes a deep breath and raises his eyebrows. "Julia's parents, your mother, and I had dinner after I got the final confirmation of my diagnosis. We all agreed there were difficult days ahead for you, for Julia. You were already in Tanzania at the time, had just left. Rather than calling you back, I said I was going to let you stay, enjoy your final trip worry free."

"That explains why you were willing to leave me there, not how Julia ended up traveling to 'bring me home.'" We both know the excuse was a decoy for Julia only.

"We were at the table reminiscing about all the trouble you and Julia used to get into."

"Trouble," I scoff. "Hardly."

"Cliff jumping, stealing bottles of wine from the cellar, rides on your motorcycle in the middle of the night, and I could go on if you like." My father chuckles.

"No need." I wave him off when my cheeks heat at the reminders.

"We all said we were surprised nothing romantic ever sprung up between you two. In fact, you seemed to have drifted very far apart. But both of you were devastated by the distance. So sad. Reluctant to talk to anyone about what went wrong." He searches my face. "So, we concocted a plan to see whether proximity would make the heart grow fonder. You can thank Julia's mother for the lack of a spare tent or bed at the camp."

"You're kidding, right?" I groan and slouch deeper into the chair.

"Phone calls were made, and I admit, this was after several bottles of wine split amongst us. Perhaps not our finest hour." He winks at me. "But it has been..." A faraway, satisfied expression settles on his face. "Very gratifying to see you both come home so happy and so clearly, utterly in love."

"I've never loved anyone the way I love her."

"It shows." My father's smile is tender.

"But then why call us home?" I ask. "If the goal was match-making…"

"One of the gossip outlets got wind of the coronation, and the story was going to break. I couldn't get it pinned down. I was afraid news of my disease would spill out with it. While I wasn't ready to tell any of you, I didn't want the two of you so far away if it came out."

I absorb everything he says, and it makes me sad to realize something so joyous, the reunion between me and Jules, will be tied to my father's disease. But at least some happiness has come out of something heartbreaking.

"I hear from Alexander that the two of you missed an important step in—" He frowns.

"Las Vegas." I fill in for him when he seems to search for the word. "Does that happen a lot?" I've noticed it a few times, even more now that I know why.

"More than I'd like. Alexander has taken on many aspects of my position I would normally be fulfilling for fear of a misstep." He shakes his head. "I realize you and Alexander aren't close, which is a shame. Your mother and I probably should have done more to foster a connection. Some people are oil and water—even if they're related." He grimaces. "But Alexander is going to need your help and support. Do you understand that?"

I nod. Alex's job will encompass the role my father used to have—his fingers in everyone's slice of life to ensure the stability of the monarchy, the Summerset's good name. I'll be answering to my brother, a reality I've bucked for years.

"We're in the process of mending some fences," I say. "I'm not sure we'll ever be best buds, but I think I've blamed Alex for a few of my own shortcomings." I give a little laugh. "This growing up thing is painful sometimes."

"As is growing old." He shrugs. "It's a privilege."

A lump forms in my throat, and I try to clear it. "I, uh, have been doing some soul searching about the referendum as well. I'm, um, going to support your wishes."

"I won't hold it against you if your beliefs don't align with mine. I've always been a proponent of open and honest debate."

For a moment I run my hands along my thighs and try to gather my thoughts, the ones that won't lead to a breakdown in my father's office. "I've been fighting this for so long because I see assisted suicide as giving up. I like to believe there's always hope. Tomorrow's a new day. A cure for anything is just around the corner." I take a deep, shuddering breath. "But I've come to realize that how anyone deals with disease is personal, and often filled with difficult choices. When either path leads to the same result, people should have the choice about which one they walk."

When I finally have the guts to meet my father's gaze, there are tears in his eyes. He sniffs and grabs a tissue from the box on his desk. "I want to be absolutely transparent. I'm not proposing this legislation so I can check out early. I'm going to fight as hard as I can, but when it's clear there's no more fight left in me, I don't want to be trapped by the shell that's left behind. Do you understand?"

No words are going to make it past my lips without a sob following behind, so I just nod and try to hold back the onslaught of tears.

My father comes around his desk, and he draws me into a tight hug, and I hug him back with the same force. I bask in the moment, file away every detail in my memory. The woodsy smell of him, the firmness of his arms around my frame, and the scent of peppermint that floats around us as he breathes.

"I love you, son," he murmurs in my ear.

His words crack the dam, and the flood gates open. A sob escapes, and we hold each other while the tears and love mingle and flow.

Julia

When Nick comes back to our suite of rooms, his eyes are rimmed in red, and he looks exhausted. After he replays the conversation between him and his dad, he falls into bed and drags me down into the thick duvet with him.

"Are you sure you want to do dinner *tonight*?" I cuddle against him in bed, and he makes absent figure eights on my arm.

Tomorrow, all of us are supposed to meet to break the coronation marriage news to Alex. My mother, the king, and the queen wanted twenty-four hours to see whether there was a loophole in the manual to give them a plausible out of the clause.

"One hundred percent," he says, and he kisses the top of my head. "Everything is all set. We just have to show up."

"The joys of being a prince." I chuckle.

"The joys of becoming my wife... again." He gives me a little squeeze.

"We should go see Bahati, Elena, and Kafil. They go back the day after tomorrow." I remind him.

"I've been meaning to talk to you about that. The doctor is worried about the amount of rehab available to them in Tanzania close to their village. The first foot needs to be in good shape before they do the second. What do you think about setting up some funded rehab centers? We can start small and see how it goes, and we'll expand if and when we can. We can figure out how to train and sponsor locals to administer the work."

"I love it." I rise up on my elbow. "That's such a great idea. Do you think we'll need to fly back there to sort it out?"

"Probably be easier if we did. We should take a look at our schedules. Do you think you can do some of the coronation setup remotely?"

"I don't see why not. I've been doing most of it from my bed in Posey's spare room the last three days."

"I overreacted." He kisses my temple.

"I'm not sure you did. I wouldn't make the same choice again, believe me." Maybe if I'd told Nick earlier, we wouldn't have fallen into such a mess of uncertainty. "I moved my stuff back in."

"I noticed." There's a hint of a smile in his voice.

"I only took one bag. How could you notice its return?" I glance up at him.

"Your glasses are on the bedside table."

"Why do you have such an aversion to my glasses?" I huff out.

He's silent for a beat and then his shoulders raise slightly. "Always felt like a symbol for a person I never got to know—Jules and *Julia*."

A truth I hadn't seen before clicks into place. "You *did* stop calling me Jules. Julia. Jensen. Secretary Jensen. Never Jules." Of course, I also referred to him as Prince Nicholas in my head once we stopped speaking. Nick was gone.

"I'm sorry for how I treated you." He runs his palm along my bare arm. "God, if I could go back. I made so many assumptions. Ruined my friendship with you. Put an additional strain on my relationship with Alex..."

We walked a terrible path to find each other again, but it gave me a lot of time and space to grow on my own. I would have followed Nick to the ends of the Earth, and I learned a lot about strength and determination from the breakdown of our friendship. Now we've repaired our rift, and maybe he can fix the one with his brother too. "I'm glad you talked to him." I stretch up and kiss his bristly jaw.

"Me too," he says. "I'm not sure we'll ever be close, but talking to him has eased a lot of my... insecurities."

"What time do we need to be wherever we need to be?" I glance at the clock on the bedside table.

"Two hours," Nick says, and then he rolls us so he's pinned me beneath him. "What could we possibly do to pass the time?"

"I need at least an hour to make myself beautiful." I grin.

"More beautiful than this?" He cocks an eyebrow. "Impossible."

"You trying to sweet-talk me out of my pants?"

"And your panties." He gets a wicked glint in his eyes. "And then your shirt and your bra, and eventually, at some point, your birth control."

"Sounds like a slippery slope." I search his face, and I can't believe he's mine. That he's going to be mine forever. Goosebumps rise across my body, and a tingling spreads throughout my core.

"So many dirty thoughts," Nick whispers before he buries his face in my neck. "God, I love you."

"I love you too." I dig my hands into his hair. "Now show me some of those dirty thoughts."

He chuckles and then draws my shirt over my head. "With pleasure."

###

Nick has my hand locked in his. After he refused to give me too many details, I settled on a dress that straddles the line between formal and casual. It's a deep purple that flatters my skin tone, and the flare of approval in Nick's eyes when I exited the bathroom told me I chose correctly. He's in a dress shirt with a jacket, but no tie. It's one of my favorite looks—formal but casual.

"Where are we going?" I ask as we exit the side door of the palace. There's no car waiting, but there are fairy lights strung up leading to the barn.

"You'll see." He glances at me over his shoulder as he leads us across the path and down the little hill to the barn entrance.

He opens the door, and inside are lanterns like the ones we used to use as kids. There's a two-person table set in the middle with a candle. My heart squeezes. I haven't been in here in years. We had so many good memories, and one awful one.

As though he can read my mind, he says, "I wanted to reclaim this place for us. Our friendship has defined my life up to this point, and our marriage is going to define the rest of it. I don't want a single piece of this property to bring either of us anything but joy."

It's a tall order, but I appreciate the sentiment. I squeeze his hand. "We're eating in here?" I ask.

"Eventually." He gives me a half-smile. "Up to our not-so-secret hideout first."

I climb the ladder to the upper level and the wide balcony where Nick and I spent so many nights in our formative years. There are blankets laid out on the ground and a bottle of white wine, two glasses, and some soda water.

White wine spritzer, some blankets, the stars, and Nick.

"Is this where I admit I haven't had a chance to get your name written in the stars?" I try to suppress my smile.

"Slacker," Nick teases. He grabs the bottle of wine and mixes us two spritzers. We lean against the railing while we sip our drinks.

"This is nice." I gaze out across the dark property. Seems like he had most of the security lights disabled, which makes the fairy lights strung up around the building more prominent. "Who'd you wrangle into this?"

"Would you believe Posey, Brent, and your dad?" He chuckles.

"Seriously?" I turn to look at him in surprise.

"Everyone has been so busy with the referendum and the news of Dad's disease. I called and asked Posey for help, and I think she arm wrestled the other two into it."

I doubt she had to work too hard. With my mother too busy to organize their personal calendar and my father retired, he's probably been itching for something to occupy himself. And I know for a fact Brent would do anything for my sister.

"Please tell me they're not serving us dinner too." Posey is a terrible cook.

Nick laughs and sips his wine. "The kitchen staff are working overtime just for us. I knew better than to them for *that* favor."

"This is perfect." I smile and then go on my toes to plant a quick kiss on his lips.

"This balcony was the scene of some pretty important moments between us." He glances at his watch. "Perhaps my favorite, the one that guided us in Las Vegas, was when you offered to fall on the marriage sword if my father ever forced me into an arranged marriage."

"How could I forget?" I smile.

"Do you remember what I promised to shower you with in return?"

I cock my head and try to replay the conversation. "Jewels, right? You said you'd shower me in jewels."

"I've been doing a piss-poor job of it, but luckily we're not legally married yet." His lips twitch, and he takes another sip of his wine.

"Still lots of time." I search his face. I'm missing something, but I can't figure out what.

"I intend to start tonight."

When the first firework goes off, I jump, and my wine sloshes out of my glass. I giggle at my own startled response and clap a hand over my mouth. Nick points to the sky as the next boom sounds.

My heart drops into my feet when I glance up to read 'Marry Me' scrawled in a bright white blaze of fireworks. "Holy shit," I breathe. I turn to Nick, and he's down on one knee with an open box, and a ring glitters in the dying light from the sky.

"I didn't do it right the first time, but I am making sure everything is right this time. Julia Louise Jensen, will you do me the honor of becoming my wife?"

"Yes!" I cup his bearded cheek. "Yes." My voice gets choked up on the second confirmation. "I can't believe you did this."

He rises to his feet and takes the diamond ring out of the box. We're so close together there's hardly any space between our bodies. My heart beats an erratic rhythm. He slides the ring onto my finger to settle over my tattoo. The diamond is so huge it almost completely covers the scrawl of Nick's name. There's a comfort in the weight of the ring and the permanence of what lies beneath. Complete perfection. How is it possible to love someone this much?

"This was unexpected." There are tears in my eyes when I glance up at him.

"Nice to know I'm still going to be able to surprise you—in a good way. I plan on being an overachiever at this whole marriage thing." He winks.

I tug him down for a kiss, and his hand follows the curve of my ass under the flare of my dress.

"Jules." His voice is rough with desire. "I think you forgot something when you were getting dressed."

"Did I?" I graze his ear with my teeth. "You know what else we've never done up here?"

"They're serving the first course in ten minutes." His breath hitches.

I've got his pants undone. "Then I guess you'd better hurry." There's already a throbbing need between my thighs at the thought of being with him up here.

Gripping my backside, he lifts me off the ground and pins me against the side of the barn. I draw my legs around his waist, and then he's sinking into me. I let out a low moan of pleasure.

"I'll never get enough of you," he murmurs against my neck.

"You never have to," I say.

It might have taken us fourteen years to get here, but we're finally where we both belong. Happy and together.

THE END

Pre-order Alex's story here: http://mybook.to/HeavyCr own

Obtain bonus chapters and exclusive content by signing up for my newsletter here: wendymillion.com

Acknowledgments

As always, my biggest thank you is to my children and my husband, who put up with my divided attention, probably far more often than they'd like while I work on bookish things. Between my day job and trying to get this writing gig off the ground, there aren't always enough hours in the day. Thank you for your patience and support. I love the three of you so much.

Thanks to Najla Qamber and her team for all their fabulous cover work on this series. I cannot recommend all of you enough.

To all of my first readers, thank you for your valuable feedback and for loving Nick and Jules as much as I did.

A special thank you to my ARC team who read and reviewed the first book in this series — Danielle Greaves, Michelle Wesley, Wairimu Kibathi, Karen Sampson, Misty Donohue, Michelle

Myers, Celeste Marie, Phyllis Pisanelli, Liana, Sigrid, Hirnakshi, Elizabeth, Anushka J, BJ, and Ilene.

And last but not least, thanks to the Nottpad and Wattpad Stars communities who are sources of invaluable information. It's so nice to have a space to learn and grow as a writer. A special thank you to two people who listen to all my writing rants (no matter when I send them)—Cole and Avery. I appreciate you both!

Also By

W Million

The Donaghey Brothers Series (Romantic Suspense)

Retribution

Resurrection

Redemption

Northern University Series (NA Sports Romance)

Saving Us

Fake Crown (straddles both Northern University and the Bellerive Royals)

With Wattpad Books (Second Chance Romance)

When Stars Fall
Miss Matched (coming 2023)
Novella (free with newsletter signup)

First Date Challenge
As W. MIllion – The Bellerive Royals Series

Fake Crown

Scarred Crown

Heavy Crown

Fallen Crown

ABOUT W MILLION

W. Million is a Watty Award winner whose contemporary romances about strong women and troubled men have captivated her loyal readers. She's the author of the Bellerive Royals and the Tuckers of Bellerive book series.

Writing as Wendy Million, she is the author of the romantic suspense series *The Donaghey Brothers,* the NA sports romance *Saving Us,* and the contemporary second chance romance, *When Stars Fall*.

When not writing, Wendy enjoys spending time in or around the water. She lives in Ontario, Canada with two beautiful daughters, two cute pooches, and one handsome husband (who is grateful she doesn't need two of those).